★

When McCall arrived at his office the next morning, he'd had very little sleep. After the conversation in the airport with Wainwright, he never got back to bed. Instead he sat in his study the rest of the night, pondering the moves he was about to make. Planning three simultaneous assassinations. Possibly four. Hiring three assassins. Or four. Three separate setups. Or four. It was going to require a great deal of preliminary work and coordination.

And all through the mental process, he felt he was standing outside himself, watching himself go through the motions of planning three murders. He wondered if he was really going to go through with it.

WILLIAM H. HALLAHAN

FOXCATCHER

A GOLD EAGLE BOOK FROM
WORLDWIDE

TORONTO • NEW YORK • LONDON • PARIS
AMSTERDAM • STOCKHOLM • HAMBURG
ATHENS • MILAN • TOKYO • SYDNEY

FOXCATCHER

A Gold Eagle Book/October 1987

First published by William Morrow and Company, Inc.,
March 1986

Copyright © 1986 by William H. Hallahan

ISBN 0-373-62109-4

Printed in the U.S.A.

FOXCATCHER

1

Brewer arrived at Sweetmeadow late that night inside a Department of Corrections van. He wore handcuffs chained to a waist-belt and leg irons.

A sleeting rain was falling and several times the van slid sidewise coming down the access road.

Someone had taped a large paper shamrock on the inside of the van door. Crudely cut from a piece of orange construction paper, it carried the lettered legend TO ALL YOU POTATO HEADS. HAPPY PADDY'S DAY FROM BELFAST.

The prison guard opened the rear van door. He stared curiously at the orange-paper shamrock, then guffawed at the joke and tore it off the door. He beckoned to Brewer with a crooked finger.

Brewer stepped down and hobbled into a bare room built into the stone prison wall. He was left standing there while the van driver, his associate, and three guards went over a packet of documents. There was a discussion, some shaking of heads, and final agreement. One of the guards signed several papers.

The van driver unlocked the leather belt from Brewer's waist, unlocked the chained cuffs from his wrists, then unlocked the leg irons. He handed them to his associate, who carried them clanking to the doorway. He threw them noisily into the back of the van. The two men rode off into the sleeting night.

One of the guards slammed the outside door. He turned the key, then pivoted around. Brewer was now locked inside Sweetmeadow Prison, facing three expressionless guards.

THEY ORDERED HIM to strip. Into a large cardboard carton he dropped his camel's hair coat, his charcoal flannel suit, his wing tip slip-ons, his tie, his shirt, socks, shorts. Personal possessions—wallet, keys, watch, pencil, loose change—went into a crumpled manila envelope.

A male nurse in green prison pants arrived, breathing heavily and bearing a white enamel pan laden with medical paraphernalia. He exhaled the odor of whiskey as he examined Brewer. He checked blood pressure and body temperature and looked for signs of hernia, piles, sore throat, bad teeth, dental prosthetic devices, gonorrhea, syphilis chancre, crabs, skin sores. With a stethoscope he listened for lung congestion and monitored heartbeat. He recorded an oral medical history, noted various scars, wrote *none* under tatoos, and finally gave Brewer four shots. Everyone watched him ineptly take blood from Brewer's arm.

Another prisoner cut Brewer's hair. He whispered questions as he clipped. They were almost the same questions the guards read off to him from a printed form.

Another prisoner stood Brewer up against a board with height marked off in feet and inches and took his photograph.

"When you're old and gray, you can look at your ID and see what a handsome dog you were," he said, peeling the skin off the film. "Fat lot of good it'll do you."

The guards sent him to the shower. Afterward, without a towel, he stood bare, wet, and shivering, waiting while sleet rattled on the window directly over his head. The box with all his clothing and the envelope with his personal property had been taken away while he showered.

He was led, still bare, still wet, still shivering, down a corridor to a large room with a broad long counter. Two prisoners watched him with basilisk eyes. The beating sleet was particularly loud in this room.

The guard pushed him forward with a finger, and the issuing of dunnage began. He was given a mattress cover to hold open, and into it the two prisoners threw his clothing allowance. The guard checked off the little squares on an inventory sheet as the items sailed through the air into the mattress cover.

T-shirts, shorts, shirts, green prison pants, socks, shaving and toilet articles, towels, stencil kit with his name and number, pillow cases, more mattress covers, a white wool blanket, watch cap, wool knit gloves, short wool jacket. One Bible. No belt.

A prisoner with white hair and downcast eyes fitted Brewer for his shoes.

"Make sure they fit. You're going to be wearing them a long time."

The guard pushed the clothing inventory sheet over the counter with a ballpoint pen.

"Sign there." The pen bore the legend QUALITY REPAIRS. NELSON'S GARAGE. "You now owe the State of New York two hundred thirty-seven dollars and sixty-four cents."

"How am I going to pay that?"

"They'll get it out of you," said one of the prisoners. "Don't you worry."

They all watched him dress in prison clothes.

The shots had made his arms ache. He felt light-headed and feverish. The mattress cover and its contents were unwieldy as he was led out of the rooms in the wall and into the dark prison yard. The door was shut firmly behind him.

Single file, a guard in front and a guard behind, he was led across the cobblestoned yard through stinging sleet that crunched under their shoe soles, around puddles and into a main building. Once they were inside, the rear guard shut the door behind them with a bang and locked it.

Odors from the prisoners' mess hung in the air, the blended reminders of ten thousand bad meals. He was led along a corridor under widely spaced lights and up a flight of steel and concrete stairs through a doorway. That door was banged shut and locked behind them. The noise echoed in the huge interior. Another long corridor, several turnings; down a flight of stairs and through another doorway went the three of them. The door was slammed shut and locked behind them. That made four. He was passing cells now, following a long line of overhead lights.

Arms were draped through the bars. Fingers grasped the uprights. Eyes from within followed him.

"Say hey, man."

"OK, Brewer."

"Asshole."

"Hullo, darling. What's your cell number?"

They turned left into another corridor, up a short flight of steel steps. The guard in the lead paused and unlocked a barred door. He nodded his head at the cell.

"In."

Brewer entered. And turned. And dropped the bulging mattress cover. The cell door swung shut firmly and the key turned in the lock.

The footsteps of the two guards receded down the corridor; then a door shut and a lock clicked. More footsteps, barely audible. A distant door faintly banged. A distant lock clicked.

He was alone with the silence.

BREWER WAS CONFRONTED with it now: After all those months of legal maneuvering, he was truly in the penitentiary. He was in a cell locked in a cell block locked inside a large prison building inside thirty-foot walls. There were five locked steel doors between him and freedom. He sat down on the cot, clasped his hands between his thighs, and drew in a shuddering breath. It had really happened at last.

Even as he sat, shivering with cold, the sweat began. It soaked his head, ran down his face and neck. It soaked his shirt and his trousers, ran down into his new socks and shoes. He rocked back and forth. Back and forth. As though consoling a child. Someone began to croon. Then voices called to him.

"Hey, Brewer. Hang tight, babe. Piece of cake."

"Piece of cake, babe."

"You're going to make it, man."

He surprised himself. He'd never rocked himself like this before. Never sweated like this before. He kept rocking.

Someone was crooning to him.

"Easy man," someone called. "Easy does it. Don't come apart. Hang tight."

The crooning, he realized, was coming from himself. As he rocked, as he sweated, he was crooning—moaning—rhythmically.

"Shit, man," called a voice with disgust. "If you can't do the time, don't do the crime."

"Don't listen to him, Brewer. Hang tight."

"Hang tight, man, or haul your ass out of here, while you still have the will. Hey, hear me? Brewer? Hey, Brewer. Listen to the man. Come to the door, Brewer. Here. You watching? Here it comes."

It was a belt with a large buckle. It leaped out of the darkness and hit the gray-painted deck in front of his cell. There it lay in a twisted coil.

"Help yourself, Brewer. That's your ticket out of here. The midnight express."

He stared at the belt. And it seemed to be staring back at him. There were many eyes watching it. They waited to see his hand reach through the bars and take it up. The midnight express.

THE BELT LAY THERE, malevolent, lethal, eager.

Through the night it confronted him while silent men watched. A number of times he heard the metal slide of a peephole click in the corridor door. The guards were also watching him. Rainwater dribbled somewhere outside. After a while he heard snoring.

DAWN WAS A DIRTY AFFAIR. He discovered that, set in the wall opposite his cell door, high up, was a window. It gradually grew from a black square to a dark-gray square, then to grim gray daylight. The sleet had turned to wind-whipped wet snow that was attacking the window like something struggling inside an aquarium.

March 17. A snowy Saint Patrick's Day: the day Brewer began asking himself questions he'd never faced before.

JUST AFTER DAWN, a guard entered.

"You'll go to breakfast early, Brewer. When some of these hopheads find out what business you were in they might give you a rough welcome."

He picked up the belt and carried it away.

Prisoner #B23424309 had begun the first day of a nine-year sentence.

2

Bobby McCall's father admonished him all through childhood: "Never let life hand you the broken hockey stick." So he should have been ready when, in the summer of 1968, life tried to do just that.

On June 3 of that year, Bobby McCall began his first day of a summer job in the chambers of Judge Lewis Lewbo, Philadelphia Municipal Court. McCall was twenty-one, with a newly minted B.A. from Haverford College and a letter of admission to the University of Pennsylvania Law School, commencing in the autumn.

"Do one thing better than anyone else," his father had always urged him, "and the world's your oyster." That one thing, Bobby intended, would be the law.

At ten that morning he was summoned from the judge's chambers for an urgent phone call. "It's your uncle," the bailiff said, holding the door open for him. He took the call at the desk of the judge's secretary.

"Bobby," said his uncle Andrew. "I have terrible news for you, son. Your father just had a heart attack."

"Heart attack? Is he okay?"

"He just slipped away. He was opening his mail in his office and—and his heart stopped. I'm afraid we've lost him, Bobby."

JOHNNY McCALL had been a professional financial adviser and portfolio manager. He had made many men wealthy, had made many wealthy men wealthier, and had impoverished very few. He had done one thing better than anyone else, and the world had truly been his oyster.

When the auditors arrived they found the accounts of every one of his clients in perfect condition, humming like little money factories even with the master's hand withdrawn.

They also found John McCall's own affairs in absolute chaos. His life insurance policies had lapsed from neglect. His medical insurance had been canceled—the letter announcing this was found in a file unopened, along with a number of uncashed checks, some two years old. Client billing was haphazard and his accounts receivable were staggeringly high; some clients hadn't received a bill in nearly a year; most of these accounts were never collected. His personal checkbook hadn't been balanced in six months. Tax forms had been neglected, urgent notes from his accountant ignored. His will, years out of date, listed assets he no longer held. With a fortune in uncollected receivables on one side of the ledger, on the other he owed everyone money.

His tax affairs were in a terrible muddle, and the IRS chose to get nasty. The Pennsylvania State Tax Collector joined in. New Jersey filed a claim.

JOHN MCCALL had lived a comfortable life in a lovely old stone house on a wide lawn that overlooked Saint Andrew's Country Club on Philadelphia's Main Line. He spent his summers in a light-filled beach house on a dune above the surf at Harvey Cedars, his winters with the yachting crowd in the Virgin Islands, while interspersed were many European vacations. His favorite expression was "I'm having a hell of a good time and I love it." On the day he died he had just turned forty-eight.

His wife, Mary Elizabeth née Carpenter, relict, was left destitute. Even though her own brother, Andrew Carpenter, a noted Main Line estate attorney, handled the probate himself—at no fee—everything went: house, yacht, beach home, even the car. Andrew Carpenter later told Bobby that his father had let various governmental bodies grab more than $900,000 unnecessarily by neglecting his affairs. "If he'd given himself one tenth of the attention he'd given to any of his clients he could easily have been worth more than ten million."

At twenty-one, Bobby McCall found himself without funds for law school and with a mother to support—a woman who had never worked a day in her life.

FROM THE GRAVESIDE, Bobby led his mother away by the elbow. He was grief-stricken and bewildered. His mother—who'd built her life around her darling Jack—was inconsolable.

Bobby overheard a man who stood beside a silver Rolls-Royce say to another: "Smartest man with a buck I ever met. We're not likely to find another like him."

"Not in our lifetimes," said the other. "Too bad he couldn't have left his brain as part of his estate."

THE ALTERATION WAS SHOCKING. At one moment Bobby McCall was a rich man's son, observing the wealthiest and most powerful men pass through his father's front door—U.S. senators, judges, famous sports figures, show business people, all bearing bushel baskets of money, begging his father to help them.

The next moment the magnificent house was gone, his mother's celebrated greenhouse stripped of its plants and aquariums, the lovely household furnishings dispersed, the cook and the housemaid released, his mother smuggling a priceless antique clock and a bombé chest of drawers into a cousin's garage late at night.

He and his mother spent four days going up and down Montgomery Avenue from one apartment building to another. His mother didn't understand that she couldn't afford an expensive apartment—her first choice was a suite with four bedrooms and maid service.

Eventually, with much sighing and with a childish petulance Bobby had never seen before, she permitted herself to be moved into a two-bedroom apartment in Ardmore. She had no idea how to cook.

Uncle Andrew—with all the diligence and concern of an elder brother—managed to scrape together an estate, including Social Security and a small pension, of some $12,000 a year for her. The night he came to tell her this, he took her hand and, with the apoplectic hue under his eyes of a sick man, looked directly at her.

"Now, Bess, you're going to have to take hold. I'm in pretty bad shape and I won't be around much longer to watch over you. You simply have to understand that there's no more money anywhere except this pittance. Now you have to show the world what a Carpenter is made of, lass— that's what Father would have said. What you've got to do is get a job. So there's an end to the tears. It's up and about for you."

Mrs. McCall expected her brother to take care of things as her husband had. She tried to decide what job she wanted him to get for her.

UNCLE ANDREW said to Bobby: "It's no use complaining, Bobby; the lost fortune is lost forever. You have to keep your eye on your own career now. And that's law school. I think I can help you there. I've got some connections with the faculty. But you're going to need a year or so to regroup before you start law school. You have to build up some capital for taking care of yourself in law school—even if I can swing some tuition money your way. You see what I'm saying? I have a connection in Washington through Senator Merson. I can get you an appointment in the Department of Commerce. Good salary. And a year from now, your mother should be on her feet and you can come back and start law school with some very pertinent experience under your belt. What do you say?''

What could he say? He accepted.

TWO WEEKS BEFORE Bobby left for Washington, his uncle's heart stopped. In his will, Andrew Carpenter left to his ''beloved Bess'' a stipend of some $10,000 a year. With careful management she could now live without working.

But *careful* was not in her vocabulary. She'd not taken any of the jobs Andrew found for her. Instead she'd run up bills everywhere. She'd had two bitter quarrels with her brother over money just before he died. Bobby could now see that his mother was a terribly spoiled woman who would not make any concessions to the facts.

''Never surrender,'' she said to her son. ''Take what you want from the world. If you haven't got the money to pay for it, someone else must pay for you. Remember your father's words: Don't let them give you the broken hockey stick.''

At Uncle Andrew's funeral she had her first quarrel with her son. She wanted him to reopen his father's office and start up the business again. She wanted him to restore her to her previous condition. She not only wanted to be wealthy again, she wanted to recover the self-same Main Line home and greenhouse filled with plants and aquariums, and the summer home in Harvey Cedars and the yacht in the Virgin islands and the car—every last jot and tittle. He could get it for her, she said.

He not only could not, he would not. He refused emphatically.

IN LATE AUGUST, on a dripping hot day, he went to Thirtieth Street Station to take the Metroliner to Washington. His mother accompanied him to the station elegantly, in a chauffeured limousine rented just for the occasion. "Wherever you go, go in style," she said, tapping his wrist with a forefinger.

That's what made men stare at her, he decided. She was a beautiful woman—but it was the way she carried herself that made the world gaze. And admire. And desire. She radiated invincibility. Majesty.

"Good luck to you, my son," she said as she kissed him. Then she shook her head. "You've taken the broken hockey stick, Bobby. You're a lumping fool."

He never returned to Philadelphia.

AT THE HEIGHT of his career with the State Department, Bobby McCall still looked back on his uncle's advice with regret. He should never have deferred law school.

The lack of a law degree had hampered his advancement in Washington repeatedly. Every day seemed to give him at least one reminder of his mistake. Every day except one— and that was the result of a child's deck of tarot cards.

As he drove to work that morning, he was shocked to look into the rearview mirror of his car and see the silly tarot predictions coming true. A blue Buick was following him. In it were three men, just as predicted: the Hanged Man, the Merchant with the Figs from Tyre, and the Masked Tumbler.

McCall's thirteen-year-old daughter had bought the tarot deck in the village drugstore in Alexandria along with a bottle of shampoo. She and her friends had spread the cards out on the card table under the bridge lamp and read the directions hastily, with muffled shrieks. The first night they'd huddled on the huge screened-in porch of the McCall home, doing forecasts on themselves and the boys they would someday marry.

There were endless wiggles and giggles and squeals of delight and dashings to the telephone. But on the second evening they were quiet. They had reread the instructions that came with the deck and were doing serious "castings." They murmured of the Monkey Man, the Woman in the Case, the Merchant with the Figs, the Masked Tumbler, and the Hanged Man. The solemn silence was gratifying.

"Dad?"

McCall looked up from his book. His daughter stood just outside the circle of his reading lamp. "Yes, my love."

"Dad. You're in grave danger."

"I am."

"It's in the cards. You have to beware of the Hanged Man, the Merchant with the Figs from Tyre, and the Masked Tumbler."

"Good heavens. I must be very careful."

She stood at his elbow without speaking, then strolled away.

A few minutes later his wife was at his side. "Could there be anything to those cards, do you think?"

"Are you serious? Can you really be serious?"

"Well, that reading they did on you is pretty serious. Debbie says three men are going to kill you and you laughed at her."

McCall took his wife's hand. "How old is Debbie?"

"Thirteen."

"Uh huh. My advice is to take the deck of cards from them and send them back to the Parcheesi. Also fill them up with ice cream."

But the next morning his wife suggested that she consult a soothsayer who was all the rage among the cocktail set in Washington. Madama Sforza.

"This has gone far enough," McCall answered. "Burn those cards and drop the whole thing."

Dinner that night was solemn. Neither his son nor his daughter spoke. They poked at their food. McCall's wife tried to brighten the conversation but she ended up doing a monologue that no one listened to.

After dinner, he and his wife had coffee on the porch. It was McCall's favorite time of day. They lived in a huge old Victorian house in Alexandria with five bedrooms and a wraparound screened porch that was the gathering place for neighborhood children in the evening. He enjoyed hearing the sound of their voices in the deepening dusk while inhaling the odor of his lawn being soaked by the sprinklers.

That night there were no children.

"I read the instructions for those tarot cards, Bobby," said his wife. "And I did a casting of my own."

"Oh boy." He put down his coffee cup and turned to her.

"It came up the same way, with a random shuffling. Twice, Bobby. Frankly I'm frightened."

"Enough."

"The Merchant with the Figs from Tyre has a sight draft with your name on it."

"Is that right?"

She glanced at him. "Oh, I know it sounds silly—" She burst into laughter. "Oh dear. But it's serious!"

"You sound like the little Scottish lady who lived in her wee cot in the Highlands," McCall said. "When they asked her if she believed in ghosts she said, 'No. And I hope they leave me alone.'"

They looked at each other and laughed again. Later, she bought a new game called Foreign Intrigue and took the tarot cards away from Debbie and her friends. Wiggles, giggles, and strident cries returned.

THE NEXT DAY, McCall drove to an early-morning rendezvous.

The night before, on his way home from Washington, McCall had placed a call to Italy from a public phone booth across from his office. He suspected that his own phone was being tapped. From Italy, his clandestine informant whispered into the phone: "I'm flying to Washington tonight. Urgent news. The usual place. The usual time." The man hung up.

The usual place was the rear parking lot of a run-down motel off New York Avenue in Washington. And the usual time was 9:00 A.M.

The city was in the grip of its unbearable summer heat, and McCall drove with the car's air-conditioner squeezing out the licking humidity from the air.

On the way to the rendezvous, he was well along on U.S. 295 when he first began to check his rearview mirror. With that sense born of experience and instinct he felt he was being followed, and soon enough he saw the blue Buick, dodging in and out of lanes, staying well back.

By the time he drove onto New York Avenue toward the motel, McCall was sure. Inside the new blue Buick were three men. They didn't crowd him; they seemed to know where he was going.

He decided to take a circuitous route to elude them. He abruptly turned left onto Queenschapel Road, sped two blocks and turned a corner, turned another and another. He was in an area of high-rise apartments and condominiums. He drove aimlessly through the winding streets, watching for the Buick. He'd lost it.

After a while he drove back onto New York Avenue. The motel was less than a mile ahead of him, an old two-story structure with flaking blue paint on the trim and cracks in the white stucco walls. The parking lot at the back was bordered by sumac trees and weeds and litter. Behind it ran a disused railroad siding.

The Buick was parked at the curb a block before the motel. The three men inside bowed their heads and half averted their faces as they watched him pass. The Hanged Man, the Merchant with the Figs from Tyre, and the Masked Tumbler who could fly through the air: three Nemeses, come in the last act to drag the hero to the underworld, as ordained by the gods. There was no question that they knew exactly where he was going.

He broke off the rendezvous and went instead to his office.

THE WASHINGTON HEAT embraced him like a hot wet towel, and he damned L'Enfant for having placed the nation's capital in a swamp with one of the most humid blistering summers in all of North America. Madness.

With some fifteen years' experience in monitoring international arms traffic, McCall had been appointed chief of Arms Traffic Control Bureau, Department of State, three years before. He had been followed many times in his career. That was an old story to him.

McCall stood at his office window and looked down at the busy street. Off at an angle he could see into Constitution Mall. The crowds of summer were thronging up the stone steps of the Smithsonian. As usual the Air & Space Museum was getting all the play.

His eyes searched the street below. There was no sign of the blue Buick or the three men. What he was concerned about was the safety of his Rome informant. And concealing the man's identity.

It was twenty after ten. Time to go. He took a deep breath and set out. When he left the building he crossed the street to the same pay phone he'd used the night before. At exactly ten-thirty he pushed in some coins and punched out a number.

"Let's do it again," he said.

"Trouble?"

"Nothing I can't handle," said McCall. "How about the second location?"

"In half an hour. I have to catch the afternoon flight back to Rome."

McCall scanned the streets, then set off on foot. They were nowhere to be seen: the Hanged Man, the Merchant with the Figs from Tyre, and the Masked Tumbler who could fly through the air.

SEVEN SEAS NEWS SERVICE was a CIA front, set up in the Simmold Center, an old office building in downtown Washington populated by news services, small specialty magazines, stringers, free-lancers, publicity agents, and various breeds of influence peddler.

Barred by law from domestic spying, the CIA used ex-CIA agents in fictitious companies like Seven Seas News Service to do its domestic spooking for it. They spent a great percentage of their time spying on other intelligence arms of the government, indeed on the CIA itself. And often, after the assignments were completed, the ex-CIA agents would then return to the CIA with their perquisites and emoluments fully restored, no longer ex.

McCall, as the chief of the Arms Traffic Control Bureau
Department of State, used Seven Seas on occasion. But to
day he was using its roof.

Sweltering, he walked north on 7th Street, past th
National Portrait Gallery with its swarm of pushcart ped
dlers. Before long, he was perspiring. Some blocks later h
went into a coffee shop and ordered a glass of iced tea at th
counter. He sat there for a few minutes, holding a newspa
per while watching the street. Satisfied, he left the pape
with a tip and strolled into the men's room. From there h
walked through the kitchen and out the back door into th
alley. He came out at 8th Street.

Two blocks later he entered the basement of an old apart
ment building, followed a labyrinth of corridors to the rear
stepped into an alley, and entered the basement of th
building next door. He took the service elevator.

At the top floor he got off and entered the stairwell tha
led to the roof. It was exactly 10:57. The heat inside th
stairwell was almost unbearable.

He paused at the stair railing and looked down six floor
to the lobby. Two double rows of lights illuminated the wel
clearly: No one was on the stairs. The well was like a broad
square tunnel straight to the bottom—the converging line
seemed eager to pull him downward. He stepped back an
went upstairs to the door that led to the roof. So far so good

When he swung the roof door open, a great wall of sum
mer heat struck him. The light was blinding. The smell o
soft hot tar filled his nostrils. Roasting under the direct sun,
the roof was an inferno.

He stepped out on the wooden platform and eased th
door to behind him. He was already dripping wet when h
moved into the shade of the stairwell cupola and waited. The
boardwalk ran the entire length of the block across the roofs

of three different office buildings. Everything shimmered in the wilting heat waves.

In the streets below him, horns sounded as the cars of bureaucrats, stealing away for a long summer weekend, struggled to get out of town through the tourist traffic. Everywhere, the streets were clotted with traffic jams. Off to the east and south, the multi-lane U.S. 295, arcing around the city, was heavy with high-speed summertime traffic.

McCall looked at the crowds of tourists along Constitution Mall. He could see Capitol Hill and the White House, the Washington Monument and, beyond, Jefferson on the Potomac and the Pentagon—all wearing noble sentiments cut in stone. Like Rome in its latter days: filled with monuments that babbled naïve epitaphs nobody read or believed.

He had been an observer of the city too long. Fifteen years in the bureaucratic wars. He knew as he stood there that everywhere about him the very freedoms that the monuments celebrated were being chopped up and stolen away. Sold. Bartered.

Illegal telephone bugs abounded, many of them authorized by the highest men in the nation, men sworn to prevent such things. McCall himself had placed his share. But it was more than bugs: Every day, white envelopes stuffed with money were passed over desks for lucrative contracts, for rigged bids, for removal of obstacles, for a congressman's vote, for influence, for silence.

Secretive bureaucrats buried the record of thousands of incompetencies, mistakes, and crimes, of malfeasance and nonfeasance—buried them in multitudinous official files by the simple expedient of stamping TOP SECRET on them. McCall was sick of his knowledge. He felt like Tiresias.

Down in the streets, History was unimpressed by the monuments. Bloodstained and gore-scarred, History fol-

lowed after mankind like a public scold who knows all the
family secrets. Men ignore History for good reason. It's hu-
manity's rap sheet.

History teaches despair.

McCALL PULLED the roof door open a crack and listened
for sounds inside the stairwell. Still so far so good: No one
had followed him; at least, no one had come up on the roof.

McCall looked at his watch: 11:00. Late in the afternoon
he would be sailing with his son out of Annapolis on a beam
reach under a rising evening breeze—if he lived through the
next half hour.

He told himself to think of cool bay breezes. He shut his
eyes and sweltered, patiently waiting for Daniels.

DANIELS FINALLY APPEARED at the far end of the roof. It
was 11:02 and McCall set out along the length of the wooden
walkway. Cupolas and elevator pillboxes, television anten-
nas and skylights—everything shimmered in the waves of
terrible heat swirling around him.

Daniels was standing in the shade of a stairwell housing,
wiping his face. He wore overalls and stood spraddle-legged
over a toolbox.

McCall smiled at him. "Love your cover," he said.
"Heavy overalls on top of a business suit on a roof in a
hundred and twenty degrees. Verisimilitude at its acme."

"Let's make this quick, Bobby," Daniels said. "I can't
believe this heat up here. Kay? Now. With this piece of info,
we're clean. Even. Quits. Kay?"

"Bad attitude, Danny. Sister agencies should cooperate
with each other. It says so right on the front page of the government manual."

"Yeah, well, you know what you can do with the government manual. Anyone from the Cookie Factory who gets

caught talking to anyone from State gets coal in his stocking."

"Alas," said McCall.

"Alas, my ass. You people are a pack of screw-ups. The whole goddam State Department. Anyway. Here's the straight skinny you wanted."

He handed McCall a spiral-bound dossier. Title: Operation Zealot. Daniels said, "Ready? This has to be fast. There's real trouble brewing in the Mideast. Those crazy Iranians are trying to crank up all that surveillance equipment that the Shah left behind."

McCall grunted.

"It's all in here." Daniels shoved the dossier at him. "There's only one ray of light in the whole thing. They don't have enough spare parts to operate the equipment. They've tried to buy the stuff but the U.S. embargo on critical equipment is killing them. So they're trying a new ploy."

"Smuggling."

"You called it. The Iranians are sending one of their best boys out with a satchelful of money to buy those spare parts. Price is no object."

"I can imagine," said McCall.

Daniels touched the dossier. "This is a military analysis of what the Iranians can do with that surveillance equipment and what it means to the whole goddam Middle East. Kay?"

"Thrilling reading, I'm sure," said McCall.

"What they can do will make you wet your pants."

"Did you get the name of the Iranian agent they sent out?"

"Attashah. Rooley Attashah. Know him?"

McCall grunted. "Couldn't be worse."

Daniels picked up the toolbox. "Okay. We're quits. No more favors, Bobby. This tidbit pays off what I owe you. Christ—get me out of this heat. It's worse than Rome."

"I got a piece of news for you, Danny. Right out of Cookie Factory ovens. You interested?"

"What's it about?"

"I can tell you who's going to be the next Chief of Station in Cairo."

Daniels put down the toolbox gingerly. "Who?"

"I hear you're an applicant for the job."

"Yeah, yeah. I am. So give. Who's got it?"

"Someday you'll return the favor maybe, eh?"

"Who is it, for Christ's sake!"

"You."

Daniels softly socked a fist into his left palm. "I'll be damned. Made it. I made it. Are you sure?"

"You'll be told on Thursday."

Daniels picked up the toolbox. "Jesus." Then he put it down again. "How about that?" He was oblivious to the perspiration rilling down his face. "How about that." He picked up the toolbox once again.

McCall said, "You'd better learn to like the heat. It's the principal product of Cairo."

"I love it. I love it." A rush of hot air was released when Daniels pulled open the roof door. He paused to point at the dossier in McCall's right hand.

"Be careful with that goddam monograph, Bobby. It's my ass. Christ. I'd rather tell the Russians than you guys in State."

MCCALL WALKED BACK along the boardwalk in the breathtaking heat. Daniels, as Chief of Station, would have access to much more information.

He glanced out over the city again. All over Washington, all over the world in fact, he'd done favors for key people useful to him. Favors that could be called in.

By the time he reached his door the heat had made him almost light-headed. He stepped through the doorway to the stairwell. Then he paused to blot his soaked face with his handkerchief. Cool breezes on his sailboat called to him. Soon. Soon.

When he drew the handkerchief away from his face and opened his eyes he was standing at the stair top in total darkness. The lights had gone out—two complete rows of lamps from the top of the staircase six floors to the bottom.

He stood listening in the dark.

From far away sounded the horns of the traffic. Even fainter was the singsong of a police siren.

He had an awful premonition that he was about to be grabbed and pitched six floors down the stairwell. His skin prickled and he stepped back out onto the roof.

He scanned the rooftops. Daniels was long gone. Quickly he walked back along the boards. Daniels had locked the door behind him. He tried the two other stairwell doors. They were both locked. There was no other way down from the roof. He was trapped with only one exit: the dark stairwell.

He walked back to his door. Sweat was dribbling off him. He wanted urgently to get away from the heat.

He opened the door and stepped in again. It was still dark. He let the door shut behind him softly, then cocked his ears. He held his breath to listen.

The flight of stairs down to the top floor was no more than twenty steps, with a turn halfway.

He sat down and, as quietly as he could, removed his shoes and tied them together by the laces. He draped them around his neck and stood up.

He listened again and heard only his own breathing. He stood there in complete darkness and slowly counted to 250 in his mind, listening, listening carefully. Concentrating on hearing. He heard the hum of the elevator moving in its shaft. Then it stopped.

He took a first step in his stocking feet. And waited. Then another. And waited. He'd crossed the upper landing. He took his first step down. Then another. He stood waiting.

Was that a sound—a sigh below him? He waited, listening. Then he took another step. And another. Then, slowly, several. He waited. He was at the turning of the stair. Silence all around him. He began the descent of the second half-flight. The door was a few short steps away.

The song of a faraway police siren grew stronger. McCall waited until it passed and faded.

He descended two more steps. Paused. Counting. Then two more. He knew he was only four or five steps away from the door. There was a faint line of light at its base. He descended two more. Then two more. Slowly he groped for the doorknob.

He touched something soft with his hand. It pressed against his forearm. Then it seized his wrist.

"Gotcha," a voice whispered. Then there was an explosion of movement and shouting.

McCall was grabbed by two extraordinarily powerful hands; one seized his left wrist and the other gripped his calf.

"Get him," said a voice.

More hands grabbed him. He was lifted out over the railing.

McCall went into a frenzy. He gripped an iron baluster and held on for his life. Arms and hands tried to raise him. He writhed and kicked and bellowed. They raised him higher.

"Get his hand! His hand, for Christ's sake!"

Groping, McCall reached his other arm around a waist. His fingers seized a man's belt.

"Higher. Goddammit. Higher."

"He's holding on to something."

"That's me! He's got me, for Christ's sake. Get his hands!"

Someone's mouth was pressed against his ear. He felt the hot panting breath. He struggled more. He was over their heads and shoulders now, at arm's length. Out over the stairwell.

"Drop him!"

McCall's groping hand seized a necktie. He wrapped it around his hand.

"Drop him, for Christ's sake!"

Out over the stairwell, they dropped him. He fell. And swung, dangling by the necktie. As the man pulled back, he pulled McCall with him.

Then the whole moving, struggling mass lurched and stumbled against a wall. Their hold on him was broken.

"Lift him, I told you."

"Wait! Get his hands. That's me you got."

There was another violent lurch. One of the forms was elevated and McCall fell back.

"That's me, godammit. Me! Wait! Stop!"

McCall got his legs free. Flat on his back, he placed both feet on the mass of entangled bodies. He concentrated all his strength in a great push. The railing shuddered and one voice shouted in terror: "No! It's me!"

"Drop him."

The terrified voice fell. It screamed all the way to the bottom of the stairwell in the darkness. The body hit with a muffled thud.

Amid the panting and wheezing, the two other men whispered to each other. Abruptly there was a square of light as they opened the stair door. The two of them stood there using the light to search the stairs. Their eyes found Mc-Call.

In disbelief they stared at him, their mouths clearly agape. One took a step toward him. McCall tried to rise to meet him.

Then both the attackers turned and fled. The door swung shut and McCall was in darkness again. He lay back, feeling his panting breath burn his windpipe and lungs, telling himself to get up before they returned to finish the job. But he couldn't move.

HE BARELY REMEMBERED getting back to his office. On that dark landing, in a brief struggle, he'd spent all the strength in his body. He ached everywhere and his left wrist was wrenched. His shirt sleeve had been torn nearly off. There was a burning scrape along the left side of his face.

And in his mind he was still gazing down that stairwell. He should have been dead. It was just incredible luck. He knew he'd passed a watershed in his life. He could never be the same again. In terror he'd wanted to negotiate with those men. He understood now how easy it was to betray. He would have done anything to save himself. Anything.

And those two men, lit by the open door, gaping at him. He was so exhausted that, even without the help of the third man, those two could have come back up the stairs, picked him up, and easily thrown him over the railing. If ever he saw them again, he would recognize their faces instantly.

THE THREE MEN had known where McCall was going beforehand. They must have tapped someone's phone—his or Daniels's in Rome. He'd suspected it all along. That's why he'd used a pay phone down in the street. He requested a phone sweep.

The debugging team arrived at McCall's office clanking. There were two of them, pushing a cart with black boxes and trailing wires. They didn't speak to him. One put his finger to his lips. McCall nodded. And systematically, in silence, they proceeded to toss his office.

They removed the pictures from the walls and studied every centimeter of the frames, probing along the edges of the paper backing with small knives. Then they removed all his books from their shelves, riffling the pages of each volume.

As he left his office, one of them was examining the picture of McCall's mother with her Main Line coiffure, holding her first grandchild.

The other one stepped into the hallway with him. "There could be a bug on your phone," he said. "Or in the main phone exchange. Or on the box in the basement. Or anywhere in your office. I can drill a hole in a vase so small you can't see it and slip a bug in there. Or it could be one of those harmonica bugs." He held up an imaginary one between thumb and forefinger. "They can turn one of those things on and off whenever they want. By telephone. From anywhere in the world. Just by dialing a number. Selective eavesdropping, they call it. If it's one of them, they're very hard to detect."

"Do what you can," McCall said. "And check the pay phone across the street."

McCall thought of his daughter. While she was doing her child's rounds on that summer morning a few miles away in Alexandria, he was struggling for his life against three men: the Hanged Man, the Merchant with the Figs from Tyre and the Masked Tumbler who had flown through the air to his death.

If they'd succeeded in throwing McCall down, his daughter would have lived out her life believing she'd predicted her father's death. He vowed he would never tell her how close the cards had come.

He thought of the tarot deck while waiting for the elevator. No, I don't believe in them, he told himself. And I hope they leave me alone.

A HALF HOUR LATER, when he returned with a new shirt and tie, the phone man put a bug in his hand. "There may be others," he said. "This city is a tapper's paradise. If I told you that there are at least a quarter of a million illegal taps in Washington, would you believe me? No?"

"Where did you get it?"

"Across the street in the pay phone."

McCall studied it, then went to the window and looked at the phone booth on the corner.

"It's your fault," the phone man said. "You and everyone else who hires these slope-heads. You put them on the payroll, teach them every dirty trick in the book, then lay them off. And what do they do? They set up for themselves, free-lancing for anyone who will hire them. They're corrupting the whole country."

McCall handed the bug to the man.

"Put it back."

"Ha?"

"Put it back where you found it."

"Oh. I get you. I see."

THE TWO MEN LEFT a half hour later with their black boxes and trailing wires and rattling cart.

McCall sat down in his chair. He was still trembling, still clammy with perspiration. Every time he thought of his struggle on the dark stair, he felt the terror anew. Every muscle ached; he was becoming stiffer by the hour, and when he removed his shirt he saw that his torso was covered with angry red bruise marks. It would be a very long time before he could enter a dark building or sleep in a dark room. He would never forget the sound of the man's terrified voice, falling. Or the thud of impact.

He looked at the CIA report he had gotten from Daniels. One of them—the dead man?—had left a heel mark on the cover. Operation Zealot: it had nearly cost him his life. But now it was his turn. He would use the report as bait to trap someone else.

He took an envelope from his desk drawer and put a stamp on it, then wrote out an address. On a piece of stationery he wrote two words: "You missed."

He folded the paper, put it in the envelope, and sealed it.

THE IDEA THAT OCCURRED to McCall was insistent. It was like a little dog trailing a traveler, impervious to thrown stones and freezing pails of water. Its name was Assassination.

Probably the incident in the stairwell had fathered the thought. Assassination, of course, was counter to all of McCall's training, his mind-set, his traditions. So he rejected it.

But no matter how many times he rejected it, the idea of assassination returned. Its appeal was seductive: a timely thrust of the blade through the arras, a push off the bridge, three shakes of a malevolent vial over a cup of tea. Whatever the form, history would change its direction.

More than that, the idea had sprung into his head complete in all its details, a whole scenario including the means, the planning, the target, the money, the motivation, even the consequences. All he needed to do was sell the idea to a sponsor who could provide the funds. The scenario even included the identity of that patron.

Selling an assassination was new to McCall. But he soon became so convinced of the need for it, he was eager to try. First he would have to get some sales aids. He had one of them: the Operation Zealot document he'd gotten from Daniels on the roof. The next piece he needed was a list of the military parts Iran needed; he got that from the file. He was all set. He put in a call to Martin Wainwright, probably the most unlikely man to sponsor assassination in all of Washington.

AT ONE O'CLOCK McCall hurried across the lobby to the front doors, headed for a crucial meeting with Wainwright. Through the glass door he could see the cab waiting.

"Any cooler, John?"

The security guard swung open the door for him. "Not a chance, Mr. McCall. It's a hundred and six in the shade."

McCall stepped out on the sidewalk. All about him he heard the wailing horns of the trapped Friday traffic. And now he would be part of it. All this effort to bring bad news to a man who hated bad news.

Wainwright was a son of a bitch. He'd flatly refused to answer McCall's urgent message. McCall had had to phone Mrs. Woolman to intercede—the one person in Washington who could cow Wainwright. God bless, you, Mrs. Woolman.

Less than a mile away the presidential helicopter rose from its pad and flew west. The Friday exodus from Washington had officially begun.

Waves of heat rising from the sidewalk embraced him. Hastily crossing the sidewalk he curled himself like a comma into the waiting cab.

The moment he sat back he realized the cab was not air-conditioned. Direct sunlight had turned the back seat into an oven.

"What happened to your air conditioning?"

"The heat wave. It broke."

"Then take me to the nearest cab stand."

"Forget it. There's no cabs there. The whole town's trying to get out of here. It's either this cab or nothing."

"Go on then. Make it fast."

"Yeah. Sure. Fast."

McCall sat on the edge of the sun-hot seat, feeling the perspiration start on his forehead and prickle down his back. Hot dusty air blew through the open windows. How he hated Washington. How he hated the melting heat. How he hated Martin Wainwright.

He was still trembling from the terrifying experience on the stairway. By now stiffness had settled in. His left arm ached where it had been seized. Every muscle in his body seemed to be throbbing. He'd been almost hobbled by the twisting of his leg. Tomorrow morning, he knew, he would be barely able to move. He was a mass of bruises. But he was alive. And at the right time he would have revenge for every bruise. Every single one.

At the very first intersection, the cab was captured by the monumental traffic jam. It was going to be a long ride.

The heat was like a tyrant who hated his subjects.

As the cab crept, McCall opened his attaché case and withdrew the manila dossier on Operation Zealot that he'd gotten from Daniels on the roof. After scanning it once more, he thumbed through a series of memos, conference summaries, and field reports, refreshing his memory on the case. He had a tough sale ahead of him.

From a clear acetate sleeve he took out a packet of black-and-white photographs, studying each one with attention. Many of them were very grainy blowups of telephoto shots taken by surveillance teams.

Next he examined a saddle-stitched report stamped SE-CRET, the linchpin of his story to Wainwright. It was titled:

A SUMMARY OF MILITARY PARTS NOW UNDER REQUISITION BY THE ARMS PROCUREMENT SECTION OF THE GOVERNMENT OF IRAN, WITH COMPARABLE U.S. ARMED FORCES STOCK AND INVENTORY CODE NUMBERS AND INCLUDING CURRENT INTERNATIONAL OPEN MARKET PRICES BEING QUOTED BY INDEPENDENT ARMS DEALERS.

He flipped through page after page of parts descriptions and catalogue numbers. On at least two thirds of the items, the price column contained N.O.—Not Offered. These were parts that Iran was not able to find in the open arms market, parts it would have to hire smugglers to steal. Every single item in the dossier was on the U.S. proscribed exports list.

McCall hefted the report. A gold mine—a smuggler's dream list: hundreds of high-tech parts that no arms dealer could supply. A skillful smuggler could name his own price for any item and walk away with a fortune.

McCall's eye selected an item at random: CRT 2374388/9. It was a part for a military computer, worth no more than $120. Iran might have to pay $12,000 to get it.

The last item in the dossier was a photograph of an olive-skinned man of about forty. McCall had seen that expression and those eyes on a number of faces in his career. Looking back at McCall were the eyes of a fanatic. A man who would kill every last soul on this lost star to achieve his goal.

This face was the reason McCall was slowly soaking with perspiration in a traffic jam in Washington in late September when he was supposed to have been sailing on a beam

each on a 36-foot Morgan on Chesapeake Bay with his son.
The thought of the cool wind on the water made the heat
seem worse.

"That's one I owe you," he said to the photo.

On the back of the photograph a label contained one
typewritten word: ATTASHAH. Someone in the Arms Bureau had penciled *The Unstoppable* after it. Below that, with
his pen, McCall wrote: *The most dangerous man in the world.*

IN THE OLD DAYS a messenger bearing news like McCall's
would have been put to death by the emperor. After the last
words had tumbled from his terrified lips—the army
crushed in the field, the summer crops flooded in the
northern provinces, an imperial city decimated by plague—
bare hands would have strangled him in front of the throne.
Wainwright would have been the kind of emperor who
strangled bearers of bad news.

"Martin," McCall practiced in his mind, "what we need
to do is assassinate a few irritating people. Please sign the
execution order here and here in triplicate."

A drop of perspiration fell from McCall's chin onto the
dossier. He fanned his face with Attashah's photograph.

GRATEFULLY, MCCALL walked into the air-conditioned
lobby and stepped into the elevator. Cool air began to dry
his soaked skin.

On the sixth floor he walked the long corridor toward the
muffled sound of contentious voices. In front of a closed
door, on a golden oak stand, was a sign: NATIONAL SECURITY COUNCIL SUBCOMMITTEE ON INTERNATIONAL ARMS
TRAFFIC CONTROL.

Through the door he heard Mrs. Woolman's scolding
voice. "Of course it can't wait. This situation has become a

real crisis now. We should have listened to McCall a yea
ago."

McCall paused to adjust his tie and wipe his face. Unde
his suit jacket, the back of his shirt was drenched.

Mrs. Woolman was saying: "It seems perfectly prepos
terous to me to have that man spend hours explaining thing
to us, then not follow his advice. And you don't even hav
the common courtesy to respond to his phone calls. You
behavior is disgraceful."

McCall pushed open the committee room door and stoo
in the doorway, looking at them.

Mrs. Woolman was standing by the window staring ou
at the long traffic lines framing Constitution Mall.

Wainwright was sitting alone at that enormous confer
ence table. Abandoned balls of paper and heaped ashtray
littered the top of it. The sour odor of pipe, cigar, and cig
arette smoke. The committee meeting had ended and all the
others had left—the legal counsels, the military advisers, the
staff members, the secretaries: the spear carriers, cupbear
ers and scene swellers. Other than Mrs. Woolman, Wain
wright was quite alone. Without the pageantry. Diminished
in size. At bay.

If it hadn't been for Mrs. Woolman, Wainwright would
have already escaped for a long weekend.

"Good afternoon," McCall said.

Wainwright quickly sat up and busied himself with pa
pers. Mrs. Woolman dropped the end of the pull cord and
went to her seat. But neither spoke.

Wainwright irritably watched McCall pull the dossie
from the attaché case. Then he cast a glance at Mrs. Wool
man. "Someone picked a hell of a time to call a meeting,
McCall. A Friday afternoon in the worst goddam heat wave
in living memory."

"There's no ideal time for this meeting, Martin."

"Suppose you tell us in one sentence what all this bad news is."

"How about one word," McCall said.

"Fine. In a word then."

"Attashah."

Wainwright squirmed irritably. "Beautiful. What's an Attashah?"

"A kind of walking disaster looking for a place to happen."

Wainwright looked at the thick dossier in McCall's hands. "How long is it going to take?"

"Ten minutes," said McCall. "Bad news is quickly told."

The chairman sighed heavily. "Start firing."

McCall opened the packet of photographs. Far away a helicopter pumped across the Washington sky. Another VIP in full flight from the heat.

"Here's the situation, Mr. Chairman." McCall handed Wainwright a photograph of President Richard Nixon and Henry Kissinger with the Shah of Iran in Tehran. "In 1971 when President Nixon and Henry Kissinger visited the Shah, they permitted His Serene Majesty to buy great quantities of our most secret military weapons. Billions of dollars' worth. Not even our allies in Europe were allowed to buy this stuff. It was our most sophisticated surveillance equipment. The Shah was able to snoop not only on the Russians but on all his other neighbors as well. And that gave the Shah an awesome amount of military power."

"I know this," said Wainwright. "Get to the point."

McCall said, "When the Shah fled his country, he left behind mountains of this sophisticated equipment. And to this day most of it is scattered in military storehouses all over Iran."

"Yes, yes, McCall."

"Martin," said Mrs. Woolman, "you are either going to let this man give his report without your editorial ragging or I'm going to tell him to leave this room."

"Okay. Okay. Get on with it, McCall."

McCall said, "Lately the Iranians have realized what enormous political power they have in their hands. So their military people have been trying to get the stuff working again. Fortunately for us, they've come up against one severe problem: no spare parts."

McCall put the parts lists on the conference table and pushed it over to Wainwright, who quickly flipped the pages and looked back at McCall.

"You have to appreciate what a gold mine that list is for a skilled smuggler, Mr. Chairman. It's the temptation of a lifetime."

Wainwright nodded. "I understand, McCall. Get on with it."

McCall slid another photograph across the table to the chairman. It was an extreme close-up of a mound of diodes and computer chips. They all rested on the tip of a human forefinger.

"These parts," said McCall, "are made only in the United States and almost all of them are on the official U.S. Proscribed Exports List. Okay? So, in a nutshell, Mr. Chairman, Iran can't beg, borrow, or steal the parts they need to get that very dangerous equipment operating."

"That's good news. So what are we here for?"

"I'm getting there, Mr. Chairman. There's only one way for Iran to get the parts they need. From an independent arms dealer who knows how to find them and smuggle them out of the U.S."

Wainwright rubbed his face irritably.

McCall said, "We think Iran is about to solve its problem."

Wainwright stopped rubbing his face. "How?"

"Rooley Attashah."

"Who's he?"

McCall pushed another photograph across the conference table. "He's a very skillful Iranian agent. And he's been sent out into the marketplace with a satchelful of money to buy the needed parts at any price."

Wainwright studied the face in the photograph. Attashah's eyes seemed to study Wainwright's face in return. "So? There must be some way to stop him."

"Name one."

Wainwright turned his eyes to McCall, looking for a sign of insolence in his face.

"That's your department, McCall."

"I wish it were that easy."

"But Iran is a backward nation," said Mrs. Woolman. "What good are a few pieces of modern equipment to them?"

"It can enable them to tune in on any communications anywhere in the Mideast. It can enable them to disrupt Israeli and Western military communications. It will give them the matériel they need to cause great dissension among the Arabs. And it will positively drive Russia crazy. They'll be able to raise hell from the Russian border to northern Africa. In the Middle East, this can be your worst nightmare come true."

"Dear God in heaven," said Mrs. Woolman.

"So. What's the answer?" demanded Wainwright.

McCall cast a glance at Mrs. Woolman and shrugged.

Wainwright looked at Mrs. Woolman, then back at McCall.

"If Attashah gets those parts—" McCall began.

"Yes, yes, McCall," said Wainwright. "You'd better have some damned convincing evidence." He slapped the mahogany table. "Thank you, Mrs. Woolman. I think I'll take our friend here out for a little drink and a long conversation."

MARTIN WAINWRIGHT was a bourbon drinker—and he drank it straight. In Dino's he ordered it in a two-ounce glass. Then he sat and scowled at it, preoccupied, with the expression of a habitually unhappy man.

There was no secret about his mood. Recently he had turned sixty. After twenty years of making himself useful in Washington, his once-promising career in public service had still not borne fruit. His future was in shadow. And the hour grew late.

Kudos, applause, awards, decorations, magazine sobriquets—these eluded him. In spite of all his efforts, all his accomplishments, his indefatigable chairmanships, speeches, newsletters, public service donations, he was still known in Washington merely as Engine Andy's grandson.

His main claim to fame was his inheritance of one of America's greatest fortunes. Yet he was a dedicated, civic-minded patrician, a man who set standards. With his noble face, he belonged in a toga.

He needed a victory and he needed it soon. Above all he wanted to be somebody, not somebody's grandson. And that was McCall's trump card.

Wainwright faced McCall with his usual brusqueness. "Okay. How do you handle this Attashah?"

McCall shrugged. "There's only one solution, Mr. Chairman. Eliminate unhappiness. Happy men do not buy guns."

"Very funny, McCall."

"It's the only answer."

"Come on. There was obviously something you didn't want to say in front of Mrs. Woolman."

McCall shrugged.

Again, Wainwright rubbed his face irritably. "We've got more spooks and counterspooks in our government than most of the other countries in the world combined. You can't tell me we're not doing something about this Attashah."

McCall said, "Yes. My bureau has had off-the-record chats with some of the bigger arms traders. We've told them that the U.S. takes a dim view of anyone supplying those spare parts to Mr. Attashah. And so far no dealer has tried to fill in Mr. Attashah's dance card for him. But now Iran is putting some real money on the table—and as Oscar Wilde said, 'I can resist everything but temptation.' So it's only going to be a matter of time before one of them eventually takes up Mr. Attashah's deal. Martin, you have to understand: Warnings aren't going to work. This one Iranian package can make some arms dealer rich beyond his dreams. And wreck the peace of the Mideast—and worse."

"I know. I know about worse. Let's get back to Attashah. What kind of a guy is Attashah? Can you buy him off—or scare him off?"

"Attashah has big brass balls. Four of them. You don't buy him. You don't scare him. He's a devout Muslim—a Shi'ite—dedicated to his country's cause."

"You're saying he's a dangerous fanatic."

"Worse. He's also one of the smartest men in the business. We've got our hands full."

"Well, what about the arms dealers?"

"We warn them. We use the carrot and the stick. And we have them watched."

"That's it? Have them watched? Christ, those arms traders have more moves than a snake. It would take a goddam army to watch them. You're holding back on me, McCall. I can feel it. What's the answer?"

McCall shrugged.

"Listen, McCall. You're the expert on arms traffic and smuggling. Not me. That's why I got you appointed as special adviser to the committee. You see what I'm saying? So come on. Just between us girls, what do you think we ought to do?"

McCall sat back and eyed Wainwright speculatively.

"Well?" Wainwright said. "Out with it, man."

McCall slowly reached into his pocket. He drew his hand out and pressed something into Wainwright's palm. Doubtfully, Wainwright glanced about the barroom, then put his fist in his lap and glanced down as he opened his fingers.

"What's this? Dear God. It's a silver bullet." He was mystified. "You want us to use the Lone Ranger?" Wainwright waited for McCall to answer him. Instead he got silence.

"McCall, will you tell me what the hell you're talking about? You want—oh—I see. Wait. Oh, come on, McCall." He leaned forward and whispered in a hoarse voice. "You want me to send hit teams out to snuff a bunch of Iranians in shit-stained sheets?"

He folded his arms and stared at McCall. "Even if we wanted to do that, McCall, we could never bring it off. Can you imagine what an operation it would take to get a hit team into Iran—the planning, the money, the time? Besides, we can't go around knocking off all these people. Here. Take it back. You have to be out of your skull."

McCall refused to take the bullet. "That's not what I'm talking about."

"Then what, man? For God's sake. Spit it out. Is it Attashah? You want us to knock him off?"

"I'm thinking about the arms traders."

Martin Wainwright looked at McCall for a very long time. Then he said, "Oh." He looked again at the silver bullet in his hand. "Arms traders. You want to ace them." He looked at McCall. "No traders, no spare parts." Then he shook his head. "Here. You take this little number over to the glory boys in the CIA—that's their department."

McCall said, "It doesn't belong over there."

"Take it," Wainwright said. "I could never get anything this crazy through the committee."

"You don't have to get it through the committee. You asked me what I would do. And I'm telling you."

Wainwright seized his bourbon like a man who had narrowly escaped death and finished it in one mouthful. "Jesus."

McCall pulled the Operation Zealot dossier out of his case and handed it to Wainwright. "Why don't you take five minutes to thumb through this?"

Wainwright took it and read the title.

"Where did you get this?"

"I have ways."

"I shouldn't be seeing this, McCall."

"Maybe when you read it you'll change your mind."

Wainwright skimmed it in under two minutes. "Pentagon stuff," he said when he was finished. "Crap. I don't trust a word those people say. I'll bet this whole thing is fabricated out of whole cloth. That doesn't convince me of anything."

McCall looked at the secret report wryly. He'd risked his life to get that thing, Daniels had risked his career, and the Masked Tumbler who flies through the air—whoever he was—had died as a result. And Wainwright had dismissed it out of hand.

The man sat across from McCall, slumped in his chair, his right fist pressed against his lips. He murmured something. Then cleared his throat and said it again.

"How many?" he asked softly. "Hits, I mean."

After a pause, McCall answered. "Three. Maybe four."

"Three total? That's all?"

"That's right. There are only three major dealers who have the high-tech knowledge and smuggling skill to bring it off."

"Are you sure? Just three?"

"Three top bananas in one package."

"I see." Wainwright cleared his throat again.

McCall said, "That way the other arms traders get the message. We'd be cutting Attashah off at the knees. None of the other traders would touch his package after that. And that would be the end of this Iranian nonsense."

Wainwright rubbed his hand over his face and bald head furiously. "It's a damned dumb idea."

"You're right," said McCall.

Wainwright looked at the silver bullet again. "Three of these and there'll be no spare parts for Iran?"

"As you say, Martin. It's a damned dumb idea." McCall took his silver bullet back.

"What about reprisals?"

McCall shrugged. "Forget it, Martin."

"No, no. Talk to me. Tell me about reprisals."

"There would be no way to trace any of this to you or the committee. No one would know for sure who did it. But they'll know exactly why. Besides, no one is going to weep over three of these animals even if they did know who did it. None of the other arms traders are going to take on the U.S. government. Which brings up one other interesting aspect to this."

"Go on."

"You asked me one night to keep my eyes open for a chance for you to make a little PR."

"Oh hell, McCall. That was too much bourbon talking."

"Brilliant careers have been built on moments like this, Martin. The Iranians could create the kind of problem that could fester for years. It could lead from one damned crisis to another. It could upset our diplomatic applecarts all over the world and put us on the defensive and finally bring on a major war. And you could stop that with one decisive act. You show all your qualities of leadership. And people would have to formulate a new opinion of you."

Wainwright looked at McCall's face as though he were reading a road map. "I need another drink."

WAINWRIGHT SAT IN DEEP SILENCE, stroking his face with his fingers. Occasionally he would throw a piercing glance at McCall. He was oblivious to the other people in the barroom.

Then he sat up decisively. "Could you do all three at once?"

"Sure. That would be the idea."

"All three?"

"All three."

"My God, McCall. What a package that would be."

"It would be a Washington legend, Martin."

"How much?"

McCall shrugged. "Oh—let's see. A package of three assassinations, all simultaneous? Say three bills."

"Three million?"

McCall hesitated for a moment, then put his hand to his mouth. "Absolutely clean work. It would mean complete deniability for the committee. It will mean no more big trouble with Iran for a long time. And no more footsie between arms traders. They'll know unofficially we have a heavy hitter in Washington who will come down hard on them if they get out of line."

"What heavy hitter?"

"You."

"Oh." Wainwright was transparent. He was picturing himself with one of those sub rosa reputations in Washington that some men dream of. A man of behind-the-scenes power. A heavy hitter. The kind of man who, entering a crowded room, would be whispered about. The kind of man Presidents would solicit advice from. A legend. Tantalized, bemused, ensorcelled, Wainwright had a third bourbon. Somebody.

He lapsed into deep thought again. At one point he looked at McCall and snorted. "It's so simple. Not bad. Not bad at all, McCall."

At last he asked, "Who are these three men?"

"Garbage. Human garbage." McCall took a bar napkin and wrote out three names on it with a felt pen. Then he wrote a fourth. He handed the napkin to Wainwright.

"There are four names here. Who's R. Roe?"

"Anyone else that might take the Iranian deal."

"Oh. I wonder who that would be."

"So do I," McCall answered. "So do I."

THEY TOOK A WALK. McCall was almost completely silent, letting things cook inside Wainwright's mind.

The September sun was merciless, and the heat seemed to have emptied the city. The few people about tried to walk in the shade.

"Christ," said Wainwright. "It must be a hundred and ten degrees." But he walked along oblivious to it, up K Street. Shopkeepers in their cool interiors looked out on the streets for customers, in vain.

Wainwright walked like a man with a pain in his gut, plodding, bent, self-absorbed, unmindful of the perspiration that flowed down his face. At last McCall could stand it no longer. He pulled Wainwright into an air-conditioned bar.

Wainwright was still rejecting the idea. But he kept coming back to it, to scoff and sniff and back off—just as McCall had done earlier. Yet he didn't leave—he couldn't stop thinking about it. It was the thing he loved: a quick solution. Simple. Clean. Safe. If only he dared.

"Lordy. Lordy," he said thoughtfully. "I wish I could go talk to my old professor of ethics and morals. I mean, this goes against the grain of everything I've been taught—everything I believe in."

He rubbed his hands together indecisively. "To stop these criminals, I have to become a criminal." He thrashed about in his seat like a whale trying to pull free from a harpoon.

McCall said, "We face questions no people ever faced before. Today's combatants aren't soldiers anymore—they're agents operating in a slimy terrain created by terrorists and guerrillas. If we're going to survive, we have to destroy them before they destroy us. History has stopped repeating itself, Martin."

"I'm not sure I agree with all of that," said Wainwright.

"The old rules of morality don't apply anymore," McCall said.

The most bemusing aspect of the conversation, for McCall, was the money. When he mentioned the price as "three bills," he'd meant three hundred thousand. Wainwright thought he meant three million—and never turned a hair at the price.

Without preamble Wainwright abruptly stood. "I can't believe I'm even considering this insane idea. I'll see you later." He strode away, through the door and out onto the sidewalk.

McCall sat finishing his drink and watching Wainwright pacing in the heat of the intersection, trying to flag down a cab. By the time he got one, his shirtfront was soaked through.

McCall pulled the silver bullet from his pocket and stared at it. A corny little trick from childhood. This time it didn't work.

He felt spent. He was supposed to pick up his son and take him for a weekend sail on the Chesapeake. But his body was so sore that he was not sure he could safely drive home, let alone raise the sails and manipulate the sheets of his yacht.

Today should have been his death day. Only a groping error had saved him from that terrible fall down, down, down in pitch darkness. He could never again accept the gift of each future minute of life as casually as he had accepted the previous ones. How could he insouciantly go for a weekend sail? More to the point, how could he have casually planned the murders of three arms merchants?

Most wondrous of all, with his new awe of death, how could he continue to plan the three murders? For he certainly intended to.

McCall dreaded the onset of nightfall and sleep. And nightmares. He wondered what the rest of his life would be like.

ROOLEY ATTASHAH arrived that evening at JFK Airport on Long Island. Wearing an ill-fitting wig and equipped with a forged Turkish passport, he passed through customs unnoticed.

An hour later he was registered at a residential hotel in midtown Manhattan. He stood at a window and looked out over Manhattan and the Hudson River at the sunset of a very hot day. Somewhere between his hotel and the Pacific Coast three thousand miles to the west was the matérial his country needed.

He knew exactly how he would get it.

BLACK-AND-BLUE, stiff, and still haunted by the memory
of the stairwell, McCall took his son sailing on the Chesapeake. The heat wave persisted and the winds on the water
were flaccid, but the boy enjoyed himself enormously and
the light airs required very little sail-hoisting or other
movement. So McCall slouched in the cockpit of his sailboat and rested his stiff muscles and various pains.

Mostly he spent the weekend brooding about Wainwright.

McCall knew that Wainwright had gotten away from him.
If he was going to change that man's mind, he needed to do
two things quickly.

First, he had to make the three arms dealers real to Wainwright. The three had to be men with characteristics and
reputations and histories and predictable futures. And he
had to make Wainwright hate them.

Second, since Wainwright didn't accept Operation Zealot's assessment of the Iranian danger, McCall had to find
another assessment that Wainwright would accept—one that
would scare the hell out of him. It had to be a sobering, valid,
historical assessment. So he turned to a historian.

THE FOLLOWING MONDAY, McCall went to see a man who
was known to his peers by the sobriquet of Cassandra. And
he brought a votive offering: food.

Cassandra was housed in one of the State Department's
oldest office buildings in Washington, down in a subterranean labyrinth—a hodgepodge of secretaries' cubicles, executive offices, mail rooms, closets, winking computers, file
areas, and twisting hallways that led nowhere. It was like
walking through the grid of a crossword puzzle.

People were talking on phones, rattling typewriters,
wrapping packages for waiting messengers, huddling in
hallway conversations, and hastily disappearing down cor-

ridors. Everything was done with murmuring voices and a sense of quickstep urgency. The flavor was exactly that of a coronary unit in an emergency ward: patient fibrillating, heartbeat below 20/minute, blood sludging, the doctor inserting the long needle of a transthoracic catheter right through the chest wall, straight into the heart to pump in 20 cc of a lovely mauve-colored heart medicine. Quick, quick, quick.

Many times over the years McCall had visited this section of the State Department—which always wore its air of crisis—yet he still wasn't sure what all those people were doing. Indeed, if pressed he could not have told you with any fullness what Cassandra did.

Cassandra's real name was Harry Hollis, and officially he was a State Department research officer. He had a Ph.D. in Middle East history and culture, and his specialty was Middle East military affairs. But he was involved in much more than that.

Bearing his box of deli sandwiches and coffee, and limping slightly, McCall followed the maze along a memorized route. It was like dialing the combination to a safe: two turns to the left, a turn to the right, twist, pause, where the hell is it?, turn again, and finally a sign looming over a doorway: ALL HOPE ABANDON, YE WHO ENTER HERE.

McCall stood in the doorway with a knowing smile. "How about just a pinch less despair today, Harry?"

"You look a sight," Hollis said. "Where'd you get the shiner?" He pushed his eyeglasses up onto his forehead and sat back from his computer screen. "Don't tell me. Wherever you got it, you deserve it."

"I was taking a flying lesson," McCall said. He put the cardboard box of food on the computer table.

"Bless my soul, Bobby. Are those sandwiches from the one and only Belly Deli?"

"They are."

"Praise the Lord. And might one of them be a corned beef on Jewish rye with coleslaw and Russian dressing?"

"The very same," McCall said.

"That's what I call a very proper bribe."

"It is."

Hollis looked down at his own huge girth, wiped a pudgy hand over his fleshy face. "I don't need it. But—I'll take it." He unwrapped a sandwich, took a large bite from it, and sighed as the juice of the coleslaw flowed down the back of his hand. "I'd kill for one of these any day—and I'm talking about shooting my own mother in Garfinckel's window. Eat, eat."

McCall tried to eat. But the memory of the stairwell was still racing around the edges of his mind and he chewed without pleasure.

"Deli food always reminds me of the uncertain positioning of moral values in our society," Hollis began.

McCall had heard this before. Food made Hollis loquacious. "You're talking about relativism," McCall declared flatly.

Hollis shook his head. "I'm talking about life's salami tactics. Life steals your soul a slice at a time until it's all gone. Then the gods abandon you."

McCall's ears were shut. As he chewed mechanically, he heard the Masked Tumbler's fading cry down the stairwell. Down. Down. Down. McCall heard it with unending horror.

While the man talked, McCall's eyes roved over Cassandra's office. It had grown worse since his last visit, a chronicler's nightmare: Piled in tilting stacks on tables and chairs and spilled across various floor areas were columns of computer print-outs, flanked and supported or endangered by pile upon pile of odd-size books with such titles as *Strategies* and Tactics: The Arab Way of War; Egyptian Idioms; On the Causes of War and the Madness of Man; Cairo, 1942; an eight-volume set of Benoit's History of the Arab; a copy of the third volume of The Mid-East Year Book 1963; an outdated calendar in English and Arabic taped to the wall with the bottom right corner half furled; a bust of the historian Gibbon, set upon a radio; abandoned take-out coffee containers; soda bottles; two blue-and-gold boxes of Grandma's Kountry Kookies—contents looted; three rifled jumbo-size potato chip and pretzel cans; a cavalry saber wrapped in an unidentifiable black-and-red pennant peeking out from under two unmarked brown cardboard cartons.

On the wall next to the calendar was a poster: CANNABIS. A STUDENT'S GUIDE. EVERYTHING YOU SHOULD—AND DON'T WANT TO—KNOW ABOUT MARIJUANA. Below the headline were two columns of staggered type outlining a full-color photograph of the plant itself.

Piles of Foreign Affairs magazines, monographs, reports in clear plastic covers, manila file folders, coffee cups, shoes, a dried-out half lemon, neckties, a dilapidated umbrella—all formed an uprising, an outbreak, an insurrection of undisciplined parts.

On the open office door was taped a sign: DO NOT CLEAN THIS ROOM ON PAIN OF DEATH.

Someone had written in ballpoint pen below it: Thank God.

Hollis had a considerable reputation among Washington's prognosticators, futurists, think-tank people, and various what-if forecasters—those identified as the Mirror Mirror on the Wall crowd. He was labeled the Cassandra of the State Department because he was said to be constructing a computer model of all of man's wars in history and their causes. Rumor had it that he had already finished it and had now predicted the time and outcome of the ultimate war between East and West.

"They say your model's finished," McCall said.

"I neither confirm nor deny, Bobby, my son." Hollis emitted his famous mocking laugh. "These idiots are so afraid of my model they are now announcing that history is no longer repeating itself. We've run off the charts and into unknown territory, they say. The last time I heard that kind of talk it helped get us into the Vietnam War, and oh boy, did history repeat itself then."

He took another bite of the sandwich and bolted it. "The trouble with the American people is they despise the past and believe they are somehow exempt from history. They suffer from the arrogance that precedes a great fall. *Hubris* is the correct term." He hooted his mocking laugh again, making his large body tremble.

"Listen." He shook his sandwich at McCall. "You don't have to make a computer model of all of man's wars to predict the future. Man's history hasn't stopped repeating itself. Why? Because man's nature hasn't changed. Even if he gets his hairy little ass to the nethermost galaxy in the universe, he will find his own nature waiting there for him. And his same brainless, selfish, incompetent little history will continue to repeat itself there until the end."

McCall grinned. "It's that optimism that has made you famous." He pointed at the screen. "Who's winning?"

"Not the human race, I can tell you." Harry Hollis chuckled. "I'm doing a paper on Assurbanipal for our office in Turkey—640 B.C. Change this ancient idiot's name to our esteemed President's and it reads like today's newspaper. The same plot, the same characters as today: the bird-brained congressman, the corrupter in the Senate, the greedy Secretary, the blindly arrogant general." He tapped the glass face of the screen. "They're all here and they're all working to bring disaster on themselves. In ancient Assyria and modern Washington. It's the same old script.'' He reached for another corned beef sandwich. ''I'm very lucky I found the computer. You know why?''

McCall shook his head.

''Because,'' Hollis said, ''I'm a born klutz. Can't hold a bat, too fat to run, too flat-footed to soldier. I walk into furniture, drop things and fall off curbs. Ergo, I stayed home to be near the cook and filled in the time with reading. See? I have a gift for failure. Even my father could see that. And that freed me from enterprise. There was no question I had no career. Can you picture a brain surgeon with these klutzy hands? So my father paid for my Ph.D. in hopes I might thereby feed myself—a large responsibility, as you can see.'' He wheezed with muted laughter. ''My gift for failure thereby left me free to spend my life reading and speculating on the madness and the magnificence of man. Being a klutz has its advantages. And when klutz meets computer, the whole town quakes with fear.'' He laughed his whistling, wheezy laugh again. ''It's called Cassandra's Revenge.'' He held out his hand. ''What have you got?''

''Listen, Harry, I have something here—''

''I know. I know. I never saw this paper, I never heard of you, and this meeting never took place.'' Hollis fitted his eyeglasses down over his eyes and thumbed through McCall's report. He absorbed it with great speed, running an index finger down the center of each page.

He looked up at last. ''Three layers down I detect the fine hand of Pentagon Intelligence in this.''

''You think it's true?''

''Is what true?''

''That Iran can cause an East-West war?''

"Do you want Iran to cause an East-West war? Okay. I can accommodate you. You want me to? All right. Here's a scenario. I did one on this subject a couple of years ago."

"I remember. Scared the hell out of everyone."

"Okay. Here's the way it plays: The biggest danger of war right now is this. There's a faction in the Kremlin that feels Russia is falling below parity with the U.S.—particularly in sophisticated technology. That makes them vulnerable, and vulnerability makes them nervous. So it's panic time in Moscow. See what I'm saying? Iran is like a knife tucked up against Russia's soft underbelly. If Iran gets that surveillance equipment operating, it can be used against not only the Arab countries and Israel, but against Russia too. Snooping against a paranoid nation can tip the balance in Moscow's eyes, and *voilà*! We're off to the races."

"Do you believe that?"

Hollis snorted. "Believe? Listen. Moscow's got problems that are so bad even Washington's worried. Their system mitigates against them ever coming up with a high-technology capability—like our Silicon Valley. So they're having a tough time keeping up with us in computerized warfare. Furthermore, each year the Russian minority is becoming smaller in a sea of other ethnic groups. The place is crawling with alcoholism, corruption, industrial incompetence. Agriculture keeps laying eggs. Nobody gives a shit. The whole economy is rickety; it's in constant trouble and the people are so dispirited they can't even raise a decent revolt. They are falling behind the West and now the Third World nations are on the move. And on and on. You understand? What I'm saying is they may figure the only way to stay in the game is to hit us before we get too far ahead."

While he talked he pulled the hard disc from his computer disc drive and rooted through a file drawer of floppy discs. He shoved one in a disc drive and snapped it shut.

"Trouble with you, Harry, is you're a pessimist."

"No. No, I'm not. But the Russians are. And they're getting more pessimistic every day."

Hollis watched the menu come up on his screen and tapped out a file number. "Here it is. Three years old. But it's pretty good. This is my assessment of the Iranian surveillance equipment and its impact on the Mideast. In fact some of the stuff in your paper was lifted from mine. All this part in here is right out of this computer. Practically verbatim. See? The kicker here isn't just Ivan's goosey asshole, although that's bad enough. Here's an assessment of Israel's reaction to Iranian surveillance. It could sabotage their military communications. See? Very dangerous. And here's the Saudis. See? Very unhappy. Then there's Egypt. She is not going to love Iranian eavesdropping. See? And more and more. The main problem is Iran is looking for anything that can make trouble. And that surveillance equipment is a dream come true. So I'd mark this all down in big red letters. D-A-N-G-E-R."

Harry Hollis took another half sandwich and bit off half of it. He chewed joyfully. "Dear God. You corrupter. I see you brought cinnamon buns." He waved the decapitated sandwich at McCall. "Listen, Bobby lad. I can put this same bleeding assessment on anything in the world today. The truth is we are all inside this jerry can filled with gasoline, and any idiot including the Iranians can strike a match and immolate us all. Remember the sign over my door."

McCall said, "I'd like a copy of that report to show to a big fan of yours."

"Who's that?"

"Wainwright. How about a copy of it?"

"How about another sandwich?"

"How about a nice piece of German apple cake?"

"My God. You brought that too?" Hollis's fat fingers rooted through the food box. "Jesus. Four of them."

ARMED WITH HARRY HOLLIS'S White Paper and other materials, McCall called Wainwright. Before he could do more than identify himself, Wainwright said, "The answer's no. Forget it."

McCall said, "I have something to show you."

"It won't do you any good."

"How about tonight around nine?"

"Okay. But it won't do you any good."

WAINWRIGHT LIVED in a compound of magnificent town houses in historic Alexandria, complete with a colonial gatehouse and a security force. His home was considered the *chef d'oeuvre* of that showplace.

A houseman admitted McCall. He was enormous, with legthick arms filling the sleeves of his white jacket. As he led McCall to the study, they passed a dining room where a dozen people in formal dress were having a lively meal.

Wainwright's study was one of the most celebrated rooms in the house. It was done entirely in Federal-period fruitwood paneling, hand-carved in China, which had come from the Danforth mansion on Long Island and had been willed by Wainwright to the Metropolitan Museum in New York City; the museum had eagerly accepted it. Included in the will were a number of rare books and four priceless Windsor chairs.

Wainwright sat with rolled-up shirtsleeves at a Duncan Phyfe desk, working on his stamp collection.

"McCall's magic lantern show," he said with a smile when he saw the slide projector that McCall carried.

McCall held up the projector plug. "Paid your electric bill this month, Mr. Chairman?" The houseman put the plug in an electric outlet.

Wainwright looked at the two dozen slides in the carousel tray. "What are we going to see?"

"The Who's Who of International Arms Trading."

"Hmm." Wainwright looked displeased. "Is this going to take long? I promised to have dessert with my wife's dinner guests."

"Fifteen minutes," McCall said. "It's a background briefing on the arms dealers Attashah is most likely to approach. We don't have much time to stop him." McCall projected the first slide. It was a photograph of a man with a bull neck and a round pink face. McCall said, "Mr. Chairman, I'd like to introduce Peno Rus."

McCall let the man's face remain on the screen for a few moments. Then he clicked to the next frame.

Slide: photograph of a huge mansion, done in a white stucco Spanish style with orange roof tiles.

McCall: "These are his modest digs on the Riviera. Beyond them at anchor you can see his yacht. No one knows how rich he is. But we do know what he sells. Arms. And for that purpose, he uses computerized direct-marketing techniques right from Madison Avenue. The key piece in his program is this glossy catalogue."

Series of slides shown ad lib: pages and spreads from the four-color catalogue.

McCall: "Peno Rus's catalogue is a war maker's dream. Here in gorgeous full color is an endless supply of bombs, detonators, binary explosives, poisons, silencers, assassin's tools, surveillance and sophisticated electronics equipment, tanks, weapons carriers, rockets, small artillery, uniforms, field kitchens, and on and on and on."

Slide: panorama of lush mountains in Africa.

McCall: "Unlike most merchants, Mr. Rus has a peculiar sales problem. Most of his customers cannot afford what he's selling. So in his wake he often leaves poverty, famine, and crowded cemeteries. This is Dadhwai, Central Africa."

Slide: photograph of capital city, blue mountains in the background.

McCall: "Rich with natural beauty. Poor in resources and capital. The World Bank gave Dadhwai money—partly to build its tourist business and partly to do some rudimentary processing of the raw materials it sells on the world market, but mostly to implement a full-scale agricultural improvements program."

Slide: Rus with Dadhwai's president.

McCall: "Mr. Rus persuaded the country's leader to spend that money on an army. And the poor man quickly got one. But then with a massive crop failure, Dadhwai soon found itself confronted by an adversary it couldn't defeat with Mr. Rus's shiny new rifles—famine."

Slide: photo of emaciated corpses in roadway.

McCall: "It took the combined efforts of six U.N. agencies and huge additional sums of money from the World Bank to put this nation on its feet again, but not until nearly one third of its population starved. And just in time for the Communists to take over—with Mr. Rus's arms."

Slide: close-up of Peno Rus on the deck of his yacht, a very beautiful girl sitting beside him in a deck chair.

McCall: "From his poop deck in the Bahamas, Mr. Rus expressed his great dismay for Dadhwai's plight. He contributed a thousand dollars to the relief fund."

Slide: photograph of Rus with another man seated inside a limousine.

McCall: "Mr. Rus with a Soviet agent in Ankara, Turkey. The Soviet Union is notorious for using independent arms dealers as covers for its cynical arming of terrorists. On occasion, to get things started in a static situation, Russia has armed both the native Communists and the native rightists simultaneously. Mr. Rus has been the obliging middleman.''

Slide: Peno Rus smiling.

McCall: "Mr. Rus has become a very important supplier to Iran. Why? Because in a world where shoddy merchandise and unprincipled practices abound, Mr. Rus has a reputation for unassailable integrity. He has never sold a bomb that failed to go off.''

Slide: photograph of Mr. Rus in the casino at Monaco with another man.

McCall: "Mr. Rus, however, is most comfortable in the company of wealthy men of good education and breeding. He maintains friendships with some of the world's wealthiest men. These men contribute staggering sums of money anonymously to their favorite guerrilla wars. Rich men like Berthe and Golpin, Landish and Fogarty, and this man—R. Thomas Dutter.''

"Dutter? You must be mistaken, McCall. I went to school with him.''

"R. Thomas Dutter," McCall repeated.

Wainwright studied Dutter's face. "He's aged.''

McCall continued: "A handful of armed terrorists can easily take over a small government in a few hours. Witness the near-coup in Africa recently. Terrorists can also disrupt production of raw materials and oil in whole regions of the world—with consequences rich men love.''

"Some rich men love," Wainwright said.

"Political power is going for bargain rates these days. And R. Thomas Dutter is shopping hard in the marketplace . . . with the sedulous Mr. Rus providing the party favors.''

"I never would have believed that of him." Wainwright shrugged. "Dutter. Imagine."

Slide: photograph of Rus examining the mutilated U.S. Embassy building in Tehran.

McCall: "Naturally Mr. Rus is one of the first independent arms dealers that Iran would turn to for a supply of military parts."

Slide: photograph of Eric Rock.

McCall: "Here is another arms dealer who could do the job for Iran—a really knowledgeable smuggler who has the technical background to understand state-of-the-art electronics. He would be an admirable choice—especially since he's very cunning, extraordinarily charming, and a compunctionless sociopath. Meet Eric Rock."

Slide: photograph of Rock with two Arabs.

McCall: "It is said that peace negotiations don't begin until the last bullet is fired. Mr. Rock agrees with that. He made a handsome sum of money last year by fracturing a cease-fire in North Africa between two Bedouin tribes that had originally been armed by Libya."

Slide: photograph of Rock with Arab leader.

McCall: "This is Mr. Rock with an Arab fanatic who was absolutely powerless until Rock armed him. Free. This Arab and a band of followers then went on an indiscriminate shooting spree against both tribes and thereby brought about the collapse of a very fragile cease-fire. Both tribes immediately ordered large quantities of arms. From Mr. Rock of course."

Slide: photograph of dead Arab girl in doorway. She is about seven and is holding a doll's cradle in her limp hand. Behind her, through the doorway, are seen several other dead bodies.

McCall: "Before another cease-fire could be arranged hundreds of people died from gunshot wounds, and a like amount died from cholera. The most important point here is: Mr. Rock was the only smuggler brilliant enough to get arms into that area at that time. He has a great gift for smuggling.''

Slide: photo of the skeletal remains of a bombed-out hotel building.

McCall: ''But that was slumming for Mr. Rock. His real specialty is explosives. As an electronics expert, he has devised some ingenious ways of detonating bombs. It is a virtual certainty that Rock sold the binary explosives that killed those two hundred people in this Damascus hotel last month.''

Slide: L. Slane.

''Number three in our trilogy, Mr. Chairman. His name is Slane. An Australian from the Great Outback. Rancher's son. Mercenary, soldier of fortune. Got his early training in Vietnam in the U.S. Army. He was fifteen at the time and very big for his age.

Slide: Slane with Richard Mann.

''He learned his trade from this man, Richard Mann, the Swiss arms trader who specializes in Oriental markets. He's done more mischief there than all the Communists in the last ten years.

''A few years ago Slane went in for himself, practically without capital, by trading in U.S. arms that were left on the Vietnam battlefield. Most of these have found their way into Central America, primarily through Slane's efforts. Slane is a man on the make, looking for his first big package that will give him the capital he needs for inventory and storage. He's very smart, ruthless, and thinks big. He'll probably be a major trader one of these days.''

McCall turned on the room lights. ''I doubt if there is one person on this entire planet who would shed a tear for these three men—except maybe Rus's tailor.''

He opened his case and pitched a spiral-bound report onto Wainwright's Duncan Phyfe desk. "Rus's history. Compliments of Intercrime. And here's another on Rock. And a third—on Slane. Instructive reading, Mr. Chairman."

Wainwright nodded at the reports without speaking.

"And here, Martin, is a White Paper from State on the Iranian situation."

"Who wrote it?" Wainwright asked.

"Harry Hollis."

"Oh." Wainwright took it and flipped the pages quickly. "Any news on what's-his-name?"

"Attashah? He hasn't been seen in public for several weeks. An informant in Tehran claims he is already in the U.S."

"Thanks, McCall, for coming over with this stuff. I'll let you know."

He was dismissed. Not by so much as a narrowed eyelid had Wainwright indicated a reaction. He barely said goodnight when McCall, projector case in hand, left the study.

He followed the houseman down the stairs, past the dining room filled with murmuring voices and scraping silverware, and out through the front door.

There was nothing to do now but wait.

McCALL WAITED THREE DAYS before he got a reaction from Wainwright. And when he got it, he got it in the middle of the night.

His phone woke him at 1:00 A.M. With his usual brusqueness, Wainwright said, "McCall? Meet me at the Skyport Lounge as quick as you can get there."

WAINWRIGHT WAS RIGHT WHERE he'd said he would be. In an upholstered chair in the Skyport Cocktail Lounge at Dulles Airport.

The man sat slumped back, legs spraddled, thoughtfully spinning his whiskey glass on the table. When he saw McCall approaching, he sat up and pointed at the other chair. McCall seated himself.

"Sorry I woke you up, McCall." Wainwright rubbed a craggy hand over his face and bald pate.

The night crews were cleaning the airport, washing glass doors and windows, mopping, running electric floor buffers. There were few passengers about, and most of them napped fitfully in uncomfortable plastic chairs. At the end of the corridor a company of marines was shaping up at an airline check-in counter.

Wainwright watched the cleaners like a choreographer planning new steps. He chewed on a knuckle. Then he glanced at McCall.

"What are you drinking?"

McCall shrugged. Anything. Nothing. He was waiting.

Wainwright spoke with an alcoholic slur. "I've been chewing over things ever since your picture show the other night. That report from Hollis made me wet my pants. And the profiles on those three gun sellers turned my stomach." He looked at McCall with haggard eyes. "This thing has me chased around the table. You know what I'm saying?"

The bartender brought drinks and a bowl of peanuts.

Wainwright rubbed his eyes. "Crazy goddam thing. I know it's wrong. We just can't do it. Kill three-four men. Yet, we can't not do it. You see what I'm saying? There are a lot of men in Washington who would grab at this thing as the opportunity of a lifetime. Meaningful appropriate action, they'd say. In a country that's dangerously drifting, they'd say. Dead in the water. Yet—well, goddammit, McCall, say something. I haven't slept in three nights."

"I think we should drop the whole thing."

Wainwright clawed a fistful of peanuts and fired them into his mouth one at a time with his thumb. He squirmed in his chair, chewing urgently.

He seized another fistful of peanuts as though he'd suddenly realized he was hungry. Many of them cascaded down his shirt-front. "I think so too, McCall." He went silent. Then he sat up. "But we can't. And do you know why we can't? We can't because there's no other action we can take."

He pointed a finger at McCall. "In fact, this is exactly the same action we should take with those goddam Russian agents over here trying to buy our military computers right from under our noses. Here we are letting these Red bastards arm themselves with our military hardware. It's the only way they can keep up with us. Shut those agents down with a couple of hits one night and we'd reduce the Russian army to a hoard of spear throwers. You see where I'm coming from, McCall?"

But Wainwright needed no answers. He was a monologist, and he would have declaimed to the walls if he'd been alone. "How can we justify murder?"

McCall turned his chair and leaned forward, touching Wainwright's arm to get his attention. "It's not the same as it was," he enunciated, as though talking to a senile old man. "It's not. The answers from your ethics course don't apply anymore. We have different imperatives now."

Wainwright writhed at that. "McCall, I think you're wrong as hell. There is absolutely no difference between me and Isaac holding a knife over his son. Things haven't changed. Not a goddam bit. And someday, out on a faraway planet, some spacemen are going to be sitting around, eating peanuts, fighting little green men, and saying: 'We have different imperatives now.' And they'll be just as wrong as you are."

"I don't believe that, Martin. Take a look around you. Just scan the daily paper. You'll see—"

Wainwright waved a hand at him. "Enough. You and I belong to a different generation. What's wrong to me is routine to you. You see what I'm saying? I wonder what the greater danger to this country is—Iran or you."

Wainwright seized another clutch of peanuts, spilling more down his front. He brushed at them irritably and chewed in a fury. "Okay. It's crazy, I know. But you listen." He pointed a finger. "I raised it. All three million. So go do it. Get all three. Four if necessary. Do it quick. Do it clean. Do it soon."

He stood up. "You handle it. Don't tell me anything. Just make sure nothing can be traced back to the committee or to Washington or to the U.S. Or to me. I curse the day you gave me this idea, McCall. May God forgive me."

He threw his handful of peanuts on the table and walked away, spilling more peanuts from the folds of his clothes with each step.

He didn't look back.

IN GLORIOUS AUTUMN SUNLIGHT, Mr. Peno Rus strolled along Great Western Road in London, accompanied by his Master of the Arsenal, Major Archbold Mudd. They had just come from the printer, and both carried proof copies of the latest Rus four-color arms catalogue, fresh from the press.

Mr. Rus walked with the catalogue held against his nostrils so he could sensually inhale the odor of printer's ink. That was the modern smell of money to him. Mail-order sales.

The first mailing of the catalogue, addressed to Mr. Rus's A List (Government Buyers) and B List (Individuals With Known Arms Interests), would be completed in three days.

There were some 40,000 names of arms buyers and buying influences on Mr. Rus's combined A and B Lists, embracing every continent and almost every nation.

His computer had already projected the probable percentage of mail response, probable average size of order, and probable total profit. And the profit was considerable. A former Russian citizen, Mr. Rus loved being a capitalist.

As they walked, Mr. Rus said, "Major. I have a fabulous arms deal in mind. It could make us the talk of the arms trade."

"Oh, yes?" Major Mudd leaned close as they walked in order to understand Mr. Rus's odd linguistic potpourri: His very correct English was heavily overlaid with a difficult Slavic accent.

"That package deal we sold to the Dadhwai government in Africa," Mr. Rus said. "It may have a happy outcome for us after all."

"Happy!" exclaimed the major. "It caused a scandal. I shall never forget the day a question was raised in Parliament. We were certainly the talk of the arms trade then!"

"Now, Major, it is not our fault a famine killed so many. We are arms traders, not ministers of agriculture."

"Hmmm," the major said.

"Anyway, it has given us a substantial cash flow that I've been planning to take advantage of."

"I should have thought that money had burned a hole in your pocket by now."

"Next week," Mr. Rus said, "I'm going to bid on those Israeli tanks the Franconi government has. All twelve."

"The Merkavas?"

"Marvelous instruments those," Rus said with his heavy accent. "There are no other tanks like them in all the world. Did you know that the Merkava completely destroyed Russia's newest T-72 with just one shot? Marvelous. The whole world is clamoring to buy them from Israel. And I can offer them to Jarrett as a deal sweetener. He's panting for them. Then—''

''I see,'' the major said. ''To get the tanks, he'll sell you the six jets—''

''Yes, yes. You do see it, don't you, Major?''

''You'll sell the jets to Chile—''

''And?''

The Major stopped walking. ''Dear God. Buy West Arms?''

''Precisely! Their entire inventory of small arms. We'll become the biggest dealer in small arms anywhere. That ought to warm the cockles of your heart, Major—master of the largest arsenal of small arms in the world.''

''Does that mean that our first major customer would be Iran?'' the major asked. ''I'm not too pleased about that.''

Peno Rus said, ''But that's a monumental deal for us, Major. We will be the only arsenal that can offer the Iranians one-source buying for all their small-arms needs. An annual master contract. It would be of enormous proportions. Attashah will snap it up in a minute.''

But the bedazzling aspect of this deal wasn't just the Iranian contract. It was Iran's shortage of cash. Iran's balance of trade was deeply negative, and the Iranian treasury was reluctant to part with money.

What that mad fanatic Attashah wanted was barter, and what an enticing barter it was—small arms in exchange for heroin. Attashah was offering heroin that could be sold on the open market for many times the barter price. Truly an astronomical profit.

This was known in the trade as a Daisy Chain Deal: Israeli Merkava tanks in exchange for jet fighters. Jet fighters to buy small arms. Small arms that garner a one-source dream contract with one of the world's heaviest small-arms buyers. And crowning it all for Peno Rus was a king's ransom in heroin. Several millions of cash dollars. Untaxed. Unrecorded. And all his. Perhaps best of all, he could acquire this dominant new marketing capability without a significant infusion of capital. No bank loan, no bank snooping, no interest payments.

All from his skill as a trader. It was the Dadhwai money that did it.

He glanced at his solemn master of the arsenal. "We've been somewhat at odds since that Dadhwai deal, Major. Perhaps this new deal will help put things to rights between us."

Major Mudd nodded. "Perhaps."

That English way of thinking sometimes baffled Peno Rus. It was a strange code the major had, selling arms that killed people wholesale, yet drawing the line at famine and drug addiction. Oh well. It was a lovely day in London. Sunlight of great clarity touched the old walls and rooftops, showing their marvelous mellow hues. Quite the most satisfactory city in the world: London. And quite the most wonderful time of the year in the city: autumn.

A sense of profound well-being almost filled Mr. Rus's eyes with tears of joy. In a few weeks he would move to his home in Monaco for the winter.

He needed to celebrate his well-being with a boutonniere. And to that end he searched out a florist with Major Mudd in tow.

At the florist's he sniffed his boutonniere and happily permitted the young saleslady to put it on his lapel. The major declined to wear one.

"Oh, come," Mr. Rus said. "You really ought to learn to wear boutonnieres, Major. They give things just the right tone."

SLITS OF HOT CAIRO SUNLIGHT slipped through the shutters on the hotel window. But on the bed it was cool from the air conditioning.

Eric Rock chuckled when the girl bared her sharp young teeth in a menacing smirk. "Ow!" Those preadolescent little razors had nipped his navel.

Rock told himself over and over that his infatuation with this girl/woman was dangerous. This was still a risky town for him ever since the binary explosives deal he'd worked with Libya. Those people in Egyptian Defense were still very shirty about it. Furthermore, every time he flew into Cairo to see the girl, the uncle's price got higher: The man could read the hunger in Rock's eyes and adjusted the fee to fit the fever.

Rock drew a finger along that petulant child's lip, then along the beautiful configuration of her ear.

There came a low, urgent knuckling on the door.

"Sir! Sir!" the uncle whispered through the door. He said something in Arabic that made the child leap from the bed. She snatched up her clothing in a loose ball, hugged it to her bare body, and ran to the door.

"Her father's coming!" the uncle said. And he hauled her down the hallway to an exit door as the girl tried to pull on some of her clothes. From seductive vamp to threatened child in a few steps, she looked smaller and younger than her ten years.

A moment later Rock, too, abandoned the room. Still half undressed, he ran toward the elevator, holding his passport and airline tickets in his teeth, carrying an attaché case in his left hand, and trying to pull on his shirt with the right.

Down in the street he entered a cab and opened his attaché case to read the airline schedule. He was sure there was a flight within the hour. He would take it no matter where it was going.

His infatuation with that child would be his undoing. He felt he was one step ahead of arrest. The last thing he wanted was to be chased by an irate Egyptian father. In the hotel room he had abandoned over two thousand dollars in clothing.

When he looked out at the street, he saw the uncle hurrying the girl in and out of the throngs on the sidewalk. Rock watched her through the rear window until she became a speck in the crowd.

Would he never see her again?

THE GIRL'S FATHER and his four sons borrowed an automobile. In the late afternoon they took Fawzi, the uncle, bound and gagged in the car trunk, out into the desert, about an hour's drive away.

They followed the old caravan trail toward the west that the camels had followed in their immemorial treks before the dawn of Western civilization. There in the vastness of the desert, where they wouldn't be disturbed, they took the uncle out of the trunk. The desert sunset was gorgeous, and all over the Arab world the muezzins were calling from their lofty minarets to the faithful to affirm their belief in the All-Powerful.

The uncle came out of the trunk on his knees, madly praying, babbling incoherently, his hands clasped, imploring his brother, then his nephews, crying out to his God. The father and his four sons stood in a circle and, indifferent to his shrill singsong litany, watched the man dancing on his knees. The father handed each son an old scimitar, then watched them draw the curving blades from the scabbards. Long afternoon shadows on the earth pantomimed their movements.

The uncle scurried about on his knees, clutching at their garments, hugging their legs, reminding the boys of past kindnesses, reciting the names of his children, calling on his brother to remember their mother and her grief. He begged and wept and called on his God's mercy.

His brother replied by pushing Fawzi over with his foot. Fawzi quickly rolled over and back on his knees, stumping after his brother, talking urgently now. From behind, one of the sons pushed him over again. Before he could rise, his brother made a slash on his buttock. Red blood soaked quickly through the slit in his trousers.

Fawzi wagged a forbidding finger at his brother, shouting "Enough." The eldest son with one stroke cut off the finger. Fawzi's voice rose to shrieks now as he clutched the stump of his forefinger, blood dribbling from both hands and spotting the desert. Another son flicked away a piece of Fawzi's left ear. A long strip of skin and muscle was surgically sliced off his bare right forearm.

Fawzi howled with terror. He groveled with pain, crawling on his knees and elbows. His brother chopped off his right hand. Blood spurted from major veins and arteries. Slashes and sliced-away flesh appeared now on all his limbs and his back. His clothes were long red ribbons that fluttered when he moved. Everywhere he was leaking blood, rapidly bleeding to death, a writhing red-wet ball, demented with pain. One slash nearly severed his left arm at the elbow. A third nephew chopped at his foot.

Fawzi tried to curl around all his many pains, his cries growing weaker, slowly writhing in his own large stain of blood.

And then his brother, admonished by his Maker to mercifulness, signaled his sons to step back. He bent over and spoke a few words of farewell to his brother, raised his scimitar, and struck off his head. They all watched it roll a few feet toward the setting sun.

Using the end of his scimitar now, the father wrote one word in the desert hardpan with its tip: the name of his daughter's deflowerer. Rock. Then he plunged the tip of the scimitar into the word. Rock.

SLANE GOT READY for the sales clincher as the four customers stood around him in the office. He took six telephone books, stood them up, and wedged them into the corner of the room near the door.

The eyes of the four customers watched with fascination as he opened his attaché case. He lifted out a rifle with a collapsible steel-rod stock.

"Length," he said, "under twelve inches." He pulled on the stock until it reached its full extension. It clicked into locked position. Next he reached down to the open attaché case and lifted out a fat tube that was slightly bulbous at one end, like a long, drawn-out raindrop. It was a malevolent gray color. "Suppressor," Slane said.

He coupled the suppressor to the rifle and held them up. "This weapon is based on the Ingram machine pistol."

"M10 or M11?" asked one of the men.

"The M10/11, with some new wrinkles," Slane said. "Total weight slightly over six pounds. Fires a dozen shots a second. Seven hundred twenty rounds a minute. Range three hundred yards—ammunition either forty-five caliber or nine millimeter."

Slane looked through the glass partitions of the office and studied the office staff at work. People were walking to and fro, talking on the telephone, and sorting papers at their desks.

"Watch," he said. They watched with mouths agape as he raised the weapon and aimed it at the telephone books. He pulled the trigger. Pfft pfft pfft pfft pfft pfft—the bullets shredded the phone books with barely the sound of a computer printer.

All eyes looked out through the glass partitions to the people in the office. Not a head was turned to them.

"Now that's what you call silent." Slane watched their bobbing heads. He lifted another fitting. "Telescopic sight. For use day or night. This weapon is whatever you tell it to be—a pistol, a machine gun, or a sniper's rifle."

The four men smirked at it, then at each other.

"It's the ultimate jungle weapon," Slane said. "A handful of men can tie up entire armies with this little item. It can kill more men in shorter time than any other gun in the history of firearms. And I can make immediate delivery of quantities up to twenty-five thousand. You could be shooting your way into Government House on Traone Square a few weeks from now."

One of the businessmen chuckled with delight, spreading the heavy odor of garlic in the room.

3

In the cell to Brewer's left was a kid named Jason Poole, from Maine. He was serving seven years for breaking and entering—a harsh sentence for a first offender. In the cell to Brewer's right was Clivedell Rine, a professional thief from Harlem. A three-time loser at forty, he was in for eleven years on six counts of burglary and grand larceny.

"Robbed the wrong apartment at the wrong time and stole the wrong things. Wroooo-ong."

The man to Rine's right was a hardball named Pelew. He was in for twenty years on assorted charges including armed robbery, kidnapping, and atrocious assault. A friendless man, he was known as a dangerous head case with a violent temper and an antisocial personality. In the past three months he'd raped two other inmates, hospitalizing both of them in the process, and was awaiting trial on both counts. He was an odds-on favorite to be committed to Creedmore or some other state institution for the criminally insane.

He had thrown the leather belt the night Brewer had arrived.

Without prompting, many of the inmates asserted to Brewer that their jail terms were passing quickly—a piece of cake you can do standing on your head. Nothing to it. Everyone wore a brave face. If an inmate lost heart and spoke out in despair it was considered a breach of faith. Despair is a contagious disease in a prison.

At night Brewer often heard men sobbing.

JASON POOLE TALKED usually of his father and his brothers, of hunting and of country life in Maine. Most of his hunting stories centered around a blue-tick hunting dog called Chili.

"She can hunt a bird right up his kazoo."

Clivedell Rine spoke of the good times he'd had when the scores were good and the fences were generous, of feeling mellow from wine and joints, of women and night life in Harlem. He'd had gonorrhea at least twelve times—and maybe more—and Old Joe twice.

"Clap's just a bad cold in your private."

He was illiterate and was learning to read so he could study the Koran. While in prison he'd become a Muslim.

IN HIS CELL Brewer was confronted with himself. For the first time in his life there was no place to hide: Brewer faced Brewer. Lying on his back in the dark with his eyes open, he engaged in remorseless and unremitting self-examination. He was shocked when he discovered a person he neither liked nor admired. He'd uncovered a naïve fool who had trusted people, who had expected the system he had defended to defend him. And with astonishing speed he reached a fatal conclusion.

Now it became clear to him that he had always been in prison. Not the wall and locked doors and grated steel decks and bars and cells, but the real prison inside himself.

For he was a prisoner of time, locked inescapably into this historical age, carried along with it like a stone in a glacier— moving, but at time's tempo, not his own.

Most of all he felt he was a prisoner of his own personality—of that given set of traits that came with birth, stayed until death, and predisposed him to see the world in a certain way, to make certain moves, certain choices. The iron maiden of his personality gave him at birth predetermined preferences and inclinations, whether he wanted them or not. It allowed him to make only these moves and these choices and no others. He had no free will. No man did.

Sitting on the edge of his cot in the middle of the night, he told himself each man is born an optimist or a pessimist, a ditch digger or a violinist, a fool or a knave, a terse introvert or a loquacious extrovert. You can play only the hand you were dealt. No other.

In short, he saw himself as the prisoner of predestination.

On a piece of paper, he wrote, "Brewer is a Calvinist." He stuck it on the wall and tried to laugh at it. He couldn't.

The Greeks had said it: Character is fate. Personality is destiny.

To change his fate, he would have to change his personality. Refuse to be the trusting fool any longer.

The fatal conclusion this led him to was even more astonishing. It was a consequence of numbers.

First were the numbers of time.

Some 1,500 prisoners in unison, with all the fervor of desperate hearts, willed time to race by. Flee, days. Fly, months. Roar on, years. With the speed of light, hurry by, Time. Get me out of here.

The least unit of time was carefully measured and judged: bad time or good time. Bad time was prison time, those bleak days and worse nights. Good time was time spent on a phone call or a family visit, on a letter or a package. Good time was anticipated, savored, and hoarded.

Each inmate was allowed 2 phone calls a month. Each phone call lasted no more than 6 minutes—minutes that were carefully planned so that each second of each minute would be filled to overflowing with love and encouragement and home news, like glowing coals placed around the heart to warm it for days afterward.

Each inmate was allowed one visitor a month. Visiting time, one hour: 12 hours a year. This, too, required careful planning and thought. Some prisoners even contrived to have regular sexual contact with their visitors.

These good-time segments meant nothing to Brewer. He received no phone calls, no visitors, no mail.

THEN THERE WERE the numbers of space.

Brewer's cell was exactly 6 feet wide. It was 8 feet 4 inches deep and 7 feet 9 inches high.

In it were 5 pieces of furniture: a steel cot with a foam mattress, a steel footlocker, a cold-water sink, a backless stool, and a lidless toilet. There was very little room to pace in.

His sliding cell door unlocked every morning at 7:00. It locked every night at 5:00. The opening was exactly 24 inches wide.

His cell was one of 50 cells on his row. There were 2 rows to a tier: 100 cells. There were 3 tiers—and 300 cells—in each cell block. There were 5 blocks in the prison, 1,500 cells. All 5 cell blocks were contained within one huge brick building which also housed the 2 prison mess halls.

It was a Noah's Ark of criminals. A living anthology of various crimes. Sweetmeadow housed 1,487 prisoners, more than 500 of them serving time for robbery, 246 for burglary, 222 for homicide, 200 for murder, 130 for drug possession, 65 for weapons possession, 56 for felonious assault, 33 for grand larceny, 53 for rape and other sex offenses including sodomizing minors, 15 for forgery. In all, nearly 1,500 failures in their chosen careers.

Numbers haunted their lives.

It was 357 paces from his cell to the left-side mess hall. He never entered the one on the right, which was identical. There were 64 tables, all bolted to the floor, and a backless bench on either side of each table, also bolted down. Each table fed 12 men. Each mess hall fed 768 prisoners.

Counting the 2 chapels, the school building, and the workshop buildings—which also contained the laundry and the barbershop—there were 26 buildings inside the walls.

The prison area covered 54 acres. And it was surrounded by a 4-sided wall of steel-reinforced concrete, 1.25 miles long, 30 feet high, 36 inches thick at the base. There were 11 watchtowers, each containing one armed guard, posted to make sure that the inmates stayed in. Prison was a deprivation of geography.

For Brewer the most significant number focused on the prison farm, where 89 prisoners were allowed to work outside the walls: 89. Outside the walls.

Jason Poole said, ''No one's escaped from here in thirteen years. Two men tried three years ago. They killed a guard. They were shot dead by the state troopers about a mile from here.''

Brewer thought about his 9-year sentence. And he refused to serve it. He refused to be the victim of predestination any longer. He refused to be someone else's fool one more day. From the library he checked out a book on gardening and farming.

He would escape.

AFTER A WHILE Brewer was old news to the prison population at large. He was just another face there to do his time. He listened to their talk. And they talked endlessly.

The most insistent subject in prison is not sex or crime or revenge. It's the art and craft of getting out. Serving the shortest possible sentence. Parole. The most important institution in a prisoner's life is the parole board. With the squiggle of a pen, the three men on the board can turn a prisoner loose, end his incarceration, put him back out on the street years before his sentence is completed. Or they can extend his stay to the full bitter length of his term.

To a man languishing in prison, such a signatory power is god-like.

Inducing the parole board to be generous requires great skill and preparation. To that end prisoners haunt the law library, become exceedingly knowledgeable in the ways of the law and in the forms that flesh out the law—the petitions and writs and the many other official documents that surround a man who has been sentenced to prison.

Brewer paid little attention to all this. He would be his own parole board.

He applied for a job on the prison farm and was put on a long waiting list. It would take years, they said. His inner ear told him that it would not take years; it would take a payoff. When the time came. He didn't want to wait. So he sought an alternative method.

His plan to escape was his balm and solace, his constant companion, his obsessive activity.

This was now Brewer's world of numbers: a count of prison doorways, their sizes and locations; the course and length and disposition of sewer lines, water lines, electrical cables, gas mains; the terrain outside the walls—the roads, their lengths and destinations. And, most interesting, several long-disused underground passageways and their dimensions.

Somewhere in that welter of lengths, heights, distances, frequency of use, method of securing, number of keys— somewhere was the way out.

JASON POOLE WAS an excellent self-taught artist. With a complex style that was part primitive and part slick technique learned from prison library books, he painted scenes from memory of his rural life in Maine. To verify it he searched travel magazines and constantly asked for photographs from the relatives who would still write to him. There were very few: his mother, his twin brother, and an aunt.

He, too, was obsessed with the parole board. Everyone said he was the ideal candidate for parole. He was a model prisoner, of good family, with no previous record, good school scores and education, and with the skills to support himself in various ways in Maine: woodsman and guide, lobsterman and commercial fisherman. If he worked it right he might be home by autumn, just in time for the hunting season. With Chili.

THERE WAS a persistent rumor that the parole board was going to inaugurate a program called Prison Without Walls. This was a plan for very early paroling of inmates guilty of minor offenses. The rules were stringent. The parolee was to be carefully supervised. In some cases he would be required to return to the prison every weekend. In others he would live in halfway houses. In yet others, he would be required to make weekly detailed reports to his parole officer. The plan was to be offered only to prisoners who were believed by the parole board to be fully rehabilitatable. Recidivists were specifically excluded.

Everything, according to the rumor, depended on the behavior of the first group of parolees. If they failed, the program would be abandoned or at least highly modified. So the future freedom of hundreds of prisoners depended on the correct behavior of the first few men.

The prisoners spent hours drawing up lists of names of men they wanted in that first batch of parolees—solid, stable men who could be relied upon not to let the rest of the waiting prisoners down. And on almost every list was the name of Jason Poole.

ONE DAY, when Brewer was in the prison exercise yard, Poole drew out a small white cardboard box from his jacket pocket. Inside was a long red leaf. To Poole it was like a messenger from a distant world.

"Sweet gum leaf. Sweet gum is the first tree to turn color in the autumn—with the sassafras. It's kind of a waxy maroon color. This coming September and October, when the sweet gum turns, my father and my brothers will start slicking up their hunting pieces, oiling the stocks, cleaning the barrels.

"And there'll be mists in the alder thickets by the lake in the morning. And the skies will be filled with migrating birds. The geese will fly across the moon late at night, way up, honking as they go. And the dogs will be getting funny and milling around, barking at nothing. They know they're going to be hunting soon. First for the woodcock in the old abandoned apple orchards. And the other game birds too. Then later comes the deer season. There'll be the first snow sprinkling the ground by then and the water in the buckets will freeze on top."

Brewer stood up. "I don't give a shit for your birds and deer and geese and dogs or mists or frosts or any goddam thing." And he walked away.

Brewer told himself he had to escape soon. He couldn't stand much more of this.

THE WHOLE PRISON knew about Jason Poole's paintings. The subjects were always rural scenes, often hunting scenes. The guards were his biggest customers; they were all rural men who hunted as avidly in New York State as Poole's family hunted in Maine. His cell was always overcrowded with paintings, and he would sell them for a few dollars just to get leg room for more painting.

His oils graced the mantel of many a guard's home. A few were even hanging on the wall of a saloon five miles away. The guards were convinced that Poole could make a comfortable living just painting hunting scenes. They said he was getting better with each painting. They expected his paintings to fetch a good price some day.

There were, however, about a dozen paintings that Poole wouldn't sell. These were his personal favorites.

ON THE FIRST THURSDAY of every month, the three members of the parole board arrived. This was the most important day of the calendar for many prisoners. Those who were scheduled for a hearing prepared and rehearsed and memorized for days beforehand. Shoes were carefully shined, hair was cut, clothing washed and ironed. The men sat in their cells with their hands clasped, reciting their lines, waiting for the three board members to arrive in their separate cars.

And everyone knew the three cars: a five-year-old red Mercury, a year-old white Saab, and a year-old blue Cadillac. Red, white, and blue. Hundreds of pairs of eyes from every part of the fifty-four acres would watch the three cars drive through the prison's main gate and park by the Administration Building. They would watch the three men walk up the entrance steps.

And everyone knew the names of the three parole board members, knew their dispositions and mental habits.

Shortly after the three cars arrived, escort guards would be sent for the eligible prisoners. Then came the long walk from the cell, along the concrete corridors, up and down steel steps, and through steel security doors. There were encouraging words called from various cells as they strode by. The walk led past the throngs of prisoners in the prison yard, past the smiling faces and waving hands in the win-

dows of various work buildings. And everywhere were
words of encouragement.

Then came the jubilant half-dancing walk back. The
thumbs up. The catcalls. The clip-clap of applause. Free!
God almighty! Free! I'll never come back here! You bastards, hear me! Never!

But not every prisoner was granted his petition for parole. For them the walk back was wracking. Now there were
no words. No one looked at the unsuccessful petitioner.
Everyone contrived to be busy with his back turned. Except the few close friends.

"Next time, Eddie. You'll get it next time."

In the night, then, on the first Thursday of the month, one
would hear soft sobbing.

WITH AUGUST came a long spell of hot weather. There was
no air conditioning, and often the prison smelled like a
locker room. On August 7, the first Thursday of the month,
the three members of the parole board arrived in sultry heat.
The quick, eager walk of the petitioners commenced, followed by jubilant dances and long slow trudges. This time
the trudgers outnumbered the dancers.

During the exercise period the inmates stood in the shadows, away from the scorching sun. A few played boccie ball.
Brewer was sitting against a shady wall, watching a delivery
truck unload provisions. It takes a great deal of food to feed
1,500 men, however badly, and delivery trucks arrived every
day. Upon departure, each one was searched carefully by the
guards. Studying the trucks now as he had been doing for
several months, Brewer knew he had found a way to escape.

Directly under the parked delivery truck was a large cast-
iron grating fitted into the cobbles. The grating covered a
storm drain. The grating itself was quite large but the drain
was hardly big enough to hold a man. However, the drain

lay buried just above an old and infrequently used underground passageway that led from the food storage building to the main building.

A twenty-minute session with a pickax would produce a hole in the ceiling of the passageway leading to the drain. It was the storm drain that presented the problem. Cutting away the drainpipe so he could crawl through the grating would surely require an acetylene torch and might take several sessions. So he would have to re-cover the hole in the ceiling after each pipe-cutting session.

What he would need then was a way of securing himself to the underpart of the truck at least until he got through the gates and preferably into the nearest town. He was thinking of a rope hammock with steel hooks that would attach to the metal frame of the truck. Then he would be able to go into the main building, unlock the tunnel door, descend to the passageway, take down the ceiling cover, climb up to the grating, push it aside, and hook himself into his hammock on the underside of the truck. *Voilà!* Freedom.

"Brewer." A blue-shirted guard stood over him. He nodded his head at the Administration Building. Brewer stood up and followed him. They walked across the exercise yard on the hot, uneven cobbles to the dished stone steps of the building and entered. Many men watched.

The building was air-conditioned. The cool air, like a hostess, greeted him with caresses and held him in her embrace up the old wooden steps to the second floor. The guard pointed at a bench. Brewer sat and waited.

Presently a man opened a hall door and leaned out like a bird, squinting up and down the hallway. He had a florid face and pate and large dark sweat stains at the armpits of his blue shirt. He pointed at Brewer with the jab of a yellow wooden pencil.

"Is that Brewer?" he asked the guard.

"Brewer," answered the guard. The man jerked his head at Brewer.

IT WAS A SURPRISINGLY small room and the long oval conference table occupied much of it. The three-man parole board sat behind it in shirtsleeves with their papers and attaché cases and their aging world-weary faces. The air conditioning was not working well in this room, and the faces of the three men were damp with perspiration. They were clearly irritable and brusque. No wonder a number of petitions had been turned down.

The guard pointed at a seat directly across from the three parole board members. Brewer sat. The guard remained standing behind him.

"Identify yourself," said the board member in the middle.

"Brewer."

"No, no, no. Your number."

"B23424309."

The three men each picked up a piece of blue paper and scanned it.

"B23424309," said the man in the middle. "Brewer. Hmm." He peered with absolute disgust over the tops of his glasses at Brewer. "Have a lawyer?"

"I don't know. No. Not anymore." For the first time since his sentencing he recalled her—the faint sensuous odor of her perfume and her long stockinged legs and her lawyerly struggle to help him with his hopeless case.

"We'll appeal," she'd said. "I'll come see you in prison."

"Don't bother. Don't come see me." He knew he'd been wrapped and tied like a fish. There was no appeal worth bothering with. "I don't want to see anyone."

She acceded to his wishes. She never came to visit him.

The man in the middle spoke to Brewer. "B23424309. Have you heard about a program called Prison Without Walls?" He didn't wait for an answer. "Under that program we will consider a petition for parole on your behalf. You say you have no lawyer. Good. You're far better off with some of those guardhouse lawyers in the prison library than with most of the members of the bar we've seen around here lately. Submit your petition in one month. Dismissed."

All the way across the main yard under the blazing sun, back to the exercise yard, the same suspicion crossed and recrossed his mind. Setup.

After his trial Brewer had been given the maximum sentence with the gravest prejudice by the judge, who sternly recommended that Brewer be made to serve every single day of his term with not one day of parole. Officially, Brewer was anathema to the whole legal system. And here he was being offered the parole he was not supposed to be eligible for. The new Brewer told the old one the truth: He was a setup. A mark. He was being released to be aced. Someone wanted him dead.

Brewer thought wryly that he might be the first man in Sweetmeadow's history to refuse to accept a parole . . . the first man to be kicked out of prison.

THE PRISON hummed with talk. There were drawn-out arguments, quarrels, and analyses without end. Every possible consequence was explored to a degree outsiders would have found absurd.

There were fourteen men who had been invited to petition for parole under the Prison Without Walls program. Seven of them would be selected for parole. Among the fourteen names was Jason Poole's.

With great diligence he set about drafting his petition and planning his presentation. He had lots of help. Nearly every man in the prison was eager to make the program a success.

Poole walked around like a celebrity. There was a strange fever glow in his eyes. He talked without end about Maine. He painted urgently, often through the night by flashlight. The paintings were almost painful in their affection for the woods, almost mawkish.

The others let Brewer alone mostly. They believed obviously that the parole board was not going to give the nod to any man who had committed the crime Brewer had.

Pools were formed and the betting was heavy. Brewer's name was not among the favored seven names. Indeed, of all the many combinations of names that were being wagered on, his name was not in one.

Brewer declined what little help was offered. He filled out the correct forms with the assistance of a small pamphlet of instructions. Writing the petition was a matter of complete indifference to him. It was easier than digging a hole. It simply saved him the trouble of escaping.

JASON POOLE walked like a man in a daze. Already out of prison in his mind, he lived and relived the first moments of contact with his family. He was terrified of rejection. He wrote letter after letter home, particularly to his father. He eagerly received advice from everyone around him in the prison on what to say, what arguments to use, what promises to make.

At last a letter from his father arrived. The first. It was painfully terse—a single sentence: "We'll talk about it." Jason was overjoyed.

"It was my mother," he said to Brewer. "He's a pretty hard guy. She softened him up. Everything's going to be all right." He almost shook his own hand in congratulation.

There was a vicious fight. One of the eligibles discovered that his closest friend had bet a list without his name on it. He considered it disloyal—bad luck in fact. The other prisoners went to great lengths to conceal the fight from the guards. But many other prisoners took sides—an ethical issue that was argued over and over and caused ripple quarrels of its own. Tempers grew shorter by the day.

If the parole board's decisions had been delayed another week or so, the whole prison would have exploded into riots.

FOURTEEN MEN: That's less than one percent of 1,500 men. Seven is less than one half of one percent of 1,500 men. It was a statistically insignificant number, yet even the prisoners on death row demanded hour-by-hour bulletins.

THE DAY of the parole board's decision began with a furious sun that leaped above the horizon balefully. The heat had been relentless—a superwarm pocket of humid, stagnant air that sat over the land without even a hint of a breeze. The earth panted and gave off slowly rising convection currents of shimmering heat. The fields turned brown and shriveled. Life waited for cool weather and rain.

For the desperately bored, there was even a pool on the order of arrival of the three board members. The first car drove through the prison gates at 1:13 P.M. It was the blue Cadillac and it was greeted with cheers and groans. The next car to arrive was the white Saab, followed almost immediately by the old red Mercury.

Prison guards gathered the fourteen applicants outside the board room. The rest of the prison paced and waited. More than two hours passed. The only information the guards gave out was the order in which the men were interviewed. Each interview took about ten minutes. The last interview ended at 3:49. Another half hour passed.

It was nearly 4:15 when the front doors of the Administration Building opened and six men came out, hugging each other and flinging their arms in the air, cheering. They ran in a group across the yard, shouting overjoyed obscenities.

The seventh man came out alone. He slouched along behind the others under the terrible sunlight, indifferent to the shouts and catcalls. Eyes all over the prison studied the group and called out the names. Even before the second group of seven came down the steps and trudged away, the whole prison knew the names of all the winners. The seventh man was Brewer.

Jason Poole was in the second group. His petition had been denied. The next phase of the program, when seven more men would be selected, would start in January. He was told to resubmit his application at that time.

Release date was set for the following Tuesday morning. During the next few days he was scheduled to sit through a series of seminars with the other six men. They would be told that they were not on parole. They were officially still in prison. In fact, one of the men was going to have to return to his cell in Sweetmeadow every night.

The seven were lionized. Wherever they went they were thumped on the back, applauded, and smiled at. Every single prisoner believed that somehow his own sentence had been shortened this day. The commonest admonition the seven heard was "Don't screw it up, bastard."

Jason Poole congratulated Brewer with a faint grin. "Best of luck, Brewer."

"You'll be out, Jason. Hang tough. January will be here before you know it."

"Yeah, you're right. I'll be out of here before you know it." Poole went back to his painting.

The festive mood carried all through the dinner hour and into the night. The prisoners laughed and talked through their favorite television programs. Periodically, a wave of birdcalls and animal imitations would sweep through every tier of the prison. It was a totally spontaneous event that might occur but once in several months. Men trilled like canaries or cawed like crows, barked like dogs, mewed, roared, giggled, chattered, shrieked, cooed, and trumpeted. And that night it happened time after time. It began with a single call, rose to a long sustained crescendo, then slowly died away to silence.

The guards were uneasy. In the manic-depressive world of the prison, such a high would surely be followed by a low—a mean, sullen time that could trigger fights and riots, especially if it was accompanied by a full moon. In the cell blocks it was dripping hot. At nine, September's full moon rose.

Brewer could tell that Jason Poole was busy in his cell. He was tearing wrapping-paper, scribbling notes, putting the last few touches on a painting, cleaning his brushes, packing things in his footlocker. It was the busy-ness of a man getting ready to leave.

Brewer was busy with his own thoughts. In less than five days he would step through the prison gates. His life would go back to that moment he was sentenced. Like a piece of movie film he would take the 118 days of his imprisonment and snip it out of his life, then splice together the day he was sentenced with the day he would walk out free and resume the ongoing action that the imprisonment had interrupted. The minute his feet hit the ground he would be on a manhunt. And at that same minute, someone might be waiting around a bend in the road to kill him.

After all the ruminating during all those nights in his cell, he still didn't have the vaguest idea why all this had happened to him.

"Hey, Brewer."

"I'm here, Rine."

"How you doing?"

"I can't be beat."

"Hey, Poole."

"Yep."

"How's everything in the high-rent district?"

"Fantastic."

"January is ice-fishing time in Maine, ain't it?"

"Yep."

"I see by this calendar that it's almost here. A few weeks."

"That's right, man. Hardly enough time to get packed."

"A right, man."

Brewer dozed in the heat. There was a faint occasional breeze flowing through the cell block and if he sat on his bed near the cell door, it flowed over his damp skin. The next few days would be the longest in his entire life. His biggest fear was a reaction by the judge who had sentenced him. If that judge heard about his release, he might raise hell with the parole board members and force them to change their ruling. Five days to sweat out.

He heard a bump. Then a struggle. Then a drumming sound.

"Guard! Guard! Hey, man!" Rine started the clamor and soon every voice in the cell was shouting. The noise smothered the soft drumming sound.

Guards came running at last but they were too late. When they opened his cell and cut him down, Jason Poole was dead from strangulation. He'd hanged himself with a length of plastic clothesline.

Poole had done a neat job of it. He'd carefully bundled up his clothing, destroyed all his personal papers, and on the back of each of his paintings he'd taped a piece of paper with the name of the recipient. Brewer received Poole's favorite, a sun-filled portrait of Chili on a perfect point in an alder thicket. The woodcock was almost invisible in the shade.

"It's probably the best thing he ever did," the guard told him. "And that's saying a lot."

PRISON WAS A RITUAL—reenacted daily, year in, year out. Prisoners came and went; generations came and went; and yet the ritual endured.

Cell doors were opened invariably at the same time each morning and closed at the same time each night. Breakfast time was fixed; lunch time never varied; supper was always supper; the mail was received, the showers were taken, the movies shown—every minute of the day was scheduled, organized, routinized. Ritualized. It was more than doing it by the numbers. It was ceremonial. Traditional. Expected. Reassuring.

And so it was with the discharge. The inmates who worked in the tailor shop prepared the civilian clothing of the dischargee the night before, itemized, invoiced, recorded. Ritualized.

THE HEAT REMAINED. There was no rain. Everything dried up. And the autumn foliage came early. The night before his discharge date, Brewer lay awake the entire night, a mass of contradictory emotions.

Sleep was a restless affair at best in prison. All night Brewer heard men yawning and pacing in their cells, heard them shout at the heavy snorer, heard the toilets flushing, smelled the drifting cigarette smoke, heard the slow pace of the guards.

He feared the last-minute hitch: the protest from the judge, the second thoughts by the parole board, the warden's objection, the chance impediment, random, unexpected. He had to hang by his thumbs until noon.

All night the prison saying haunted him: "You're not out until you're out." Meantime—sweat.

HE MUST HAVE eaten breakfast. He knew that he had been braced against the wall several times by small knots of men with furious faces. "Don't fuck up, Brewer, or it's your ass. You come back here on a parole violation and your life ain't worth two farts on an old penny. Hear?" He was numb most of the morning with a roaring in the ears and a somnambulistic pace.

At nine the paper-signing began. And the settling of accounts. The directions on signing in with the halfway house in New York City—once a month. He smiled. By telephone, if necessary. A thimblerigged parole. He was being turned loose—flung from the prison. And into the arms of an unknown, for an unknown reason.

He would accept it—freedom—under any terms. Just get out. He would take his chances on the street. He would beat the odds.

By eleven he was convinced the fix was in. The parole board would sit at one, and he was to be dressed and ready to receive the last words. Kiss the ring in the throne room.

They gave him early lunch at eleven but he didn't remember seeing it or eating it. A guard touched his arm and he followed the man.

It was a reverse of his arrival: He picked up his dunnage from his cell and horsed it on his shoulder in a mattress cover, following the guard, through one door—slam!—with shouts of farewell and curses in his ear, through another door—slam!—and another and another in succession, up and down corridors and steel catwalks, then down a long flight to the main door, then crossing the yard to the receiving and discharge rooms.

They took his dunnage and they counted it and examined it and gave him a receipt for it. He was stripped naked again, surrendering everything down to his socks and shorts.

Then he was led to the tailoring room and given street clothes. As he took each item, the guard sang out the name, and another inmate checked it off on the tally sheet.

"One pair shorts, size thirty-two. One pair socks, size fourteen. One T-shirt, size large. One dress shirt, fifteen and a half, thirty-four. One pair of street slacks, waist thirty-two. One street jacket, size forty-two. One pair of shoes, size twelve. One belt. One necktie. Sign here, please." To the end it was a world of numbers and numbering.

These weren't the clothes he'd worn in. Those had gone long ago on someone else's back. And what he now received had *prison* written all over it. Gray stretch polyester pants, washable brown jacket with badly cut lapels, prison shoes, black, and a worn string of a tie for a shirt that was pilled around the collar. It badly needed ironing.

It is said that you can tell how many friends you make in prison by the clothing the prison tailors give you. And what Brewer got was a token of the friendless man.

"Hey, asshole." One of the tailors put a hand on Brewer's chest. "Story is you bought your way out of here. You got Poole's slot. And that sucks, man."

AT ONE O'CLOCK he was led to the counter in the same room he'd entered six months before in a sleeting rain. As he was signing the last papers, he heard the catcalls and whistles and looked up. He saw the three cars of the parole board arriving, framed perfectly in the open doorway—first the red Mercury, then the white Saab, and last—not the blue Cadillac, but a new green Mercedes-Benz. And that's what had drawn the whistles.

Brewer bowed his head and laughed softly. His life was worth at least one German automobile to somebody. Or at least his death was.

He signed his name with a flourish on the last piece of paper.

4

Brewer walked through the gateway and out of prison.

About twenty yards ahead, in a No Parking zone, was a powder-blue Mercedes convertible. At first he didn't recognize the woman who stepped out of the car. It had been six months.

Later he thought it was the way she held her head that he remembered. Or the legs: All through his trial the jury had stared at her legs.

"Hello," she said.

He nodded at her.

"How are you?" she asked.

He studied her cautiously. She looked younger. He wondered what he looked like.

She tried again: "Handsome painting. Did you do it?"

"How'd you know I was getting out?"

"The court. Have you forgotten? I'm still listed as your attorney. If you'd called me, I would have helped you fill out the forms."

He nodded and stared boldly at her, at her tailored suit, her hair, her legs. It was shocking—going from that walled-in locker room, that bricked-up madness with its violence and street ways to this soft and civilized, money-pampered loveliness.

He stepped past her to the trunk of the car and waited for her to unlock it.

He remembered the quarrels they'd had.

She had told him he could not defend an innocent plea. No one cared whether he was innocent. It was a different game. What he had to do was use the few moves that were open to him to negotiate a lesser sentence. He must spend as few days as possible in prison.

He insisted. She entered a plea of innocent, defended it resolutely, and gave the prosecution a good fight. But it was hopeless. A jury of his peers didn't believe a word he said. They found him guilty. And the judge gave him the maximum sentence with the stern recommendation that he never be paroled.

And not once did she say "I told you so."

WHEN HE FIRST MET HER he thought she was Irish—she had the marvelous coloring of women in the West of Ireland he had seen so often when he fished for salmon there. A gift from the rain, they would say.

Not Irish, she told him later. Vermont stock, originally English. Cornish, in fact. From Land's End.

He looked again at all those other features he had seen day after day all through the trial. The thick black hair, all soft waves and loose curls. And under black brows, blue eyes set in whites as unblemished as a baby's. Eyes with a direct, open look that held the complete attention of the jury.

She had rarely smiled during his trial—he had given her little to smile at. And when she did, it was mirth mixed with a dash of cynicism at each corner of the mouth. The wary smile of a lawyer who had been lied to by many clients. In sunshine, beside her automobile now, she smiled—warmly.

Lastly, on her finger, the ring he had stared at every time she'd made a lawyerly note on her courtroom pad. Mrs. Madeline Hale.

He looked at the bus ticket he was dumbly holding in his hand and flung it in the air. They drove off in silence.

In spite of the panting summer heat and the grave still-
ness of the air, autumn was arriving. Under a cerulean blue
sky, fall colors swept from horizon to horizon—umbers and
tans, yellow and reds, magentas and golds, on the trees and
on the ground and falling through the sunlit air. Sweet gum
was the first to go—a waxy deep maroon color—along with
the mitten-shaped red sassafras. Jason Poole had told him
that.

The extraordinary beauty of the countryside filled him
with rage. That patient acquiescence. He was not ready for
acquiescence.

He looked at her, and her femininity was almost over-
whelming. Those prison officials were insane to have let him
ride off in a car with an attractive woman after six months
behind those walls.

He wasn't prepared for this tide of rage that was welling
up in him. He wanted to kill someone. Anyone.

"I reserved a room for you," she said.

"Don't talk."

They rode back to the city through the beauty of late
summer under that limitless sky in silence.

SHE DROPPED HIM OFF at the Hotel Ashbourne—"A Residential Hotel with Amenities." On Second Avenue in the
Twenties.

"I reserved a room for the next two weeks," she said.
"Cooking facilities included. I got your trunks and suitcases from storage and put them in the room. Here." She
handed him his checkbook. "If you'll stop around the office, I'll give you all your other papers. And the power of
attorney."

He thrust the painting at her. Chili on a perfect point. Tap
tap tap went Jason Poole's heels on the wall. As he watched,
she put it back into the trunk of her car and drove off.

Brewer stood on the street corner in the wilting heat, observing her Mercedes blend in with the auto traffic. It was a Mercedes that had gotten him out of prison. Then he looked at his "Residential Hotel with Amenities" and drew back. He was not quite ready for that. He turned and walked away.

Free. He walked unimpeded. He felt naked and exposed under the dangerous sky, without those protective prison walls and the guards.

His anger had a new companion. Fear. He felt as though he'd been ejected from a womb. Reluctantly born. And helpless in a hostile world.

He paused in a doorway and looked around him. Where was the attack going to come from? A sniper from a rooftop? A passing car? What baffled Brewer most was—why would anyone pay off a parole board with a new Mercedes plus two other unspecified gifts to get him out of prison? It had to be to kill him. But he wasn't worth killing.

He knew no state secrets; he wasn't a potential blackmailer; he knew of no one who wanted revenge on him. He shook his head at the puzzle. He could die from an assassin's bullet without ever knowing why.

On Third Avenue, he found the Tipperary Pub. It was dark and cool inside, and the cold glass of beer tasted like benediction. His sense of freedom—the enormous range of options after the optionless world of prison—was intoxicating. A leaping joy mixed with a lurking rage: Brewer didn't know whether to hug the world or go on a rampage.

Or to go into hiding. He carefully avoided sitting with his back to the door.

BREWER KNEW what he should do next: find Marvel. Marvel had been his backup in Central Park during the arms sale. Handy Andy Marvel, the no-show. His testimony could have kept Brewer out of prison. What had happened to Marvel? Had he set Brewer up?

The fastest way to find Andy Marvel was to find his brother Freddy. Brewer finished his beer and went back into the city's heat. In the hotel he opened his trunks from storage, changed into his own clothes, threw his prison outfit down the garbage shaft, and went uptown to Murray's.

There was always a hush at Murray's—an air of tension and concentration. This was no neighborhood billiard parlor. This was Murray's. Pumping balls with a cue stick was a serious activity—on twenty pool tables, all in championship condition. At this hour of the day many of them were covered in dark green rubberized cloth. Draped corpses in a morgue.

Voices barely murmured. Eyes scowled. And the only sounds were the clicking of the balls and the whack and bump in the pockets, and the occasional thumping of a cue handle on the linoleum floor to call for a new rack-up.

Along the back wall were four huge cathedral windows curtained in thick green baize to block the sun. At Murray's, it was always three o'clock in the morning.

Many great confrontations had occurred there; the walls were covered with photographs to commemorate them. Near the entrance was a huge glass case exhibiting silver cups and plaques.

Brewer hired a table with a clear view of the entrance and began pumping balls while watching the stairway entrance.

After a while a few familiar faces appeared. Regulars. They hardly glanced at him but they'd seen him. Brewer finished off a rack of balls, then turned and made a delicate survey of the faces. That was the first time he saw the man in the black suit, sitting in the disused shoeshine chair, looking out of place.

He sat there stiffly, exuding a severe and disapproving air. In his lap lay clasped hands that had never held a pool cue. The black suit was nondescript, the white shirt noncommittal, the blue polka-dot tie an afterthought. He had the lean and authoritative air of an undertaker's man come for the body.

Brewer decided to try the Off-Track Betting center.

THERE WAS A LISTLESSNESS in the sweltering streets, the exhausted air of a city too long under siege, waiting for rescue. A bus with broken air conditioning rolled by, shooting a cloud of dirty exhaust; bare arms projected from the open windows; sweat-wet faces looked out at Brewer with gaping mouths. All the buildings seemed to sway in the rising heat waves.

Marvel's brother Freddy loved the ponies and his favorite Off-Track Betting center was down at 34th and Lexington. Men stood in the small room, leaning on elbows on green wall-counters, reading the charts: PREVIOUS DAY'S RESULTS, TUESDAY, ROOSEVELT, MONTICELLO. The signs over the betting windows said SELLING or CASHING, SELLING. The men all held betting slips about the size of an open book of matches which they marked with great thought, furtively. Over their heads were television screens posting the races, the horses, and the odds.

One of the horses in the third at Belmont was named Marvel.

"A cold front," said one man. "Tomorrow, they say."

"Twelve days in a row over a hundred degrees."

"I told you. It's the greenhouse effect."

The place was all windows; he would be visible in there from a block away. So Brewer took up a position in a coffee shop across the street. He sat on a stool near the back where he couldn't be seen too easily, and from there watched the OTB doorway.

And that's when he saw the man in the black suit again, strolling past the OTB office. With black hair and olive skin, he could have been any Mediterranean type—Spanish, Italian, Greek, Arab. Perhaps Turkish. In a few steps he was gone around the corner.

BREWER QUIT AT FIVE. Marvel's brother Freddy was probably holed up until dark. So Brewer went back to his hotel.

He was out on the street again at nine that night, ate dinner somewhere—he couldn't have told you where an hour later—and clambered up the steel-edged stairs to Murray's. Each stair riser had an enameled sign, many of them badly chipped, advertising defunct cigarettes and hair oils. The Burma Shave sign warned: HE MARRIED GRACE WITH A SCRATCHY FACE. HE ONLY HAD ONE DAY OF GRACE.

The night pace at Murray's was brisker. The tension greater. Most of the tables were in use. And some serious games had drawn small bands of spectators. Brewer positioned himself at the rear in the midst of a crowd and watched the front door. And in walked the man in the black suit.

He walked from table to table, observing the games, looking at the faces, then moving on. At one point Brewer glanced up and found the man staring back at him. The eyes were humorless and unwavering. Then the man turned away.

After an hour and a half, Brewer quit. When he left, he crossed the street and stood in a doorway to see if the man in the black suit came out. He did and hailed a cab without a glance at Brewer.

IT HAPPENED SO FAST Brewer almost missed it. It was after nine the next night in Murray's as he sat with a group of spectators, watching a game. He kept his eyes on the stairway. Abruptly, through the railing, Freddy Marvel's head came just level with the floor and paused. He could have passed for his older brother's twin. Freddy's eyes studied the crowd. Then the old man at the counter said something to him. Freddy's head ducked. When Brewer got to the street, Freddy was gone.

So. The kid brother had been tipped. And now he would avoid his familiar haunts. But Freddy Marvel was the only way to Andy Marvel. Brewer had to find another way to tag him.

BREWER TANKED UP on beer at the Tipperary Pub, brooding in the midst of laughter and banter. The clientele was largely Irish and largely middle-aged and elderly, from the apartments and rooming houses in the neighborhood.

There were signs on the wall; one with a huge shamrock said GET OUT OF MY COUNTRY, BRITAIN. Another was a poster with Bobby Sands's face: REMEMBER ME. Along the bar, amid the smiling faces and the chat, were conspiratorial little knots of men: huddled heads, angry scowls, murmured words.

Brewer's anger still smoldered, and the beer just made it worse, taking him down into the depths. He left.

As he walked back to his hotel, a woman's voice from a dark doorway called to him. "Goodnight, Mr. Horny."

He paused. Black, young, in a thin, flowered dress. "Like to see what twenty-five dollars will buy?" She undid the belt around her waist and held the dress open. He stepped into the doorway, counting out the money.

"Here," she said. She pushed a long-necked beer bottle into his back pocket, then raised her right leg around his waist and hooked it on the bottle's neck. "Welcome to the Ritz, baby. Seconds are free." And she laughed throatily in his ear.

Later, when he stepped back, she said, "Take her easy, baby. Calm down. You don't want to do any more time in that place."

He paused and stared at her.

She smiled again. "Takes one to know one, honey."

BREWER LAY AWAKE in the dark. The waiting was maddening: After two days, no one had attempted to shiv him yet.

At three in the morning a great thunderstorm struck. High winds caught up garbage cans and, with a great clatter, rolled them like tumbleweed down Second Avenue. The gutters were awash, and streaming rain carried summer's litter into the sewers. The rain slashed at Brewer's window, and the wind seethed at the pane. The temperature dropped twenty degrees in minutes.

Up at Sweetmeadow, the inmates, damp with sweat, would be cheering as that chilly air blew away the locked-in heat. Many hands would reach for blankets. A good sleep under the patter of an autumn rain. The simple pleasures of the poor.

Brewer recalled Jason Poole's description of a rainstorm in the Maine woods that blew all the autumn leaves off the trees in minutes and dragged in winter's killing frost behind it.

Faintly he could hear Jason Poole's heels kicking the prison walls. Galloping in air, running away from life. That haunting sound.

IN THE MORNING, autumn weather was in the city. Brewer took a bus up to Central Park, then walked in to the little stone bridge and stared at the spot where he'd been arrested.

Cyclists and joggers passed by. And a horse-drawn carriage.

He placed his feet in the approximate place: There he had stood, on that roadway right about there, two years before in March.

It had been bitter cold. And he'd called Andy Marvel's name. Many times. And the answering silence sent him to prison.

BREWER should have known better.

On that cold day, everything had been wrong. The meet had been set up by a guy that Brewer had never heard of before. A guy named Rumbh. He'd contacted Brewer in Rome by phone, so Brewer had no idea what he looked like and no means of checking his credentials. He could have been calling from anywhere in the world.

Still, this had happened before in Brewer's career. Midnight phone calls, abrupt transfers halfway around the world to confiscate contraband arms, to pose as an arms buyer, to shadow and observe.

Rumbh had used the right code words. And he detailed the job with great authority, including Marvel's role. Whoever he was, he was a pro, and he knew the innermost details of the System. He'd even sent Brewer a round-trip airline ticket to New York.

WHEN BREWER had gotten to the park, Marvel wasn't where he was supposed to be. In fact, Marvel wasn't anywhere in sight. The meet was in the worst place, out in the open in the middle of Central Park in broad daylight. And this guy, the buyer, Giuseppe, was giving all the wrong vibrations.

Make the sale and make the bust: That's what Rumbh had ordered. Money in one hand, cuffs in the other.

Following Rumbh's instructions, Brewer had driven into Central Park at 72nd. He'd followed the serpentine roadway that was clogged with cabs taking a shortcut to the West Side. He turned right into a lane and followed it to a high-backed stone bridge arching over a dry rivulet. And there he stopped.

His breath was a damp white plume. Leaves of snow fell now and then from the dirty-gray March sky. In all directions the bare trees made a beige haze against the sky. Here and there the park showed green patches. Springtime in the wings waited for her cue.

He leaned against the rented car and waited.

A few minutes later, Giuseppe came rolling down the road in his dented and scraped green Volvo. "Ha," he said as he got out. "Florida it ain't. Would you believe snow on March twenty-third?"

Still no Marvel. No cops. No backups.

"You got my goodies for me?" Giuseppe crossed over to him and clapped a hand on his shoulder.

Brewer was looking at a man who was about to do three-to-five for arms violations.

He shook his head at Giuseppe. "Nah. The deal's off."

"Come on, cupcake. What kind of off? We got a deal and I got the cash."

"Buy yourself a lollipop."

"Hey, *que pasa*? You got something I want and I got something you want. So what's with the lollipop?"

"Later."

He saw Marvel. At last. Under the bridge. It was just a piece of him, part of his head and shoulder. And there was someone else down there too.

"There's no later," Giuseppe insisted. "Now. Deal now."

Brewer shrugged. He made a beckoning motion to Giuseppe and watched the man pull a white teller's envelope from his jacket pocket.

"Count it, champ."

Brewer counted it and grunted. He took one long last look at Giuseppe. Coming up: a fall for Giuseppe of at least three-to-five for arms dealing. Still the vibrations were bad. He hesitated one last time. Instinct.

Then he walked to the trunk of his car and unlocked it. Giuseppe bent over and pulled back the olive-drab army blanket.

"There's a dozen of them there, ha?" Giuseppe lifted one and grunted. "Sweet, sweet, sweet. Okay. You got a deal, Mr. Cupcake. Assume the position, please."

Brewer was looking at an armed New York City detective.

"Oh, beautiful," said Brewer. "Another screw-up." He peered down under the bridge. "Hey, Marvel, get your ass up here."

But the man who scrambled up the side of the embankment wasn't Marvel. Whoever he was, he arrived with handcuffs. Behind him came a uniformed New York cop. They put the cuffs on him.

Now it was Brewer who was looking at three-to-five. Maybe more. Maybe a lot more.

REMEMBERING IN THE MIDST of the autumn leaves, Brewer felt his rage rise again. He walked hastily away from the site. When he came down the lane to the road, he saw a parked cab abruptly start up. Through the back window he glimpsed a familiar Mediterranean face.

EVERY THURSDAY NIGHT at Slosberg's Gym, the boxing committee put on a card of young comers, drawn mainly from the local talent pool—New York, north Jersey, occasionally Connecticut. Raw talent in varying stages of development. The bouts were three-rounders mostly, with head guards and heavy gloves so no one could get hurt.

This was far from the Olympics class. It wasn't even at the Golden Gloves level, but for the dedicated fight fan it was always an interesting card: young kids, eager, still learning the basics of their trade. Lots of action, one quick three-round bout after another. This was the fight game's own minor leagues and it had a large following.

There was always the chance you'd see a new Sugar Ray or Hagler in his first bout. That would be something to talk about.

"I seen the champ in his very first fight ever, and I pegged him then as a comer."

Marvel's brother Freddy loved the Thursday night fights almost as much as he loved shooting pool and hustling the ponies. He never missed Slosberg's Thursday night card.

So Brewer went there. He put on a big Spanish moustache and a baseball cap and mixed with the others.

There was a good crowd. It was a cool evening after all that heat, and everyone seemed glad to be out. They were all talking about a black kid from Bedford-Stuyvesant who had all the right moves. Eighteen he was, with a couple of years in the Police Athletic League. They said he already had a left jab that could drop an ox.

When the kid walked in, even in his street clothes, you could tell. You could see the way the head was screwed down on the neck—and the neck on the shoulders. He could take a punch, you could see that. And then there were the shoulder muscles and the legs.

He had the right build for throwing jabs. And they said he was a converted left-hander which figured too. Best of all, the crowd liked the look in the kid's eyes. Young and naïve, skittish like a colt, but behind that the eyes of the hungry hunter. He would stay the course, that one.

What made it all the more interesting, he was slated to fight a Hispanic kid who had scored a first-round knockout in his last bout. Beat that: With a heavy glove and head guards he took out a guy with one punch, an overhand right smack on the button, and goodnight, Charlie.

It was a fight not to be missed by fans like Marvel's brother. He was sure to show up.

The early bouts took place in rapid order. There were mistakes in every round, awkwardness, cross-footed jabs and hooks, headhunting without finesse, scores of missed punches, dumb right-hand leads—but there were sudden flashes of real talent, a beautifully executed combination finishing with a head-rocking straight punch that made the crowd yell.

Brewer hardly noticed.

The kid from Bed-Stuy came out in purple trunks. He stood dancing in his corner, shadowboxing in the Sugar Ray style. His opponent was a tank: a head like a cannonball and no neck. The shoulder muscles seemed to be rooted to his skull right behind the ears. The overstuffed gloves looked like mittens a size too small. He was just the type of street brawler that makes even the best boxers look bad.

The kid was overmatched.

The bell rang and the caller introduced the two fighters. Marvel's brother was nowhere in sight. The two fighters went to their corners, whispering urgently to their handlers. The mouthpieces were shoved in and the bell rang.

The tank strode across the ring, upright and open as a crab, and threw a punch that the kid dodged, then threw six more, wild, without finesse, totally exposed to counterpunches. But the sixth one was a major-league ace that caught the kid flush on the jaw and rolled him like a pole along the ropes. The crowd yelled.

And Brewer saw Marvel's brother, standing in shadow behind a heavy punching bag, peering out and shaking his fists in excited silent pantomime.

The kid pedaled, the tank charged, the crowd stood on its feet, and Brewer moved to the side toward the wall, working around to Marvel's brother Freddy.

The kid danced, cleared his head, and turned to fight. But the tank was swarming all over him like surf. An experienced fighter would have known how to slip the punches, to roll, to straighten up that battering charging head, and to tear the tank's face to pieces.

At the bell the crowd sat, and Brewer got a clear view of the punching bag. Marvel's brother was gone.

Brewer skipped down the stairs.

The street was dark and empty. Slosberg's was in the middle of the block, and even at a dead run Freddy Marvel couldn't have made it to either corner. So he was hiding in a doorway. Or behind a car. Or in a car.

Brewer worked hastily down one side of the street, watching the shadows and peering into dark parked cars. Through the open windows of the gym two floors up, he could hear the crowd at ringside yelling. He heard the bell ring. And he heard the applause.

He didn't find Marvel.

He turned and worked down the other side of the street, hearing the round bell and the renewed shouting. At the middle of the block he saw a figure in a doorway and paused. The Mediterranean undertaker's man. They faced each other briefly and then Brewer went on.

The noise as he passed under the gym windows was one long bellow. At the end of the street he turned and looked back, just in time to see, all the way at the other end of the street, a shadowy figure dodging around the corner. It was undoubtedly Freddy Marvel. Brewer must have gone right by him.

The caller's voice carried clearly as he awarded the decision to the tank. It must have been a dubbing; nobody booed the decision. And now the kid from Bedford-Stuyvesant would take his battered body home and wonder if he was really cut out for the fight game. A beating like that had driven many a man out of the ring before him.

Too bad about Marvel's brother. It had been just the kind of fight he loved.

THE NEXT MORNING Brewer went down around the Bowery and found a pawnshop. For twenty-five dollars he bought an unclaimed segmented cue stick in a leather-trimmed case. He carried it back uptown and near Murray's found a wino rooting through a trash Dumpster.

For five bucks the wino took the cue in its case and walked up the metal-edged steps of Murray's and presented the case at the counter.

"For Mr. Marvel," he said.

"I'll take it," said the counterman.

"Your ass is out. I have to give it to Mr. Marvel."

The counterman told him Marvel's address.

The wino carried the cue back down the stairs and through the streets at an eager shuffle. The five dollars was burning a hole in his pocket. Each time he passed a bar he turned and glanced back at Brewer following him, then hurried on.

He turned in at an old, battered brownstone apartment building, three stories with crooked blinds and potted plants in the windows. He dashed up the outside steps and into the vestibule and pushed a button. When the door buzzer went off, he flung it open and ran down a hall.

"Who's there?" a woman's voice asked.

"Me. I mean—I got a package for Mr. Marvel."

"Put it under the door."

"It won't fit. It's a cue stick."

There was a murmured conversation behind the door. Then the door opened a few inches and a woman's bare arm reached out. "I'll take it."

"Nah! This is an expensive stick. I have to give it to Mr. Marvel."

The door swung open. "Come in," the woman said. "And be quick about it. I'm not dressed."

Brewer stepped into the room behind the messenger.

The woman gaped at him. All she had on was Marvel's suit vest and a brown bath towel, which she had wrapped around her hips. Unbuttoned, the vest barely covered her large breasts, and the towel left a four-inch gap around her ample hips.

From the bed a tousle-haired man lay glaring sullenly at him.

"Hullo, Brewer."

"Yeah." Brewer took the cue stick and dropped it on the bed. "First prize for last night's foot race. Where's your brother?"

"That's a funny question coming from you."

"Where is he?"

"He's in Joliet."

"What for?"

"What for, he says. For you! You set him up in Central Park. Three-to-five."

THE WINO HURRIED toward his favorite bar with his five dollars. It was something between a trudge and a scurry but it quickly carried him down the street and around a corner, followed by his own long autumn shadow.

Brewer sat down on the brownstone steps. He had been trained all through his career to expect the unexpected. But here in his own personal affairs he'd been surprised.

Hour after hour, day after day, for more than two years he'd pictured himself finding Bobby Marvel and beating the truth out of him before dragging him to court to vindicate himself. And now it turned out that Marvel was in Joliet, sitting hour after hour, day after day, planning to club the truth out of Brewer.

He had to find Rumbh. The road to vindication led to a man he'd never seen and no one else had ever heard of. And for that he needed money and lots of free time. Years perhaps. He would have to make a career of finding Rumbh.

Meantime he had to find a job. It might just be that he would go to his grave, embittered and furious, his entire life blighted, haunted by that voice on the telephone. And never finding it.

Meantime, he waited for someone to try to kill him. It was like waiting for the other shoe to drop.

Brewer stood up. At least he wasn't in Marvel's boat—in prison on a bum rap while his wife, in a vest and a towel, is screwing his own brother.

HE HAD TO ASSESS his situation. So, up the street from Marvel's apartment he bought a *News*, went into a bar, and ordered a double with a beer.

The first thing he did was count his money. In his pocket and in his checkbook. Enough for a couple of months. Four or five weeks more likely.

So.

No money. No way of clearing himself. No moves on the board. An unemployed ex-con on the dodge, expecting someone to try to kill him.

He opened the newspaper and read the classifieds. But there was no job there for him.

On the margin of the newspaper he penned an ad. *Situation Wanted: Ex-con, ex-government agent. Specialist in illicit high-tech arms smuggling. No reasonable offer refused.*

All his expectations had focused on one event: getting the truth out of Marvel. And now the bottom had dropped out of that plan. He saw no other moves on his board. He heard the soft padding paws of Despair approach.

Life was snickering at him. He looked at the rows and rows of bottles, lined up like an audience in a theater, come to laugh at the great fool Brewer. Innocent. Framed. Ruined. Show me the man who did this to me. Point him out. God deliver him into my hands.

Brewer tossed off the double, then grasped the empty shot glass in his palm. Target practice; his eyes selected a half-empty bottle of Old Fitz whiskey on the upper row. Two for one: The shot glass would smash the bottle and the mirror behind it.

A figure blocked the light from the door.

"Mr. Brewer?" The undertaker's man, come for the body. "May I have a word with you?"

Same black suit. Same inquisitor's eyes.

"I must apologize for following you. Perhaps *observing* is a better word."

Brewer put the shot glass down and picked up the newspaper. He turned to go.

"Come, Mr. Brewer. I wish merely to talk . . . I'm sorry to have upset you. But I did want you to find out for yourself about your partner, Marvel. It was your last piece of hope, don't you see? I needed to wait until you lost it. You understand?"

"No."

The man sat down slowly on the stool next to Brewer. "I'm the person who got you out of prison. Do you understand that?"

AT THE MAN'S SUGGESTION they moved to a booth. He carried Brewer's newspaper for him.

"What are you drinking?" Brewer asked him. He knew the answer before he heard it.

"Nothing. I won't stay long."

"Muslim?"

"How perceptive of you, Mr. Brewer." He smiled a tight smile.

"Why did you get me out?"

"I must tell you that I got you at bargain rates. The art of the bribe is not practiced with a high degree of finesse in your country, Mr. Brewer."

"Why did you get me out?"

"I wasn't sure it was such a wise move until now. But here I see considerable intelligence, Mr. Brewer. And a few other desirable characteristics. Like your anger. Very useful. In fact, I'm praising myself on my choice. I have an enticing offer to make to you."

"Do you have a name?"

"Yes. My name is Rooley Attashah. I'm from Iran."

"LET ME ASSESS your condition for you, Mr. Brewer. You've been betrayed by your country, put on trial for a crime you didn't commit, sent to jail wrongfully, sentenced to an excessive term, had your good name besmirched, your career destroyed. You are now unemployed and unemployable, with no friends, no money, no family, your life in ruins, with the bleakest possible future. You are an outcast in your own country. Neither dead nor alive. Is that an accurate inventory?"

Brewer shrugged indifference.

"You are not blessed with many options, I would say, Mr. Brewer. Surely it is time for you to reexamine all your loyalties to discover who merits them and who doesn't."

"What's the deal?"

"A few things are all I need," said Attashah. "A few small things."

"You pay the equivalent of three Mercedes in bribes and you want just a few small things?"

Attashah frowned at the newspaper, reading Brewer's handwritten ad, then tapped it with his surgical forefinger. "Ah! Precisely what I want."

Brewer nodded. "I know what you want, Attashah. Military parts. For Iran. Let me guess: American surveillance equipment. You want to eavesdrop on your neighbors."

Attashah turned his right palm up. "Ah. You are too quick, Mr. Brewer."

"But I'm not crazy."

Attashah leaned forward on his folded arms. "But you do need to get back into the game, is it not so? You need to get a stake. Because it will take much time and much money to find the culprits who framed you and to clear your name." Attashah waited for a reaction from Brewer. But Brewer never blinked.

Attashah tapped the tabletop with his index finger, a minister in his pulpit. "Who will help you, Mr. Brewer? No one. No one in the whole world. You are alone and helpless. You can do nothing without money. But—I can give you that money. I can give you the means of finding your enemies, clearing your name, and restoring your life."

Attashah waited again for a reaction. He sighed in exasperation. "Mr. Brewer, in my land, letting your enemies flourish while you languish is a disgrace."

"Marvelous people, the Iranians."

"Upon reflection, Mr. Brewer, you will discover I am offering you the only option you have." Attashah stood up. "Well—I see I've approached you too soon. You are not ready to strike a bargain. Yet."

He leaned over the table of the booth and with a black felt-tip pen wrote a phone number on a very small and white square piece of paper taken from a pocket pad. His index finger then pushed the little scrap across the table slowly to Brewer as though it were a rattrap liable to crush his fingertip.

"Call me. When you're ready. I can make you rich. Rich beyond your wildest dreams." He leaned closer and tapped the newspaper again. "I am the only one answering your classified ad, Mr. Brewer. No reasonable offer refused."

FOR A LONG TIME after Attashah had left, Brewer sat looking at the small square of paper. He'd been put back into the pot to cook a little longer.

Attashah had read him like the label on a beer can. With shrewd insight he'd pushed every secret button, touched every hidden nerve, called out every reason why—exploring another man's soul with the hot, dancing eyes of a fanatic.

Brewer had seen those eyes before. Every one in his trade had: the terrorist.

The terrorist standing on top of an embassy in Beirut, holding a pistol to the head of a young woman—an American file clerk—and demanding something impossible, the release of PLO prisoners, was it? Or jailed Libyan bomb throwers? Eventually frustrated, his demands unmet, in front of five hundred people, holding the weeping girl in his brutal embrace, the terrorist pulled the trigger. With one shot, he killed a person he had never seen before and whose name at the moment of her murder he didn't know.

Terrorist's eyes. Attashah's eyes. Here comes the great troublemaker of the world: the true believer.

The undertaker's man, come for the body.

ATTASHAH HAD ACTUALLY brought him a measure of joy. Brewer realized he wasn't going to be shot from a dark doorway after all. At least not right away. And he was out of prison—free to make his own moves. He could turn his attention to getting on with his life.

But what he sat and thought about was Attashah's offer, and all the compelling reasons Attashah had given him. In the end, though, he decided to try to do it his own way.

For starters, he would get a job. Any job. Nothing thrilling. But a job to pay the rent, to feed himself and give him the time he needed to vindicate himself.

He read the want ads again. Busboy. Dishwasher. Gasoline station attendant. Night orderly. Bartender.

Bartender.

ROARKE, THE OWNER of the Tipperary Pub, had taken to Brewer.

Several times he had talked about his saloon-owner's problems: three sons and none of them wanting anything to do with owning an Irish pub, a brother-in-law wanting to be a bartender only, with a weekly paycheck and no headaches. And Roarke himself wanting to sell the place and retire.

"I'm looking for work," Brewer announced that afternoon.

"Oh, that's wise. What line of country might that be?"

"Tending bar."

"Oh. Good choice. Myself, I like a bartender who's not too gregarious, don't you see? A good listener is what I'm referring to. This place doesn't have the clientele that take very readily to the new kind of bartender you get from these bartending schools these days. You know what I mean—very young men with beards and girls with tight-fitting blouses. What's wanted here is the older bartender who's seen his share of life—if you get my drift. One who would eventually take an interest in the business, don't you see?''

"Someone who would eventually like to own an Irish pub.''

"Exactly.''

Roarke served the eleven o'clock crowd, retirees heading for a racetrack somewhere. As he worked, he would cast an appraising glance at Brewer now and again.

He made up his mind. He said to Brewer: "My brother-in-law will be off visiting Ireland for a few weeks. Seeing his Da and Ma in Cork. You get my drift? It'd be only for a few weeks—but he's usually First Broom, you see? He sweeps out the place first thing in the morning, polishes up the glasses, stores the ice and such, and takes care of the dog patrol. You know, dog patrol. The early-morning drinkers come to get a hair of—ah, you see. Well now, it ain't all that much but it is a way to learn the business from the bottom up, don't you see?''

Brewer nodded. He saw.

"I'll let you know when.'' Roarke set up a free beer.

LATER, WHEN BREWER LEFT, Attashah stepped from a parked car and entered the bar. He drank a glass of club soda and had a nice chat with Roarke.

BREWER SPENT the rest of the afternoon checking out various marginal jobs in Manhattan. Just in case. Amazingly enough, he was turned down for busboy, a job category jealously guarded by Puerto Ricans. The gasoline pumping job was up near Harlem, in a station that had been robbed at gunpoint seven times in six months.

This was going to take more scratching than he'd thought. Late in the afternoon he went back to the Tipperary Pub.

Roarke barely spoke to him, stayed at the other end of the bar talking to an old man who fulminated against Eamon de Valera for having visited the German Embassy in Dublin to express his condolences on the announced death of Adolph Hitler.

"The most unforgivable thing that perverse old idiot ever did!"

Brewer had a difficult time catching Roarke's eye for another beer.

Roarke served him quickly. "It fell through," he said hastily to Brewer. "The whole deal. You get my drift?"

AND THAT WAS THE WAY it was going to be: Attashah going around after him, queering every job he would get. Attashah had invested three Mercedes in Brewer and then reduced his options to two. Smuggle or starve.

When I am the hammer I will strike. When I am the anvil I will bear.

Brewer reached in his pocket for some coins and walked to the phone. Don't get mad, Charlie. Get even. He dialed Attashah's phone number.

"That offer still open?"

BREWER WAS TRYING for the third time to fit everything into the box. On the wrapping paper he'd printed in block letters Clivedell Rine's name and prison address.

This would be the first package Rine had ever received in prison, and Brewer grinned, imagining the expression on Rine's face. But he had to admit there was more stuff there than he could get into the box. He was going to have to leave something out.

Brewer heard a light tapping on his hotel room door.

"Who's there?"

"Madeline Hale."

When he opened the door she said, "Don't you return phone calls?"

"You're a long way from Washington."

"May I come in? Or shall we talk in the hallway?"

"Testy, testy."

"Yes, quite, Mr. Brewer."

She glanced around the room as she entered, noting the documents and the pad on the table. It appeared to be an inventory list from which he had been transcribing selected items. He removed the papers.

She said, "I've brought back your file, including your power of attorney."

He nodded at her. "You could have mailed it to me."

"No. I need your signature on several of these. And there's something else that can't be handled by mail. Thank you for inviting me to sit down."

Brewer removed the papers from one chair for her and seated himself in another. He waited for her to speak.

"When I first met you," she began, "I asked you if you were guilty. And you said, 'More or less.' Those were your exact words as I noted them. And I believed you."

"Sounds about right."

"But you weren't guilty, were you?"

"More or less."

"But what does that mean? I thought it meant, 'Yes, I'm guilty with extenuating circumstances.'"

Brewer shrugged. "We're all guilty of something."

"But you weren't guilty of selling guns, were you?"

"I have a lot of work to do, Mrs. Hale."

"You're not going to dismiss me that easily, Mr. Brewer. You and I formed a relationship when I took your case. And you misled me. Now I want this straightened out. Our relationship is not ended yet."

"It's all over," Brewer said. "The trial is history."

"No, no. It continues. It always continues. Because of the trial, you went to prison. Because of prison, your career is ruined. Because your career is ruined, you have limited options. Because you have limited options, you are liable to do something that can ruin you completely. And I participated in that sequence, albeit unwittingly."

"What makes you think I'm going to do something that will ruin me completely?"

"Because," she said, "in your world there are only cops and robbers. And you can no longer be a cop."

"That's pretty simplistic."

"I've seen it happen too many times, Mr. Brewer. Now, I'm asking you again—were you really selling guns from the back of that car for your own gain? Are you guilty of that crime, yes or no?"

Brewer sighed. "I'm satisfied that you did as well as any lawyer could have. No recriminations. No regrets. I can handle it from here."

"Well, I have recriminations. I want a rematch."

"Mrs. Hale. What will it take to have you leave here?"

"The truth."

"Some other time, maybe."

"I conducted your trial on the basis that you were guilty. I took the strongest defensive position I could muster to minimize your sentence. And you absolutely refused to cooperate. You insisted on a plea of not guilty, which involved a trial and infuriated the judge. I felt, and still feel, you could have gotten a far lesser sentence if you'd changed your plea. Do you understand that?"

Brewer sighed again.

"And now, Mr. Brewer, I have a nagging suspicion that you were innocent."

Brewer shrugged at her in silence.

"Over the years," she said, "as a trial lawyer I've defended many a guilty person who claimed to be innocent. But I have never handled an innocent person who claimed to be guilty."

She waited for a reply. "No answer?" she asked. "If you are innocent, then I would have conducted a different trial. I might have gotten you acquitted."

"No. You never had a chance. Nothing you could have done would have changed the outcome one whit."

"Explain that, please."

"When pros set out to do a job on you," Brewer answered, "you get trapped, wrapped, and delivered with a big red bow. The job gets done and it stays done."

"Then you are saying you were framed by professionals? You were innocent?"

"Believe me, it doesn't matter a bit."

"It does to me." She pointed at the inventory document in his lap. "Before you make a fatal turning in your life, I want to make an offer. If I reopen your case and find that you were truly framed, and if as a result of that you are restored to your career and your job—if I can do that, will you stop doing what I think you're doing here?"

"You think I'm doing something nefarious?"

"How about answering my question?"

"My name cleared and my old job back? Sure. I would certainly drop what I am now planning to do."

"Okay. Then I think we have a deal. Are you innocent?"

"More or less."

"Oh, dear God in heaven. Explain that to me. Now. Please."

"It's called relativism. And, as the ministers love to point out, relativism makes sinners of us all."

"What does that mean?"

"Salami tactics, Mrs. Hale. Life doesn't take your soul all in one go. It does it a slice at a time. Like salami. Do you understand?"

"No."

Brewer looked down at the document in his lap. "You know, I have a lot to do and I'm desperately short of time."

"Don't stop. Tell me about relativism."

"I can give you just a couple more minutes. Okay?"

"Yes."

Brewer pitched the document and the pad onto the bed. "When I was a young agent, just starting out, I was very naïve. I believed that the Feds were good guys and the arms dealers were the bad guys. So I was very careful about obeying the law.

"For example, I never never put a phone tap in position until I had the paper from the judge. Then one day, because of an urgent situation, I put a tap in while waiting for the judge to sign the papers—which he did. I had done something legally illegal. I bent the law a little. Okay so far?"

"Go on."

"Next time I put on a tap before I had the papers, the judge refused to sign them. So I took the tap off. But the next time a judge refused to sign the papers, I left the tap on because the judge was clearly an idiot with a political motive. A few days later, sure enough, another judge did sign the papers. Later I put taps on even before the papers had been drawn. After that I often just put the tap on and let my conscience be my guide. See? I went from legally illegal to illegally legal."

"Those are weasel words," she said.

"Yes. They are, aren't they? Next I started putting taps on as a service to other agents. Those taps picked up a lot of information—helped stop crimes and helped put criminals in jail. Okay so far?"

"Go on."

"Then I was given a reward here and there. Now I was putting taps in for money but only if I felt the tap was justified. Finally I stopped asking for justification. The world of politics was too corrupt for me to sort out. Some judges would sign a paper other judges wouldn't. There was no rhyme or reason. Legal merit didn't seem to have anything to do with it. So my conscience had to be my guide. Then I saw that everyone was guilty. Everyone deserved to be tapped. See? A slice at a time. I lost myself a slice at a time. From there it was easier and easier. I eventually committed every crime in the book, from breaking and entering to bribery and blackmail to assault, mayhem and even murder. Right and wrong became relative terms. They had no real meaning to me anymore. Until I was arrested. And that changed everything."

"Why?"

"Have you ever been arrested and locked in a jail cell?"

Madeline Hale shook her head. "No."

Brewer said, "When you're put into a cell, even innocent people feel guilty. All kinds of feelings of guilt come to the surface. I knew that I belonged in prison for many of the things I'd done as an agent. And when you walked into my cell, I told you the truth. I'd sold arms a number of times. Mainly to entrap people. But sometimes I never bothered to turn in the money I made on the deal. Do you hear what I'm saying? I'm guilty of a string of crimes that would knock your hat off. And I can't even say I did them all for my country."

She was biting her lower lip in anger. "Mr. Brewer—"

He held up his hand. "Wait. One more thing. I was framed and I knew there was no way out. I was going to prison. And I did. There's nothing more you can do legally to help me. Nothing. You understand?"

"You're going to take the law into your own hands?"

"I'm going to find the man who framed me. That's all I'm interested in."

She shook her head at him. "Judge, jury, and executioner."

Brewer shrugged.

"Mr. Brewer, permit me to ask you about these."

She pulled out a packet of white business envelopes. He recognized his own handwriting: letters he had written to himself, care of her law offices.

"I respected your wishes and left these envelopes unopened. All except one. This one. Our mail clerk sent this one through the electric letter opener. And then came to ask me who Segrue is." She removed the folded sheet from the opened envelope and held it out to him.

He read the message:

SEGRUE ADDRESSES THE GODS:

From you, there are two Greek gifts: birth and death.

The latter's the better. It's what makes the former so palatable. Life without end would be hell on earth; there is no greater punishment—no more exquisite torture— than endlessness.

But there is one gift greater than either birth or death. Not being born at all: that's best by far.

Next best: not being born again.

With heel taps on my wall, I hear the arrival of your second gift. With heel taps I hear death.

Accept my petition: I do not want your gift of life after death. I do not wish to return here. I do not wish reincarnation. I do not want to see again what I have seen. Do not want to feel again what I have felt. I do not wish to be a victim—nor see the other victims—of the gods again.

Keep your spurious gifts. Leave me alone.

"Who is Segrue, Mr. Brewer?"

"Someone I know."

"Is it you? When I read this I was devastated. It was one of the blackest days of my life. This is the petition of a person who is horrified, sickened by life. If this was your mood in prison, and I had something to do with it, it will haunt all my days."

"Mrs. Hale, we are all grown-up here."

"This has nothing to do with being grown-up."

"Yes, it does. We both know life is not fair, never has been. Most lives are not worth living. Most people would be better served if they'd died in their cradles. That piece about Segrue was written the night an inmate hanged himself in his cell."

"Oh." She studied his face. "How terrible." She touched the paper. "That makes it even worse. Whenever I read this it leaves me depressed for days. Now it will haunt me."

"Mrs. Hale," he began.

"I want a straight answer from you, Mr. Brewer. Were you selling guns out of the back of a car in Central Park for personal gain?"

Brewer sat back and folded his arms. He looked insolently at her, at the soft waves of her black hair and at the pale-blue eyes that were fixed so unflinchingly on him.

"You have beautiful coloring, Madeline Hale. Are you sure you're not Irish?"

"I'm not Irish and neither are you. Will you please answer my question?"

"I know women who would kill to get skin like that."

"Were you selling guns in Central Park for personal gain?"

Brewer shrugged at her, finally. "No. I was there on orders of a man named Rumbh."

Madeline Hale took out her notebook and a pencil. "Mr. Brewer. Start at the beginning. And describe every detail. I want all the facts. From the beginning. Slowly."

"On one condition."

"What?"

"Don't call me Mr. Brewer anymore. Do people call you Madeline?"

"Yes."

"Then so will I."

IN THE MIDDLE of a question she was phrasing, Madeline Hale stopped and asked, "Do you like Chinese food?"

"Sure," Brewer said.

"I noticed there's a place down the street, and I do a great act with chopsticks." She smiled at him. "I haven't eaten since this morning."

SHE PUT THE FOOLSCAP PAD on the table next to the soy sauce and Chinese noodles.

"Okay," she said. "Next question. Who had a motive for wanting to frame you?"

"Nobody."

"Someone did."

"Nobody in the arms trade. Framing is too much work. It's easier to use a gun or a bomb."

"I don't see us making much progress here," she said.

"You'll know when you're making progress. These people will bomb your car. Or burn you in your bed."

"Is there anything else you can tell me about this framing?" she asked.

Brewer shrugged.

She put her pencil down. "You don't really think I'm going to get anywhere, do you?"

"No."

"I'm going to surprise you."

"The soup's very good," said Brewer.

LATER she consulted a pocket calendar. "How much— Are you Charles or Charlie?"

"Charlie will do."

"Okay, Charlie. How much time do I have?"

"For what?"

"To clear your name before you do something irrevocable."

"How much time can you put against it?"

"As much time as it takes. I'm winding up my affairs in Washington, and your case is my last piece of unfinished business."

"Where are you going?"

"Back to Vermont to open a law practice and get married."

"I thought you *were* married."

"I'm a widow, Charlie."

"Oh. Sorry to hear that. How did it happen?"

"A shooting in a Washington courtroom. A prisoner got a policeman's gun and killed four people. One of them was my husband. Do you like the life of an agent?"

"Okay, change the subject. The life of an agent is simple enough. All you need is a simple mind."

"I don't think it's very simple at all. And I don't think you're simple. In fact I've always found you a very complex man. And very private. After all those weeks and months working on your trial I didn't know you any better at the end than I did at the beginning."

"I'm just an ordinary dogface cop."

"Come on, Charlie. That's a pose. I've handled a number of government agents and I've never met anyone like you before. Certainly not anyone who wrote anything like your 'Segrue Addresses the Gods.'"

"I'm no different from any dozen other agents. It's all the same world."

"Same world, yes," she said. "And on the surface it seems very romantic. Wild chases, smuggling, arms deals, double crosses, shots in the dark, car bombs. But it's an abnormal life. I haven't met one agent yet who had a successful marriage. And that includes you."

"Maybe I just never met the right girl."

"Charlie, there isn't any right girl. Have you ever really pictured yourself dashing home on the five-fifteen to go to the supermarket with your little wifey after a big shoot-out on the waterfront with arms smugglers? You live out of a suitcase. You sleep each night on a different airline. Ten cities in ten days. You never know in the morning where you'll be at night—or even if you're still going to be alive. Most agents eventually get sick of it and complain about the constant danger, the endless travel, the loneliness and isolation, the bad pay, the indifferent front office and all the rest. But you—it's quite obvious you love it. You're fascinated by the game, playing cat and mouse on a worldwide scale. Addicted to it, in fact. I figured that out the day I met you. And you're a loner. Any woman who tried to make a marriage with you would have to be crazy."

"I thought you hadn't learned anything about me."

"Lawyers say if you want to learn about a man, watch him when he's on trial. But I didn't learn much. You kept it all locked in. Except the anger. That's evident. You're still angry."

"That doesn't sound very admirable."

"On the contrary, I came to admire you greatly. When they led you away after the trial with the handcuffs on, you turned once and looked at me. I'll never forget that look. And all I could think of was 'I'll never see him again.'"

Brewer shifted in his chair.

Then she smiled delightedly. "I do believe that's as close as you can come to blushing. I'll tell you something else. One of the happiest days I've had in a good long time was the day you got out of prison. Try that necktie on."

Brewer said, "How about some more tea?"

"I went out," she said, "and bought that suit just to go to the prison to pick you up. I can't tell you how excited I was about seeing you again. But when you came out through that prison gate, my heart dropped. I thought, Dear God, what have they done to him. You were a walking bomb. You were literally ticking."

Brewer cleared his throat. "Convicts say if you want to learn about a lawyer, sit through a trial with one."

"Oh, I see," she said. "Turnabout. Okay. What did you learn about me?"

He looked at her speculatively. "Very quick-witted. Well prepared. Good strategist. Poker face. You never once tipped your hand. A very tough competitor. A real fighter. And you love the game too. I'd say you're just as bad a bet for marriage as I am."

DURING THE MEAL the questions continued. What time was the flight from Rome? How did you contact Giuseppe? Who got the weapons from the baggage check, you or Marvel?

He laid his hand over hers. "Do you know, Madeline, you hardly ever make a direct statement? Your whole conversation consists of questions."

"Is that bad?"

"See? Another question. No. I don't think it's bad. I think it's a way of keeping people from getting close."

"And why would I do that?"

"Maybe to keep me from saying what I think about moving back to Vermont."

"You don't think I should go?"

"No."

"Now how did you reach that conclusion?"

"It's easy. You've got a top-drawer law degree. You're connected with one of the best law firms in Washington, and you've been trained by some of the best trial lawyers in the business. You've already got a major reputation. Right in the power center of the world. Other lawyers must point you out in a crowd. You're young and good-looking, with all the money you want. And a great legal future. It's all glamour and headline trials, expense-account restaurants and famous people. On top of that you're fascinated by your own cat-and-mouse game too. And you're going to go from that to changing diapers and writing wills in a country town in Vermont? No major leaguer ever opts to go back to the minors. I don't believe it."

"Believe it. I come from a long line of country lawyers in Vermont."

"Nah. After Washington, you're going to lay an egg in New England. It's a low-percentage shot. Won't work. You can't go home again."

"I was born and raised in Vermont. I know exactly what I'm getting into."

"A boy for him, a girl for you, in an old Victorian house down a lane."

"That's the goal of a lot of people, Mr. Brewer."

"Charlie."

"Charlie."

"That's true," Brewer said. "But not after Washington. What does he do?"

"Professor of humanities in a small college."

"How old are you, Madeline?"

She pushed back her chair. "I have to leave."

Brewer laughed. "Now who's aloof and hard to reach? I think we're a matched pair."

"Thanks for your time, Charlie. I'll be in touch with you."

"Admit it. You're never going to find a case like mine in Vermont."

She nodded solemnly. "And I'm not going to meet anyone like you in Vermont, either, Charlie."

"What does that mean?"

"Well, that got your attention, didn't it? You can figure out for yourself what it means." She stood up. "You still haven't answered my question. How much time do I have?"

"For what?"

"To clear your name before you do something irrevocable."

"I do believe you're trying to save my soul."

"I do believe you're right, Charlie. Goodnight."

"How much time do *I* have?" Brewer asked her.

"For what?"

"Before you move to Vermont."

"I'm getting married Christmas Day," Madeline Hale said. "Down a country lane in an old Victorian house I was born and raised in." She leaned over, put her two hands on his cheeks, and kissed his lips softly.

5

When McCall arrived at his office the next morning, he'd had very little sleep. After the conversation in the airport with Wainwright he never got back to bed. Instead he sat in his study the rest of the night, pondering the moves he was about to make. Planning three simultaneous assassinations. Possibly four. Hiring three assassins. Or four. Three separate setups. Or four. It was going to require a great deal of preliminary work and coordination.

And all through the mental process, he felt he was standing outside himself, watching himself go through the motions of planning three murders. He wondered if he was really going to go through with it.

He took out a yellow foolscap pad and consulted his list.

1) Locate Attashah. And watch his every move.

2) Put a watch on the shipments and exports of all items on the Iranian parts list. Discover if any of the suspect arms dealers are buying them.

3) Locate Rus, Slane, and Rock. Determine exactly where they will be on the key date. November 26.

4) Hire three assassins. And another in reserve—just in case.

McCall stared at the list. The key date: He'd chosen it. November 26. Five weeks.

Number one on his list was to locate Attashah. He summoned his assistant, Borden, to his office. "Bring over whatever you've got on Attashah."

HE HAD ALREADY DECIDED that the quickest way to get a lead on the three targets without drawing attention to what he was doing was to check the computer dailies for the last month or so. He was after three simple pieces of information: Where would Peno Rus, Eric Rock, and Slane be on November 26?

He sat at his computer and punched in his code number, then the access number. A moment later in reply, the computer displayed its menu. Mirror, mirror on the wall.

Search, McCall ordered.

The screen scrambled and a second menu appeared.

McCall decided to punch in the names of more than just the three arms dealers:

() Peno Rus
()L. Slane
()Eric Rock
()Thomas Reilly
()Stanislaus Winiski
()Giuseppe Nero (a.k.a. John Black, Jack Black, Black Jack, Twenty-One, and Ventuno)

Then he added three words: *current data only.*
The screen blinked and blanked.

When Borden arrived he had a very slim manila folder. Before McCall could speak, Borden held up an arresting hand.

"Now, Bobby, before we get to Attashah, we have to talk about Dice. In fact, we have to do something about Dice before he gets someone killed."

"I know. I know."

"You haven't heard the latest."

"I have. He went moonlighting to remove a whole bunch of legal FBI taps."

"No. You haven't heard the latest latest."

"Do I have to?"

"He made an unbelievable hash of Time Sector four. We just caught it in time. He never showed it to anyone. He was just on the verge of sending it out. When I saw it I goddam near wet my pants. He came within a whisker of compromising four of our people. That's four coffins, Bobby. If you don't move on this, someone is going to wax his skis for him. I hear they've already drawn lots. You have to move on this today. Today."

McCall silently read Borden's scowling face.

"Bobby, listen," said Borden.

"I am."

"Arms Control can turn into a shooting gallery. They're going to put that son of a bitch in the river. This thing could destroy the whole organization."

"I hear you. I'll take him to lunch at the Khyber Pass."

Borden sighed. "I'd give a box of chocolate gumdrops to have Brewer back."

"So would I," McCall said.

"Christ, what a loss that was."

"Tell me about Attashah," McCall said. "Where is he?"

Borden opened his thin folder. "Ask me where he was."

"Okay. Where was he?"

"In the Merrill Hotel in Manhattan."

"Manhattan? Are you sure?"

"Yes." Borden held up the paper he was reading. "He apparently got in on a Turkish passport."

"Go on."

"He was there some six weeks. Didn't do much. Never used the telephone. The only thing we got a lead on—he bought a car. A Mercedes. For export. Papered for shipment on a Turkish freighter."

"Six weeks under our noses and all he did was buy a car?" McCall rubbed his nose. "You know what? He made a contact. You have to find that car."

"It's gone to Turkey."

"Check. Make sure. Attashah never would have bought a Mercedes here to ship to Turkey or anywhere else. It would have been much cheaper to buy it in Germany. Besides, Iranian officials don't buy Mercedes. Not on their austerity program."

Borden shrugged.

"Check!" McCall insisted.

"Bobby. This could take—"

"Don't tell me. Do it. And I want a work-up on every arms dealer on List B. Find out if any of them were in New York City during the six weeks Attashah was there."

Borden got up and walked to the door.

"Hey," McCall said. "You didn't give me the key piece of information. Where's Attashah now?"

Borden shrugged. "Checked out. Three days ago. Maybe he's on the Turkish ship with the Mercedes."

BEFORE TEN, McCall's computer screen came on:

()DDL: Slane. Excerpt from USBSPERSO-710918CYZ Mexico City: Random. During surveillance operation Project Catspaw, arms trader L. Slane was observed in lobby and bar of Orizaba Hotel with

Caucasian male answering to the name of Joli or Jolly.
End.()

()DDL: Peno Rus, Thomas Reilly, Stanislaus Winiski, Eric Rock, Giuseppe Nero. Nothing found in
dailies. Continue search? End.()

McCall frowned at the first message. Joli? It was a new
name to him. A new playmate for Slane. Caucasian male.
Answers to the name of Joli or Jolly. Who might that be?
And what is Slane doing in Mexico City?

He asked the computer to do a name search for Joli or Jolly
plus seven spelling variants.

Then he sent a request to Chief of Station, Mexico City,
for a complete list of names from the guest register of the
Hotel Orizaba.

At one he took Dice to Khyber Pass for lunch.

KHYBER PASS was an intelligence hangout. And McCall,
sitting with Dice near the door, watched with interest as a
whole miscellany of people ducked inside, shaking their
dripping umbrellas, shucking their raincoats and hats, and
smoothing their hair. Many headed right for the bar and the
day's ration of gossip. Others circulated among the tables.

McCall was looking at an anthology of Washington
spookdom passing before him, what Charlie Brewer had
once called the parade of bad boys.

It was the ideal place to be seen if you were a spook looking for a new connection. And Dice didn't need anyone to
tell him he was a spook looking for a new connection.

Two ex-CIA types came in, wiretappers now working for
Senator Ritter of Wisconsin, who had unofficial friendly taps
on at least three other senators' telephone lines. Reelection
in Wisconsin was such a chancy business these days, a candidate had to have all the help he could get.

"Hullo, Bobby," said one of them. "How are the gun-runners treating you?"

Another agent, now with Naval Intelligence in the Pentagon, arrived in the company of a marine engineer who was a registered lobbyist for a naval construction firm. It was a not-so-subtle announcement that the agent would soon be leaving government employ for a job with the construction firm. What he had done for the construction company while in Naval Intelligence was worth a guess. And McCall made a silent one.

All about him men sat at tables over white linen table-cloths and conducted spooks' business. Charlie Brewer had once said going to lunch at Khyber Pass was like putting the light on in the kitchen and seeing the cockroaches scramble.

McCall realized that Brewer's name had kept turning up for one reason or another all day.

The current piece of chat among Washington's within-walls personnel was the discovery by a congressional investigation committee of fifteen different illegal taps on its telephone lines. The FBI was supposed to be investigating, although rumor said that three of the taps at least were put there by people in the FBI.

The biggest laugh was drawn by Congressman Storm Pacek of New York, who bellowed that such conduct was subverting the government's business and destroying the Constitution. One of the taps was purportedly his.

Dice smiled broadly at the crowd. "Kind of reminds you of the fall of the Roman Empire, doesn't it?" And he emitted his obnoxious cynical guffaw. He stared boldly back at those who were looking at him. Their glances were furtive and they were making sotto voce remarks to each other. Such a lunch was a commonplace; all the agencies practiced it. It was said that Khyber Pass was the place where each agency abandoned its strays. Brewer had been blunter. He called it the human garbage dump.

McCall saluted Dice with his wineglass. "Cheers."

"And jeers," Dice replied.

"I wanted to talk to you," McCall said, "about your performance."

Dice nodded and glanced at his watch.

"You almost did it for four of our people."

"Yeah."

"They're ready to float you in the river, Dice."

"Imagine."

"It isn't just that you've done a poor job, Dice. I feel you're doing the wrong job. You're a street man, not an administrator."

"I suppose."

"Don't take this so lightly, Dice. There are those who want you flogged through the fleet for what you did."

"I appreciate the favor, Bobby."

"Then there's also the matter of the taps you removed. Perfectly legal taps. Installed by the FBI."

"How did I know they were legal? All taps look alike. When a well-known candidate for President asks you to sweep out his Senate telephone lines and you find seven separate taps—"

"That's just the point. You were moonlighting. What you did was illegal."

"So were five of those seven taps. Hell, Bobby. Everyone knows this town is crawling with thousands of illegal taps. Put in by the very people who are pissed because I took them out."

"Those are hardly excuses, Dice."

"I suppose."

"It's too bad this isn't working out, Dice. You were given the assignment in my group because you wanted it—in spite of the contrary recommendation by your superiors. There's a lot of I-told-you-so going on in the corridors right now. I'm sorry. Maybe you can put the pieces back together in another outfit. Okay?''

"Okay." Dice looked at his watch. "Not bad," he said. "Under two minutes. Now we can enjoy lunch." He guffawed and signaled the waiter for another martini.

They ate without talking. And all the while, Dice's eyes shopped the faces at the other tables, seeking his next job.

"I must say, Bobby," he said at last, "it's a very peculiar world we live in. The people in this room are slowly but surely destroying the whole goddam country, and I get fired for filling out the wrong form."

"A form that would have exposed four men in a very sensitive operation."

"Do you believe that, Bobby?"

AFTER LUNCH, Dice strolled into the bar and chatted with a knot of men. And soon everyone knew he was among the walking dead, a man with a paycheck but no assignments. And no desk. No place to go to in the morning. He had become part of the day's gossip.

Several times McCall heard Dice's insolent laugh carry from the bar and shook his head. Even in a town where screw-ups flourished, Dice was going to have a tough time finding a berth. He was now known as a bungler who had nearly caused the deaths of four field men. By filling out the wrong form. Silently McCall answered Dice's question: No, he didn't believe it. And neither did anyone else. Wrong forms don't kill. They're excuses to get your enemies—like Dice.

Dice was a casualty of office politics.

McCall went back to the office alone.

AROUND THREE, Borden looked in expectantly.

"We had lunch," said McCall.

"They say Khyber Pass is a good place to get rid of a headache," said Borden.

"So they say."

"You're too nice, Bobby." Borden shook his head. "I would have sent him out on a Dawn Patrol."

"There are more than a few around here who should be sent out on Dawn Patrols."

"That son of a bitch is going to haunt you."

"I hope you're wrong."

"I am never wrong."

CHIEF OF STATION, Mexico City, was polishing up the handle on the big front door: Before five, he had sent to McCall almost two hundred names of guests registered in the Orizaba Hotel.

McCall sat scrolling the list on the computer screen. Slane, he noted, was registered for two nights. He asked the computer's data bank to match up the two hundred names with his agency's master list of more than 100,000 names of "watchables."

Then he sent a message to all Chiefs of Station for a current status on Code List 12—Leading Arms Dealers, Traders, and Smugglers. Forty names. And among them were the three men from his list: Slane and Rus and Rock.

In the morning he hoped to know the whereabouts of all three. He went off to dinner with his boss. Sufficent unto the day.

IN THE POLITICAL monetary system, the principal unit of value is not a dollar or a piece of gold. It is the favor. The richest person in the capital is the one with the most favors due. A power broker is someone who can assemble a number of favors due from a coterie of powerful people and then use that agglomeration of callable favors to work a deal. Sometimes the deal borders on blackmail.

To build a fund of favors due, Martin Wainwright always exacted a little something extra on the side from every deal he worked in Washington. The extra then went into his little black book of political debits and credits.

Most of his side extras were aimed at subordinates and lesserlings and amounted to school-ground bullying, usually as harmless as swapping baseball cards. In fact, some of his detractors called him the one-horse-power broker.

McCall knew that Wainwright would demand something for the deal he'd worked on the three assassinations. And he had suspected from the beginning what the demand would be.

Now, as he waited in the small committee room on the second floor, he knew. The little something on the side was Monroe.

WHEN HE FIRST ARRIVED in Washington, McCall had been told: "It's the double standard in the State Department that will ultimately drive you away. Either get connected with one of the old boy networks or get out."

McCall hadn't listened. He'd not joined any network. And now each year he found himself growing more cynical. Daniels, on the roof that day, had uttered the general opinion of other branches of government: All you guys in State are screw-ups.

And up the stairs came a screw-up named Monroe.

Monroe was a member of the same eastern private-school Ivy League network as Wainwright. And McCall's little side payment to Wainwright was to brief Monroe on the Brazilian situation.

Wainwright had said, "He'll be off on a special junket in a few days, and it's just the kind of background stuff he needs."

But to get McCall to sit down with Monroe, Wainwright had had to ask three times and then insist.

McCall had been working on the Brazilian material for months, and as part of his program to promote his career he was planning to present it in a speech to the Washington Press Club. Not even Borden had seen the material.

McCall had seen Monroe in action before. Friendly, tentative, with a diffident air and a drinking problem, Monroe was trying to put things back together after making a hash of a job in Athens. There had been other hashes in Monroe's career, a string of them.

If he'd had the same status as Dice, Monroe would have been taken for his last lunch at the Khyber Pass long ago. But Monroe was connected. He was part of the privileged network, protected by that double standard that had thwarted McCall so many times.

McCall stood at the top of the marble stairs and watched Monroe climb them. State was awash with Monroes, all wearing the same protective coating: Choate, was it? Or Deerfield Academy? He would still be known among his network cohorts by his school nickname: Buffy, was it? Or Frog?

After his fiasco in Athens, he was sporting a new image. Or, rather, trying to drop the old. Thinner. Trimmer. New tailor. New haircut. New wife: His original, an alcoholic, had been seen as a liability; the replacement was younger, attractive, with money, and related to a State Department ranker—in short, a career asset. Also she made him seem younger, more contemporary. She mixed Monroe in with the right younger people.

You could see it in the man's eyes: Monroe was shopping for a new hobbyhorse. And Arms Control was one of the items on his shopping list.

He called affably up the stair: "McCall? Yes. Monroe. Awfully good of you to see me. I won't keep you but a minute." He came skipping up, bobbing his head. Then the condescending boneless handshake. The runt of the litter, but he was in the right litter.

McCall felt a touch of pity for him. Pale hair, pale face, and pale-blue eyes. It must be lousy to be incompetent, and to know it and to hate it and to know others know and to hate their knowing. And to know you can't do anything about it.

It must be lousy to wake each morning with the same pathetic prayer on your lips: Oh, God, don't let me screw up today. Amen.

Each day, the weak hand reaches for the bottle for just one more drink. One more drink, then I'll be good. I'll amaze the world. I'll pull myself together. I'll salute with my glass all those who find achievement so easy, and I'll join them. They'll say: How decisive he's become. He's a lion. He's been posted to Paris and in weeks he shaped up the whole place—a model operation now. He has restored our faith in man and in the American system. They'll praise me and they'll feel good about me. I salute them all with just one more drink. (Oh, let my hand not rattle the neck of the bottle on the glass.)

Oh, God, keep me out of trouble today.

Every bureaucracy had its Monroes. The British did. So did the Russians. And the French. Affable, well-intentioned, filled with goodwill and with a gift of charm often given to the weak. But unable to make things work. Could never throw a football. Never catch a pass. Never get the school newspaper out on time. Always missing planes. Nodding off at meetings. Yet clinging like a limpet in the heaviest sea.

His glance said it all as he stepped past McCall. "In here? Ah, I see." He was the kind of man who decorates himself with others' feathers.

He sat down in the meeting room, facing the blank screen. "How long does it take?"

"How long do you want it to take?"

"Oh. I don't know. Ah—let's see." He scratched the back of his head, the scholar searching for the answer. The year of the Pelopennesian War? The definition of the ablative absolute? He was baffled by McCall's question.

McCall sat down across the table. "I understand you are interested in the international arms trade."

"Oh, yes. Quite right. I'm going on a junket, mainly European capitals. And I need some backgrounding."

"I see. Have you had any previous experience in the arms trade?"

"Oh, here and there." Monroe watched the screen expectantly, almost like a child at a matinee.

"I have spent quite a bit of time gathering this material on Brazilian armaments," McCall said. "I'm giving a talk on it later this month. So what I'm telling you is still confidential."

"Quite right. Quite right," Monroe said airily.

McCall commenced his presentation: with slides and overheads, a recitation of Brazilian arms and their effect on world arms and on the domestic arms market.

McCall identified his thesis: An avid student of the U.S. system, Brazil was now a serious, tough competitor to the U.S. arms industry.

It was storming through the worldwide markets with good stuff. Simplified. Equipment that can take rough wear, that can be fixed in minutes with a simple tool by unlettered Third World soldiers. Priced right. Stealing market after market from the complicated, higher-priced American arms.

Brazil was making more than half of all wheeled armored vehicles and selling them to buyers from China to Libya and Surinam; well over three hundred companies in Brazil were making a $3 billion full-course dinner for military customers: jet trainers, military aircraft, military helicopters, small warships, submarines, artillery rockets, cannon—whatever the market wanted.

Over strong U.S. objections, Brazil was also selling nuclear power material. It was Brazil that sold the uranium dioxide to Iraq for its nuclear power plant—the one that so alarmed Israel she sent her jets to destroy it.

Some military specialists doubted that the Persian Gulf War would have been possible without Brazil's eager arms selling. Brazilian antitank missiles were fired from both sides.

Brazil was carrying arms sales to their logical conclusion: Anyone with the money gets the merchandise. Anyone.

With more and more nations relying on armaments sales to improve their international trade balance, the world was awash in warfare potential. Since it was the United States that had largely shown the way, it was the U.S. that would have to find some means of reducing the threat. Even if it meant reducing its own enormous arms sales abroad. If it could find the will. Before it was too late. If it was not already too late. In the last five years, the potential for warfare around the world had increased twentyfold.

Monroe never asked a question. Didn't seem unduly alarmed. In the end he said, "I would like to borrow a copy of your White Paper overnight. I'll return it by messenger in the morning before I leave."

McCall hesitated and Monroe, with unexpected firmness, picked up the White Paper and saluted McCall with a finger. "Thanks. Much. Big help. Return it tomorrow. Don't worry. Mum's the word."

McCall watched him with contempt.

WHEN MCCALL came into his office the next morning, the computer had matched its 100,000 names of "watchables" with the 200 names from the Orizaba Hotel guest list. It had isolated three names and they sat neatly stacked in the middle of his computer screen:

1) L. Slane
2) Aubrey Joli
3) Florian Gomez

The computer had also searched its Summary Reports for the name Joli or Jolly, with seven variant spellings. It had found a Summary Report on just one: Aubrey Joli. McCall punched it up on the screen:

()DS/Lon/V182243/580213/PSPT-J137465   Aubrey Joli, British national, b. Liverpool, 09/09/50. No criminal record. Former manager of the Duchess Club casino, London. Subject of three investigations into questionable casino practices, 1978, 1981, 1982. On all three occasions closely interrogated by British casino authorities. Also suspected of connections with organized crime. Once questioned on drug smuggling operations. After scandal at Duchess Club involving four dealers and two known gamblers, Joli voluntarily resigned casino position and vacated his gaming license June 12 last. Same day all charges dropped. Now persona non grata in British casinos. Reported to be working with Los Angeles office of Ampersand Film Productions, London. Application for American visa

denied 85/12/12BTR. See also FBI files passim; US
Embassy/Lon #R-107-28453.

McCall now asked the computer for a Summary Report
on Florian Gomez.

()DS/Wash/K239476/477121/PSPT   NK   Florian
Gomez: AKA Colonel Gomez, Captain Hook, The En-
forcer; national, Leeward Island Free State. b. Vincentown, LIFS, 07/04/46. Former Director of Security,
Leeward Island Free State. Right hand man to Antonio
Cappi, Lifetime President of Free State. Falling out
three years ago over question of building a gaming
casino in Vincentown. Gomez left Free State. Some say
he fled. Currently living on French Riviera near Nice
with widow of former Minister of Finance, Leeward
Island Free State. No known economic activities. Car
bomb destroyed his vehicle, killing chauffeur, with ex.
damage to his residence, 09/10/84. For political history LIFS and for citations against F. Gomez see Am-
nesty International file. Also Commission on Human
Rights, extensive Gomez dossier. Three applications for
American visa denied: US Embass/Par (dossier); FBI
reports, passim.

McCall found the combination worthy of considerable
speculation: an unfrocked casino manager from Britain now
doing something in or to the film industry; an exiled Caribbean political thug and bomb target who wanted to build a
casino; and a notorious arms trader and smuggler—all in the
same hotel at the same time. What interesting scenarios that
suggested.

But it didn't tell him where Slane would be on November
26. He addressed the computer once more. He asked it to

check all commercial airline computers for airline reservations in Slane's name from present to November 26. For good measure, he threw in the two other names: Joli and Gomez.

Then he summoned Borden.

"I'm still trying to place Attashah's Mercedes on that Turkish ship," Borden said, entering.

"That's not why I called you. I want you to put a watch on these Iranian military parts." He handed Borden the Iranian parts list. "Go over to Export Control at Commerce and request a monitoring. We want full details on anyone who applies for an Export License with Exceptions Certificate on any of these items. Go back at least two months. Also monitor any reported thefts or disappearances of any of these items domestically. And anything of any suspicious nature concerning these parts." He watched Borden riffle the pages. "And don't tell me how long the list is."

"The thought never crossed my mind."

BEFORE NOON, the computer reported on airline reservations for Slane, Joli, and Gomez. All had multiple reservations during the following four weeks, and in a pattern McCall found most interesting.

Slane had a round-trip reservation on November 1 from Dallas through Miami to the Leeward Island Free State and back to Dallas three days later. Gomez was a citizen of the Leeward Island Free State.

Gomez had a round-tripper New York/Miami on November 1, the same day Slane was to be in Miami. And Joli had a round-tripper L.A./Miami on November 1. So the three would be in Miami on the same day. Slane was then slated to go to the Leeward Island Free State that evening. A gathering of ghouls.

What was more interesting, Slane and Joli held one-way ticket reservations to Mexico City on November 7: Slane from Dallas; Joli from Los Angeles. And Gomez had a one-way ticket from New York to Miami on November 25.

How were Slane and Joli to leave Mexico City? And where were they going? And how would Gomez leave Florida? Of course they all could be renting autos. McCall was fascinated. But none of this told him where Slane would be on November 26—where an assassin could find him on that day.

And none of the bureaus had filed any information on Peno Rus or Eric Rock.

McCall asked Chief of Station, Mexico City, for a monitoring on the three: Slane, Joli, and Gomez.

IT WAS PURELY BY ACCIDENT that McCall saw the article in the newspaper. It was *The Washington Post,* lying folded on a desk; as he passed by, the headline stopped him: *Monroe Scores Arms Sales.*

> In a prepared speech before the National Press Club last night, Eliott Monroe, career diplomat with the U.S. State Department, issued a solemn warning against the growing volume of arms sales around the world.
>
> "Too many nations have become dependent on arms sales to maintain a favorable balance of trade," he told nearly 200 news people. "The prognosis is for vastly increased arms sales and sharply increased competition among the selling nations."
>
> To prove his thesis, Monroe gave extensive statistical documentation on the growth of Brazil's arms manufacturing capability.

The rest of the article was a summary of the speech, interspersed with extensive verbatim quotations. Eliott

Monroe had read McCall's speech to the National Press Club without changing a word.

When he returned to his office, McCall found an envelope on his desk, left by a special messenger. Inside was his speech with a cover note: "Thanks much. Very interesting. E. Monroe."

McCall looked at the quavery, alcoholic handwriting of Eliott Monroe. Why was it that no one had ever tried to throw the Monroes of the world down a stair shaft? McCall told himself he was a fool. He'd allowed himself to get stuck with a broken hockey stick.

ON THE FOURTEENTH FLOOR of the Orizaba Hotel at ten that night, Slane emerged from the elevator and strode down the carpeted corridor to Room 1434. He rapped four times.

Colonel Gomez opened the door and beckoned him in. "Your pleasure," he said, pointing at a small bar set up on the bureau.

Slane sat down on the chair by the small guest desk. "Joli will be here in a minute." He looked out at the Mexican nightscape: the world's largest city with 14 million people, a megalopolis out of control.

"Have you read the script?" Gomez asked.

"Yes. It's shameless."

Gomez shook his head. "Shameless," he echoed.

Four knocks sounded on the door. Gomez admitted Joli, who entered busily with an attaché case.

"Have you both read the script?" Joli asked.

They nodded.

"Then," Joli said, "it's your move, Slane."

"That's right, mate," Slane said. "It's my move. I'm going to take this shameless movie script of yours to my great good friend, the saintly President of the Leeward Island Free State. And as one old comrade to another, I'm going to tell him that, as I promised, I have put together a great team of film experts to make a movie of his life. And I can tell you without hesitation he'll love this script. Gawd. It makes him out to be some kind of latter-day Jesus Christ.''

Joli pulled out a folder and consulted his timetable. "Okay. We have to have his final approval of the script by November fourth. Along with a certified check for one third of the total estimate. Okay? On November eighth we go to his old training base in the Baja desert here, and we set up to shoot the training camp sequences. That's next week. Shooting is set between November eighth and November twenty-fourth.''

"This will have to look absolutely authentic," the colonel said, "in case he decides to drop in.''

Joli shrugged. "It'll be a complete movie set including one hundred extras. You won't be able to tell it from the real thing. We are going to reenact the training episode exactly as it happened and also the invasion and take-over of the Free State. We even have the original boat the President sailed in. It will look exactly as though we're making a movie. Okay?''

Gomez nodded.

"And all paid for with the President's money," Slane said.

Gomez asked Slane: "You have the hundred mercenaries signed up?''

"I only need about ten more," Slane said.

Joli said, "Then on November twenty-fourth we break camp and sail the whole movie crew, including the hundred glorious troops, to the Free State and reenact the beach landing. That will be dawn of the twenty-sixth. Only now the movie crew turns into a unit of one hundred mercenaries who keep right on going from the beach landing to the presidential palace, where they arrest the President and his whole staff.''

"Can't wait to see the surprise on his face," Slane said. "His movie turns into a take-over—paid for with his money."

Joli asked, "Colonel Gomez, you have made arrangements to secretly get onto the island?"

"I have."

"You'll stay concealed until the beach landing is complete?"

"Correct. Then I lead the troops to the palace, where I announce myself the new President of the Free State."

"Your speech is ready? We don't want Washington slipping a company of Marines onto the island. That could ruin everything."

"No, no. This will be a purely domestic political situation. No Communists from Cuba. I announce immediate elections and a five-year plan. Also I announce construction of the new casino, the establishment of a new bank, and new projects to bring jobs to the island." He touched a briefcase on the bureau. "I have all my speeches and official documents and proclamations in here."

Joli looked at Slane. "You'd better get the President to approve that script fast. If he diddles around with it, this whole thing will fall apart."

"The trick is, don't give him any time," Gomez said. "His ego is unbelievable and if he convenes a committee to go over that script, it'll never be finished."

Slane nodded. "If he wants that film for the anniversary of his invasion, he won't have time to change a comma."

"This is the only part I don't like," Gomez said. "Getting that animal to approve the script."

"Leave him to me, mate," Slane said. "He trusts me. After all, it was my idea to make the damned movie and I'm also going to play him in the film. You watch my smoke."

"Preposterous," said the colonel. "How tall are you?"

"Six feet five."

"And he's barely five feet two."

"It's even better than that," Slane said. "I promised him that all the mercs I hire will be under six feet. I'll be head and shoulders over everyone else in the film."

Gomez shook his head.

"Don't disapprove, Colonel," said Joli. "It's that enormous ego that's making the whole coup possible."

Slane said, "It'll be a piece of cake."

"I wish I were as sure as you," Colonel Gomez said. He looked doubtfully at the script that lay on the bed. "All our futures rest on this little pile of unspeakable flatteries and lies."

Slane held up his glass. "Here's to November twenty-sixth."

ROCK HOLED UP IN PARIS. It wasn't the child's father that had him concerned. It was the gooks in Egyptian Defense who were still pissed about the Libyan deal he had made; if they heard that he was messing around with a ten-year-old Egyptian girl, they could start that crap about Egyptian national honor all over again. Then they would send one of their lumps around to pat him on the popo.

After a few days he became restless. There were no knocks on his door, no other signs that he was a target for anyone, and he was getting very bored. So he went out.

He had hidden himself pretty carefully. Some twenty miles north of Paris, in a combination of tourist hotel, American-style shopping center, and low-income housing development. It was called Les Flandres.

It was dark when Rock left his hotel, but the shops were all open, flashing their lights and playing loud music. The place was crowded with people. The well-lit promenade was teeming with Algerian and black kids kicking soccer balls.

As Rock came out of the hotel, a restauranteur in his long white apron and black vest was shouting at all the children. He held one of their soccer balls.

"You hit my window again and I'll cook you in my ovens! Get out of here!"

One black youth, big enough to be a man, said, "We have no place else. We have to play here."

"There are five football fields around here," the restauranteur shouted.

"They're dark!" one of the kids yelled back. "No lights," protested another.

Angrily the restauranteur drop-kicked the ball over a wall and down into a subterranean car-park.

The youths ran off in a throng after the ball.

"Don't come back here!" he shouted after them.

"Is your couscous as good as your kick?" Rock asked him.

"My couscous, monsieur, is the honor and glory of Algeria." With a flourish of his arms he ushered Rock into his restaurant as though it were the gateway to Paradise.

Rock ordered the specialty of the house, a couscous composed of barley, potatoes, green peppers, pumpkin, hard-boiled eggs, carrots, chick-peas, okra, and chicken, laced with a tongue-tingling sauce.

It was high autumn back in Pennsylvania, and while he ate his couscous, Rock thought about polo. He had come late to the sport. His youth had been spent learning the type-setting business in his father's type shop in New York City. An immigrant from Germany, his father had allowed no time for sport. Then in college, he'd majored in electronic engineering. With his father footing the bills, there was no time for sport there either.

Rock had seen his first game of polo in Saudi Arabia, played by Arab princes on blooded Arabian horses. And a few days later he had sat upon his first horse, a trained polo pony with explosive energy. What had drawn Rock to the sport was the mad abandon in both rider and mount.

After several riding lessons, he'd taken a polo mallet and tentatively driven a few balls. He discovered the polo pony was as eager to chase the ball as he was. He scrimmaged a few weeks later and knew he'd found his sport. It gave him exactly what he wanted—what his Arab riding instructor called madness with style.

Rock proved to be an outstanding horseman.

It was late October now. Autumn would be splendid in south-eastern Pennsylvania—one brilliant, clear, dry day after another. The foliage would be spectacular. Perfect weather for polo.

In the mornings there was heavy dew with thin mists along the Brandywine and a chill in the air. The horses in the paddocks were snickering and feisty. Before dawn they were led out and exercised, dancing sideways, kicking at each other and lunging with their teeth.

John Sherman, the eighty-four-year old honorary polo team captain, said those ponies were the meanest pack of roughnecks he'd ever seen—and that included ten years in the cavalry. "There's nothing meaner or crazier than a polo pony."

Rock ate his couscous and remembered how the exercise girl had handled his favorite mount, Tabnak. The animal was snorting and rolling his eyes in his paddock—eager to make trouble. He refused the bit.

The exercise girl grabbed him by the mane. He reared up, raising her dangerously close to his front hooves. She grabbed his lower lip with her right fist, sank her fingernails into the soft tissue and twisted. Next time he tried to rear, he shrieked with pain and anger. Still holding his lip firmly, she forced him to back up and jammed a snaffle bit into his mouth. When she mounted the saddle, he knew she was in charge. She took him off for a morning jog into the rising sun, wreathed in Tabnak's steamy breath.

The girl was perhaps fifteen and weighed maybe ninety pounds. She reminded Rock of the Egyptian girl.

And so did the couscous. With every bite the child became more vivid in his memory.

Afterward, Rock had cups of hot mint tea and, for dessert, a sesame and almond samsa. The pastry was similar to her favorite Egyptian sweet. He ate it with a sigh. He had to see her again.

TO SET THE SCENE, Peno Rus invited Ney, the arms dealer, to dinner at the Ballaster's Club in London. Things were still done the old way there: crisp white linens, real Waterford crystal, and silverware two hundred years old. The service was the old kind too—superb.

Rus had bespoken Irish salmon for the main course. The chef, Robert, had an affinity for fish; with the merest whisper of a sauce he could create an unforgettable bouquet. With it would come those delectable small potatoes with fresh parsley. Tantalizing. It would be a memorable meal.

The way to the Israeli Merkava tanks was through Ney's stomach. For Ney was a sensual eater.

The meal was flawless. Ney ate it with glittering eyes. Rus himself had made the wine selections, a superb white Bordeaux and several reds of flawless pedigree, one from Rus's favorite vineyard near Moulin-à-Vent. With each bite Ney dabbed his heavy lips with his linen napkin and exhaled the faintest of ecstatic sighs.

"With each bite," Rus told Ney, "I remind myself of my childhood years of near-starvation under the tender ministrations of the Comrades."

"Incompetent Russian barbarians," Ney agreed.

"You must pay close attention to the flavor of this salmon, Ney," Rus announced. Ney's eyes followed the silver tray as it was carried triumphantly into the room by Chef Robert himself.

"I have often regretted," Ney said, "that I have but one stomach."

All through the meal Rus kept the conversation focused on food—on other great meals he had eaten, favorite dishes, rare culinary finds, great restaurants, and great chefs. Ney's measuring eyes gazed at each course to estimate the number of mouthfuls he would ingest. When he finished the last of the main-course wine, he kissed the glass like a lover.

"A great Frenchman once said," he observed, "that his favorite wine should be drunk on the knees with the head bared. I applaud the sentiment but disagree with the choice of wine. Surely it is this one." And with that Ney poured the last few drops from the bottle into his glass and, kneeling, drained it. Once more he kissed the glass.

Rus softly applauded.

After the café espresso was served, cigars were passed, Ney settled his heavy form back in his chair, comfortably fed, rolling the cigar under his nose; then, wafting the smoking tip under his large nostrils, he drew in the ambient smoke.

"Marvelous," he sighed, his eyes mutely bidding a farewell to the dishes as they were wheeled away. The door was shut. The meal had ended and the business was about to begin.

With the brandy they talked. Times were changing, they agreed.

"Look," Rus said. "Twenty, thirty years ago there was no such thing as an arms consultant. Your occupation simply didn't exist. Now consider the substantial fees your client countries pay you to work out their arms buys—even though their own defense departments are top-heavy with arms experts. You read me?''

Ney did.

Rus said, ''Today, we have to use all the modern tricks—telemarketing, videotex, new channels of communication, training programs of arms salesmen, marketing studies, closed circuit and portable video, pull-through and program selling. Is that not so?''

Ney shifted in his chair, became more attentive. ''What is program selling?''

''The wave of the future, my dear friend,'' Rus said. ''The days of selling on price alone are gone. The client no longer buys from the lowest bidder; he buys a total package. Before he issues a purchase order, he must know that the supplier can supply the matériel he orders; has the inventory, the delivery system, the staff, the entire infrastructure. You not only ship to him but you maintain his inventory for him; you give annual analyses of his military equipment, showing him ways and means to update before he falls behind. In short, the supplier acts before the purchase order is issued.''

Ney rubbed his chin thoughtfully. ''My present suppliers never move until I give them a purchase order.''

''Ah! That's exactly my point. I don't wait for such things. I'm on the inside; I can do in-depth studies, a complete analysis of the assignment. Every detail. Things you'd never think of. Do you see what I'm saying? It is no longer enough for me to go schlepping from capital to capital, living on airlines, asking 'Any orders today?' I analyze your needs. Then I take your low-percentage shot and turn it into a winner. This is program selling, and it truly is the wave of the future in the arms world. Fortunes will be made, Ney. Fortunes.''

''I see,'' said Ney.

Rus poured more brandy. ''Here's what I propose. Take me to your most difficult client. Let me analyze his needs and discuss them with him. Then let me make a proposal—it will make him happy, you happy, and me happy.''

Ney scratched his chin again. ''Are there any conditions you haven't told me?''

''No. None at all. I ask only that you let me make a serious bid for those Israeli tanks. I have a superb offer that will make your client beam.''

Ney savored his brandy. ''Mmmmm,'' he sighed appreciatively.

''Come with me, Ney,'' Rus whispered. ''I can make you rich.''

6

Attashah had the nocturnal habits of all conspirators. He was making each successive appointment with Brewer later than the one before.

He chose to meet Brewer at Murray's Pool Hall at eleven at night. And Brewer found him there in the midst of a small crowd watching a game of nine ball.

Brewer stood beside him. "You ever shoot pool?"

"No. No." Attashah was shocked.

Brewer said, "You know what the Koran says about idleness and foolish games."

Attashah's eyes didn't smile. Deep in their sockets, they were filled with self-reproach. Have I, the eyes asked, lapsed even momentarily into frivolity or silliness? The eyes were scanning the pages of a memorized Koran.

"Do you know the Koran, Mr. Brewer?"

"My instructor is Mr. Clivedell Rine of Sweetmeadow, New York."

"I'm not sure I find anything in the Koran that—" He frowned at Brewer's smile. "Ah. Levity."

Ah. Levity. That was as close as Attashah came to humor—a faint acknowledgment of its existence. Not once had there been even a shade of a smile on the man's face. At an auto-da-fé, Attashah would be the one who remembered to bring the matches.

In his now familiar black suit and polka-dot tie, he led Brewer on foot through the night streets to a basement restaurant in an old brownstone building.

Even before they reached the steps that led down to the door, Brewer's nostrils were filled with the odors of garlic and lamb shish kebab. Syrian. Faintly through the door he heard the weepy tones of Arab music. Inside, the place was crowded with men, all drinking tea and watching a belly dancer.

Attashah stepped past three musicians and walked around the tables to an empty one in the back. A tent card on the tablecloth said RESERVED. He gave an order in Arabic to a waiter, then cast his eyes over the faces that crowded the room. Each face was examined carefully. Next he studied the belly dancer. She had a lithe, voluptuous body which the men watched with rapt attention.

Attashah leaned over and murmured to Brewer: "She's dancing an ancient love poem to a lover who is far away." Then he pushed a spiral-bound book across the table to Brewer. "For you."

Brewer flipped the pages and found what he expected: column after column of proscribed-parts numbers. He looked at Attashah. "All these parts are on the American shit-list. None of it can be exported. Even domestic shipments are monitored by Washington."

Attashah nodded. "I understand."

"I don't think you do. Uncle Sam doesn't want your people to have this stuff."

Attashah put a finger to his lips. Silence.

Brewer leaned closer to Attashah's ear. "Are you an idiot? You can't buy any of this stuff except through standard invoicing. You have to have Certificates of Exception. Waivers of Regulations. Notarized Bills of Lading. End Users' Declarations of Application, and on and on. It's a nightmare of red tape. It takes months to process and even then you'll be refused."

"Yes. It is a difficult assignment."

"And that's just gathering the material. If you think that's tough, try to smuggle it out of here to Iran. It's a goddam nightmare. It can't be done, Attashah. Iran is going to have to find another way of being a troublemaker."

Attashah leaned over and whispered, "Can you hear me, Mr. Brewer?"

Brewer nodded.

Attashah said, "I assure you, Mr. Brewer, my country does not need instructions on how to conduct its foreign affairs. You understand?"

Brewer nodded.

Attashah said, "You will do this—for me and for yourself both. I am giving you no choice, Mr. Brewer. You will do it. Do you understand my exact meaning?"

Brewer beckoned him to lean closer again. "Just how do you think I'm going to accomplish this?"

"You are more capable of doing this than any other person in the entire world. The Koran says God does not require any man to do more than he has been given the ability to do. And God has given you more ability in this area than any other mortal. For us, there isn't even any second choice. It's you or no one."

"Don't overestimate me, Attashah."

Attashah said, "Delivery will be made in Damascus, Syria."

"Syria? I will get it to the nearest U.S. seaport and you take it from there."

"That is as useless to us as a half-built bridge, Mr. Brewer. You must make delivery in Damascus."

"How? How do you think I can do that?"

"Ah, Mr. Brewer, it is not given to me to know that. You are a leading expert on smuggling. Not I. That is your assignment. Delivery must be in Damascus, Syria, and we will take it from there. We will expect the parts within the month."

"Month? You want me to get all these parts from—what?—a hundred different companies? And smuggle them into Syria, all in a month?"

"We feel you can do it, Mr. Brewer."

"You people are a bunch of wackos, Attashah. I'm telling you it can't be done."

"Mr. Brewer, once you accept the idea that it must be done, your eyes will find the way. Necessity is the mother of invention."

"Necessity is the argument of tyrants."

"So be it." He took out a pencil and a pad. "I am no longer at that same phone number."

"The Merritt Hotel," Brewer said.

"Yes. I felt it prudent to move just in case you had decided to turn me in. Here's my new phone number. And—" Picking up his small leather portfolio, he held it open for Brewer to peer into. It contained packets of American currency.

Brewer nodded at it, then flipped the pages of the parts document. Columns of numbers: the stuff that wars are made of. He shook his head at it, a dreary poem of hatred. It was a formidable list of failures of the human heart.

Attashah concentrated on the dancer as she swayed through her dance of love. His face wore the same expression it had when he looked at the parts documents.

DELIVERY IN A MONTH. Every time he thought of the deadline, Brewer shook his head. He knew he was going to need help. But he also knew that finding the right man was going to be as difficult as getting the parts.

First he went out and rented an address. That was easy. The newspapers were filled with classified ads for mail drops. It was all done by telephone. He called a number in one of the classified ads, described his needs, and contracted for Plan Two: For his fictitious company name—Manifold Technologies Ltd.—he got a telephone number, a telephone answering service, and a mailing address, all for one monthly charge. When he received the contract in the mail, he signed it and returned it with a money order.

Then he went to a printer and ordered some letterheads. Then he went to the main branch of the New York Public Library on Fifth Avenue. In the Reference Room he got a copy of Standard Rate and Data Services' *Business Publication Rate & Data*. He turned to the section on electronics magazines and read through the summary of each publication. He selected six likely candidates.

He took his list to the librarian and began calling up current copies of the various trade magazines from the stacks. He spent hours going through the pages, reading the "New Products" columns, making notes, then reading the trade ads and making more notes. It took the best part of the day to get all the leads he wanted.

He drafted a letter for all his leads and took it to the public stenographer. He gave her sixty letters. All to be sent express mail.

He then went downtown to Federal Plaza where he found the New York branch of the Government Printing Office. In five minutes he walked out with one of the key pieces to his smuggling plan. It was more than an inch thick and was titled "Military Part Numbers and Their Civilian Equivalents."

In his hotel room he sat down and began the laborious process of reading every single U.S. military-part number on Attashah's list and finding its equivalent civilian-part number. Fully a third of the parts on Attashah's list had equivalent civilian numbers. Now how to get them?

It was time to get help. He had to find the right man, and soon.

7

Brewer needed help. And it had to be someone he knew—a known quantity. Washington was full of men he could use. But he was out of touch with things. He needed an insider's guidance. Who's loose? Who's available?

So late Thursday, Brewer caught an evening flight to Washington and took a cab to Joanie Walsh's apartment. It was around ten when he tapped on her door.

She was stunned. "Charlie. Oh, how wonderful. You're out." She took his hand and led him into the apartment. "Oh. I'm so glad." Then still holding his hand, she studied his face. "I've thought about you every day."

First they talked about his letter to her. "I tried to get at your personnel file, Charlie, but it would have meant getting permission from Bobby or Borden. I'm sure either one would have given it but you said you didn't want anyone to know. So I have no idea what's in it. Someone said your termination was stamped 'extreme something or other,' even though Bobby fought against it."

"Extreme prejudice." Brewer hid his disappointment.

"Charlie, I don't know about these things. Selling a few guns out of the back of a car. If you say you didn't do it, then it's true—you didn't. If you say you did do it, then that's true—you did. I mean, it doesn't mean anything to me, one way or the other."

She went to fix them a drink. Her apartment was as usual—neat as a packet of pins. Home. After ten years she still had Warner's picture on a side table, taken a week before he was killed in a car bombing in Turkey. That's what you get for marrying an agent.

On the coffee table were a number of tour folders. "Three Glorious Days in the Great Smokies." "Walk in Jefferson's Footsteps at Monticello." And "Sail the Fabled Chesapeake. Three Bracing Days, Two Star-filled Nights." Widows' weekends: In Washington the women outnumber the men ten or fifteen to one.

"Going on a tour?" he asked her.

"Of course. Three of us." She smiled at him. "What else do you do if you're A Simple Girl from A Good Home in Boston with A Strict Catholic Upbringing?"

"Bowl," he said.

"Oh, you remember. And quilt with my quilting group. And I was just elected treasurer of the Women's Sodality."

He smiled at her. "And two dozen nieces and nephews all with a Boston accent—"

"And vacations in the summer on Cape Cod with my family. My God. How predictable my life has become, Charlie." She shook her head. "I can't believe it's been twelve years since we both started working there. Where did the time go?"

She knew: The easy days dropped astern quietly in the dark each night. Twelve years toward her pension and twelve more coming up.

Brewer knew another side to her. She secretly loved limericks—scatological, sick limericks. She had a hearty, dirty laugh. Liked a glass of whiskey. And was open, warmhearted, caring.

She hadn't learned a thing about agents. She had once proposed marriage to Brewer. "We're as alike as two peas in a pod, Charlie," she had said. "Two single socks in a drawerful of pairs."

"How's Bobby?" he asked her.

"McCall? Oh, as softhearted as ever. Borden says he's soft-headed. He turned Dice loose without firing him. Borden is quite buzzed by it. Says Dice should be shot."

"So where's Dice now?"

"Hanging around. Spends his days at Khyber Pass. So far no takers, I hear. He'd better move his butt. They're not going to carry him on the payroll forever. Even Bobby McCall has a limit to his patience."

He saluted her with his glass of scotch. "Here's to you, Joanie. How have you been?"

"Grand. And here's to you, Charlie Brewer. I'm sorry for your troubles. May they end soon." She tapped her glass against his.

In an hour, he'd caught up with the shoptalk and had a list of possibles for his Attashah job. Dice headed the list.

BREWER COULD SEE DICE through the window of Khyber Pass. And the way the man was standing at the bar told the story: He'd quit fighting. Hands at his sides. Whipped. There were no takers for Dice in Washington.

The place pretty much emptied after two; most of the patrons went back to their spooking. And that left Dice bending over his glass, talking to the bartender. Finally he, too, left the bar—about three.

Brewer followed him for a few blocks, then called his name.

"Well, bless my big blue eyes," Dice exclaimed. "Brewer."

"How's it going, Dice?"

"Very nicely indeed, Brewer. And how is it with you?"

"Got a couple of minutes?"

"What did you have in mind?"

"A chat. A little chat."

"Charlie, I had nothing to do with anything that had anything to do with you. Okay?"

"Sure. That's not what's on my mind."

Dice led the way to a worn old taproom, and they knocked back a few. Dice was drinking old-fashioneds.

"I hear you're on the loose, Dice."

"Nothing I can't handle. When did you get out?"

"You available for a job? For about two or three weeks?"

"Yeah? What did you have in mind?"

Dice had no sense at all. He named a weekly price that must have been lower than his salary.

"You'll never learn, Dice." Brewer doubled Dice's asking price. "There'll be a bonus at the end of it, too. Another five grand. Okay?"

"Okay. What's next?"

"I'll be in touch." Brewer started toward the door, then returned. "I don't have to tell you that you didn't see me today, do I?"

Dice uttered his insolent guffaw. "Charlie who?"

"For your own sake, Dice."

BREWER GOT DICE a hotel room in Manhattan and put him immediately to work. He handed him a thick trade directory. "I want ten printed invoice forms from ten different companies. All fictitious. And each one from a different city. Okay? Go through this directory and pick out ten names, then figure out a similar name for each one and use the same street address. Then take each name to a different printer—that's ten printers—and get each printer to print one name and address on a standard invoice form. Say a hundred copies of each. Okay?"

Dice never asked questions. By the end of the day he had created and printed invoices for ten different fictitious companies.

"Okay, it's done," he said. He looked at Brewer's handwritten list of civilian parts. That was the thing about Dice that Brewer didn't like. He was openly nosy.

"Some of these numbers are one point off," Dice said. "I mean—like—the universal code number for this part is CW 84647 and what you wrote here is CW 84646."

"That's right, Dice. The part I want is CW 84646. Not seven. Okay?"

Dice shrugged. "If it makes you happy, Brewer, that's all that matters."

"It makes me happy."

Dice put the list down. "What's next?"

"A little dinner and a little nine ball, Dice. And tomorrow we go to Philadelphia to see the big bad wolf."

THE NEXT MORNING they rented a van and drove it down to Canal Street, where they shopped in the electronics and secondhand-parts stores for telephone equipment. By ten they were through the Lincoln Tunnel and on the New Jersey Turnpike.

Brewer said, "We're going to see a guy down in Philadelphia, Dice. But before we do, I want you to put a tap on his phone and record everything that happens. Okay?"

"Sure."

"We've got to handle this guy with care. He's a real wacko."

"Yeah? Who is he?"

"His name is Wolf. He's connected with the family in Philadelphia and the mob in Atlantic City."

"So—how does he fit in?"

"He's an industrial parts distributor. If I can bring him around, he can clean up a lot of parts on my list in one shot. It could save us weeks of running around. But I have to tell you going in, Dice, he's the most treacherous bastard I ever met. If he thinks there's a buck in it for him, he'll turn us in. We could be looking at a federal rap with a big jail term. Okay?''

"Thanks for telling me," Dice said.

By the time they'd passed the Bordentown exit, a needle-like drizzle had settled in.

THEY TOOK THE Walt Whitman Bridge over the Delaware into South Philadelphia and drove to Wolf's warehouse near Veterans Stadium. It was shortly after noon.

Dice went into his big dumb harmless act. Carrying a phone installer's tool case and a spare phone, he entered Wolf's warehouse by way of the loading platform and disappeared inside.

About forty-five minutes later he returned. "Piece of cake," he said. "Got two taps on Wolf's personal phone." He climbed into the back of the van, set up a tape recorder, and plugged in two pairs of earphones. "Okay. He talks. We listen. What's next?"

THEY DROVE TO A PAY PHONE and Brewer made the call to Wolf. "I got an interesting deal for you," was all he needed to say.

Wolf agreed to meet them at Donzi's, a longshoreman's saloon down near the Packer Avenue docks. Two ships laden with containerized freight were being off-loaded, and Donzi's was crowded with longshoremen in rain slickers and hard hats, drinking, playing hand-shuffleboard, and talking about the Eagles' game with the Redskins.

"That's him," Brewer said. The two of them watched Wolf step out of a hot-pink Cadillac and swagger arrogantly toward the entrance with a cold cigar in his mouth.

He looked meaner than ever to Brewer. Running to flab around the middle, he was still a powerfully built man, maybe in his mid-sixties now, with a shock of bristling gray hair, a long scar that traversed his forehead, and intense wild eyes.

"You're right, Brewer," Dice said. "He does look like a real wacko."

"Wait till you see him in action," said Brewer.

Wolf shouldered his way through the crowd of longshoremen at the bar, then stood looking bleakly down on Brewer and Dice. He pointed with his cigar. "You I remember. You I never saw before."

"Okay," said Brewer. "That'll do for the introductions. Sit down."

"What are you guys into?"

"Got a nice deal for you, Wolf."

Wolf slid into the booth. "I'm listening."

"I want some parts and I'm ready with the cash."

"Let me see."

Brewer pulled the list out of his pocket. "I need these parts—from these manufacturers—in these quantities," he said.

Wolf studied the list for a few moments. Then he used his cigar as a pointer again. "Why do you have to have this one from Superior? I can give you the same part from Ruflex and for less."

"Make it Superior, okay?" Brewer said.

"You're the doctor. What kind of paper you got?"

"Straight stuff. Legit invoices. From six or seven outfits."

"Why so many?" Wolf asked.

"You want to sell seventy grand worth of these parts to one buyer? The Feds would come to visit in nothing flat."

"Are you telling me how to run my business?"

"What do I care? You want to put it all on one invoice, Wolf, be my guest."

Wolf looked at Brewer, then at Dice. "You guys don't want much, do you? Every one of these parts is on the Feds' shit-list. I could turn you in just for showing me this paper."

Brewer slapped some coins onto the table. "There's the phone. And here's the money. Go make the call."

"Do I need you to tell me when to make a phone call?" Wolf looked at the list again. "This ain't going to be easy. Maybe I can't give it all to you."

"It's all or nothing at all, Wolf," Brewer said.

"Then maybe it's nothing."

"If you're not interested, just say so." Brewer stood up.

"What's the rush?" Wolf asked. "Sit down."

"I haven't got time for games," Brewer said. "I'm offering you twice the going price in cash—all of it off the books. It's your move. So shit or get off the pot."

There was a pause as Wolf's face began to flush.

Wolf put a crooked finger under Brewer's nose. "Don't you give me any lip, you hear?"

"It's a nice piece of change, Wolf. Seventy grand. You want it, you got it. You don't, take a walk. Put your fucking finger down."

Wolf's face turned a murderous purple. "I don't need this shit," he said.

"It's your move, Wolf," Brewer said.

Wolf took the cigar out of his mouth. "Let me see your paper."

Brewer eased out of his pocket a set of blank invoices.

Wolf raised his eyebrows. "Altoona. You know where Altoona is, for Christ's sake?"

"Right inside your territory," Brewer said.

Wolf pointed with his dead cigar. "We haven't done any business in Altoona for twenty, thirty years. Sheesh. Scarsdale. Easton. Stroudsburg. Landsdowne. How many you got?"

"How many you want?" Brewer asked.

"Eight would be nice."

"Help yourself."

"Cash with the order."

"Sure. No problem."

"In small bills."

Brewer nodded. "No problem. When do I get delivery?"

Wolf studied the list again. "Most of this I can give you right now. In fact I can get all of this to you. Day after tomorrow."

"I need it tonight," Brewer said.

"Don't be a pain in the ass."

"I need it tonight, Wolf."

Wolf shrugged. "Okay. Tonight. After six. Loading Bay two. But the price is one hundred."

"Forget it," Brewer said.

"Ninety is my best price," Wolf said.

"Seventy. Take it or leave it."

Wolf stood up and leaned over the table. "Seventy grand in small bills. Right? Six o'clock. Loading Bay two." He swaggered toward the crowd of longshoremen at the bar like a linebacker looking for the ball carrier.

Brewer sat frowning. "He didn't ask the right questions."

"What's that mean?"

"It means he could be planning to blow the whistle on us."

THEY FOLLOWED WOLF back to his plant and parked the van a half block away where they could keep the pink Cadillac in full view.

"Let's see what he does when he gets back to his phone," Brewer said.

They didn't have long to wait. Within minutes after he got back to his office, Wolf was on the phone. He called a Mr. Harris.

"Okay," he said to Harris. "I got two live ones for you. They want parts from here to there and all of them are on the shit-list."

"Get any names?" Harris asked.

"One of them I never seen before."

"Who's the other one?"

"I don't know. Some guy. A smuggler, I think."

"When are you going to pass it to them?"

"Couple of hours. Six o'clock."

"Okay. Do it. And the minute they drive off, call me and we'll take it from there. You read?"

Dice disconnected his earphones. "You want to drive?" he asked Brewer.

"Where?"

"Back. To New York. You're not going to hang around here, are you?"

"I'm not leaving without those parts, Dice."

"Charlie. You don't have a prayer."

"Ever hear of Mr. Micawber? His favorite expression was 'Something will turn up.'"

"No, I never heard of Mr. Micawber," Dice answered. "Where did he do his time?"

DICE LISTENED on the earphones half asleep. "Christ," he said. "All this Wolf talks is numbers. All kinds of numbers. He says one two three four, and the other guy says five six seven eight. Then he says we have three eight ninety-seven five bee. And the other guy says forty-four dozen. Then they talk shipping from inventory and invoice numbers. That kind of stuff. I can't understand it." He looked at Brewer. "Charlie, let's get out of here. They're going to have a dozen cars in this area in a short time. We haven't got a prayer."

Brewer nodded without speaking.

"I know. I know," Dice said. "Mr. Micawber."

DICE TAPPED BREWER'S ARM and pointed at his earphones. "Wolf's just called some broad," he said. "They're set up for a little matinee in her place, then dinner at the Coq au Vin."

Later he said, "Now he's breaking a date with his wife. They were supposed to go to dinner and a show in town. He says he's working late in the office, but she's really ticked."

He looked at Brewer's impassive face. "Charlie, you like shows?"

"Sometimes. Why?"

"Call Wolf's wife, Charlie. Get a nice evening for yourself. Dinner, two seats on the aisle, and hugs and kisses. If you get out of this you'll deserve it, Mr. Micawber."

DICE MASSAGED HIS NECK and sighed. "How did a cretin like that get a business like this?" he asked.

"It's an inspirational story, Dice," Brewer said. "He started with stolen military parts in a garage. His best sales tool was a maniac's temper and a tire iron. Sometimes he used a sawed-off baseball bat."

"And he got from that to this?"

"His sons did. They both have Harvard M.B.A.'s. If it wasn't for them he'd still be peddling stolen parts from his garage."

THE WAREHOUSE STAFF quit at four. The office staff left at five. At five-thirty Wolf's two sons drove off. Dice said, "Lay you eight to five there's a dozen cars staked out around here."

At quarter to six, Brewer said, "Make me a copy of that telephone tape."

At five to six, he said, "Okay, Dice. Here's the rundown. There's no sense both of us taking a fall. You get out and walk. If I make it I pick you up four blocks that way on Packer Avenue. If I don't, you go home on the train and no one will be the wiser."

"Brewer, I never walked out on a guy before. But you don't have a prayer. I want you to know that I think you're crazy, and I expect to take the train home." Dice stepped out of the van, put his raincoat collar up, and walked north toward Packer Avenue.

"Just follow the streetlights," Brewer said to him.

"Good luck, Mr. Micawber."

Brewer drove the van around to the loading platform and backed up to Loading Bay two. He put the van's lights out and waited.

After a while Wolf stepped through a small door and knocked on the van roof. "Open up."

He led Brewer inside to a hand truck holding several dozen low stacks of small-parts boxes. "That's the whole thing. Every item on your list. Only the price is one hundred, not seventy."

"How come?"

"Price increases and one thing or another."

"Seventy," Brewer said.

"Like I said," Wolf replied. "One hundred. I got the only game in town."

"Forget it. I'm making a fishcake on this job as it is."

"It's your choice," said Wolf.

"You wasted my time, Wolf." Brewer turned and walked through the door. He crossed the loading platform, jumped down, and had opened the van door when Wolf called him.

"Okay, okay. Hold it. You got the cash?"

"Don't do me any favors, Wolf," Brewer said.

"Take it easy, babe. We can do business. Let me see your money."

"We have a deal at seventy or what?"

"Yeah, yeah. Seventy. Come on back in." He watched Brewer climb back up on the loading platform. "You got a very short fuse," Wolf said to him.

The two of them returned to the hand truck.

"Where's the money?" Wolf asked.

"First I count the order," Brewer said.

"Sheesh." Wolf watched Brewer go through each box and check the contents against his list. It took nearly forty-five minutes.

"Okay," Brewer said. "Seventy big ones in twenties, tens, and fives." He held out a large brown paper bag tied with string. "You want to count it, Wolf?"

"You bet your bippie." Wolf opened the bag and pulled out some stacks of currency bound by paper bands. He counted the bills in several stacks; then he counted the stacks and shrugged. "Seems to be all here. If it isn't I know where to find you."

"You'll never find me, Wolf. Count it now. I don't want any complaints."

"I counted it. We got a deal."

"One more piece," Brewer said. He held out the reel of telephone tape. "If Harris and his team pick me up, my partner drops a copy of this in the mailbox. You read?"

"What's this?" Wolf took it doubtfully.

"It's a few phone conversations you've had lately, Wolf. Enough to send you up for ten or better—not counting income tax evasion."

Wolf's face turned purple. He crushed his cigar in his right fist and shook it at Brewer. "You've been tapping my phone!"

"Bet your ass. Including the chat with Harris this afternoon."

Wolf threw his shattered cigar down.

"Call them off, Wolf. If you don't, my partner makes his drop, and the big boys come and hang your asshole over a doorknob for a few years."

Wolf hefted the reel in his hand.

"Call them off, Wolf, or you'll be in the cell next to me."

"Get out of here," Wolf said.

"Call first."

"No! The deal's off."

"No. The deal's on. You got the money and I got the parts. Now call them off."

"How, for Christ's sake? The place is crawling with them." Wolf's face was purple and his eye was maniacal.

"That's your problem. Move your ass."

"Dummy up," Wolf said. "We gotta call this deal off. They'll nail both of us."

"No. This deal is on or I drop the tape anyway. There's no moves on the board for you, Wolf. Call."

Wolf's eyes rolled wildly.

"Call," said Brewer.

Wolf threw the tape against the wall and walked over to a phone on the shipping desk. He dialed a number and murmured a few words into it. Then he walked back.

Brewer slammed the brown paper bag against Wolf's chest. "Here. If anything happens to me, Wolf, it happens to you. Now help me load the van."

BREWER DROVE AWAY from the loading platform, back toward Packer Avenue. It was all or nothing now. The parts in the van could get him a very long federal prison term; with his prison record, a very long term indeed, plus the completion of his gun-selling jail term. He would be a very old man before he'd served out his years.

He would know in a few moments; ahead were two parked cars, both with men inside. As he drew closer, one of the cars put on its headlights. It rolled forward slowly toward him, then paused. The second car put on its headlights. They were ready for him.

Brewer looked ahead, seeking a rabbit hole to dash into. But there was none; a low-powered rental van chased by two high-powered pursuit vehicles had no place to hide, no place to run to.

He continued driving towards the two cars, drew abreast, and passed them. Both cars made U-turns and drove after him. Now they picked up speed and came up fast behind him. They split, one coming up on his right side, the other on his left.

As they came abreast they studied his van and looked accusingly at him. Then the right-hand vehicle raced ahead; the left-hand followed and they quickly disappeared around a corner.

At Packer Avenue he found Dice on the corner and let him in. As they drove off, they passed another parked car with men in it.

Brewer said, "We've got to get out of here before Wolf finishes playing the telephone tape." They passed two more parked cars with men in them.

"Jesus God," Dice said. "How many did they have?"

They drove back on the Jersey Turnpike to New York in a slow, steady rain, accompanied by the rhythmical bump-bump bump-bump of the windshield wipers.

Brewer had put a sizable dent in his parts list.

"This is better than taking the train," Dice said.

8

The paralegal assistant carried Brewer's portfolio in his left hand to Madeline Hale's desk. She opened the flap and pulled out the miscellany of papers, writs, transcripts, and depositions connected with his trial. Compared to most of her other case files it was not very fat.

Hale felt like an archaeologist in an ancient midden, piecing together shards to discover a lost tale.

Among the papers was her trial journal, and she idly opened it to her first meeting with Brewer in prison. They were holding him then in the Tombs in lower Manhattan, while they decided whether to try him in federal court or state court. He was brought into the lawyer's conference room and locked in with her—with a guard on either side of him.

The first thing about him she'd noticed was anger. A smoldering anger. He must have given the police a very difficult time, because wherever he went he was accompanied by the two guards. She decided after that first interview that his anger was aimed at himself.

To her, Rumbh was a fabrication, as was the story of Rumbh's instructions, as was Brewer's description of his actions in New York—all manufactured by Brewer for the trial. It hadn't really mattered, because more than anything else it was Marvel's testimony that had convicted Brewer.

On the margins of the pages of her trial journal, she found jotted the titles of the books he'd asked for. There was no pattern to them: history, literature, philosophy, contemporary affairs, biography. No light reading. She was impressed anew by how much he had read.

In all, he was like a strange fish to her, brought up from some random toss of a net. He didn't fit the usual mold of intelligence men, the slightly rumpled, quick-minded lot who were not given to much introspection. They didn't have Brewer's perception of salami tactics. Their easy moral codes permitted many things without any discomfort to their consciences—the wire tap without papers, the lie casually rehearsed in the cab, the planting of heroin in a coat pocket.

Now she had to start with the first page of her trial journal, and go through every single word of every document, exactly as she had before, but with one vital difference: Before, everything she did was guided by one word—*guilty*. Now she would review the same material with its opposite—*innocent*. It was like a completely different case.

She looked up at the old Monitor clock on the wall with its slowly wagging pendulum and wondered how much time she had—how much time before Brewer committed himself irrevocably to whatever crime he was planning. Did she have weeks? days? hours?

She also wondered if she was doing this for him or for herself.

She sat at her desk all through the afternoon while jets from Washington National Airport shook her windowpanes. She read the transcripts and the depositions and the other papers that accrue in a trial, searching for some fact or combination of words that would strike a spark of hope.

Hour after hour she sought for something that would indicate he was telling the truth.

She heard the secretaries and the paralegals call goodnight to each other. Several partners pushed their behatted heads into her half-closed door and nodded curtly at her.

She reread a transcript of Marvel's testimony with close attention. This bothered her. One of them was lying, Marvel or Brewer. As a lawyer she'd been lied to by almost every client—either in a small detail or in a major way. So she had no illusions about Brewer. She'd never forgotten the words of the firm's senior partner on the day she started her career there.

"Never forget! All men lie. And especially they lie to their lawyers."

But then explain Marvel. His words, if they were lies, not only jailed Brewer, they had jailed Marvel.

This was shaping up to be the strangest case she'd ever handled. If the facts bore her hypothesis out, then Marvel was the only man she'd ever heard of who'd lied his way into jail.

Enough: At eight o'clock she decided to call it a day. She sat back wearily and looked at the pile of papers from Brewer's portfolio. An airline ticket stuck out from the bottom and she picked it up. Brewer's round-trip tickets: Rome to New York, and New York back to Rome. Only the first half of the ticket had been used.

She examined the return ticket. It had been issued through the Washington office of the airline. And for the first time she realized the significance of that. The ticket had been purchased in Washington. Brewer couldn't have purchased it, not from Rome. Someone else had to have done that. Someone in Washington.

She turned the voucher in her hand thoughtfully. She had uncovered her first gleam of hope.

Before she left for the night, she made arrangements to visit Marvel at Deepford Federal Prison in Deepford, Ohio.

MARVEL WAS A TYPE she recognized immediately. She sat in the visitor's room in Deepford and watched him approach down a long corridor, slightly duckfooted, gone soft around the middle, a careworn face, and thinning pale hair.

He arrived in the meeting room with the expression she'd seen on so many prisoners' faces: a combination of anxiety and hope. He was a born policeman, patient, shrewd, with no illusions about human nature and with the ability to size up a situation quickly. She handed him her card.

"I'm trying to reopen Charles Brewer's case," she said.

He looked at the card, then skeptically at her. "Why?"

"I believe he's innocent."

He looked down at the card again. "Jesus."

"I came to talk to you about your testimony at his trial."

"What makes you think he's innocent?" he asked.

"There are a few things that don't ring true."

"There're a lot of things that don't ring true."

"Like what?" she asked.

"Oh, nothing to do with Brewer. Lawyers. You're a pack of wolves, the lot of you. Cop a plea, he said, and walk away. Otherwise you go down with Brewer."

"Who said that?"

"That high-priced shyster they sent me," Marvel answered. "Donovan."

"I see."

"We worked a deal. I plead to a lesser offense, testify at Brewer's trial. And walk away with a suspended sentence. Only the judge doesn't go along. And I end up with a three-to-five. That Donovan hasn't been near me since. This is just great. If you prove Brewer is innocent, he gets out and I do my time."

"Brewer is out."

Marvel's mouth fell open. "Jesus Christ."

"It's possible you can help clear him."

"Clear him?" Marvel shook his head in disbelief. "You said he was out, didn't you?"

"Yes. But the conviction stands. His career is ruined."

"His career is ruined? Jesus God on the Cross, what about mine? What about my whole life?" He shook her business card at her. "Give me one good reason why I would want to clear Brewer's name? He's the guy that got me in here."

"Because if he gets off, you might get off. With a full pardon. You want to talk or fight?"

He looked at her card once more, then scaled it onto the table. "Lawyers."

She sat quietly waiting.

At last he said, "What the hell. I've got everything to gain and nothing to lose. What do you want to do?"

"Tell me your side of it."

"That's easy. It's a tale briefly told. I was in London. Brewer was in Rome. We're putting together a package on this guy Peno Rus, who sold a carload of guns to some Africans and caused a famine. I get a phone call to drop what I'm doing, go to New York, and help Brewer put the arm on a guy in a gun-selling scam. I go. I do like I'm told, and the next thing you know, they have the cuffs on me. The home office in D.C. says they never heard of this scam, and they never ordered me and Brewer to do it. So right away I see that Brewer set himself up for a little something on the side and muffed it. And I get left holding the smoking gun."

"What made you think it was Brewer's doing?"

"Who else? And what for?"

"Who ordered you to New York?"

"Some guy. Said his name was Rumbh. Gave the proper clearances and such. European deskman—a fill-in, he said. So? Happens all the time. That night, there's the airline ticket waiting for me at my hotel with a baggage claim ticket."

"Did you save the airline voucher?"

"Save? Hell, that was a long time ago."

"Do you remember what city the ticket was issued from?"

"No."

"Go on. What was the baggage claim ticket for?"

"Guns. Stolen guns. When I fly to New York, sure enough there's Brewer. I take the baggage claim ticket downtown and get a suitcaseful of handguns. Mint forty-fives. Collector's items. Over fifty years old and never been in service. U.S. government property. Later it turns out they were stolen from Fort Benson arsenal. What do I know? I'm to meet Brewer at the rendezvous in the park. Brewer makes the contact, and I wait in the ravine to help with the collar. Instead, they cuff me—three of New York's finest—while I hear Brewer yelling my name. Black day for me, I can tell you."

"Are you telling me you were innocent?"

"Does a bear shit in the woods?"

"Then why—"

"Because that knucklehead Donovan tells me I had to. I've been jobbed, he says. Brewer is as guilty as Judas and I'm going to sink with him if I don't make my move right away. Son of a bitch. Now I'm in and Brewer's out."

She referred to her note pad. "Do you remember the name of the man Brewer was supposed to sell the handguns to?"

"Sure. Pines, Russell Pines. Instead, he ended up dealing with a guy named Tony something-or-other or Giuseppe or someone, who turned out to be a detective."

"I must say, Mr. Marvel, I think you were rather hasty pleading guilty."

"What could I do? I had no case. Washington said I wasn't authorized to leave London. Nobody ever heard of a guy named Rumbh. And it looked like Brewer and me stole those forty-fives and tried to peddle them for a little ready. My lawyer was blunt as could be. Cop a plea or go in for the big count. Besides, Donovan gave me the strong impression that Washington wanted me to cop a plea, like it was part of a script or something."

"Who did you cop the plea with?"

"The Feds. There was a long period of time when the Feds and the N.Y. district attorney argued about where we would stand trial. New York State has a very tough gun law."

Marvel began to fold her card into meticulously formed squares. "One of the federal lawyers was sure we were part of something bigger. He was the one who separated us and got us in federal court because the weapons were stolen U.S. government property and because they were transported across state lines. I was afraid Brewer would cop a plea and leave me holding the bag."

He unfolded the card and tried to smooth away the fold lines with a fingernail. "Then they tried to work on me. We don't want you; we want Brewer. Tell us the whole story and you might be able to walk with a suspended. What could I tell them? They were very unhappy."

"Why should they be unhappy? You creamed Brewer."

"They figured there was a bigger story behind this one."

"Who paid for your lawyer?"

"I don't know. He just told me it was paid for. Like I said, I secretly kept expecting to get sprung from Washington. I figured I was part of some kind of script, and we were all going through an act. I wasn't too worried even when I was sentenced. I figured I'd go in the front door and right out the back, and be in London for breakfast. Then when I didn't, I figured Brewer pulled something and I got the pie in the face."

"Did you know Donovan is an ex-FBI agent?"

He raised his eyes from the folded card and looked at her with shock. "What are you saying?"

"They weren't interested in you or Brewer. They were interested in the people who broke into the arsenal."

"For a dozen lousy handguns?"

"It was all the other material that was stolen—high explosives, rockets, launchers—a truckload of terrorist weapons. None of that material has turned up yet."

He studied her face thoughtfully. "I'm not the fastest guy in the world, so spell it out for me. If you knew what game they were playing, then how come it took you so long to decide to help Brewer now?"

"Because when you made your guilty plea, I made the same assumption everyone else did. I believed you two had done the arsenal job."

"Beautiful."

"How well do you know Brewer?"

"Pretty good, I guess. We worked a lot of jobs together, mainly in the European sector."

"Yet you figured he was a thief who was going to finger you. Does that mean you didn't like him—or trust him?"

"Let me tell you a story, Mrs. Hale. Brewer took me fishing once. In Ireland. Showed me his secret fishing place over in the West of Ireland. He really loves it—the outdoors, the trees, the flowers, the birds, the fish, the lot. One day he leans over this little pool in a stream and, with his bare hand, grabs a trout from the water. So help me.

"We had a great time. He can be great fun, that Brewer. Make you laugh till your sides hurt. Great storyteller. Good guy to be with. We stayed in an old inn, and he showed me how to fish and it was fantastic. Then we brought back the fish, and the innkeeper's wife cooked them. And while she was cooking we drank pints and talked to the owner in the bar. I remember standing there in the pub, by this fire in the fireplace, waiting for dinner and watching this great sunset and feeling terrific and thinking what a great guy to be with this Brewer is. Then we ate this delicious fish. And we talked until three in the morning, drinking pints. It was one of the best times I ever had in my whole life.''

''So you liked him?''

''Yeah, he was okay. But he's a thinker. Reads all the time—like a guy looking for something. You never know what's going on inside his head. I mean, in there he could be plotting to take over the world. How could you tell? That fishing trip was the closest I ever got to him. And I knew at the time I wasn't within ten miles of the real Brewer.''

MARVEL'S LAWYER, Donovan, had offices in the building next to Hale's in Washington. She called him three times. He never called back.

One of the partners said to her: ''Donovan has two specialties—criminal trials and drinking. You'll find him either in court or in the bar across the street.''

He was in the bar across the street. When she walked in she saw him down at the end, waving a hand and talking loudly to two men. He fit his description to a T. Former tackle for Notre Dame, All-American, six five, corpulent and barrel-chested, white hair and a beet-red face.

She walked up to him. ''You're a tough man to catch up with.''

''Not for you, princess. I am at your disposal.''

''It would be easier if you were at my disposal on the telephone. My name is Madeline Hale.''

''Oh. The arsenal job. Well, what can I tell you?''

''I'm reopening.''

''Well, good luck.''

''You are aware that Marvel is probably innocent.''

''Sure. And cows give beer.''

''Can you tell me something off the record, Donovan?''

''Shoot.''

''Who paid your fee?''

"I don't know. Who paid yours?"

"The same man."

Donovan laughed. He exhaled a long wheeze; then his red face turned purple, the wheeze became a guffaw, and the guffaw became a cough. He struck the bar with a hammy fist. "Touché, princess, touché. Let me tell you something."

He picked up the shot glass brimming with whiskey and deftly lowered it into a glass of beer. While the beer was still briskly foaming, he drained the glass. He made a bitter expression. "Hooo," he said and slid the glass across the bar. "Again, Johnny." Then he turned to her.

"I got this phone call," he said, "from a guy who said he represented the friends of Marvel in the government. Civil service people. Passed the hat, they did. Now I did get his name and his check. But he made me promise not to reveal it."

"Did they ever catch the men who broke into the arsenal and stole the weapons?"

"Sure. Brewer and Marvel."

"Did you ever suspect that Brewer and Marvel might not be the ones who broke into the arsenal?"

"I wouldn't lose any sleep over it, princess."

"They do."

"You're breaking my heart."

"Mr. Donovan, I suspect that you worked with the FBI to try to coerce Marvel into identifying the man who stole those weapons from the arsenal. When he couldn't or wouldn't, I think you hung him out to dry. If that turns out to be true, I'll be back to see you and your old buddies in the FBI."

"Cheers, princess." Donovan tossed off half a glass of whiskey.

MADELINE HALE next called the person who had paid all the costs of Charlie Brewer's trial: her aunt, Constance Woolman. She was told her aunt was attending a meeting with Martin Wainwright and other members of the Arms Traffic Control Committee.

Later, her aunt called her back. "Sorry I took so long, dear. Is it important?"

"Aunt Connie, I want to ask you a question. It's about the Brewer case."

"Go ahead."

"When you paid Brewer's legal fees, you led me to understand that you were serving as a conduit for other people who contributed to Brewer's cause."

"That's right."

"What I need to know is who those people were."

"Mr. Brewer's friends, mainly, and people in the government who worked with him."

"But who in particular?"

"Oh, I'm sure I don't know. The man who organized it was Bobby McCall. He raised most of the money himself. From a number of people. And many stipulated that their names not be revealed. So I don't really know who-all contributed. Martin Wainwright I'm sure gave some money. And other members of the Arms Control Committee. And Bobby McCall's secretary, Joan Walsh, gave five hundred. I gave a thousand. I think most of us gave for Bobby's sake. He was quite upset. Brewer and Marvel were his two best agents. And he was quite concerned that they might not get the best legal defense. Why are you bringing this up now?"

"Because I've begun to suspect that Brewer and Marvel were used to cover up a conspiracy right here in Washington."

WAS THERE anyone named Rumbh?

She went first to the office library and got down the Washington, D.C., phone directory. No Rumbh. Then she took down all the regional directories for Virginia—including Northern Virginia Washington Area, Peninsula and Tidewater Area. No Rumbh.

She went through all the regional directories for the states of Delaware and Maryland. No Rumbh.

Was it an alias?

She decided to try another tack. With Brewer's power of attorney, she went to the State Department's personnel office. She filled out a form to examine Brewer's file and took a number: 304. Then she waited until her number was called; she presented the clerk with her papers.

The clerk went away and didn't come back. The room was crowded and warm. Banks of microfiche sat in the other room where petitioners diligently studied the microfilmed contents of files and made xerograph copies of selected documents. Many of them were preparing pension claims; she recognized one lawyer who specialized in immigration and naturalization cases.

Other people came after her, handed in their forms, read through the microfilmed files, and were long gone while she still waited. Many others. She paced.

At last her number was called: 304. Instead of being assigned to a microfilm console she was summoned back to the desk and handed a form: Request to Examine A Personnel File Denied.

Printed on the sheet were eighteen reasons why the State Department could refuse to open a personnel file, each with its own check box. The box for reason #3 was checked: National Security.

The refusal was unexpected. To see the file now she would have to apply for a court order under the Right to Know Act. On a hunch, she requested to know if there existed a personnel file for the name Rumbh. The reply this time was much faster. No such name in the personnel file.

MADELINE HALE went fishing for the first time when she was eight years old. Her father had taken her in his boat far out on Lake Winnipesaukee in New Hampshire. The entire lake was shrouded in a heavy morning mist and when he turned off the outboard engine, the muffled silence was awesome. Forbidding and isolating.

In that strange whited-out world, she dropped her line into the water with a sinker and a flasher and waited. After a few minutes she felt a sudden hard tug on her fishing line. She yanked and came away with an empty hook.

But she never forgot the sense of having reached into the unknown, of having touched something mysterious and dangerous. She was delighted and frightened at the same time.

In the State Department personnel offices, she now felt the same way. She'd put her line into the bureaucratic maze and felt the response on the other end. Somewhere back in the labyrinthine corridors and alleys of bureaucratic red tape, someone had given her hook a hard tug. That someone was blocking the way to information. Why? She felt her first twinge of excitement.

What had happened was quite clear. Bearing Hale's written request, the personnel clerk had gone to Brewer's file and found a red flag on it. She'd called the person who had authorized the flag and reported the official request to see the file. The person she called had declined.

That told Hale several things. Only a ranking bureaucrat could authorize a red flag. And whoever that ranking person was, he wanted something in Brewer's personnel file concealed. She was convinced it had nothing to do with national security.

She walked away staring at the pencil check-mark on the refusal form. She'd uncovered an adversary.

The next step was to see Brewer and submit a court paper to open the file. But that took time. More time than she probably had.

BREWER, AS USUAL, hadn't returned her call, and Madeline Hale sat at her desk, drafting a telegram to him. She heard the secretaries leaving and glanced at her watch. The last thing she wanted to do that evening was go to that 6:30 fitting for her wedding dress.

"Significant new development," she wrote. "Must talk to you immediately."

There was a tap on her door.

"Yes?"

Brewer pushed the door open.

"Well, this is a nice surprise, Charlie," she said. "You've gone from not answering your phone messages to answering them in person." She pointed to a chair. "Join me."

"I didn't know you called," he said. "I'm here for another reason." He sat down across from her and waited.

"The reason I called," she said, "was to give you an update. I've hit a glitch in my investigation."

"I figured you would."

"It's your personnel file. Someone is blocking access to it."

He grunted. "A red flag? I thought so."

"The reason given is national security."

Brewer considered that. "So—someone baited a trap with my file." He looked at her thoughtfully. "And he snared you."

"I'd hardly say I've been snared," she said.

Brewer shrugged. "You tipped your whole hand to him. He knows that someone is snooping into the Brewer case. And he knows who. And he can easily guess why."

"What difference does that make? He would have found out sooner or later."

"The difference is that this is the end of your investigation."

"End? I can file in court for access—"

"There's nothing in my personnel file worth hiding. The red flag is just an early warning system for him."

"Well, at least I can find out who it is who put the red flag on the file. It seems to me—"

"They'll kill you," he said quietly. "Without any fuss or muss they'll just come around and kill you."

She stared at him thoughtfully for a moment. "How can you say that? We don't even know who these people are."

"Yes, we do," said Brewer. "They're the people who framed me. They may be the people who broke into the arsenal to steal the weapons. They're covering up something. And you're trying to uncover it. They're not going to let you do that. Believe me. They will kill you. And that's the name of that song."

"Are you telling me I have to stop?"

"Yes. Stop. Right now."

"Charlie. If we let the criminals intimidate us, they'll soon be running this country."

"They're running it now." Brewer stood up. "I'll handle this from here on."

"I can't let myself be intimidated."

"The answer is no. No more investigation. Okay?"

She looked down at her clasped hands. Then she raised her head to look at him. "You want a rematch on the wonton soup and egg roll? There's a Chinese place down the street here that really does it all."

"You're not going to change my mind, Madeline," Brewer said.

She stood up. "I think I'll have the hot-and-sour soup."

THEY WALKED toward the restaurant.

"I'm supposed to be at a fitting for my wedding dress at six-thirty," she said.

"Why aren't you?"

She took his arm. "Because I'd rather have dinner with you, Charlie Brewer. I can't always find a fellow Chinese food fancier."

Brewer halted. "I'm sorry about what I said about Vermont and the little white house down the lane. That's what you should go for. And leave the red flags to me."

She said, "Marvel says no one can get to know you. He says you think too much. Do you think that's true?"

"Ah," he said. "You saw Marvel."

"I think he's right. Why don't you let me worry about me? And you worry about you?" She put her hands on his cheeks, drew his face to hers and kissed his lips. "There. I've wanted to do that for a long time. In case you missed it, Charlie Brewer, I just made a pass at you."

Brewer looked at her face, at the deep blueness of her eyes, then drew her into his arms. He kissed her.

"I think I should have gone to that dress fitting," she said.

"I came to say goodbye, Madeline."

She stepped back, astonished. "Goodbye?"

"It's dangerous just to be seen with me. You understand? I can't protect you. And I can't be responsible for you."

"Now wait."

"Your investigation is over, Madeline. You have to get off and stay off. Understand? Off. Right now."

"Wait a minute. I have something to say."

He gripped her shoulders and rocked her back and forth. "I warn you. Don't make me tell you again. It's all over. It's goodbye." He released her shoulders. "Go to your fitting. And leave the red flags to me. I hope you have a wonderful marriage."

Charlie Brewer turned and walked away.

Holding her fingers to her lips where he'd kissed her, she watched him walk away into the dusk.

ONE OF AMERICA'S favorite games is called Find the Runaway. Among the practitioners, it's a fully developed art form. Any number can play.

Skips, scamps, deadbeats, absconders: They all try to leave town without a trace. Policemen, federal agents, bill collectors, bounty hunters, tracers, irate spouses: They use a large number of techniques to try to locate the runaway.

There is one overriding reason why the runaway can't always make a complete disappearance. It is exceedingly difficult to live in this society without being snared by one official form or another. Driver's licenses, motor vehicle registrations, state and federal tax records, Social Security numbers, post office forms, credit cards, court records, magazine subscriptions, checking accounts, contracts, lawsuits, insurance policies, subpoenas, unwitting relatives: The number of places to seek the hidden is extensive.

Lawyers in particular are skillful practitioners of the art of tracing. And as a criminal lawyer, Madeline Hale was more adept than most.

The next morning, she resumed her search for a man named Rumbh.

WHEN SHE got to her office desk, the first person she called was a professional skip tracer she had worked with many times.

"Arthur, I want some fast action on this one. Ready? The name is Rumbh. I don't have a first name or a date of birth. But I want you to run it through the driver's license bureaus in all fifty states. I'll take any and all names in the Rumbh family. Six spelling variations. Yes: male or female."

Next she called contacts in a half-dozen mid-Atlantic state tax offices. Then, assuming that Rumbh might have used a credit card to pay for the airline tickets from Rome and London, she called the skip tracer back and authorized him to put a check on a half-dozen credit cards, and the ten leading gasoline credit cards.

She then called the Retail Credit Bureau and asked for a personal credit file on anyone named Rumbh. She was interested in any credit information, including bankruptcies, judgments, and court orders. Next were the automobile insurance companies, life insurance companies, prison records, and much more. She had a busy day ahead of her. She ate lunch at her desk.

Shortly after two, the skip tracer called in with a partial report on the driver's license bureaus.

"We've got about half the states done and we've turned up only one Rumbh. Mrs. Abigail Rumbh of Dallas. She's eighty-two years old. You want her address and phone?"

MRS. ABIGAIL RUMBH was loquacious. She was also a family genealogist. "I am," she assured Madeline Hale, "the last living Rumbh of my branch in America to bear that name."

Hale extracted the information she needed: Within the last ten years, the last three male Rumbhs had died, all of them Miss Abigail's brothers and none with sons. Louis had died in Dallas. Edgar had also died in Dallas six months after

Louis. And Anthony had died two years ago—in Washington, D.C.

AT THREE she got her first break. One of the files she had put a trace on was that of the Immigration and Naturalization Service. An unlikely source, it had been added to the list in the interest of thoroughness. So Hale was completely surprised when the name turned up: An Anthony Rumbh had been granted citizenship thirteen months before in federal court in Washington, D.C. His address was the same as Miss Abigail Rumbh's late brother's.

Hale was bemused by the information: Anthony Rumbh, a native-born citizen from Dallas, Texas, had been granted U.S. citizenship as an immigrant seven months after he'd died.

ALL THROUGH THE AFTERNOON other reports came in. No one named Rumbh had a driver's license (other than Abigail), nor a gasoline credit card nor any of the major credit cards. No one named Rumbh was on the tax records for Virginia, Maryland, Delaware, West Virginia, Pennsylvania, New Jersey, or New York. No one named Rumbh had a record of bad debts, bankruptcy, mortgage foreclosure, or of prison incarceration.

Someone had been granted U.S. citizenship under the false name of Anthony Rumbh and had promptly disappeared.

Just before five she encountered another surprise. She went over to the Immigration and Naturalization Service and asked for the records on Anthony Rumbh. The request was denied. The reason: national security.

Another red flag. She'd tipped her hand again to her adversary. Brewer's words came back to her. "Without any fuss or muss, they'll just come around and kill you."

Five times that day she'd called Charlie Brewer and left a message. She tried not to think about that threatening look she'd seen in his eyes the night before when he'd gripped her shoulders.

"Don't make me tell you again," he'd said.

But the information was too important to be ignored. He wouldn't be angry, she told herself, when he heard it. Before leaving the office she sent a telegram. *IMPORTANT NEWS. PLEASE CALL.*

FOR THE FIRST TIME, she had a slight qualm when she opened her apartment door and stepped into the dark interior. She turned on more lights than usual, then went to the kitchen and put the kettle on. A cup of tea would set the world aright. She kicked off her shoes and reached for a cup in the cabinet.

There was a sharp click. She put the cup down and walked into her living room. She heard another click, then something sliding. She walked to the dark bedroom and leaned in through the doorway. The drapes over the sliding glass door were twisted and the door stood open.

"Who's there?" she demanded.

An arm seized her from behind. A hand covered her mouth. She was wrestled into the middle of the bedroom.

A voice whispered into her ear: "I'll give you a choice. I can cut your throat or throw you off your balcony." He turned her around. "Which way do you want to die?"

Charlie Brewer stood there, angrily holding her by the shoulders. "Which one?"

She tried to shrug off his hands. "I don't let people intimidate me," she said defiantly. "And I don't run from red flags."

"I came all the way down here the other day to warn you. And now you've made me come all the way back to tell you again."

"This is as much my case as it is yours."

"It's very easy to get in here," he said. "Right through your balcony door. The doorman didn't see me. No one saw me. And no one will see me when I leave. You understand?"

"So I'll get a bigger lock."

"You're not listening," Brewer said.

"Maybe *you're* not listening. I can solve this case and I'm not running away from Mr. Red Flag."

Brewer heaved an angry sigh.

"Okay," he said. "I'll have to show you." He stepped back from her. "When I became a government agent, I was sent to Fort Bladenberg for training. I was just like you. Right Makes Might. Virtue Is Invincible. I wasn't afraid of anyone. I was bulletproof. So you know what they did to me? I'll show you."

He grabbed her suddenly and turned her in his arms. "Five muscle-bound D.I.'s came into the mess hall where I was eating and right in front of everyone, dragged me off."

"What are you doing!" she shrieked. She fought to get away but he merely leaned back and lifted her feet off the floor as he pulled her across the room.

"Are you crazy?" she cried. She got her leg up against a wall and pushed. It barely staggered him. As he pulled her along she reached her right foot for the bureau and missed. Her foot upset a small lamp.

"I can't believe you're doing this!" she shrieked. "Stop!"

"Make me," he said. "Show me your best moves. Go ahead."

He had dragged her over to the balcony door. " 'If you're going to be a good agent you have to learn how puny you are.'

That's what they said. And they carried me over their head to the base firehouse. And they put me in the cherry picker and lifted the basket five stories up in the air. And then they held me head down by the ankles. And there, Madeline Hale, dangling by two very puny human hands in midair, I learned humility and common sense. And that's what you're going to learn right now."

He held her by the wrists. "They're going to send a slope-head around to kill you. And they're not going to care how he does it. Do I have your attention?"

She tried to pull her arms free. "I'm not impressed. Stop this right now."

"For starters, maybe he'll rape you. Every sickie thinks that's great fun. Then—" he drew his forefinger down her blouse from her throat "—he might carve on you a bit with a knife before—" he slashed his fingernail across her throat "—he cuts you open from ear to ear. And then, Madeline, if he's feeling generous he'll do a quick finale on you." Brewer picked her up in his arms and stepped out on the balcony. He held her out beyond the railing.

"While the tears are still wet on your face, he picks you up and drops you from here straight down. Seven stories down, screaming all the way."

She tried to clamber over his shoulder to safety. "Enough! Enough!"

"Oh, no, Madeline. You're a big-time lawyer. Let's see you get a court order now. Where's your knife-proof writ? Show me your subpoena with the parachute." He stood there firmly holding her out over the balcony. "Can I make it any plainer? This has nothing to do with virtue or justice or physical strength. If the slope-head doesn't get the job done, they'll send around six bigger slope-heads. And if that doesn't work, Madeline, they'll use a bomb."

He put her down and turned her roughly to face the parking lot below. "Down there," he said into her ear. "In your car. They'll blow it to the moon. Sooner or later one way or the other they'll come for you. And I'm telling you I can't protect you. And I don't want to come to your funeral. Understand? Do you hear me? You have a lot of living to do up in Vermont, and I don't want you to die for me. Go live. Live."

She was panting, spent, quaking, unable to talk. The pounding of her heart was thudding in her ears. If she'd had a gun—if she'd only had a gun—she would have shot Charlie Brewer dead as he stood there.

"How dare you!" she shrieked at last. She paced back into the bedroom. "I can't believe you did this. It's unforgivable! Outrageous!"

But when she turned he was gone over the balcony railing. She had no idea whether he had gone up or down. Or sideways.

IN THE MORNING Madeline Hale ordered a steel-rod lock for the balcony's sliding door. She purchased a police special .38, applied to the police for a handgun permit, and signed up for lessons at a local gun club. Lastly, she enrolled in a karate class.

Then she went to her office and resumed her search for Anthony Rumbh.

HER THOUGHTS returned constantly to Brewer and his assault the night before. She still couldn't believe he had done it. He'd terrified her. He'd reduced her from a professional attorney in Washington to a trembling silly woman terrified for her life. There were moments when she had feared he really would rape her, then had been equally sure he would pitch her off the balcony. She remembered the dangerous anger he'd shown the day he was released from prison.

It had taken years to struggle into her current position and status, and it had taken a great deal of confidence-building. In one violent event, he'd almost wrecked that. He'd almost upended her confidence. His action had been primitive, outrageous, never to be forgiven.

Brewer had ruined everything. She felt silly having kissed him. Yes, she could see it clearly: Vermont was the right path for her. She would continue her quest for Rumbh, solve the case, clear Brewer's name. And never see him again.

Then she remembered that on the street in front of the Chinese restaurant he had kissed her.

HER FIRST STOP was the library of the Central Intelligence Agency in McLean. The Biography File contained biographic data on tens of thousands of international figures.

SHE HAD BEEN preparing for bed, sitting in her housecoat just before midnight. Her phone rang.

"Hello," she said.

"Mrs. Hale?"

"Yes."

"Can you see your car down in the parking lot?"

She looked down from her window. "Yes. The powder-blue Mercedes. Why?"

"I have a message for you. Ready? One. Two. Three."

The Mercedes exploded. The hood sailed over a half-dozen cars; the trunk lid burst open; all the windows blew out; a fireball shot up more than fifty feet in the air. Burning parts from her car showered down and bounced all over the parking lot.

The driver's seat was filled with furious flames.

Where's your bomb-proof subpoena, Madeline?

BREWER ARRIVED IN A CAB at dusk that evening. He walked around the parking lot, looking at the scorched concrete. Four people stood nearby, talking and gesticulating.

Pebbled window glass from Madeline Hale's car crunched under his shoe soles as he studied the marks. It had been a large bomb. And it had been detonated by remote control. Probably from a car: a cellular telephone in one hand to call Hale and a small battery-operated detonator in the other. One, Two, Three, Boom. "A message for you."

WHEN SHE OPENED her apartment door, she stood looking at him. Then she said, "I'm okay as long as I don't think about it."

"Don't think about it and it'll go away," Brewer said.

"Okay, Charlie. I have to swallow my pride and say you were right the other night. Your methods are atrocious. You are also a latter-day Victorian romantic who has women on some kind of a pedestal. But you were right." She stepped back to let him in.

When he crossed the threshold, she said, "One more point: That bomb doesn't change a thing. I'm not going to run and hide. I intend to persist until I get Rumbh."

"My money says Rumbh wins."

"Whether you believe it or not, I can handle this."

"Handle it. There's only one way to handle it. If you're really serious and if you were trained to handle situations like this you would still have to go underground. Disappear. So he can't get at you. Then you throw out your nice-Nellie book of rules and ethics. Instead you dog him relentlessly. Work behind the scenes. You bribe; you deceive; you break in. You use telephone taps. You use muscle and threats and blackmail until you get him. And at all times stay underground. To get him you have to become just like him. See? The salami tactics of relativism at work and play."

"Force and violence," she said. "Those are your methods. Not mine."

"They're his. Just go look at the scorch marks."

"If you're so concerned, then help me."

"You could be forever, getting this Rumbh," said Brewer. "Leave him to me. I'll find him and settle with him when I get the time and the money."

"I have plenty of both. Let's clear your name now."

"Come on, Madeline. If anything happened to you while we were working together—"

"Then we're at an impasse. You won't stop and I won't stop."

"You'll stop, or he'll stop you."

"We'll see."

"You're a hell of a woman."

"And you're a hell of a man, Charlie Brewer. I wish we had met at another time under different circumstances." She reached up her arms and kissed him. "Take good care of yourself."

"If anything happens to you—"

"No long faces, Charlie."

DOWN IN THE PARKING LOT he watched his cab arrive. He opened the door, then paused to look up at her windows. He could see her face looking down at him, the black hair and pale skin, that quizzical tilt of her head. He was glad he couldn't see those pale-blue eyes.

She lifted a hand to him and dropped it. Brewer hesitated, stepped back onto the sidewalk, hesitated again, then turned, and without another glance got in. As he drove off, he took a long last look at the bomb's scorch mark.

9

No one knew where Eric Rock was. Each day McCall checked his dailies, looking for some word on the man. But Rock was as elusive as a ghost.

After a week of waiting for someone to report on Rock's whereabouts, McCall took matters into his own hands. He would locate Rock personally.

The only hard fact McCall had gleaned was a phone number in New York City—Rock's message center. People reached Rock by speaking to a message unit at that number, then waited for him to call back—which he sometimes never did.

But the man himself could be anywhere in the world. He got his messages by telephoning his recorder once or twice a day from wherever he was at the moment, and that could be Rome, New York, Delhi, Singapore, or San Francisco. He seemed to have no fixed home.

It was that message center that McCall focused on.

MCCALL ARRIVED at the disused safe house later than he had planned. By the time he'd parked, sunset was less than an hour away. Quickly he lifted the two cases by their handles out of the trunk of his car and carried them across the sidewalk and up the concrete steps to the doorway.

He paused to check the pedestrians, then studied the parked cars, then the windows of the brick row houses that lined both sides of the street. Most of them were apartments with professional offices on the first floor. Windowpanes reflected the red ball of sun.

McCall took bare note of the flawless autumn weather before he unlocked the door and stepped into the inner hallway. The building was supposed to be empty, and he stood listening for sounds: footsteps, scraping chairs, shutting doors. But the interior was quiet—almost as though the building were listening to him.

It had been used variously over the years—as offices for a special Latin American disinformation program, as a duplication center until the new one was completed, and periodically as a safe house.

By the time he'd reached the third floor, his arms were shaking from the heavy cases and he was panting. He unlocked the door to the front room and pushed it open.

The phone was sitting in the middle of the bare floor. Beside it stood the folded mattress cot he'd ordered. McCall put down the two cases, then crouched and picked up the telephone receiver. He got a dial tone. Good.

He took a pad from his pocket and looked at the number on the telephone and compared it with the number written on the pad. They were identical. Then with a screwdriver he removed the base of the telephone.

Now he opened the larger case. This was a highly sophisticated computerized telephone-tap unit. The top face of the unit was covered with toggle switches, phone-jack receptacles, and digital-number squares. From the side of the unit he drew out a sixteen-inch cable and attached its two alligator leads to the contacts inside the base of the telephone. The other wire he plugged into an electric outlet. He worked several toggle switches and watched the computerized numbers dance on the display face.

Now he opened the larger case and revealed a multi-headed tape recorder. He checked the tape deck reel, drew out the electric lead, and plugged it into an outlet. A second lead with a magnetic head he attached to the headset of the telephone.

One last piece: He withdrew a set of earphones from a drawer in the phone tap unit and plugged the jack into the audio circuit. He was ready.

McCall referred to his pad again. He looked at the second telephone number written on it, then placed it on the floor. He picked up the phone from its cradle and dialed the number. He replaced the phone on its cradle and put on the earphones. He could hear a phone ringing. On the third ring it clicked, and a recorded voice greeted him.

"This is Eric Rock. Please leave your name, your phone number, and any message, and I will get back to you. Wait for the tone."

The harmonica bug went to work. It probed Rock's telephone message recorder, identified its code number, and then displayed that code number in its green digits for McCall to note down. Next it signaled the number to Rock's message unit. A moment later Rock's message unit was feeding its collected messages into McCall's tape recorder. Messages from all over the world were pumped out.

"Rock, this is Petersen. Give me a call. Use the Athens number."

"This is the Angel Gabriel. You recognize my voice, Rock? Call me. I'm back in Paris and I have news on Fawzi."

From a marine radio telephone: "Hello, this is *Lipstick Two*. We'll be docking at the Cove in the Bahamas on the twenty-ninth. Can you come down? I have someone here who's dying to meet you. And she's just the right age. Also I have a very interesting deal for you."

In all there were fourteen messages on the recorder. McCall knew the identity of several and guessed at the identity of the others. A ghouls' gathering: itinerant arms peddlers, failed intelligence agents trying to scrape a deal together, mercenaries stirring up small wars, terrorists with their beggars' bowl garnering money, then shopping for bombs, and corrupted arms buyers from various governments around the world, looking for kickbacks. One voice he was sure belonged to a Polish defector who specialized in selling biological and chemical horrors.

They were never at rest, this parade of monsters, twisted minds, and mass murderers. Not all the arms control people in all the governments in the world could keep up with them.

With the last message, the harmonica bug shut down except for the camp-on circuit that waited for Rock to telephone to his message center. When he did, McCall's unit would trace the call and identify the number Rock was calling from. With fourteen messages on his recording unit, Rock must not have called in for a day, perhaps two days. He was bound to check in at any moment.

Now all McCall had to do was wait. He looked at his watch. It was after five, Washington time. Around ten P.M. in London. Midnight in Jerusalem. Seven P.M. in Tokyo. The wandering Rock might be anywhere, awake, asleep, dancing, eating, planting a bomb—but wherever he was, sooner or later he would call his message unit.

As soon as the harmonica bug identified the number Rock was calling from, it would switch on another circuit to monitor the new number and record any phone calls Rock would make from it. It would also simultaneously continue to record all calls to Rock's message center.

All that was needed was one phone call from Rock.

MCCALL SAT THERE on the floor cross-legged like a swami about to utter an oracle. He looked at the slanting autumn light on the wall. It filled him with sadness. It was the wan-ing time of the year, when he usually did his annual summing-up and found things wanting: How many Eliott Monroes had there been this year? How many others flourished on his work? Another year of use and abuse.

The wan autumn sun on the wall reminded him that the whole magnificent season was slipping by almost without his notice. On the Chesapeake this was some of the best sailing weather of the year, a marvelous time he always looked forward to, especially now that the children were old enough to share it with him.

How in the world had he come to this empty room on this bare floor, in this unused building, to stalk a fellow mortal with the avowed purpose of having him murdered?

He looked at the illegal wiretap he had just installed. How one crime quickly leads to another—a series of others. Plotting murder was just the beginning. But where was the ending?

Man began in the mud, crept from the slime, grew his three or four brains, evolved into a mammal, and lived his thundering history: Horsemen galloped across the plains to sack cities; the assassin's knife flashed in the harem and changed the course of a civilization; men invented numbers, scratched the earth with bent twigs to discover formulas, dammed rivers, devised tools, machines, weapons, flung rockets into space. And all of it was just a preamble to this moment when a man sat cross-legged before two boxes to snare and murder another. The only thing that had changed since the first murder was the sophistication of the weapons.

McCall stretched and sighed. This was liable to be a very long wait and he didn't need thoughts like that. With the earphones on, he lay back on the cot and yawned.

THE LIGHT FAILED and soon he was in the dark room of a dark empty house in Washington, D.C., watching the green digital clock on a computerized tap count off the seconds, the minutes, and the hours.

He dozed.

THE PHONE RANG. It was 6:46 in the evening. Rock's machine droned its instructions, and a woman replied: "Eric. This is Valerie. Will I see you Saturday?"

McCall paced through the darkness. In the ambient light of the streetlamps, he walked from room to room and back again, hearing his heels bump on the bare floor. Standing in the middle of the empty kitchen he could hear faint noises from the building next door. He stood at the window and looked down into the street: people walking dogs, carrying packages, car cruising for parking spaces, traffic light on the corner going through its endless iterations.

McCall lay down on the cot again.

A NIGHTMARE WOKE HIM. He lay on his back with the earphones on his head and heard the Tumbler cry his last as he fell through the air. It had become a regular occurrence: At odd whiles, unexpectedly, when brushing his teeth, conducting a meeting, telling a joke, he heard the Tumbler's horror-stricken shout call to him. The ultimate hockey stick.

He thought of law school and wondered what had ever happened to his great plan to conquer the world. Love had happened to it; marriage happened to it; babies happened to it; salaries and the need to feed happened to it. Reality had happened to it. The great plan lay buried under the rubble of years. He placed the crook of his right arm over his eyes and wished that Rock would call.

THE PHONE RANG hours later. McCall sat up, disoriented for a moment. He looked at the computer clock. It was 2:10 A.M. The message unit began playing its fifteen messages. Rock was opening his electronic mail.

And while he listened, McCall's unit was tracing the call. The first digits that appeared were 763. Then 891; 993; 444; 582. Gotcha.

A few moments later, when all the messages had been played, Rock punched his code and the message center erased its messages and reset itself to receive a new batch. Rock hung up.

But McCall had what he had come for. His harmonica bug unit had already set up a new monitor to tap the phone Rock had called from. It would record any phone calls Rock would make from that number.

McCall waited a half hour for Rock to make his calls. He didn't, and McCall decided the man had gone to bed. No matter. The machine would wait for him. In the morning McCall would pump Rock's phone number into his office computer and learn the address.

He stood up stiffly and left the equipment set up on the floor. He went down the stairs in the darkness and out of the building. There was a sweep of stars in the clear sky and a chilly breeze at his ankles. No moon.

McCall drove home. He paused in the upper hallway, peered into his son's room, then listened at his daughter's door. The tarot cards must have a lot to say now.

He got into bed next to his wife and wondered still if he was actually going to kill those three men. He felt a great loneliness.

THE NEXT MORNING, McCall's first business was Rock's telephone number. He looked at the piece of paper he had written it on, exactly as it had appeared on the digital read-out of his telephone tapping machine. It took his computer only a few minutes to identify the owner of that number, an unlisted number about ninety miles from Washington:

Sherard Pawlson
Windmere Polo Farms
Chadd's Ford, Pennsylvania

What in the world was Rock doing on a polo farm? And more important, where was he going to be on November 26?

Meantime other things were beginning to jell. On his desk he found a report from London:

"Re: Peno Rus. Reliable sources says Rus is planning an arms seminar in the Hotel Royal Bestwick in London November 22 through 26. Attendees' names n/a yet."

So now he knew where Peno Rus would be on November 26. Talking to a roomful of arms dealers in London.

Also on his desk McCall found a tape from the Chief of Station, Mexico City. It was a recording of Slane's meeting with Joli and Gomez in the Hotel Orizaba. He played it, bemused, then played it again.

The ingenuity of the arms traders often amazed him: taking over a country through the pretext of making a film. His former chief, Dan Dempsey, had told him years ago: "Remember, it takes as much hard work and brilliant planning to be a successful villain as it does to be successful at anything else. Your better grade villain is a very busy cat."

Slane's game didn't concern him; if everything went the way McCall planned it, before the coup Slane would be dead—somewhere between the Baja California desert and the Leeward Island Free State on November 26.

NOW MCCALL knew where Slane and Rus would be on November 26. Two down. One to go. Where would Eric

Rock be? At dusk, he returned to the safe house and picked up the day's taping of Rock's phone calls.

He sat on the cot and listened to the tape. He was fascinated. Rock was charming, witty, solicitous of his friends. He was a delightful raconteur and highly intelligent withal. He might prove to be the toughest target of the three.

Rock had been very busy, telephoning all over the world, chatting, listening to offers, swapping tales. But the most interesting piece of information McCall picked up was Rock's contretemps with a ten-year-old Egyptian girl. Rock regaled several of his friends who shared his interest in children.

"You would love this kid," he said to an arms dealer in Frankfort. "A fascinating little tart. Too bad I have to give Cairo a wide berth for a while. I can't wait to see her again. But I hear her father owns the biggest scimitar in Egypt and you know what he'll do with it if he catches me." (Laughter.) Rock added wistfully: "I wonder if I'll ever see her again." (Laughter.)

Dmitri in Alexandria had a sobering message. He told Rock how the girl's uncle, Fawzi, was killed by her family. In detail.

"Jesus Christ," Rock said. "Inhuman bastards, aren't they?"

The only other conversation of interest to McCall was about binary explosives.

Rock was speaking to a man named Beeldad in Madrid: "I have to deliver some binary stuff to six different locations in the next two weeks for you-know-who. So you have to get me what we talked about within the next few days. Can do?"

Beeldad assured Rock he could do. He was delighted to be working once again with such an old friend.

"Meet me in Paris," Rock said, "and we'll talk."

There were twenty-three phone conversations on the tape, but at the end Rock had not revealed where he would be on November 26. Probably because he himself didn't know. Yet.

THE MOMENT McCall had been dreading had arrived. It was time to sign up two assassins, one for Rus and one for Slane. And he knew just whom to turn to. He told his secretary to book a flight to Paris with a stopover in London.

At the end of a long day McCall picked up his phone and called Borden. "Have you any news about Attashah yet?"

"We're still working on it," said Borden.

McCall sat back wearily at his desk, rubbing his eyes and gathering himself for the drive through traffic to his home. Where the hell was that wily Iranian? Had he signed anyone up yet?

Without preamble, the Tumbler shouted his last mortal utterance, falling, falling, falling. Silence.

LATE OCTOBER in the Baja Californian desert: It reminded Slane of home—the Australian Outback.

He stepped down from the truck and felt his boot-soles crunch on the wind-polished hardpan. Before him stood the abandoned barracks and service buildings. The terrain rippled away in all directions, a desert dotted with saguaro cactus. The sun made him squint.

Behind him, coming up the road, the other trucks whined, laden with military matériel, movie equipment, and base supplies.

He was following the dictator's original route to the presidential palace of the Leeward Island Free State. Using the man's own map to the vault.

On November 26 he would be dining in the presidential palace, a very wealthy man.

"NOW, MAJOR," said Peno Rus, "we must make this the most impressive seminar on arms planning and usage ever offered. After it is over, I want a spontaneous outcry from all those who weren't invited, demanding a repeat performance."

"Time is very tight, isn't it?" Major Mudd asked. He looked at the unwavering small brown eyes of his employer. Mongol blood in there somewhere.

"Yes, Major, but we can make it. Understand, please, that in a very short time we will be the world's leading independent small arms merchant. I want our customers and prospects to turn to us not only for their hardware needs but with their problems. This seminar will establish our expertise."

"I'm talking about issuing the invitations. November twenty-second is a very short time away."

"Ah! That's no problem, man. We are limiting this first seminar to less than one hundred. I've already chatted informally with dozens of our best customers, including Ney. The danger is we'll be oversubscribed. By the way, who do you suppose was one of the first to sign up?"

"I haven't the foggiest."

"Ney himself. Even he can see times are changing."

"What will the fee be?"

"Five thousand pounds per head."

ABRUPTLY A MAN was standing in front of Rock's table in the Café Chanticleer in Paris.

"Mr. Rock, may I have a few words with you?"

The guy looked as if he might be an American businessman. Tall, thin, and fair-haired, he wasn't an arm-bender and certainly not an Egyptian. Rock said, "That depends. Who are you?"

"May I sit down? My name is Rumbh."

ROCK AND RUMBH drank new Beaujolais and talked the evening away.

Rumbh said, "I have an assignment that only you may be able to handle. But first let me give you some background. Recently I used a group that calls itself the Third of September. You know them?"

"No," Rock said. "There are hundreds of gangs like that."

"I gave them a car bomb assignment from my client. They made three attempts and failed. Their leaders are in jail. And in the last bombing attempt their explosives expert blew all the fingers off his right hand."

Rock grinned at him. "Sounds like you need help."

"Wait. There's more. My explosives vendor has also let me down. Bad merchandise. His bombs go fffffffft! I get blamed. My batting average is down around my socks. And my reputation is damaged."

"Things are no longer the way they were," Rock said. "You can't use amateurs anymore."

"Tell me about it," Rumbh said.

"With all the terrorist groups that are active," Rock said, "you have to have a higher kill rate just to get in the papers. And if you want front-page stuff, you need state-of-the-art binary explosives that can really take out a lot of people in one shot. One or two deaths and a lost leg won't do it anymore. You have to blow away forty, sixty at a time. I don't think the papers in New York, London, or Paris will touch the ordinary bombing with less than sixty dead anymore. I'm talking front page. You can't trust that kind of heavy-duty hitting to the nonprofessional. Especially since security is tighter than a flea's ass. And getting tighter every day. You see what I'm saying?"

Rumbh nodded.

"I can't sell sticks of dynamite out of the back of a truck anymore," Rock said. "And you can't hire guys to just jump on the nearest airplane with a suitcase full of explosives anymore, either. Opportunism is for small fry. This is the age of the specialist. You know what I mean?"

"It's obvious."

Rock pushed his wineglass out of the way. "No, it's not obvious. Look. Suppose I sell a man a bomb to tuck under the chair of his enemy. And the bomb goes off. But if his enemy's not in the chair at the right moment, it's no consolation to my client that he got the bomb from the lowest bidder. It didn't get the job done. His enemy is still living. All my client got for his money was a loud noise. I've sold him a perfectly good bomb but I haven't solved his problem."

"So—"

"So I don't go in and say, 'I can sell you your bomb cheaper.' No. I say, 'What do you want the bomb to do? What is your problem? Let me help you solve it.' Once he tells me, I can see he has the wrong plan. All his bomb is going to do is make chair splinters. Do you see what I am saying, Rumbh?"

Rumbh grunted. "Go on."

"So I sell him a package—not just a bomb. And not just a criticism of his plan. I give him a plan that will work. I find out when the enemy is scheduled to sit on the chair. I discover how to get into the building and out again. I make maps and timetables. I plan the entire operation. And I deliver the explosives that will do the job. And no junk either. Nobody knows more about binary bombs than I do. I handle only the best stuff. Okay. What I've given him is a plan that will work. You see? He didn't want to buy a bomb. He wanted to buy an assassination. My competitors sell him a bomb. I sell him a dead enemy."

"What makes you think you can make a better plan?"

"Because I'm an expert. Your September guys don't have access to the information I do. Or the knowledge and skill. All you have to do is follow my instructions, and I have a satisfied customer."

"I see." Rumbh scratched his chin thoughtfully.

"Okay. Tell me what your problem is."

Rumbh cleared his throat. "My clients want to plant a bomb in a hotel in Cairo."

"Cairo?"

"Right down your alley, Rock. I want to disrupt a love feast."

"Meaning what?"

"A regional conference between rival factions," Rumbh said. "They're going to bury the hatchet."

"Go on."

"I want to break it up. I want them to get suspicious of each other. You read me? I want a bomb planted that they find before the big sit-down."

"Find?" Rock held up a hand. "You mean you don't want it to go off?"

"Oh, no. That's the whole idea. Each side will accuse the other of planting it. It took the State Department nearly two years to get this sit-down. After they find the bomb, it'll take State ten years to get these gooks to come within ten miles of each other."

"Okay," Rock said. "What's the big challenge?"

"Getting the explosive into the hotel. The security is tighter than the skin on a snake. You may just be the only guy in the whole world who can get the bomb into that conference room."

"What hotel is it?"

"Hotel Royal Nile."

"Well, it's all very tempting, Mr. Rumbh. But the answer's no."

"Come on, Rock. I haven't even put the money on the table yet."

"Sorry, but Cairo is off-limits."

"Off-limits? What does that mean?"

"Just that I don't get there lately."

"Okay. Look. I need this job done. If you have a problem with some people in Cairo, I can take care of things for you. You read?"

"You will, ha?"

"Just give me the name and address, wait a day, and send a funeral wreath."

"Hmmm. That's interesting. There's more than one."

"How many?" Rumbh asked.

"A family. Six or eight. Goddammed monsters, the lot of them. They just hacked a family member to pieces with swords."

"Swords?" Rumbh smirked at him.

"So help me," Rock protested. "They're right out of the fourteenth century. These people don't know what the word *civilized* means. But I don't want them dead. I mean, there's a girl and she'd hate me if—you get my drift?"

"Okay. Listen, I can arrange to have the whole crew locked up for a few days so you can get in, plant the bomb, and get out again. All except the girl. What does that do for your libido?"

"How do you arrange that?"

"Friends in high places. I want this job done on November twenty-sixth. So tell me now who you want me to take care of."

Rock thought about the girl. Quickly he pulled out a pencil and a pad and wrote on it. Then he handed it to Rumbh.

Rumbh stood up and pushed back his chair. "I'll be back in a couple of days. Where do I reach you?"

"Call my answering service." He wrote the number down for Rumbh.

"I'll be back," Rumbh said. "Pack your bags for Cairo."

Rock watched the man leave the restaurant. Was he really going to see her again?

10

Part #2XJT557 turned out to be a nightmare.

Brewer's first problem was identifying the maker. After searching through a number of directories and parts catalogues, he finally found the maker's name in the Technical Resources Library of the American Microminiature Engineering Society on West 38th in Manhattan.

Their "Annual Directory of Microchips" gave a brief history: #2XJT557 was an eighteen-year-old microchip and had recently been removed from seven different classified military parts lists. It had been used in only one piece of equipment, a military radar unit. Just below the entry for #2XJT557 was an entry for a second-generation chip—#2XJT557/A—listed as classified. Brewer had hit his first serious problem—and maybe his ultimate one: #2XJT557 was listed as a discontinued part. Finding one hundred new ones was out of the question.

He sat by a library window in brilliant sunshine, watching a janitor across the street push-brooming autumn leaves into the gutter. When he finished he went down a flight of basement steps. The wind blew the leaves back onto the walk.

DICE ASKED HIM: "If that chip is so hard to find, why don't we get another model?"

"Different circuits," Brewer said. "No other chip will operate the equipment."

"Then let's get a blank chip—a *prom*, I think they call it—and make all the copies you want."

"You don't know much about military chips, do you, Dice?"

"Nah. It's not my rice bowl. Too complicated."

"Well, once upon a time the Russians were able to duplicate a top-secret military computer by buying a kid's video game computer in toy stores. The toy had the same chip. Ever since then, more and more military chips are coded to prevent duplication. And that includes 2XJT557."

"Then let's get a chip house to make a copy."

"To make a copy of that chip, we'd have to get the original tapes and masks from the manufacturer. Or we'd have to get the original chip and make accurate photographic blowups of it. Then we'd have to hire a semiconductor outfit to copy it, set up production, and make us a few hundred. Cost would be out of sight. And even if my client was willing to pay for it, no company would make it; the penalties are very stiff, and most semiconductor makers have more business than they can handle anyway."

"Okay okay. I thought I'd ask."

Brewer drew a square on a bar napkin, one-quarter inch by one-quarter inch. "That's all it is, not much bigger than a pinhead. And that little chip is a whole computer—a microprocessor. In that tiny area are maybe a couple of hundred thousand transistors that operate thousands of integrated circuits. And I need one hundred of them programmed as number 2XJT557."

"So where do we go from here?" asked Dice.

"Try to buy used units from surplus dealers."

THE NEXT MORNING, Brewer and Dice sat down in adjacent hotel rooms, each with a directory of military surplus dealers. They worked steadily, calling cities across the country from the East Coast to the West Coast and asking each dealer in turn for used rebuffered slave radar units. They were finished by two in the afternoon; they hadn't found one unit.

Dice sat slumped back in his chair, wearily. "Now what?"

"I have just one move left. You wait here until I get back."

This was one move Brewer dreaded.

HE TOOK A CAB over to the East Side and got out in front of an old high-rise residential building on 24th Street. He took the elevator to the tenth floor and, after pausing, reluctantly knocked on the door just below the nameplate: MYRON ELANDER.

"Come in. It's open."

The place hadn't changed a bit. Elander's apartment was as neat as a box of checkers except for the second bedroom. That was Elander's office.

A long white Formica counter that ran the length of one wall held a row of thick industrial-parts directories, each on a metal lectern. Elander sat at the counter, wearing a telephone headset and deftly turning the pages of one of the directories as he talked into the phone. He was sitting in a chrome and leather motorized wheelchair.

All around him on the floor were piles of telephone directories from all over the world. Behind him, at a console, a woman sat typing invoices into a computer.

When he saw Brewer he stopped in mid-sentence and gaped.

'Listen, Anthony," he said into the phone, "I'm going to have to get back to you. In an hour or so." He looked again at Brewer. "Lucy," he said to the secretary, "why don't you take that stuff to the bank?"

The two men watched her leave. The front door closed softly behind her.

"Is my mouth hanging open?" Elander asked him.

Brewer raised a limp hand in reply.

"I never thought I'd see you again."

Brewer nodded mutely.

"It must be important," Elander said. "This is no social call. Right? Right?"

"Business looks good."

"Well, now that you ask. If I was still with the Feds, I'd be earning the usual fishcake. This year I'll probably make more than seven agents together. But if it's any consolation, I'd go back to the way things were before—before the accident."

He looked old—much older than his thirty-five years. And he looked unhealthy. A roll of fat bulged over his belt, something he never would have tolerated a few years before. His face had the colorless chalky finish one sees on hospital patients.

"It still haunts me night and day," Elander said. "And it's going to hound me into my grave. Four years and eleven days," Elander said.

"Enough," Brewer said.

"It still hurts you? Think how it hurts me. She was my sister."

"Enough."

"What do you mean, enough? It's never enough. Every day, day after day, life extracts another pound of flesh from me. There's never enough penance."

"No one dumped that booze down your throat," Brewer said, "or put you in that car but you."

"Tell me about it. That's big news to me."

"Enough. Enough," Brewer said.

"No. It isn't. It was very bad around here eleven days ago. That would have been the fourth wedding anniversary for the two of you."

"Mike," Brewer said. "I can't handle this."

"Then what did you come here for?" Elander waited for Brewer to speak, then said, "Well, there must be some reason you walked through that door on this particular day at this particular hour. Am I supposed to guess? Let's see. You came to hear me apologize again. You came to make sure I'm not enjoying a minute of my life. Maybe, even, you came to forgive me. That it? Forgiveness?"

"I came for a chat," Brewer said.

"A chat. That's nice. I like chats. What do you want to chat about?"

"I'm looking for a part."

"A part? You came for a part? Be damned. I was right. It's not a social call. You came because you need something."

"That's it, Mike. One part."

"A part. We don't see each other or speak for—how many years now? And what do we talk about? A part. Welcome to the Court of Last Resort. That's my business motto: If I can't find the part, it doesn't exist. Elander the pack rat."

Brewer said, "You look terrible."

"Go look in the mirror. I wrote you three letters during your trial. I wrote you two letters in prison."

Brewer nodded.

"When did you get out?"

"Couple of weeks ago."

Elander snorted. "Weeks. I'm in for life." He banged a fist on the arm of the wheelchair.

Brewer sat down and waited.

"What the hell," Elander said. "What's the part you're looking for?"

"Number 2XJT557."

"Isn't that interesting? The notorious 2XJT557. Of all the parts you can name you pick that one. Somehow I knew it. It was like printed on your forehead when you walked through the door: 2XJT557." He sat back and studied Brewer's face. "You know, I haven't asked you what business you're in. And I'm afraid I know."

He turned his wheelchair to face Brewer. "Well, I'm sorry for your trouble, Charlie. And I'm sorry about 2XJT557. You're not going to find it anywhere."

BREWER LOOKED around the room at the piles of directories, the file cabinets, the spare wheelchair in a closet, and through an open door, an unmade bed. Welcome to Myron Elander's world: a two-bedroom apartment, a three-line telephone service to everywhere on earth, the ghost of a sister, the ghost of a friendship.

Myron Elander, finder of lost military parts; he had remembered the anniversary date. Brewer hadn't—on that date, he was getting out of prison. Sometimes now, he had difficulty remembering what she looked like.

BREWER SAID, "If I can't have that part, then I'll take surplus radar units I can cannibalize."

"No, you won't. There aren't any."

"I see."

"And I see too, Charlie. You working for the Iranians?"

"What makes you think that?"

"Never kid a kidder, Charlie. The Iranians are the only people looking for that part."

"Great."

"It's a tip-off. You say 2XJT557. And anyone in the business will say Iran. Just like that. You want me to tell you why you won't find old 2XJT557?"

"In for a penny—go ahead."

"After the Shah got chased out, Washington decided to do a number on Iran's surveillance equipment. So some smart guy in Defense got a great idea one day. Just change the design of one microchip—put in a different one and stop making the original, and *voilà*! Iran is stuck with obsolete radar units with no replacement chip. And Iran's the only country we ever sold that unit to. About six months ago Iran was running around trying to buy up used units. But there aren't any. And that's why Charlie Brewer is shit out of luck today.''

Brewer stood. ''It's that simple.''

''It's that simple. Please. You'll let me give you a word of advice. If you're working for the Iranians, you're going to end up in the river. And if they don't ace you, Washington will. You're in the middle and you'll lose. Robbing banks is safer.''

''Okay.'' Brewer had walked to the door when Elander called to him.

''Hey, Charlie.''

''Yeah.''

''Once we were good friends.''

WELL. THAT WAS the end of that. It was over. Without that part, the other matériel was worthless. Brewer felt a grim pleasure in picturing the expression that would be on Atta-shah's face when he told him the news.

Brewer felt a sense of release. He could be a good boy again. But there was also a feeling of defeat. He didn't like being beaten, didn't like being a loser. He didn't like fail-ure—even failure at treason.

There was another reason to drop the whole thing. Elan-der had said that only the Iranians would be shopping for 2XJT557. That meant Washington would already have been alerted. Agents would be on his trail in very short order now.

The sunlight was a great glow of clarity in clear air over Manhattan—a gorgeous late-autumn day when people stepped along the streets with a certain swing. A bad day to remember his wedding day and the wedding that never took place.

He walked uptown. He'd have to tell Dice it was all over and pay him off.

He found himself walking over toward the West Side to the library of the American Microminiature Engineering Society again. He'd had a thought.

THE MAKER OF THE CHIP #2XJT557 was an outfit in California called Straek Inc. In the library Brewer pulled down the *Corporate Red Book* and found the summary on Straek: the address, the corporate officers, annual sales, regional offices, credit ratings, memberships in various societies, stock issued, quantity, stock exchange abbreviation, then a list of products and trade names. Among items made for the Defense Department, the navy, the air force, and the army were computerized fire-control units, rocket-launching computers, army tank-control units, radar black boxes—a list of more than thirty items.

Below that was a shorter list issued by its consumer products division. A radar detector for passenger cars to avoid police speed traps, and a personal computer designed for schoolroom training. The latter was listed as discontinued.

A brief corporate history told him that Straek had started eight years before on a shoestring, with a single military contract for a radar unit. The second unit they made was the classroom computer.

Brewer sat gazing at the list, making a bet with himself about human behavior. He went into the catalogue library room and got out Straek's various catalogues and product bulletins.

In the product bulletin folder, he found Straek's announcement to its military customers of the declassification and discontinuance of #2XJT557 with a highly magnified diagram of its construction. And a list of classified codes that had been lifted.

He turned to the consumer products literature. First he studied the sales brochure for the passenger-car radar detection unit. Then the maintenance and repair bulletin. He studied the schematic for wiring. Nothing.

Then he leafed through the sales literature for the personal computer and discovered why it had been discontinued. Almost every personal computer on the market had standardized on MS DOS. Straek's CPM model was incompatible with any other maker's MS DOS equipment and software. Patiently he read through the product bulletins, price sheets, maintenance advisories to distributors, modifications in circuitry and design. About two months before the computer was discontinued, a bulletin was issued alerting repair people that the replacement microchip was no longer to be available. There was a diagram.

Brewer sat back in his chair for a long time, afraid to verify what he had discovered. He turned and looked around the room. Then he carefully knocked a knuckle on the wood of his chair and compared the diagram for the classroom computer chip with the diagram for #2XJT557.

There was no doubt. Straek knew a good microchip design when it made one: #2XJT557, the restricted military microchip, had led a secret and illegal life as the core of the now discontinued Straek CPM personal computer.

STRAEK'S VICE-PRESIDENT in charge of marketing was named Rollins and he had the ringing voice of an extrovert.

"Last computer in that model was made two years ago," he told Brewer. "We've gone to all our original customers and offered them our new MS DOS computers as replacements for the old CPMs. It's a more powerful unit, more versatile. And it's compatible with all the major p.c.'s. We gave them a terrific deal because we wanted to hold on to our market segment.''

"The CPM was a terrific unit," Brewer said.

"Tell me about it!" Rollins roared with laughter. "If it had been compatible for modem use, we'd be eating gravy potatoes every night."

"What did you do with the trade-in units?"

"Junked them," Rollins said. "The crusher got them all."

"I got some customers who want theirs repaired and I can't find parts for them."

"Well, that's a tough one, sir. Offhand, I don't know of any of them that are still around except for a few like your customer's. Did you try running classifieds in the computer magazines? Bound to turn up five or six from the hackers, enough to cannibalize anyway."

Classified ads in computer magazines. That could take months and the odds against turning up a quantity of the Straek unit were too great to bother with.

Another faint spark of hope had burned out.

ABOUT TEN MINUTES LATER, Brewer's phone rang. It was Rollins. "I was looking through our records. We just sold a hundred and fifteen of our new computers to the Meadowbrook School District in New Jersey. They traded in a hundred and twenty old CPMs. So far as I know, those units were supposed to be picked up and destroyed last week but I don't have any confirmation of it yet. Of course it could be in the mail but it's worth a shot."

Two hours later Brewer and Dice were in New Jersey. The secretary to the president of the Board of Education led them down the hallway, talking.

"They were supposed to take them away last Tuesday and I'm sure they did. We put them in the east-wing gym and there's to be a game there tomorrow night—a real grudge fight between our girls' basketball and Morristown's. Now let's see.'' She was sorting through a ring of keys. ''Oh, don't tell me I don't have the key? Is this—? Yes. Let's try it. There.''

The door to the east-wing gymnasium swung open. There in the fading daylight, the gym floor was bare.

''I guess we're too late. But here's the custodian. Mark! Did you move those old computers?''

''Yep. Every last one of them.'' The custodian pushed a bank of switches and the gym was filled with light. ''Up there.''

One hundred and twenty old Straek classroom computers sat on the benches of the gymnasium, lined up like a cheering section.

There will be joy in Tehran tonight, Brewer thought.

11

Borden stuck his head into McCall's office. "Someone is trying to buy #2XJT557."

McCall rose slowly from his chair. "At last. We've got some action. Okay. Lay it on me. Who did that Iranian monster finally hire?"

"We don't know. Whoever he is, he called every surplus dealer in the country, looking for that chip. I've detailed four grunts to talk to the dealers. Maybe one of them recognized the guy's voice."

"Don't hang your hat on it," McCall said.

"Like you said. Finally got some action."

"Okay, Borden," McCall said, "drop whatever you're doing and get on this full time. And don't stop until you find Attashah and the guy he signed up. Get over to Commerce and talk to the Export Control people. Find out if there's been any movement in any of those parts on the Iranian list. Check for End User's Certificates, Applications for Exemptions, Export Licenses, anything. And keep in touch with the dealers. Spread some money around. I don't care how many men it takes. You find that guy, Borden. Find him."

Borden had hurried away before McCall had finished.

"Find him!" he shouted after Borden.

Then he socked a fist into his palm. Someone was nibbling on the edges of his trap. And whoever it was, he would soon be looking for another part: ANAC/23419.PRN. When that happened, the trap would snap. McCall would have his man.

ANAC/23419.PRN. An acronym for cheese.

BREWER PURSUED the contraband merchandise avidly, and by his side Dice worked without cease or complaint. The acquisition of parts for Iran proceeded.

Early in November the city had a premature snowfall. Brewer sat at his hotel window, reading part numbers over the phone to a used-computer dealer in Denver. Down on the crowded sidewalks large wet flakes fell on bobbing umbrellas. In the midst of the shuffling throng he saw Dice walking toward the hotel. He was carrying a parts directory triumphantly.

Dice walked with that odd duckfooted stride of his, coat open, coattails swinging, unaware of or indifferent to the snow, with that silly expression on his face, half clown and half wolf, bearing the heavy volume that he had happily stolen from some library or parts dealer somewhere for Brewer.

Brewer read off the part numbers mechanically over the phone to the computer dealer as he watched Dice in the snow and thought: If you'll steal for me, you'll steal from me.

IT WAS the interconnecting cables and wire harnesses that took the longest: In most cases Brewer and Dice had to purchase civilian cables and modify them. They bought precision hand-crimping tools intended for breadboard designers and then used them to attach a whole range of circuit connectors—bayonet, sliv, kaplex. Some parts had direct civilian equivalents—a marine radio booster pack (quantity 36) came from a ship's chandler in Providence by UPS. Others were made equivalent by changing the cable couplings or the mounting frames. No part was larger than a shoe box.

Dice was brilliant. Gadgetry, as he called it, was his game; he flew to Cleveland to find the right RAX; then to Boston for the precision grommet tool; to Washington for shielded, nonmagnetic XBR leads. He worked out the circuitry patterns for cable modification, located the right terminals and connectors, and found a box of brand new BQS harnesses in a surplus dealer's warehouse across the river in Hohokus.

Dice named the whole operation The Great Easter Egg Hunt. And not once did he ask Brewer where the parts were being stored or where they were going to be shipped.

And as they worked through the list, Brewer kept looking down at the end of his list at the last great problem: ANAC/23419.PRN. He hadn't mentioned that part number yet for fear Dice would walk out on him.

McCALL WAITED twenty-four hours. Then he summoned Borden.

"Nothing," Borden said. "None of the surplus dealers could tell us a thing about the guy who called them about that 2XJT part. There may have been two voices. But there was no accent of any kind that anyone picked up. Sounded like straight American. And nothing unusual about the voice quality that anyone remembered."

"Did anyone make a recording?" McCall asked.

"Nah."

Who could it be? It had to be one of the three—had to be: Rus or Slane or Rock. Who else could it be? No one else really had the smuggling background in electronics parts they did. Slane was tied up with his phony movie. Rus was playing college professor with his London arms seminar. That left Rock. Rock. The only one of the three that was at loose ends. The only one with an American accent. It had to be Rock.

"Okay," McCall said. "We need to borrow some men from another agency—in San Francisco. I want them to watch the Prysbyl plant like a hawk. Part number ANAC/23419.PRN. I can recite it in my sleep. Whoever this guy is he has to have that part. And the only place he can get it is from the Prysbyl plant. So I want a red alert around that plant for the next few weeks at least. Okay?"

Borden nodded.

McCALL LEFT HIS OFFICE later in the afternoon and drove out M Street to the safe house in Georgetown.

When he entered the empty building, sunlight was streaming in all the front windows. He stood briefly in the vestibule and listened. He still had that strange feeling of the building's holding its breath in expectation. His feet seemed to boom on the stairs as he mounted them to the third floor.

The phone recording equipment sat in the middle of the floor in a spotlight of sun. He crouched and pushed the playback button. Then he settled onto the cot and listened to Rock's telephone life.

McCall had gotten to know some of the voices and accents of Rock's callers. The message traffic was familiar: bombs and explosives, yachts in the Bahamas and smirking references to young girls, Rock's current aversion to Cairo, and more and more telephone talk between Rock and Beeldad in Spain about the binary explosives. Six bombs were needed.

"It'll make a bundle, for Christ's sake," Rock said to Beeldad. "I guaranteed delivery."

Then came the phone call with a new voice.

"I have good news for you, Rock," the voice said.

"What is it?" Rock asked.

"I have to deliver it. When can we meet?"

"How about tomorrow, Rumbh?"

"I'm out of Paris for a few days. How about Thursday? At the Chanticleer?"

"Okay," Rock said.

"And Cairo on the twenty-sixth of November." Rumbh hung up.

AT 1:00 A.M. the phone rang in Brewer's hotel room.

"You were sleeping?" Attashah asked.

"Yes."

"Gathering parts is hard work, Mr. Brewer. You will meet me in the billiard hall?"

"Yes." Brewer got up and hurried uptown to Murray's. He found Attashah sitting in a referee's chair watching a game of nine ball. He wore the same outfit as before: black suit, white shirt, and blue polka-dot tie. He was studying the players and their body language with fascination.

"There is a game in Iran—an old Persian game," he said to Brewer in lieu of a greeting. "The player who is the best psychologist always wins. And this game rests on the same psychology. This fat man at table three. He is not interested in winning the most points. He makes side bets on various shots. So the fat man is winning on points anyway—why? Because his opponent is distracted—he's watching the side betting instead of his own game. The fat man walks away with a pocketful of money and the most points, even though his opponent is clearly the better player. And that man with the blue sweater—I can tell if he's going to win or lose before he does just by the way he stands. I think all your diplomats ought to master this game so that they can learn how to deal with the Iranians."

"No one can deal with the Iranians, Attashah," Brewer said. "Not even the Iranians. You people are crazier than the Arabs."

Attashah shrugged. "Perhaps this game of billiards would teach you how to deal with me."

ATTASHAH LED HIM to an all-night coffee stand. There was brisk business in the hotel next door. The prostitutes were busy, arriving in cabs from all over the city, leading the johns triumphantly into the lobby and up the elevators. The weather had turned milder and some of the cabbies stood beside their cabs talking to the police patrol. Others sat in the coffee shop reading the sports pages of the *Daily News*.

Attashah led them to a booth in the back.

"It goes well?" he asked Brewer.

"We're nearly three quarters through," Brewer replied.

"Truly? Three quarters? It does go well. What's left?"

"The last big job is California—Santa Anita. We're going on Tuesday. Another five days could wrap it up. Then I have to get an End User's Certificate. And then after that, I have to set up the smuggling operation into Syria."

"How about 2XJT557?" Attashah turned a spoon nervously in his hand.

"I have it. One hundred chips."

Attashah stared at him astonished. "Are you sure? Number 2XJT557?"

"Yep. Number 2XJT557. One hundred chips manufactured by Straek."

"That is most remarkable. We were told that part was extremely rare."

"It is. You hired the right guy."

"Yes I did, Mr. Brewer."

Brewer had always thought fanatics were cold-blooded. Yet here was Attashah looking at him with the eyes of a fever victim: He was squirming with elation. The Iranian smelled hope; it beckoned to him like woodsmoke drifting over a frozen terrain. Maybe, his Persian eyes said, just maybe—

"I am very impressed, Mr. Brewer."

"We are very far from home, Attashah. Don't dare dream yet. The worst is ahead of us."

"The ANAC part?"

"Yes."

"How will you get it?"

"Have to break in and steal it."

"My people looked into that, Mr. Brewer. It's impossible. The plant is impregnable. You'll have to find another way."

"No. I'll have to do the impossible. There is no other way. We'll steal it."

"You will fail, I assure you."

"There's no other way."

Attashah was dismayed. "Do you think your assistant will help you do that? Dice, I mean. I think not—unless the man is a complete fool."

"I haven't told him yet."

"When you do, he will flee."

"Maybe."

Attashah's elation was gone. He was cast down now, slowly, abstractedly stirring his tea. He'd put his customary five packets of sugar in the cup.

"Mr. Brewer," he said, "that ANAC part is so vital that without it all the other parts are useless."

"I understand."

"Do you understand that the United States government watches the movement of that part like an eagle?"

"Once I was one of the eagles, Attashah."

"If you get caught, it will ruin the whole operation."

"I don't plan to get caught."

"Perhaps. But it is an eventuality I have to consider. You had best turn everything over to me before you try to get the ANAC part."

"I'll do it my way."

"But surely you can tell me where you've put all your acquisitions. If anything happens to you, at least some of the parts can be recovered. Where are you storing them?"

"No one knows that. Not even Dice."

"Then you should tell me."

"No."

"But why?"

"Because if you know where those parts are, you're in control of the situation. As long as you don't, I'm in control."

"I must insist."

"I'll do it my way or not at all."

Attashah's eyes said he was not accustomed to letting other men do things their way or not at all. A rage smoldered in those eyes. With a single stroke of his sword, Attashah would have beheaded Brewer. Then the eyes relented. No one beheads the goose that lays the golden eggs.

"As you wish."

Attashah remained silent for a few moments, recovering his composure. He put a sixth packet of sugar into his cup. Then he changed his tack.

"Have you thought about your smuggling operation to Syria, Mr. Brewer?"

"It's a bit early for that."

"You must have a plan."

"Some thoughts, yes."

Attashah nodded. He was summoning vast reserves of patience; dealing with this stubborn Brewer was trying his very soul.

"Would you please describe your plans for me?"

"No."

Attashah's eys slitted with rage. He sighed. "I see. You'll have to do it your way. You do appreciate that if you fail, it will have great consequences for Iran. Your failure would be catastrophic for our plans."

"If I fail, you fail, Attashah. And your buddies will hang your asshole over a doorknob. So we're in this together. Like it or lump it."

Attashah turned his face away and clutched his throat like a man being strangled. He gazed heavenward for assistance. Brewer ordered him another cup of tea.

LATER, WHEN ATTASHAH had grown weary of trying to pump Brewer, he gathered himself to leave. He said to Brewer: "This Dice. Was he necessary?"

"If you want the parts, he is."

"How much does he know?"

"As little as I can tell him. After California I'll be through with him."

"He could upset our program, Mr. Brewer."

"A lot of things could upset our program."

"After California, Mr. Brewer, I think you should eliminate him. I mean, Mr. Brewer, kill him. And be sure he's dead." He stood. "That is not a request. It is an order."

He left Brewer to pay the bill: one cup of coffee, seven cups of tea. Nearly forty packets of sugar.

BREWER BARELY SLEPT for the rest of that night. No traitor ever worked harder at his treason. He felt weary. Yet he was getting in deeper and deeper. Now Attashah wanted murder.

Brewer recalled with irony that he had written a paper in high school on treason; he could still quote the Constitution from memory.

ARTICLE III, SECTION 3

Treason against the United States, shall consist only in levying War against them, or in adhering to their Enemies, giving them Aid and Comfort.

Brewer was certainly adhering to an avowed enemy. Part #2XJT557 was certainly going to give aid and comfort to Iran. And part #ANAC/23419.PRN would surely bring Attashah and his pals out in the streets of Tehran, dancing in a daisy chain around the ruins of the U.S. Embassy. Tra la, tra la, tra la.

Brewer wondered if his motive for arranging the smuggling operation was apparent to Attashah. Perhaps not. One motive is as good as another if it gets the job done.

About Dice's murder, the Iranian was right: He should zap Dice. The man could betray him and the smuggling operation. Brewer understood traitors. It takes one to know one.

But there was another facet to consider: If Attashah wanted Dice dead after California, would he also want Brewer dead after Syria?

All this enormous effort so that little Charlie Brewer can turn the Mideast into a boiling cauldron, all by himself. War, slaughter, famine, death, courtesy of Charlie Brewer.

All this enormous effort to get a bullet through the skull, courtesy of Rooley Attashah.

BORDEN REPORTED to McCall just before five that evening.

"Okay," he said. "We picked up a scrub team out of Frisco from three different agencies. They've conferred with the Prysbyl people, and the whole security system is on maximum alert around the clock. There's no way in the world that you could break into that plant and steal those ANAC parts."

"I've heard that before. So be a pain in the ass and tell them to reconfirm their plans to us."

"They're pretty ticked-off as it is. This is a dog job and nobody wants to help us. Come on, Bobby, you couldn't float a fart through that plant."

"Push them again."

THE SILICON VALLEY: an unbroken string of computer companies paving the Santa Clara valley south of San Francisco. The hope of the nation.

Brewer and Dice arrived at San Francisco's International Airport in a light fog. The city itself was muffled and invisible, although Oakland across the bay was in full sunlight.

They drove south from the airport to the valley in a smog caused by auto exhaust. Brewer had Attashah's words on his mind as they drove. Without ANAC/23419.PRN, all the rest was so much junk. He glanced at Dice and wondered if he was going to cut and run as Attashah had predicted.

"Jesus," Dice said. "I can't believe it. The last time I was here this was all farmland—peaches and stuff—with some computer plants here and there."

He was looking out at one industrial plant after another, lining both sides of the highway and covering the hillsides that flowed away to the horizon.

Brewer looked out at the buildings as he drove by. "It's all going to go back to farmland again if the Japanese pull another 1981 on these guys."

"What happened in 1981?"

"Around here they call it the second Pearl Harbor. In '81 these computer companies went to market with a revolutionary new product, only to find the Japanese had got there firstest with the mostest. Nearly ruined them." Brewer stopped the car. "Here we are, Dice."

"What's this?"

They stopped on the soft shoulder of the road, across from a large plant surrounded by a high chain link fence. Along the front wall of one building, plastic letters announced PRYSBYL COMPUTER ENGINEERING.

Dice smiled at him. "You're kidding. We're going to crack Prysbyl?"

"Yes."

"You got to be nuts to try that, Charlie. Take me back to the airport."

MCCALL PHONED BORDEN at his home in Annapolis at 1:00 A.M. and rousted him out of bed.

"Listen, Borden. I just had a hunch that woke me up. I think they're going to hit Prysbyl's in the next forty-eight hours. You call your contacts in San Francisco and stir them up. Get them to do a stakeout around the plant."

"Bobby, that goddam plant is impregnable."

"There's no such thing. The Iranians have to have those parts and the guy they hired is going to be working full time finding a way into that plant to get them."

"Bobby, God Himself couldn't get through that alarm system."

"God is not a class-A smuggler."

"Oh, come on, Bobby. No one can get through that system."

"I know someone who can. It woke me up. Where's Dice?"

"God knows."

"Find him. Quickly."

Borden sat down sleepily on the bottom steps of his staircase and thumbed through his pocket address book. He yawned mightily as he dialed a San Francisco number. He wondered how he was ever going to find Dice.

DICE SAT IN THE CAR outside the Prysbyl plant and drew diagrams on a piece of paper in his lap. "It's like five redundant systems in one," he said. "First of all, there's TV surveillance of the whole operation—along all the main corridors and hallways, in the offices, and in the plant and the warehouse. Then every door and window is wired for sound. On top of that there's an airflow monitoring system that detects the temperature of human bodies—ninety-eight point six plus or minus one and a half degrees. Furthermore there's electric eye circuitry at all key stations. And there's a pack of guard dogs locked inside for the night. And each one has fangs that long."

Brewer nodded. "And there's two guys sitting in a car who need some parts from that plant."

"Correction," Dice said. "There's one guy sitting in a car who needs some parts. There's another guy sitting next to him who's getting ready to fly back to the East Coast—allll by his little self. Sorry, Charlie."

NOW BREWER WAS drawing diagrams in his lap. "Not one of those systems is foolproof," he said.

"Yeah, but when you put them all together—"

"But why do that? Consider them separately."

"Oh, come on, Charlie. It's just crazy to try. If you'd told me what you were up to, I wouldn't have come out here. They make a lot of secret stuff in there for the military. You try to break in there and you're up not just for B and E and the local stuff. They can get you for spying, stealing state secrets, and a whole list of federal goodies that will get you put away forever. Guaranteed."

"One person can crack it, Dice. You."

"No."

"Okay, then show me how to. One system at a time."

Dice sat and thought. "You really want to give it a whirl?"

"Yes."

Dice took the pencil. "Charlie, if you make one miscue in there, all the inner doors automatically shut, the alarms go off, and you're locked in there with a bunch of dogs that eat you, starting at the toes and working up to the nose. Anyone still living when the guards come will wish he was dead."

"Tell me about the temperature system."

"They have a system that constantly circulates air through the whole installation. It also controls the heating system and the air-conditioning system. Then they have these monitors that are constantly measuring the air as it circulates. If any monitor detects a temperature of ninety-eight point six, plus or minus one and a half points, it signals the control panel in the security room. Maybe if you got a guy who had a fever of a hundred and four, he might get through. That's why the dogs don't set it off. Their body temperature is a hundred and two or something like that."

"Has anyone ever cracked it?"

"Not to my certain knowledge. The manufacturer says no."

"How can we lower our body temperatures?"

"Die."

BREWER NOW ASKED HIM: "Have you ever defeated a TV monitoring system?"

"No."

"How about a phaser? You know—it's like a television zapper. It shuts down the sound."

Dice sat up warily. "You mean the phaser on a jet fighter?"

"Doesn't that cut off every second or third TV impulse?"

Dice said, "It breaks the signal into pulses so it becomes too weak to make a picture on the enemy's monitoring screen."

Brewer smiled at him. "That's exactly what we need."

"Great," Dice answered. "We just walk up to the nearest jet fighter and unscrew a phaser and lug it into Prysbyl's with us like a coffin."

"Can you make one?"

"Believe me, Charlie, if you could make one, somebody would have already done it."

"Why can't you make one?"

Dice shrugged.

"A jet fighter," Brewer said, "needs a unit that will operate over a tremendous distance. We're talking a few thousand feet at the most."

Dice was staring with disgust at the Prysbyl sign. "Face it, Charlie. Prysbyl's has us beat. We're not going to get in there."

ON THE WAY BACK to their motel, Brewer asked, "What can we do about the dogs?"

"That may be the toughest part of all. The dogs wear a sensor in their collars. It measures heartbeat and blood pressure. If you kill the dog the sensor reports that the heartbeat stopped and the alarm goes off. If you don't kill the dogs, they chew your leg off, which makes it very hard to steal the parts you want."

Brewer considered that. "Tell you what. I'll solve the dog problem if you solve the other four."

"No. I tell you what, Charlie. I go home and you work on all five problems and I'll come see you on visiting day in the sneezer."

"You don't have much faith, Dice."

"You're going to fail and go to jail," he told Brewer. "And I'm not going with you." Echoes of Attashah.

"Okay. Here's a better offer: I'll solve the dog problems and the temperature problem if you solve the others."

"Go shit in a hat and pull it over your ears."

DICE LOVED CHINESE FOOD. Brewer ordered a large quantity of it and brought in several cases of cold beer. Then when Dice was relaxed, softly burping and gargling his beer, Brewer had another go at him.

"Dice, I've solved this whole problem. Are you ready?"

"Entertain me."

"First of all about the ambient temperature gauges. I can beat them."

"How?"

"With dry ice. I can strap pieces of it in special containers on my arms and legs and waist and on my head. That will hide my true temperature."

Dice grinned at him. "You're pretty damned smart, Charlie. I would never have thought of that in a million years."

"You ain't heard nothing yet. I can beat the television surveillance with a frequency impeder. What that will do is turn each TV screen to snow as I walk by the camera. Of course, I have to strap the damned thing on my back with an automobile battery for power, but it'll do the job."

"Beautiful," Dice said with a smirk. "What about the electric eyes?"

"Oh, they're easy. You know they're set high so those dogs won't set them off. All you have to do is crawl under them."

Dice's smile broadened. "And how about the circuit breaker alarms on all the doors and windows?"

"Easy. We cut through the roof or through a wall."

"Marvelous," Dice said. "Fantastic. Now what do you do about the police dogs? And don't tell me you're going to feed them steak. They're trained to ignore it."

"I've solved that problem brilliantly," Brewer answered. "Are you ready?"

"Oh, I just know it's going to be wonderful."

"We'll bring our own dog."

"What can one dog do against four or five trained attack dogs?"

"I'll bring a girl dog."

"So?"

"She'll be in heat."

Dice studied Brewer's face for a long time, bemused and shocked.

"Well," Brewer said, "how do you like my plan?"

At last Dice caught the glint in Brewer's eye. And then as he chewed on his egg roll, he began to laugh. "What a picture. You drive right up to the building in a truck with a heavy-duty compressor and a jackhammer. You drill through the wall. That beats the window and door alarms. Then you climb through the hole, pouring off smoke from the dry ice to fool the temperature sensors. And, to beat the television monitors, you're wearing the frequency impeder and the automobile battery on your back—Christ, what a hernia you're going to get from that. You're on your hands and knees to avoid the electric eyes. And behind you you're dragging a hundred-and-fifty-pound police dog in heat plus another one who's on her back making new police dogs. And underneath it all, you're wearing a suit of armor so the other dogs can't chew on your legs." He burst into peals of laughter. "Oh, God. I'm going to die. There you go crawling down the hall, clanking and honking and sparking and smoking and kicking the dogs, trying to find the parts in a dark warehouse. Christ, I'd pay money to see pictures of you."

"Why don't you come along, Dice, with a camera? It's a story you can tell your grandchildren?"

But Dice didn't answer. He sat laughing until the tears streamed.

IT WAS HOPELESS. Dice would have no part of the break-in. There was simply no technology available to them that could break through so many alarm and surveillance systems.

Indeed, Dice was so set against the idea, he insisted on getting away from the whole valley. He didn't like being confined to their motel rooms when there was a perfectly good and convivial bar down the street. He didn't like bringing in food to avoid being seen in restaurants. He was bored and lonely.

"We'll have to find another way," Brewer said.

Dice became wary. "What other way?"

"Well, if we can't break in after hours, maybe we can go in during the day."

"Oh yeah? Let me see you write that scenario."

For the rest of the evening, Dice watched television and drank beer. When he went off to bed, Brewer said to him: "If you want, you can catch a flight for New York tomorrow."

"What about you?"

"I have to get those parts, Dice."

Dice shrugged and went off to bed.

To MOLLIFY HIM, Brewer took Dice out to breakfast in the morning.

"Sorry about this caper, Charlie," Dice said. "It's just too dangerous."

"It's okay," Brewer said. "I've solved it."

"Yeah, how?"

"It's no big thing, Dice. I'll handle it after I put you on the plane."

"Yeah? What are you going to do?" Dice put on a preparatory smile, ready for another absurd solution.

"Don't worry about it." Brewer read his newspaper.

"Hey, Brewer. You think I let the side down, don't you?"

"Not a bit of it. You're the security-system expert. If you say it can't be done, it can't be done."

"Then how are you going to get in?"

"I won't. If I can't get in, I'll make the parts come out to me."

Dice began to smile again. "Okay. Lay it on me."

"Finish your coffee, Dice. You're going to miss your plane."

"Charlie, I'm sorry."

"Don't be sorry. You did your best."

THERE MUST HAVE BEEN fifty places between their motel and the airport where Brewer could kill Dice and dump the body. And he examined every one as they drove.

Dice became a chatterbox, trying to smooth it over with Brewer. He must have asked two dozen times how Brewer planned to get the parts.

Brewer barely heard him. He studied the road ahead, searching out secluded spots. If Dice got on that plane to New York, he was a ticking time bomb that could blow the whole operation.

The miles rolled smoothly under the wheels of the rented car, getting ever closer to the airport. And still Brewer didn't stop. At last he found a turn-out that led to a weed-grown thicket, choked with litter and blown newspapers. He pulled in there and stopped.

"What are we here for?" Dice demanded.

"The payoff."

"What payoff?"

"This is the end for us, Dice. The last job. It's been nice working with you." Brewer pulled his attaché case up on his lap and popped the latches. Watching Dice's doubt-filled eyes, he lifted the lid and reached inside.

"You know, Charlie, you got a hell of a mind. We could go into business together. Working for corporations. Lots of bread. They'll pay big bucks for your kind of thinking. I mean legitimate stuff, showing them how to make better security systems, preventing people from stealing their industrial secrets, catching spies inside the company. Stuff like that. Big money. Real big bucks."

Brewer shrugged. "I've got other fish to fry, Dice. But why don't you do it?"

"Nah. I don't have your smarts, Charlie. I'm good with the equipment but not with the selling and the contacts and the angles. I'm pretty bad shooting the angles. It takes a shrewd cookie like you to handle those animals in the business—worse than anything in the arms racket. Nah, you and me—that's a combination."

"Thanks for the invite, Dice."

Brewer drew his hand out of the attaché case and held it out to Dice. "Here."

"What's this?" Dice took the packet of bills.

"Count it," Brewer said.

Dice counted it. "Jesus, Charlie, this is more than generous."

"That's okay. You were a big help."

"Honest to God, Charlie, I'm sorry about this caper. I mean you got to understand that—"

"It's okay. I do understand."

"Charlie. It was great working with you. I learned more about shooting the angles from you in a couple of weeks than I learned during my whole career with the Uncle. I'd sure like to work with you again."

Brewer started the automobile engine. He drove the car to the airport.

BREWER WATCHED Dice's plane take off and wondered how much time he had left before Dice would telephone Mc-Call. In McCall's sunny, book-lined office, in front of the pictures of McCall's mother and wife and kids staring out from their frames like a Greek chorus, Dice would cut a deal with McCall.

And then Dice would spill his guts.

AT FIVE THAT EVENING, Brewer was preparing to break into a San Jose business office. The company name was Argosy Ventures Inc., and it made components on contract to the military.

Argosy's complex of manufacturing buildings itself was as carefully protected by security systems as Prysbyl's was. But Brewer wasn't interested in that. After putting Dice on his plane, Brewer had spent most of the day checking out companies in the Silicon Valley that specialized in military hardware. Driving up and down Route 101, which ran like a vein through the valley, Brewer examined some twenty companies that were listed in the Military Purchasing Manual he held in his lap.

It was almost five and getting dark when he found Argosy. He made a careful study of the company's manufacturing complex first—the fencing, the dog kennel, the guards at the gate, the flood lights. Beyond them, he was sure, were the redundant security systems, elegant state-of-the-art monitoring devices and hardware that had made Dice run for home.

But it wasn't the manufacturing complex that attracted him. It was the executive offices. These were in a separate compound a few blocks away, where the security was considerably less determined.

He parked in the executive parking lot and sat studying the building. Employees were coming from various exits in the building, and the parking lot was rapidly emptying. He could see one security man at the front door seated at a desk. The building itself was fully lit, and the cleaning people were already working in some of the lower offices.

Inside the glassed-in lobby was a company directory. A small sign said PURCHASING SUITE A310. At the back parking lot were four Argosy Ventures delivery vans.

Brewer felt Argosy was ideal for his needs.

He drove off.

BREWER RETURNED shortly after ten that night. Carrying a box and several shopping bags stuffed with rolls of paper, he went up to the main entrance and rang the night bell. The security guard came to the glass door and looked at him.

Brewer held up a job order so the guard could see it through the glass. The guard opened the door.

''What's it for?'' he asked.

''I'm supposed to decorate the rear wall of the main purchasing department. Let's see—room A310. It's a farewell party for tomorrow morning. It's a surprise.''

The security guard scratched his head. ''Never heard of this before.''

"Never heard of it?" Brewer said. "It's how I make my living. Office surprise parties."

The guard stared dully at Brewer's packages. "That's all you're going to do—put some streamers on a wall?"

"That's it. Takes half an hour or so."

"Okay." The guard led him down a hall. "Through that door. Don't mess with anything in there."

"Perish the thought," Brewer said.

ONCE INSIDE THE MAIN ROOM, Brewer went right to work with tape and crepe paper rolls, standing in his stocking feet on desks to reach up high on the wall. When he got several streamers attached, he jumped down and went through a desk, then another.

He looked around the room for more desks, then walked into one of the cubicles. Quickly he riffled the various blank forms in the drawers. No luck. He went to the cubicle next door and checked the drawers.

This time he found what he was looking for: a neat stack of blank Special Delivery Purchase Order forms. With them he found another form: Military Procurement Restricted Parts Purchase Order Authorization form #PUF/USMIL/86767549. He quickly folded several of each form, pushed them into a white envelope, and put the envelope into his box containing festive decorations.

Then he jumped up on the desk and strung the crepe paper along the back wall. In ten minutes, he had several streamers intertwined high up near the ceiling. In the middle he'd affixed a card that said GOOD LUCK. It was time to leave.

The guard returned.

"What do you think?" Brewer asked. He picked up his staple gun and reels of tape and rolls of paper and dropped them back into the carton.

"You do that for a living?"

"Sure."

"I'd rather be a guard." He carried Brewer's shopping bags with the leftover signs and ribbon clusters as they walked to the front door.

Brewer drove back to his motel and carefully filled out both forms with a word processor, printed them on dot matrix printer, and signed them. Then he went to bed.

BEFORE DAWN the next morning, two men met in the parking lot adjacent to the Federal Court House in San Francisco. They both got into one car and drove off toward the Silicon Valley.

"Bobby McCall better have this right," the driver said. "I wouldn't get up at this hour to save my mother from a burning building."

"I wouldn't get up at this hour to leave a burning building," his partner said. "What's the name of this outfit again?"

"Prysbyl Computers."

"That's where those guys tried to break in last year."

"That's right. Five-to-ten for the three of them. They should never have carried the guns in with them."

"Maybe this guy we're after is smarter."

"I don't know. I think they make them dumber every year. I wish I was back in bed."

AT 6:00 A.M. a cab picked Brewer up at his motel and drove him back to Argosy Ventures' executive offices. It let him off at the diner across the road.

It was still quite dark, a half hour before dawn, with a bare tinge of light in the eastern sky. Brewer walked across the highway and down a side road to the back of the executive parking lot. The four Argosy Ventures delivery trucks sat under floodlights. Through an office window, he could see his streamers and the sign: GOOD LUCK.

"Good luck," he echoed.

Brewer hurried along a line of trees until he got within twenty feet of the vans, then crossed a concrete apron. With several quick movements of a locksmith's tool he popped the door lock on one of the vans and stepped inside. He cut the wires to the ignition switch, stripped them, and twisted them together. The truck started on the first try.

With the lights off, he drove the truck along the back of the parking lot and out through the rear exit. Two blocks away he put the headlights on and hurried through the darkness to Prysbyl Computer Engineering.

THE TWO MEN drove in silence down Route 101 from San Francisco. They were just outside East Palo Alto when the driver said: "Gotta weewee. That's French for yes yes."

"Time for a coffee break," his partner said. "How much farther?"

"Not much." He drove into a diner parking lot.

PRYSBYL'S LOADING PLATFORM opened at 7:00 A.M., and Brewer was the first delivery truck through the gates. The guard took one look at the Military Procurement Restricted Parts Purchase Order Authorization form and waved him through. Brewer drove to the rear of the complex and backed the van up to the long loading platform.

Most of the warehouse doors were open; inside, the parts department was already busy. Men in coveralls worked behind long counters, pushed hand trucks, and climbed ladders in front of ten-foot shelving filled with parts. A large sign said JUST-IN-TIME PURCHASE ORDERS GO TO SECTOR 14.

Brewer climbed up on the loading platform and walked to sector 14. He laid both forms on the counter.

"Just-in-Time P.O." Brewer said.

The inventory man behind the counter took a look at the forms, then at Brewer.

"Never saw you before. You new?"

"No," Brewer said. "I've been around a while. Can you hurry this order, please? They're really screaming."

The counter man shrugged and pulled out a directory. He checked the company name against a master list. Then he studied the Military Procurement form.

He said, "Well at least someone's on the stick. This is the first time I see this new procurement form. Beats the socks off the old one. Too complicated." He walked away.

Brewer watched him: He walked far down a long, narrow corridor to a wall phone and dialed a number. Brewer wondered what it was about the papers that the counter man didn't like. Brewer turned and studied the cyclone fence. If anything was wrong with that paper, he was trapped. No place to hide. No way out. His instinct told him to get into the van and drive off.

He stood and waited. The counter man had disappeared.

THE TWO AGENTS from San Francisco arrived at Prysbyl's and pulled up to the gate. The driver showed his badge. "We're here to see Metzer."

"Security building," the guard said, pointing. "Park your car there and walk through that door."

TEN MINUTES LATER, the counter man returned with another man. The other man held Brewer's papers.

"Where did you get these forms?" he asked.

Brewer sighed. "Hey. You got any problem with the paper, call the office, okay? I just drive the truck."

"Uh huh." The man studied the forms again. "Hmmmm." He looked at the counter man. "It's okay, I guess. I mean, you people—" he looked at Brewer "—aren't using this part for anything so far as we know. Now you order it out of the blue. From Just-in-Time inventory."

Brewer pointed at the form. "See that number. You call it and tell them your problem. And I'll go back and tell them you're holding up the order. I get my pay in either case."

The man took a long questioning look at Brewer, then handed the paper to the counter man. "Fill it," he said and walked away.

The counter man went down another long corridor. Brewer waited again. He turned and surveyed the loading platform. Maybe that second guy was making a phone call to Argosy. Brewer fought a strong impulse to get into the van and drive away.

Then another Argosy Ventures delivery van drove around the corner and down the line. The driver pulled into the platform five spaces away from Brewer's van.

Brewer quickly turned away and lowered his head. The driver got out of the van and clambered up onto the loading platform. He stepped through a doorway.

Brewer told himself to run like hell. Instead he held his breath and waited.

He saw the counter man at the end of the corridor. He was chatting with another man, nodding and stepping away, then resuming the conversation. He turned and looked directly at Brewer. He talked again, nodding again. He walked toward Brewer carrying a small box. He paused again to speak to another man. Both of them looked at Brewer. Then he made his way to the counter.

"Sign here," he said to Brewer.

Brewer signed a scrawl. The counter man shoved the small box across the counter along with carbons of the order forms.

"Pass," Brewer said.

The man wrote out the gate pass, looked at a clock and penciled in the time, and pushed the pass across the counter. Brewer saluted and turned to leave. The driver of the other Argosy van was standing on the platform looking at the truck, then at him.

Brewer skipped off the platform and waved to the other driver. Trying to be casual, he stepped into the van, started the engine, and deliberately drove toward the gate. In his side mirror he could see the other driver still staring after him.

"Seven come eleven," Brewer said. "Let me have it all, Lady Luck." He drove up to the gate and waited in line as the guard handled two trucks in front of him. It took forever. When Brewer drew up to the guard shack, he saw the other Argosy van driving toward the gate.

The guard checked Brewer's papers and waved him through. As he drove off, Brewer saw two men from the security shack waving at the guard and running toward him.

Brewer headed south. In his side mirror he saw a car pull through the gate and follow him. It was driving very fast.

"Hot damn," Brewer said.

The car openly pursued him now. About a mile ahead was the motel. Brewer pressed the accelerator to the floor. In his mirror he could see the car still racing after him.

Brewer passed the motel and turned at the next side street. He turned into a driveway and rolled behind a garage. He jumped out. He hurried through a thicket and across a field toward the back of the motel. A woman at a kitchen window watched him go.

A moment later the car turned in and raced by the driveway, then stopped and backed up. When Brewer reached the motel, he saw the woman hurry from her house to the car.

The car turned and hustled back to the intersection. Brewer would never get to his car. He turned and ran back across the field to the van and got in it. He raced it down the driveway onto the side road and drove away, making a big loop. Five minutes later he arrived back at the motel from the other direction and drove the van to the back. Quickly he jumped into his own car and started the engine.

As he pulled out of the motel, the other car was just turning in. The two men were searching for the van.

Brewer turned north and raced off.

HE DROVE the entire distance to the airport expecting to encounter a police roadblock at any moment. He abandoned the car at San Mateo. From there he took a cab to the airport.

He felt he was leaving a trail a mile wide.

He checked in with the airline, kept his overnight bag, and walked toward the departure gate. He had twenty minutes to go. He went to the metal-detecting station, put his bag on the conveyor belt, and stepped through a metal-detecting frame under the eyes of a guard. No alarms sounded. He recovered his bag and commenced the walk toward the departure lounge. Fifteen minutes to go.

The plane was delayed. Fifteen minutes turned into twenty, then twenty-five. Brewer paced. He watched the long corridor back to the metal-detecting station, looking for police.

He told himself he was safe. They might not have found the van yet. And if they did, they might not have gotten his rental car's license number. And if they did, they certainly couldn't have found the car itself yet. And if they did, they would not know that he'd taken a cab to the airport yet. And if they did, they had a whole airport to search and— And if he escaped, it would be only with the greatest good luck.

The flight attendant called all passengers to board the plane.

Now he sweated out the slow shuffle of passengers filing up the passageway to the jet, the shuffle along the aisle to his seat. The stowing of gear, the chatting with the stewardesses, the fooling with newspapers and glasses and seat belts.

Finally, the doors were shut and sealed. The plane rolled out on the runway to take off. Six hours nonstop to New York.

When the plane was airborne, he opened his bag and eased out the Prysbyl box. Inside were 144 chips. ANAC/23419.PRN. The last pieces on Iran's shopping list.

12

McCall returned to the empty safe house to pick up three days' taping of Rock's phone calls.

Rock had a long conversation with the yacht *Lipstick Two* in the Bahamas. Still in Paris and still pining for the child in Cairo, Rock discussed her at length. *Lipstick Two* tried to entice him to the Bahamas with "someone nearly as nice." But Rock declined. There was a chance he might see the child in Cairo after all.

There were a number of other calls he didn't return.

Only Beeldad in Madrid was called regularly. And then they both spoke in a code with innuendo. Rock was insisting on the absolute trustworthiness of the explosives. "The usual sources won't do, Beeldad. This stuff has to be absolutely reliable." Beeldad agreed to redouble his efforts.

AT 7:30 THAT EVENING, Brewer took the British Airways flight from JFK in New York to London. At 10:00 P.M. McCall flew from Washington. His destination was also London.

HARROW SCHOOL lies about twelve miles northwest of the center of London.

Brewer arrived there in a rented car in late afternoon. He gazed about the grounds, then glanced skyward. The brilliant and dry autumn weather was about to end. The streaming sunlight would soon be smothered by flotillas of black clouds sailing from the North Atlantic.

On the playing fields, young athletes from some of Britain's wealthiest families scrimmaged, shouting urgently to one another. Beyond them, straggling into the first Harrow building, constructed in 1611, was a late-season tour group.

Brewer found the boy's room without difficulty, at the top of a winding stone staircase probably three hundred years old. Brewer rapped on the door. Then again. He tried the door and it opened easily.

Brewer stepped inside. The boy was a sports jock: Cricket bats hung on the wall. Photographs of a soccer team holding a silver cup. A pair of tennis rackets leaned against a wall. And peering out of a closet at Brewer was a golf bag. Hung over the closet door, tied by shoestrings, was a pair of track shoes.

Brewer heard the sound of steps on the stone stair. A boy. He called to another boy angrily: "Half an hour, I said, dammit!" He was just outside the door. "No, no, Rogers! That's the wrong one." His steps descended.

Brewer looked out of the window. The boy was wagging a finger at another, smaller boy. Both wore cycling gear, including a leather box cap.

Brewer stepped into the closet and rooted in a canvas bag. His hand found just what he wanted. He straightened up, crossed the room in three strides, and exited through the door. He walked along a stone balcony to another stairway and descended to the courtyard at the other side of the building.

The boy waved Rogers off with another admonition. "In a half hour, Rogers! Be there!" And he mounted the steps to his room.

THE DIFFICULTY with the clandestine life is the paranoia that trails after it. It induces a permanent state of mental furtiveness. The eyes are forever glancing over the shoulder.

A simple meeting for even the briefest of conversations becomes fraught with problems that match those of a major diplomatic conference. Where shall we meet? Is it safe? Does it have escape routes? Is it too much in the open? Do we blend into the surroundings? What are the chances that we will be observed? It mustn't be too secret or the opposition will read all kinds of meanings into that. But not too public—for chance and bad luck happeneth to all agents.

Then there's the problem of getting to the meeting. Evasive action is employed to elude shadows. Switching cabs, taking the Underground, then jumping off the train at the last possible moment, making feints, using decoys. The antics can be amusing.

Brewer dispensed with all that. He simply got on the Underground near his hotel and rode to the British Museum.

But he knew that Attashah would make elaborate maneuvers, especially in London, where he was well known to the exiled Iranian community. Attashah knew his name was on more than one anti-Khomeini hit list. He was very careful to conceal himself in that city.

In fact it was Attashah himself who chose the meeting place: the British Museum, late in the afternoon, in the hall of the Elgin marbles.

From the Underground, Brewer walked in a drizzle to the museum. Guards at the door were searching packages, attaché cases, and handbags routinely.

Attashah was already there, playing the assiduous tourist, staring at the marbles and tapping his chin with the guidebook. He wore as usual his black suit, white shirt, and muted blue polka-dot tie. Over his left arm hung a raincoat and the crook of a large black umbrella. London, the land of the black mushrooms.

There were only two other people in the whole room: an elderly couple, deeply engrossed in animated conversation in front of one of the friezes as they thumbed through several texts.

Brewer walked up to Attashah directly and nodded at him, then watched the pained expression on Attashah's face as the lidded eyes glanced about. Attashah cleared his throat irritably.

"You've got good taste, Attashah." Brewer swept a hand in the air. "The Elgin marbles."

"Stolen, I believe, from the Greeks," Attashah said.

"Saved from destruction by the Turks, some say." Brewer grinned at him. "Aren't the Turks related to the Iranians?"

Attashah's back stiffened. Did anyone call him Rooley? Or Roo? Did he ever roll a passionate maiden in the hay? Did one ever say, "I love you, Roo," in Iranian or in English— in pig Latin, for that matter? Better still, did Attashah ever, with an erotically husky voice, say, "I love you, duckie?" Was he ever a carefree boy writing love poetry or was he always an implacable, humorless fanatic? Would the world be better off without him?

The fanatic was a fanatic without choice. He was born that way, with the genes arranged that way. And as soon as life set him on his little feet, Attashah had scurried into life looking for a cause to dedicate himself to. No choice. No free will. It was stamped on his rump like a manufacturer's label: Fanatic.

"These marbles belong in Greece," Attashah said. "They are part of the Greek heritage—no matter what reasons the British give for bringing them here." He fixed his judgmental eyes on Brewer. "The thief always has his excuses."

"Yes, I do. My excuse is I was paid handsomely by the Iranians."

"The situations are hardly comparable, Mr. Brewer," Attashah answered. His eyes said, "Someday I will kill you, Mr. Brewer."

"Why not? I'm a thief—a very successful one."

Attashah's eyes searched Brewer's. "Did you—are you saying you got the ANAC parts?"

"Yes. A hundred and forty-four of them. Would you like more than that?"

Attashah lost his composure. He exhaled sharply, then tried repeatedly to clear his throat. He was clearly stunned. In his eyes was barely concealed joy. "Splendid," he said at last.

"That's the lot, Attashah. I've got your grocery list safely stowed and ready to move."

Attashah looked at him with something close to admiration. "You are a very gifted man, Mr. Brewer."

Brewer ignored the praise. He still heard other words from Attashah from another time: "You have no choice, Mr. Brewer," he had said in his executioner's voice.

With his eyes roving over the Elgin marbles on a damp day in London town, Attashah was daring to dream. He was trying on his role of Iranian hero, the man who engineered the American parts caper. How rapidly his star was rising in the Persian sky.

THE MINISTER'S SECRETARY signed for the package. Without touching it she quickly called a gentleman from security, who hurried it off in a bomb truck across London to the laboratory where a group of explosives experts waited to have a look-see.

There the wrapping was carefully photographed. Then the package was weighed. Then the interior silence was explored by a medical stethoscope which searched for the sound of ticking or a movement of parts within. Magnetic detectors sought some sign of lethal life—a battery or two, perhaps—or for metallic parts (there were none). Later, a series of X rays revealed a perfect sphere inside with no contours to suggest a detonator.

One of the experts, groping for a simile, noted that it was about the size, weight, and density of a cricket ball. Or a plastic hand-bomb, said another sourly.

Before opening the package, the lab men submerged it in a tub of water for half an hour.

Then, with great care, the soggy wrapping was pulled off. The carton was snipped open. Within, the tissue wrapping, now in sopping shreds, was pulled away with tweezers. And there was revealed a cricket ball—a combat veteran of many innings, gore-scarred and grass-stained. On its surface was the single word HARROW.

Sheepishly, the security man hastened back to the Minister's office, bearing the ball in a large manila envelope. Inside, along with the cricket ball, was their official laboratory report outlining procedures used and conclusions drawn: a used cricket ball from Harrow public school, mailed from Harrow three days before.

AFTER A PLEASANT LUNCH the Minister returned to his office to find the manila envelope containing the ball and the lab report. To him the message was quite clear.

He called his son at Harrow. The boy was hunted up and brought to the telephone. His father asked after his health and chatted with him for a few moments.

"Did you send me one of your cricket balls?" he asked his son.

The boy was stunned. Why on earth would he ever mail a cricket ball?

Afterward, the Minister sat in his office, staring at the cricket ball on his desk and waiting for the phone call that was sure to come. On a hunch, he had a protective squad dispatched to Harrow to watch over his son.

Charlie Brewer called at four. He identified himself as Mr. Cricket and the Minister immediately accepted the call. They arranged to meet the next day at three.

THE WAYS of seducing a man who controls power are many, and Charlie Brewer had seen most of them used. He was guided by an old cliché tirelessly reiterated in the arms trade: All men are corruptible. There are no exceptions.

Even a British departmental Minister who wields great power behind closed doors is vulnerable: He may harbor shameful secrets; he has been passed over in favor of another; he has an ambitious wife; he has created a bleak, impecunious future through gaming indiscretions; he has deep affection for his young son at Harrow. No matter. Any one will do.

The pattern is usually familiar. After the question "What do you want me to do?" once the deed is done, a whispered phone message or a written note imparts a seven-digit number—a Swiss bank account number, in the name of a research group or a fund with a resounding philanthropic name. The Minister can use the money as he wishes—to pursue research or altruism (he is the sole holder and user of the secret fund) or to spend on his son who has so heedlessly lost his cricket ball. Such a handsome lad. Such a vulnerable child. Another politician is rendered submissive to the secret government of ruthless men.

SHORTLY BEFORE THREE that afternoon in Saint Paul's Cathedral, a group of Americans lumpishly strolled along behind a tour guide who pointed with still-dripping umbrella at statue after statue of British heroes. Here's Nelson, embodiment of Britain's dauntless spirit. And Wellington. And there in the shadows, peering quizzically out at the world, is the legendary Kitchener.

As they bumped along in their damp raincoats, the group craned their heads upward at the vast high dome, their coughs and sneezes carrying clearly.

It was a slow day for visitors. Arctic turbulence had sent a marine low-pressure system spinning down from Greenland. The meteorological service reported severe storms on the North Sea and predicted a week of rain. November was not a tourist month even in the best weather, and with the downpour outside, the tour group had the cathedral almost to itself.

The guide was discussing the lofty cathedral windows and the effects of the Luftwaffe bombings, when the left-most large cathedral door swung open. In dirty gray light the Minister entered, collapsing his large black umbrella and shaking it three times. He then walked to the last pew on the left and sat down, hat in lap.

The group, coughing and snuffling, continued on scuffing feet to the altar and to the memorial to the American war dead of World War II in the Jesus Chapel. It proceeded down a side aisle past the apse, the guide still wagging his umbrella skyward and calling off the features in practiced tones.

The damp little group proceeded along the aisle to the rear again. The doors swung open. The Minister was quite alone.

"Good afternoon, Minister," Charlie Brewer said.

The man turned in the pew and looked up at Brewer. "I don't believe we've met," he said.

"Quite right," Brewer replied. "We haven't."

"Yes, yes," the Minister said impatiently. He rubbed his hands and looked unhappily out at the vast world of interior cathedral walls and rising arches, reaching for heaven.

Brewer read the circles under the man's eyes, the drawn expression, the sallow complexion—classic signs of a man in a trap.

Brewer entered the pew behind the Minister and sat. "I have had a delightful tour of your most impressive cathedral, Minister," he said.

"I see." The Minister was unable to mask the anger and scorn he felt. With both hands resting on the crook of the umbrella, the man radiated imperiousness and arrogance. From one end of the year to the other, he would rarely address a Brewer. A man with enormous financial needs, he was also circumspect: He would never have permitted Brewer to approach him with a bribe. He dealt only with men from his own circles—school, party, class.

He betrayed his impatience. "How may I help you, Mr. Cricket?"

Brewer studied the side of the man's face in the sullen light. "A small assistance. Nothing to trouble you too much. Something you have done for others a number of times. And of course a little something for you from me in return, to express my appreciation."

The Minister seemed to relax a bit. His expression sifted Brewer's words. Something manageable. With compensation. Not blackmail. No threat to his son.

"You will accept my apologies, Minister, for the cricket ball. It served merely to get your attention."

"And as a threat?" The Minister leaned forward.

Brewer shrugged. "That won't be necessary. Your son is of no interest to me. I'm sure we can do business, Minister."

"What is this business?"

Brewer drew from his inner raincoat pocket an envelope. "A certificate, that's all."

The Minister opened the unsealed envelope, unfolded the sheet inside, and in the poor light studied the document. "An End User's Certificate."

"As you see."

"That's it?"

"Yes. That's it."

The Minister reread the document. "I see."

"Excellent, Minister. It will naturally require the usual 'walk through' for the appropriate authorizations. One doesn't want U.S. Customs impeding the shipment for lack of proper documentation. You can appreciate that, of course."

The Minister seemed flaccid, spent. He was expecting a threatened kidnapping of his son. And now that he was relieved of that concern, he was beginning to react to the bribery offer.

"I feel as though I am being raped," he said.

"But then, Minister, you are hardly a virgin. Shall I quote some appropriate chapter and verse—going back ten years to Mr. Peno Rus?"

"Enough. I will do this as quickly as possible."

"Excellent. To seal the bargain, I present you with a Habana Classico." Brewer extended a glass tube hermetically sealed and containing a cigar. "And, of course, the matches."

The Minister accepted the cigar. Then he took the matchbook and opened the flap. His eyes read the seven-digit number, then looked at Brewer.

"The usual fee, Minister."

The Minister tucked the envelope into his breast pocket. He handed the cigar back to Brewer. "Not my brand," he said. And the matchbook was thrust into a side pocket of his coat.

He arose without another word, strode to the large door at the left, placed his hat on his head, and stepped through the doorway, popping open his large black umbrella as he went. A moment later the huge door swung shut, and Brewer was alone in the dusk. Somewhere he could hear a jet of rainwater spattering on paving.

He looked down at the glass tube in his hand. Not his brand either. He would give it to the Syrian Fat Man in Paris. The Fat Man's brand was anything burnable. Brewer stood up. Now came the toughest part of his whole smuggling operation.

LONDON ALWAYS excited McCall. Bad weather notwithstanding. Even after a rain-filled two-year tour of duty in that city, he still liked rain. He recalled again that his son had been born there sixteen years before—while it was raining.

London was crowded. The attraction was an international bill of fare: The city offered a new play and two musicals from the United States, a ballet from Russia (complete with human-rights pickets), an Italian opera, the Berlin Philharmonic, an art exhibit from France, a Japanese trade show of new electronics products, and, at the Victoria and Albert Museum, a special presentation of Indian Art Under the Raj.

The British had put up new signs for their foreign visitors. LOOK RIGHT BEFORE STEPPING OFF KERB.

PENO RUS had his penthouse off Green Park in one of the most expensive areas of downtown London. In the late afternoon McCall strolled through the park in a heavy drizzle to examine the building. According to the report, Rus owned the entire structure.

In just thirteen years Rus had gone from the status of penniless Russian journalist who had been granted political asylum in England to a ranking among the wealthiest gun-runners in the world. Every stone and steel beam in the building had been bought with human blood and agony.

Like all great salesmen, Rus had dazzling charm and graciousness. A great psychologist and reader of men's souls, he knew instinctively to whom to offer a bribe and to whom to extol altruism. He had a paunchy body, like Pan piping through the woods with his nymphs—a body he dressed with British tailoring. The only flat note in his appearance was the almost Oriental flashiness of a diamond ring on his left pinkie.

It was Rus's throat, the fullness and fat of it, that intrigued McCall. That throaty wattle told McCall more than Rus's small Russian eyes did. It was a public confession of his sybaritic greed.

McCall had practically memorized the psychograph on Rus: claustrophobia, terror of heights, rarely flies, rarely travels except to his chateau near Nice. How did he manage to live in his penthouse? How could he use the elevator to get up and down? It must take a superhuman act of will for a claustrophobe to enter that shut-up steel box and ascend or descend six stories. McCall pictured Rus fighting his phobias every inch of the way, the damp brow, the shortness of breath, the mounting terror until the door opened to free him from his terror one more time.

But in Rus's eyes, wealthy British gentlemen lived in penthouses. And he was determined that he would have all the outward trappings, regardless of the terror. Give us this day our daily dread.

Well, how do you kill a man? In his career, McCall knew of possibly a hundred murders in the arms world. It was not a difficult art in itself. But to kill a Peno Rus—that was going to take great skill. Rus took every precaution, from burglar alarms to bodyguards, from bulletproof cars to anti-bomb patrols in his offices. He would not be the victim of a cheap shot. Still, he had his vulnerabilities. Everyone did.

McCall walked past Rus's doorman, who saluted him. Were there any flats to let? The doorman assured him there weren't—hadn't been for years. He went to a drawer in a lobby highboy and took out a card of the rental agents. But there was little hope, you see.

No matter. McCall had decided how Rus would die. It was extremely simple and appropriate: inside the elevator. Rus would drop down the shaft six stories from his penthouse to the bottom. He would do an appropriate imitation of the Tumbler's last cry. All that was needed was the man who would do the job. And McCall already knew who that would be. Major Mudd.

MAJOR ARCHBOLD MUDD was Rus's Master of the Arsenal.

He was a small and smoldering, peppery man. He had slick black hair and an unpleasant ferret's face which he had half-hidden behind a large guardsman's moustache. A graduate of Sandhurst, he was known to have many excellent contacts in the British bureaucracy and in the British military, an invaluable attribute that Rus exploited eagerly.

Unpleasant tales followed after Mudd. A story persisted that he had been discharged from the military for cowardice. He was accused of being a sneak. Some said he was vengeful and vicious, a back-shooter, a sniper from behind the garden wall, a house burner, a letter-bomb practitioner. Eager to be offended, he cherished his resentments.

McCall had taken some pains to learn about Mudd's ambitions and game plan. The key word was *snob*. A man of no particular antecedents, Mudd was a dedicated social climber who wanted to get his two sons into the best schools in England. He was raising them to be gentlemen in the City. Stockbrokers. Barristers, perhaps.

He was just the man to assassinate Peno Rus.

BEFORE GOING TO DINNER, McCall called Major Mudd at his home.

"You need to sharpen up your skills, Major," he said.

"Who's this?"

"Now who else would it be, Major?"

"Give me your number. I'll call you right back."

So Major Mudd was worried about wiretaps. Some ten minutes later he telephoned McCall.

"What is it you want?"

"It's not what I want, Major. The question is: Are you sure you want a piece of this quarrel between Rus and me? And are you sure you're siding with the winning team?"

"Where can we talk?" Major Mudd demanded.

"How about a nice chat in my car?" McCall suggested.

"Make it mine."

"Fine. Would you like to pick me up at the Marble Arch in, say, an hour?"

WHEN MAJOR MUDD picked him up in his Jaguar, the man was distraught. He was as carefully dressed as a tailor's dummy, in a custom-made houndstooth hacking jacket and a military-cut raincoat—but he nervously tugged at his cufflinks and stretched his neck out of his shirt collar.

"Well, how have you been, Major?"

"Bloody awful, now that you ask."

"You really botched the job, you know. I'm supposed to be in my grave."

"I didn't do it. Not me. It was Rus. Bloody fool. I told him not to use those hacks. That idiot they dropped down the stairwell could hardly make change of a pound note, and the other two—if their brains were dynamite, they wouldn't have enough to blow their noses." He looked at McCall with the ghost of a smile. "He nearly had a stroke when he got your note. 'Missed.' Dear God, I thought I was going to be rid of him that day. Deep-purple face he had. It's a bleeding miracle he didn't have a fatal heart attack. 'Missed.' Aha."

"Still in all, Major, it was not a nice way to try to kill me. Dropping down a stairwell."

"I told you, I had precious little to do with it. I think the man's gone mad. I mean, he's taking on the entire U.S. government, isn't he?"

"Then it's time to leave him."

"Leave him!" Mudd narrowly missed hitting a bus. "You and I have been through this before, haven't we, McCall? You know bloody well Rus has no ex-employees. He's paranoid about betrayal. If you quit, you die. And if he thought I was going to leave him—sweet Jesus. I'm master of his arsenal. I know too much. I'm a constant danger to him. I also have a personal score to settle with him and he knows it."

"What's that, Major?"

"It's personal, I told you. But Rus knows I could do him in for it."

"He must have done something terrible to you."

"To my family," Major Mudd said. "He's bound to make a move against me anytime now. Every day I wake up I say, 'Today's the day he's going to do it.' It'll be my bedroom that goes up. Or my car. I'm damned if I stay and damned if I leave. Imagine him taking on the U.S. government. I mean, you don't have to read tea leaves to know how that will turn out, do you?"

"It has already turned out, Major. Peno Rus is a dead man. Here's your chance to escape with a whole skin."

"What are you telling me? You're going to do it for Rus?" Major Mudd swerved widely around a truck, then slammed on his brakes to avoid hitting another car.

"Yes."

"Deliverance. Dear God. Deliverance." Major Mudd glanced sharply at McCall. "I don't want to know anything about it. Not a bloody word."

"Major, you're going to know everything about it."

"I am?"

"You're going to do the job."

Major Mudd skidded violently, flinging gravel and dirt as he rode his brake to a violent stop on the shoulder of the road. Then he looked with disbelief at McCall. "If you think I'm going to do away with Rus, you are a bleeding fucking madman."

"Now come on, Major. You're the only one who can do it and you know it. You don't have any other options. You can't run and you can't stay. And if you don't beat him to the punch, he's going to ace you."

The major's face had gone bone-white. He bunched his two fists in his lap and stared down at them. "Sweet Jesus."

"You've known in your heart for a long time you have to do it. And I'm just the man to help you. We share a common objective."

"How?"

"How what?"

"How am I—how is the job to be done?"

"Very simple. His elevator."

Major Mudd took a long time to read McCall's face. "Elevator." He shook his head slowly. "Bleeding monster you are."

"It's no worse than pitching a man down a stairwell, Major."

Mudd looked solemnly at him. "But it pulls you down to the same level with him, doesn't it?"

McCALL LEFT LONDON for Paris on the late-afternoon flight. It was pouring at Heathrow when he left and it was pouring at de Gaulle when he arrived.

He sat in his hotel room near the Pont de la Concorde. He watched the rain on his window and wrote some notes and letters, fighting off a strange feeling of depression. Later he had a leisurely and solitary meal in his hotel dining room.

At nine he left the hotel to keep his rendezvous with Jamil. He slumped in the seat of the dark cab listening to the beat of the windshield wipers.

McCall sat in the brasserie on Avenue de Clichy behind a large pane of glass and watched the rain pound down on the outside tables and chairs.

He was bemused with himself. In a few moments, he would set into motion a plot to kill another man. It would be violent, cold-blooded, premeditated murder. Without an indictment. Without a hearing. Without a jury trial. Without even a warning of any kind. It would be done in the back in the dark.

There were only a few people in the bar, and they sat in their raincoats, separate, turned inward, twisting their glasses morosely, stirring their coffee endlessly. No one talked. Occasionally, outside, a few people dashed up the rainy steps from the Metro and disappeared running into the darkness. The sad side of Paris.

Three murders. And all the while that he was considering this, in his memory, ineluctably, his Constitutional Law professor uttered two words over and over, wrote them endlessly with chalk that stuttered with passion across the blackboard: DUE PROCESS. DUE PROCESS. DUE PROCESS.

"It's the only thing that keeps man from a tragic slide back into the cave. Never, never forget: It was due process of law that made modern civilization possible. We cannot survive without it. Due process!"

Due process.

McCall told himself to get up, drop a few francs on the saucer, put on his raincoat and leave the brasserie, step down into the Metro and ride back to his hotel, and get the morning flight back to Washington. And find another way.

"There is no other way," he said almost audibly. He'd been over this ground so many times, he was weary of it.

Stand up. Leave. While there is still time to turn back. Before it is too late. He wondered if there really was a hell.

McCall decided to play a game with himself. A form of Russian roulette. He would prepare to leave the brasserie. If he got to the Metro steps before Jamil arrived, he would go back to Washington and cancel the whole plan. But if Jamil arrived first, the plan would go through. The fates would decide. Ready. Aim. Pull the trigger.

McCall stood. He put a few francs on top of the white cash-register slip in the saucer, deliberately slipped his arms into the sleeves of his raincoat, picked up his collapsible umbrella, and turned to walk the few steps out in the rain to the Metro stairway and the ride back to his hotel. Back to Washington. Back to Due Process.

Like Nemesis, a cab hurried out of the darkness and stopped at the curb. The gods had made their decision. Jamil stepped out.

SLIM AS A BOY, impeccably turned-out, Jamil walked grandly under the large black wheel of his umbrella, across the sidewalk, past the outside tables and chairs, and into the café. A regal procession.

He was expensively turned-out, as usual—tailored gray flannel suit, custom-made white shirt, and maroon foulard necktie, all elegantly contrived to set off his handsome olive boy's face and chestnut hair. He languidly cast off his raincoat, capewise. Then he sat. Or rather, he arranged himself in the chair.

He nodded at McCall. "So," he said.

"So," echoed McCall. So: there would be no flight back to Washington. There would be three assassinations.

"You will forgive me, I know, for insisting on a public place." Jamil waved an arm in benediction. "As you can see, no one we know comes here."

He watched McCall's unconvinced expression. "Well, you do see. It is a workingman's neighborhood. Just a corner brasserie on a rainy night with no one about. We are perfectly safe here."

"Your words are a great comfort," said McCall.

Jamil smiled at the sarcasm. "Alas. You are upset. But one cannot be too careful."

"Meeting in public is hardly careful."

"Meeting in a less public place is, for me, even less careful." Jamil had spoken on the matter. He dismissed it by changing the subject. "So, Mr. Smith . . ." He waited.

"I have some work," said McCall.

"Good."

"For you."

"Good. Anyone I know?"

"Perhaps."

"Indeed."

The waiter approached. Jamil favored him with a small smile as he gazed at the youth's blond hair.

"Alsace?" Jamil asked.

The waiter shook his head. "Brittany."

Jamil gazed frankly at the boy's body. *"Vive la Bretagne."* He ordered a Sambucca with a coffee bean and watched the waiter walk off.

"So. Someone I know." Jamil lit a cigarette with a gold lighter.

"Slane."

Jamil raised his eyes from the lighter flame and looked at McCall. "Oh. Slane. Yes. Slane." He pocketed the lighter and looked thoughtfully at McCall. "So you know about Slane and me?"

"I thought you'd be interested."

"Oh. Indeed."

"I've come to you, Jamil, because you have a reputation for discreet management of your affairs."

"Of course. I have never botched a job."

"I was talking about silence."

Jamil breathed smoke through his nose. "Yes. Well. That's essential, isn't it? Careers like mine are built on silence."

Jamil watched the waiter serve the drinks. He cast the youth a grateful small smile and watched him walk away. "Have you ever been to Brittany, Mr. Smith?"

"This project is going to take a good deal of planning, Jamil."

"Oh, yes. To do Slane will require a masterpiece. A great deal of planning. And time. It will take some time." Jamil turned large brown eyes to McCall. "It will also be expensive. Very expensive."

McCall's face remained expressionless.

Jamil reached a manicured fingernail into the Sambucca and hooked out the drowned coffee bean. "Fascinating, you know. This could be my *chef d'oeuvre.* What a marvelous challenge." He put the coffee bean into his mouth, kissed his wet fingertip, and contentedly chewed. The flavor of

Sambucca in the bean made him shut his eyes languidly. "Marvelous."

The conversation drifted. Jamil seemed to lose interest in the offer. Then, decisively, he drank the last of his Sambucca.

"I see." He sat back. He placed a thoughtful thin finger on his lips. "The first question one must ask is, can it be done at all? Is it doable?"

"There's more," said McCall.

"Oh?".

"He's to be killed with his own favorite weapon."

"Ah. His rifle. Poetic justice. You are an artist, Mr. Smith."

"Do you want to handle this, Jamil?"

"Handle it? I think this could make me the uncrowned king of my profession."

THE BRASSERIE EMPTIED and the waiters watched television while Jamil and McCall held a long conversation, exploring every aspect of the subject. Much of the time Jamil sat pensively turning his glass, deep in thought.

"Very clean," he said at last. "You will provide the setups, the locations, and the weapons. And I will provide the action. Very clean indeed."

He cast an eye at the white plastic shopping bag at McCall's elbow. FRERE JACQUES TOYS AND GAMES was printed on it in merry letters. In four languages.

McCall touched the bag. "Do you play pinochle, Jamil?"

"I think I should say yes."

McCall slid the plastic bag across the small table. Jamil took it and slipped out a cardboard box. *Pinochle* was printed on it in a flowing script. Inside were two decks of cards and a row of black chips. Jamil slid his fingernail along the spine of the chips, he counted fifty. He plucked one from the stack and glanced at the legend imprinted on it: PE-DRO'S CASINO LONDON.

Jamil raised his eyes to McCall's. Each black chip was worth $1,000.

"I have just become an avid lover of pinochle."

"The balance on delivery. Another fifty chips."

"A Slane might cost somewhat more than that."

"I see."

"I was thinking more in the range of a quarter of a million. After all, there are very few men with enough cunning to do Slane."

"It's too high, Jamil."

"Alas."

"One hundred fifty chips is all I can offer."

"I can't possibly do it for less than two hundred."

McCall reflected. Then he nodded. "Two hundred."

"Plus expenses of course."

"*Oui*, Monsieur Jamil."

Jamil smiled. Then he stood and draped his raincoat over his shoulders. "Then that is the end of Slane. *Au revoir*, Monsieur Smith, until November twenty-sixth."

Under his large black umbrella, Jamil walked into the pelting night. In his hand he carried the plastic bag containing the pinochle box. A creature come from darkness, he soon disappeared back into it.

On Rue Fontaine, Rock stood on the walk opposite the Café Chanticleer and studied the scattering of people seated at the tables inside. Several waiters stood with arms crossed, looking at the rain, murmuring to each other. It was a very slow night.

Rumbh sat at a central table reading a paper. Rock studied him carefully, then crossed the road and stood outside the café and looked even closer. There was something about the man he didn't trust. He seemed too well connected with the Egyptians. Maybe he was a Judas goat for the gooks in the Egyptian Ministry of Defense in Cairo. Rock told himself to be careful. He stepped into the café.

"Ah. Rock," Rumbh said, folding up his newspaper.

Rock nodded. "You said you had very good news."

Rumbh reached into the inner pocket of his suit jacket and pulled out an envelope. He handed it to Rock.

"What's this?" Rock tore the flap and pulled out a folded sheet of school paper. He opened it to see a note written in Arabic, a child's scrawl. Within the folds was a photograph. It was a shock, on a rainy night in Paris, in a café ababble with French, far away from her, far away from her Egyptian sunlight, to see her face looking directly at him. The photographer had caught that glance, that mixture of innocence and wantonness. Rock nearly gasped.

"Her parents have been persuaded to visit relatives in Alexandria. Upon their return, the father has been promised a position with the government of Cairo, a lifetime career."

"And the girl?"

"She remains in Cairo. With an elderly aunt."

Rock sat tapping the letter on his thumbnail, regarding Rumbh severely. "How do you do this? Who are your connections with?"

"Do you want my background, Rock?"

"I got your background."

"So?"

"I got a rundown on you. You have what is described as a long and distinguished career in crime, mainly in Asia. I know about your involvement with Ho Wat, selling U.S. arms left in Vietnam. I know about your caper in Malta. I know about Hong Kong and Broboff."

"Quite right, Rock," Rumbh said. "That breaks the ice very nicely."

"Yeah, well I know a lot of things about you. But I don't know anything either. I want to know what's your involvement in Egypt?"

"I have a client—an Arab gentleman of international stature—who does not want this hatchet-burying ceremony to take place. He wants to keep these two Arab factions at each other's throats."

"Yeah? Why?"

"Have you got a few hours?"

"Okay. Forget it."

"Oh, one other thing." Rumbh pulled out another piece of paper. "A translation."

"From her? You saw her?"

"Yes."

"What did you think?"

Rumbh looked frankly at Rock. "I prefer boys myself."

Rock read the translation. He frowned at it.

"She's studying English," Rumbh said. "In school. That's as close as she can come."

Rock now grinned at it. He could see her struggling with English block letters. Half of them were indecipherable.

"The coast is clear, Rock."

"Hmmmm. You know anyone in the Egyptian Ministry of Defense?"

"No. Should I?"

"You said you had a client."

"Oh, yes. Highly placed. You would recognize the name. Incidentally, it was he who recommended you for the job. A critically delicate matter, you can appreciate."

"Hmmmm." Rock looked at the photograph again. *The coast is clear*. He looked at Rumbh. "What if I say no?"

"No is no. If you turn us down, there isn't anyone else my Arab client would trust with this job. It would be a catastrophe if the bomb actually went off. You're the only one with the deft touch this job needs.''

Rock scratched his neck with the edge of the envelope. ''Okay. Let's go through the drill again. It's going to be in the Hotel Royal Nile on November twenty-sixth. Right?''

Rumbh looked past Rock out at the wet night. It was raining harder. ''Right,'' he said.

13

The rain had followed Brewer from London. But it was a different rain in Paris. London was unaffected by rain—a customary occurrence that was part of the setting. The city didn't miss a beat.

Paris became introspective and sad. It seemed to withdraw until the rain ended.

Brewer sat in the tiny lobby of the Taft hotel in Paris, not far from the Gare St.-Lazare. He read *France Soir* with scant interest, looking up occasionally at the wet street. He could see the fine drizzle dimpling the puddles.

The Taft was an old hotel, one of the many that at one time flourished around the train stations of Paris. Five floors and no elevator.

The lobby was a tiny affair. Marble flooring with an umbrella stand, one chair, and a small registration desk under the stairs. It told the inquirer exactly what the rooms were like abovestairs: all furnished alike from the same hotel outfitter sixty years before, all the same, and all in the same state of decay.

In each room a threadbare rug, a rickety double bed with an exhausted mattress that curled along the edges like a hammock, a creaking, sagging wooden chair. Old and discolored pseudo-lace curtains, a badly battered dresser, a sink, perhaps a bidet, and time-darkened wallpaper that once showed a garishly colored floral print. The woodwork would be scraped, scratched, peeling in places, and hand-rubbed along the door edge. There would be one light, overhead, hanging from the ceiling with one bare bulb that made anyone inside the room look ill and aged.

Day or night in any season, the hallways and stairways would be in darkness, lighted only by a lamp that would stay lit for about fifteen seconds. One spent one's time, going up or down, repushing fifteen-second light switches.

And throughout the hotel, from top to bottom, all five floors had the same deeply imbedded, ineradicable, offensive garlic odor from sixty years of cooking. And that was a puzzle because the Taft had no restaurant.

The census of such rooms in Paris must have been in the thousands; the recollection of them must have been burned into the memory of uncounted hordes of students, budget travelers, itinerant Algerian workers, and prostitutes.

THE FAT MAN was taking a long time. And that amused the young girl behind the desk. She smirked at Brewer, then barely but eloquently shrugged her left shoulder.

In the newspaper Brewer read a dismal account of the Paris traffic problem: The Boulevard Périphérique, which circled all of Paris, was suffering gridlock from the impossible traffic. It was jammed night and morning, turning a normal fifteen-minute commute into hours and hours of sitting and crawling while too many cars tried to use the same road at the same time. Paris was strangling. And no one knew what to do about it.

At last, Brewer heard a sound in the hallway. Two voices, low and urgent. The stairway light went on. "*Voilà*," a man's voice said on the stairway.

"But, monsieur," a woman's voice said, "it is only half the fee."

"So?" the man whispered. "I had only half the pleasure."

"But it is not my fault if—" The light clicked off.

"If what? When nothing happens, nothing happens in the wallet either." The stair light was put on again.

"Ah, monsieur. It was a failing on your part. I was ready. I did everything." Her whisper was barely audible now as she recited a list. The light went off again.

"So?" The man was unsympathetic. He switched the light on to descend.

"So, this is the third time you have failed."

"I see. Are you counting?"

Her voice became intimate, concerned. "*Cheri*. You worry. And the more you worry, the more difficult it is for you to—but you understand. I have other clients who occasionally—as you see."

"Other clients? Do you discuss me with your other clients?"

"Monsieur!"

"Listen. You don't discuss me with anyone." The light went on again.

"Monsieur, shall I give your appointment to a new client?"

"Another! No!"

"But I cannot afford half-fees, monsieur."

"Eh. *Voilà*."

"*Merci, cheri*," she said. "The next time—the very next time—anytime night or day, when you are ready, you come to me and we will accomplish this thing. Without charge! Do you understand? My honor is at stake."

"There is more than your honor at stake here," the man said. He began to descend the stairs.

Behind him the woman descended partway, her ample breasts swinging freely inside her gown. She made a pitying face at his descending back. She drew his fat shape in air with her hands and shook her head.

Then she descended another few steps and clutched his rotund face in her hands and kissed his mouth. She nibbled his lips. "I will not fail you. Do you understand?" She pulled him closer to her.

"Aha," she exclaimed. "What is this? See. You still have the capacity. Aha."

They embraced.

"You are a lion, *cheri*," she said. She pulled him up several steps. They embraced again in the dark hallway. "Aha," she said softly.

There was a scuffling and a stamping of feet, ascending. A door banged shut.

Brewer went back to the gridlock on the Paris Périphérique. A while later, the stair light went on again.

"Ah, *cheri*," the woman said. "Do not be disappointed."

"Enough. I must go."

"You will see. All men have these moments, you understand. Be not afraid. You are still the man you always were. The fault is the couscous."

The Fat Man descended with a heavy tread, gravely, frowning with concern. "Couscous."

"*'Revoir, cheri,*" she called. "Remember, anytime, day or night."

He waved an impatient hand to dismiss her.

Brewer laid aside his newspaper and stood. "Monsieur."

"Monsieur." The Fat Man looked with profound suspicion at Brewer.

"It is a pleasure to see you again."

"Yes?" His suspicion remained. He put his hand on the brass door-push.

"Perhaps you would join me in a coffee."

"Ah, no, monsieur. I am told I need the exercise."

"Shall we walk?" Brewer asked.

"I have very little time, monsieur."

Brewer nodded. "I need but a few moments."

"I cannot place your face, monsieur. Where have I seen you before?"

"On several occasions. Perhaps you recall Cahors?"

The Fat Man grunted. "Well, yes, perhaps. As one ages, various parts of the anatomy begin to malfunction. My memory—you see."

"Yes," Brewer said. "I understand."

Under the Fat Man's enormous umbrella they strolled slowly along the street. The Fat Man had bad feet, and he rolled from side to side as he walked.

"Couscous," he said.

"Pardon?" Brewer frowned at him.

"Couscous, monsieur. I am passionate about eating my wife's couscous. But I am told—" he glanced back at the hotel "—that couscous and love make strange bedfellows. So I walk. Tell me what is on your mind."

"I have some merchandise, monsieur."

"Ah."

"I have it here and I want it there—you understand."

"We have met, you say?"

"I will mention Gorki Sembranovich."

"Ah."

"And Sanders Elliott."

"Ah."

"And I have a very clean all-cash deal for you."

"Ah."

As they walked, Brewer felt the man's eyes upon him. A light film of perspiration made the Fat Man's forehead glisten. He walked more slowly,

"Perhaps now, a coffee." He led Brewer into a small café of some nine tables. The waiter stood in deep reverie holding an iron pole for the awning.

The Fat Man sighed as he sat.

They ordered two demis of coffee. The Fat Man put five cubes of sugar in his. He took a sixth and dipped it in the coffee, then put it between his teeth and sucked the coffee out of the cube. He drew the cube into his mouth and swallowed.

He stirred his coffee slowly as he gauged Brewer's demeanor.

"So, monsieur. We are quite alone. Merchandise, I think you said."

"I want it transferred from Paris to Damascus."

"Damascus. Very sensitive place. The Syrians are very excitable these days. Very wary. What kind of merchandise is it?"

"Mainly electronic parts. Computer parts."

"I see. Computer parts. Small pieces?"

"Yes. Nothing larger than this." Brewer drew a small square with his two index fingers.

"Uh huh. Uh huh. Small pieces. How many?"

"Perhaps seven, eight hundred pounds."

"Uh huh. Destined for Israel?"

"No. Not Israel."

"You understand, monsieur. I do not touch merchandise that is destined for Israel—directly or indirectly. I do not approve. Also it is very bad for my health. You must tell me where this merchandise is going ultimately."

"I would rather not say at this time, except that it is very bad news for the Israelis."

The Fat Man studied Brewer's face again, trying to place it. "Well, we will discuss that at a later time. For now, we say the destination is Damascus. What are your thoughts on this movement of merchandise? Will it be soon?"

"Yes, soon," Brewer answered.

"And the merchandise—how will it be brought in?"

"End User's Certificate."

"Ah. That means we will have a very short time to re-package it." The Fat Man made a doubt-filled mouth.

"Perhaps seventy-two hours."

"Seventy-two! That is exceedingly tight."

"Yes," Brewer said, "it is."

"Monsieur. Do you have a preferred method of trans-portation? That is, you understand—the airlines, for ex-ample, are impossible lately. The terrorists and hijackers have done it. The airlines are so closely guarded and watched, I no longer use them. Forget the airlines. This time of the year I do not like small boats in the eastern Aegean. The storms, you see. Besides, the Israelis and the Ameri-cans and the Russians are all fiercely patrolling those wa-ters, especially around Syria. And of course, with such a tight time schedule, we cannot break up the shipment into small parcels and ship over an extended period of time. So you see we do not have many options. Perhaps I will make a suggestion."

"I had an auto caravan in mind," Brewer said.

"Precisely, monsieur. My cousin, here in Paris, does a used-car business in the Mideast. It's a shoestring opera-tion, you understand, monsieur, but he makes a profit. The cars, they are driven individually by homesick Arabs who cannot afford the airfare. So they get a free ride home and my cousin, he gets free chauffeurage for his used cars. You see? All it costs him is gasoline. I am told that small things can be shipped in such vehicles with great success."

"We are in accord."

"Ah, you know my cousin?"

"I know of him. A large man with a passion for couscous and walking in the rain."

The Fat Man smiled and nodded his head. "I think, monsieur, you and I will do some business."

BREWER WALKED IN THE RAIN, turning over in his mind the pros and cons of using cars to smuggle the parts.

The one advantage was also a disadvantage: Most of the cars could be expected to get through the various customs checks on that long road to Damascus. But then some surely would not. If the important items—like the ANAC parts—were to be intercepted, the whole shipment would be almost useless. What he needed to do, according to the Fat Man, was to divide up the parts among all the cars so that at least some of each type would get through.

Brewer pictured the long drive across Europe, from Paris south through Provence to the Italian border, then into Liguria, across the northern plains of Italy to the Yugoslav border, traversing that nation to the Turkish border near Bulgaria, across Turkey, another long ride, to the Syrian border, then a long run south to Damascus.

SLANE WATCHED THEM go through the military drill: one hundred mercenaries re-creating the original training mission. By his side stood Malpina, El Presidente's personal counselor, who had been sent as technical adviser to the filmmakers.

No one knew this was a fake movie they were making. The film crew, the cameramen, the grips, the prop people, the director—an alcoholic old queen—all diligently went through each item on the shot list, screening the rushes every night and bickering with the film editor.

The mercs had been told they were in a movie and comported themselves like stars. They watched the rushes at night and each became an expert cinematographer eager to advise the film people.

Malpina, who had been in the original camp with the original band of patriots, had grown soft, he missed his city and his comforts. The food was basic and not to his liking.

There were no women. There was fine dust everywhere. And every evening, Slane managed to get from the capital, to feed Malpina, some gossip that made the man run to the phone to talk to his associates at length. Malpina cast his eyes longingly eastward. He was bored and hungry, dusty and eager to get back where the action was.

About midmorning he made a solemn announcement: Full of regret, waving his hand at the disappointment of Slane, he indicated that he was returning to the city. By midafternoon he had left to make a glowing report to El Presidente.

Slane had slapped him on the back and assured him that he would see him on the beaches November 26. A few scant days away.

ROCK SAT in his hotel room in Paris. He had before him on the desk a tablet of white paper, a supply of pencils, a fresh pot of coffee, and several expensive cigars. From his neck, on a leather thong, dangled a stopwatch. He was about to create another masterpiece, a nonexplosive explosive.

He lit the cigar, then surveyed all the papers that were carefully arranged around the room. On the couch in a neat row was a series of photographs of the Hotel Royal Nile in Cairo. On the Fifteenth of July Street. Beside them rested a schematic plan of the buildings on either side of the hotel and the adjacent streets.

On the floor before the couch was another row of photographs: interior shots of the hotel lobby and many more of the conference room, which was on the third floor, street side.

Rock took from a large manila envelope a packet of 3x5 color prints. Additional close-up photographs of the conference room. He could see the air-intake vents, the air-conditioning ducts, the control panel for the room's lighting, the screen for films and slides, and the closets and service pantry adjacent.

The fee he had extorted from Rumbh was most reassuring. No one could possibly want to kill Rock badly enough to pay such a fee just to get him to Cairo. It would have been far cheaper to send a grunt after him. The key word in the transaction was *guarantee*. Guaranteed delivery. And performance.

Rock had to devise an authentic bombing effort that was so arranged that it would most assuredly be discovered before it went off. He lit a cigar and almost hugged himself. His idea was brilliant. Absolutely brilliant. This was panache; this was high style.

Rock looked down at the photos and the schematics of the Hotel Royal Nile. Then he looked at her photograph. *The coast is clear.* Soon. Soon.

PENO RUS fussed with the agenda. Each speaker had to be flawless. Rus insisted on rehearsals. There were slides and films, and maps and pieces of equipment. There were the coffee breaks and afternoon teas to be reviewed with the hotel staff. And the evening meals—each a masterpiece.

Nothing was to be left to chance. Rus was determined that this seminar would be the talk of the arms world. He had winnowed the number of attendees down to twenty. Twenty of the major arms buyers in the world. The aristocracy of arms customers. It would be a status symbol in future to have attended a Rus arms seminar.

Rus was making a fortune. But he was spending a fortune.

He nearly drove Major Mudd round the bend. Checking and rechecking every detail, calling him at the arsenal, at the office, at home, all hours night and day. And as the opening day drew closer, the frenzy grew worse. Rus flogged and bullied and berated, roared and shouted, flung papers, pounded tables, and walked about with his face an apoplectic purple.

Major Mudd carried one picture in his mind. That large teddy bear's body capped by that Mongol face with the small black eyes squeezed by the high cheekbones—and the open mouth screaming all the way down to the bottom of the shaft. It would make a boom not heard in London since the days of the Hitler raids.

November 26: independence day for Major Mudd.

McCALL HAD BEGUN to feel like the protagonist in a Greek play caught up in the toils of ineluctable Destiny. Messengers were arriving from all over his kingdom bearing news of disasters.

The moment he returned from Paris, Borden told him about the successful heist of the ANAC parts from Prysbyl. "The stolen van was finally found in a motel but the guy was gone by then. Like the earth swallowed him."

"With the chips?"

"A hundred forty-four."

McCall shook his head wryly. The joy in Iran must be unbounded. Those 144 chips were equal to a major victory on the battle field. The Iranians had decked the United States once again.

"How about the motel registration records?" he asked.

Borden shrugged. "It's a hot-sheet operation. Dozens and dozens of guys in and out of there every week with women—rent a room for an hour or two and gone. All phony names, phony license plate numbers."

McCall grunted. "A guy steals a couple of authorization forms and blows away Prysbyl's whole bloody security system. A fortune in security hardware. That's a new wrinkle."

"That's chutzpah," Borden said. "We're up against one smart cookie."

"Yes, but who? Who?" McCall chewed a knuckle.

"We'll find him."

"Will you, Borden? When?"

Borden looked away and cleared his throat.

"An End User's Certificate," McCall said, reaching in his desk drawer. He threw the Iranian parts list on the desk. "Even if this guy is Houdini, he's going to have to get an End User's Certificate to get all this junk out of the country. That's where we'll have to nail him."

"Now, Bobby. You know what a killer of a job that is. We just can't borrow that much manpower to check every EUC in the country. We're talking about millions of items."

"He's not going to get those parts out of the country without an EUC. And he has to file all his papers at the port he's shipping the stuff from."

Borden turned away in his chair. "Oh, Jesus. We'd have to borrow all the staffs from the CIA, Military Intelligence, and the FBI."

McCall shook a finger at him. "No. Play the odds. Ninety-nine percent of those End User's Certificates are open-and-shut export cases. We know what the shipment consists of and a lot of the history of the cargo. So, play the hunches, Borden. Check out just the likely suspects."

Borden started to object again.

"Don't," McCall said. "Just do. Follow my direction and I'll make you a legend in your own lifetime. What about Dice?"

"No one's seen him in a couple of weeks."

"Dice is involved in this, Borden. You can make book on it."

"We're still looking, Bobby."

"Find him. Find Dice."

Borden got up to leave.

"Who's doing it, Borden?" McCall asked him.

"What?"

"The smuggling. Is it Rus? Slane? Rock?"

Borden shrugged again. "Whoever he is, he really knows the ropes. I get the feeling this guy knows things even people like Rus don't know. Like an insider."

"Dice," McCall said, "is an insider."

"Yes. But he's a dull-normal. The guy we're after is a real fox. He's as smart as Brewer."

BORDEN WAS hardly out of McCall's office when he came back in.

"Okay," he said. "They found the Mercedes that Attashah bought."

"Where?"

"Some guy in New York State. He's a lawyer. A lot of political accounts. He's also held a couple of political jobs on the state Republican Committee. And he's a member of a prison parole board."

"Which prison?" McCall asked.

"We're working on it. We just got this."

"Not Sweetmeadow?" McCall asked.

"Don't know."

"Oh, Christ. Not Sweetmeadow."

IT SEEMED TO TAKE BORDEN forever to learn what parole board the man was connected with.

At last, McCall heard Borden's dreadful step in the hall. Borden, the Greek messenger.

But the man who stood in his doorway wasn't Borden.

"Hullo, Bobby," said Dice. Dice, bulking in his wrinkled suit, hat in hand, visitor's badge clipped to his lapel. And that silly expression on his face.

"Why," McCall asked, "am I so unhappy to see you, Dice?"

"Got a minute, Bobby?"

"By all means. Sit down."

"I want to cut a deal." Dice sat down on the edge of the chair. "Okay?"

"Shoot. What have you got?"

"If the stuff is right, can I get my job back?"

"How good's the stuff?"

"It'll blow your socks off, Bobby."

"Well, what is it?"

"We have to cut a deal first, Bobby. I want my job back with all the perks—uninterrupted government service going back to the day I started."

"That'll practically take an Act of Congress."

"What I have is worth it."

McCall took a measured look at Dice and played his hunch. "Are you going to tell me about Charlie Brewer?"

"Oh. You know."

"Yes. We know." And now McCall did know—and wished he didn't.

"Do you know everything?"

"Probably."

Dice sagged in his chair. A man in despair.

Borden appeared in the doorway.

"Sweetmeadow?" McCall asked him.

"Yes. There's more."

"Stay there, Dice," McCall said. He walked into the hallway with Borden.

"Brewer's been paroled," Borden said.

"I thought so. Dice was about to spill his guts."

"They're together?"

"They were, anyway."

"Jesus. We're up against our own best man."

McCall nodded thoughtfully. "Did you ever have those days when you wished you were dead?"

MESSENGERS SEEMED TO BE arriving with disastrous news from every quarter now. The last man on earth that McCall ever wanted to confront was Charlie Brewer. Especially a renegade Charlie Brewer. After all those years of a close working relationship, how did they ever become adversaries?

What a brilliant move that Attashah had made. While McCall was running around trying to nail Rus and Rock and Slane, Attashah had reached out and plucked up the one man who could beat them all. And Attashah had even got him out of a federal prison.

McCall had only one more card to play. Brewer had the parts Iran needed. Now he was ready to smuggle them out of the country to Iran. To stop Brewer, McCall realized, he would have to have the man assassinated. But first he would have to find him. He went back into his office.

"Okay, Dice. Where is Brewer now?"

"I don't know, Bobby. We split in Frisco."

"You know he got the ANAC bits?"

"Holy Christ! From Prysbyl's? I can't believe it. Nobody can get in there. How did he do it?"

"Dice, if you want your membership card back, you have to help us find Brewer."

"Jesus, Bobby. That's a tall order. I'm out of my league with Brewer."

"Just find him. Let us know where he is and we'll take it from there."

"And I get my stripes back?"

"Everything I can possibly get back for you. Your job and most of the perks. I don't know about your seniority."

Dice stood up. "I'll see what I can do."

"There's a lot riding on it, Dice—for you and for me. You find him and you're back in. Before you go, you see Borden and spill your guts, addresses and telephone numbers and parts numbers and every dingdong thing you can think of about Brewer's little caper."

Dice stood, hulking and doubtful. "Bobby, you're not going to catch him. You know? Brewer is the smartest man in the world."

MADELINE HALE was alone now. And she was faced with a homicidal adversary who was restrained by no rules. And by trying to find him within the bounds of the law, she knew she was operating at a tremendous handicap. Worse, she would find no help anywhere. Brewer was gone. Her partners were no help outside of legal matters. And the police didn't have the facilities to give more than token help. It was Hale versus Rumbh.

She recalled Brewer's words and decided to go underground to some extent. She packed her suitcases and closed her apartment, and one Saturday afternoon she moved into a furnished apartment in Georgetown. She didn't use a car at all now. Instead, she did all her traveling by taxicab. It wasn't much of a precaution but it made her feel better.

She resumed her search for Rumbh by looking into the arsenal robbery.

It was a tale quickly told. And it was fully documented in the transcript of Brewer's trial, for the prosecution had made a big parade of the arsenal theft.

A truckload of weapons and ammunition had been stolen from the Fort Benson arsenal. Among the list of items missing were twenty-four mint-condition sixty-year-old Colt .45's.

After generations of service as the official sidearm of the armed forces, the .45 was to be phased out of service. Orders had been issued to all bases to commence gathering every .45 for shipment to a destination to be announced later. The .45's had been gathered from miscellaneous sources at Fort Benson and were waiting transshipment. Aside from their nominal value as military sidearms, these mint-condition .45's were worth a fortune to gun collectors.

No one had seen the vehicle that had carried off the weapons. It wasn't even clear exactly when the theft had taken place. The absence of the weapons was discovered during a routine inventory procedure. So the military carried the case on their books simply as mysterious disappearance. From the day of discovery there hadn't been the slightest clue to the theft until the .45's turned up in the trunk of Brewer's car. Brewer and Marvel said they had picked up the weapons at a baggage check in lower Manhattan.

Hale called the federal attorney who had tried Brewer.

"Is that file on the stolen weapons still open?" she asked.

"Dambetcha," he said. "Open forever or until all the weapons and ammo are recovered—whichever comes first."

"Any developments since the trial?" Hale asked.

"Nah. We shopped hard for the rest of the stolen ordnance. Checked all the known terrorist groups and all the loonies. Whoever got them has them well under wraps."

"You ever hear any more about this man Rumbh?"

"Mrs. Hale, you want my opinion? Rumbh is Charlie Brewer."

NEXT, HALE TURNED TO Russell Pines. The police had testified that a man identifying himself as Russell Pines reported that a man named Charlie Brewer was trying to sell him some .45's. But since he suspected they were stolen, he felt the police should handle the matter. Pines had declined to give an address or a phone number.

Hale began the investigative process anew on one Russell Pines. She ordered a search of the usual laundry list of records: state driver's license and car registration bureaus, credit cards, court orders, bankruptcies.

Then she turned back to Rumbh. Her check of Immigration and Naturalization files had upset Rumbh no end. He had blown her car up. The logical question now was, who put the red flag on Rumbh's Naturalization file?

THE INVESTIGATIVE REPORTS came in like clockwork. In all the fifty states of the Union, no one named Russell Pines drove a car, owned a car, owed money, was involved with the law courts, or had been in jail. Legally at least, Russell Pines didn't exist.

She now commenced a study of all the name files containing aliases, noms de plume, and a.k.a.'s. There was a long list to check through. Each state, the FBI, and the CIA biography file. She asked for a search of two names: Rumbh and Russell Pines.

At the last minute she included Interpol on her search list.

SHE HAD LITTLE MORE than a month before her departure from Washington.

If she had ever had any doubts about it, Bradley Joyce, the senior partner, now made it clear: She was his favorite trial lawyer in the firm. And he didn't want her to go.

He sent her things. The classified real estate section from *The Washington Post* with a notice circled:

A Bit of Vermont in Virginia. White clapboard Victorian, lovingly finished with gingerbread. Huge old windows, turrets, wraparound porch, 5brs, 4 1/2 b, lr, dr, breakfast nook, fmly rm, big ktchn, pantry, 3 acres, a/c, h.w.heat. Come see. Hurry.

From the Law Journal he picked out an article on the growing incidence of crime in New England. A clipping on the low income of lawyers in Vermont. From *The Washingtonian*: Seventeen senators from various parts of the United States pick northern Virginia as the ideal for raising a family.

His little notes were gasoline on a fire. Washington seemed more alluring every day. Vermont, in contrast, was a defeat, a turning back. But worst of all was Brewer's voice, so positive, telling her she would never make it in Vermont.

She wondered where he was. How he was. He didn't answer his phone—it had been days.

THEY CAUGHT HER by surprise—two responses from Interpol. One was on Russell Pines. But more astonishing was the other—on Rumbh.

Interpol had a wealth of information on one Anton Rumbh. He had a long criminal record. Nationality unknown. Date of birth unknown. Education and background unknown. But his criminal performance was well documented. He had long-term connections with the Communist government in Vietnam, functioning as their agent to sell the enormous quantities of American arms left on the Vietnam battlefield. He had definite connections with a notorious Asian bandit, Ho Wat, through whom he had done a thriving business gunrunning in Malaysia. He'd flooded Asia, the Mideast, and South America with American weapons. The police in New Delhi wanted him for smuggling. Athens wanted to question him about two murders there. Malta had an arrest-on-sight writ standing, a result of an arsenal robbery there. He was cited by five intelligence groups for gunrunning in Africa, again with American arms from Vietnam. There was more, a long litany of arms trading, theft, smuggling, and troublemaking. But never once arrested. Never once photographed.

How on earth had he obtained an American passport?

The Interpol report on Russell Pines was almost an anticlimax.

Russell Pines was a.k.a. Peno Rus. And his life was well documented. Born in Russian Georgia, Communist education, training as a journalist, defection, and a highly lucrative new career as an arms trader. Never arrested but ample photographs available. British citizenship.

Hale returned to the Rumbh report. So there really was a Rumbh? And he was an arms trader. Why had he chosen to frame two American agents? And how had he obtained an American passport?

Perhaps some of the local police had more information. She sent inquiries to Malta, Athens, and New Delhi.

Then she took the latest real estate section sent by Bradley Joyce, decorated with red circles, and threw it into the wastebasket.

14

The guy went by the name of Poke, and he owned an old Super Constellation.

He was a gypsy wandering the earth like a solitary frigate bird; an independent nonscheduled freight carrier who was always in search of payloads to carry. Price negotiable. Not very fussy about what it was or where it went. Poke periodically had his Connie grounded for FAA or customs infractions—or for bank payments. Customs men all over Europe, the United States, and Latin America frankly called Poke a smuggler.

A small man about sixty, in an old leather flight jacket, he had the deep voice and the leathery face of a heavy smoker. He never drank anything but soda, and no one had ever seen him eat. In the last half hour in Brewer's presence, he'd already had five glasses of cola. He sat, cigarette in one hand, glass in the other, staring at the Brooklyn Bridge through the saloon window and nodding at Brewer's words.

In a booth behind them, by herself, waited his companion, a large woman with two glasses of beer who was reading a Gothic novel.

Brewer was explicit about what he wanted: "I'm having my air freight shipped to Cargo City terminal at JFK from six or seven locations in the city. Today. I want you to load it on the Connie tomorrow. You can make two refueling stops—one in Gander and another in Shannon. Flight time should be about twelve to fifteen hours. Okay?"

"Okay," Poke said. "I figure it'll take me couple of hours to load—then it's over the hill and far away." Poke spread his arms like wings.

"Now look, Poke," Brewer said. "You have to be clean as a cat. I can't have you load my stuff, then get grounded by some FAA regulation. Or by somebody putting a lien on your kite. This cargo has to move fast—from the time it gets to Cargo City to takeoff time. It just isn't going to stand up to much scrutiny from customs. You read me?"

"It'll move like shit through a goose. See you day after tomorrow on the other side." Poke stood up and started to walk away. Then he stopped. "Say, Brewer, this is on the up-and-up between us? I mean, you're not setting me up for something, are you?"

"Perish the thought, Poke."

"I mean I don't forget you was once a Fed." He shrugged at Brewer. "I never done a day of time and I'd hate to do it now. Okay?"

"Okay," said Brewer.

Poke and the woman left and went slouching up the street, in close tête-à-tête.

IT WAS TIME FOR BREWER to start worrying again. For one thing, Poke could screw up—he could be stopped for any number of reasons he didn't tell Brewer about. Then there was the plane, a thirty-year-old antique. It could develop engine trouble and be grounded anywhere along the way. Worse, it could drop into the ocean.

Brewer's main concern, however, was the paper. He had spent his career around export/import documents—manifests, bills of lading, certificates of exemption, export licenses, and all the other forms of paper impedimenta. The two documents he was most concerned about were the Rated

Commodities Watch List and the Table of Denial and Probation Orders Currently in Effect.

Both documents were issued and regularly updated by the Export Control System in the Bureau of East West Trade of the Department of Commerce. Both documents were carried by every customs officer. And every item on Brewer's shipment was on the Watch List.

As long as U.S. Customs accepted the End User's Certificate—which certified that the parts were all destined for use inside Britain—there would be no problem. But if customs challenged the certificate, just the litigation could take months. Worse case—if they nailed Brewer, it was back to Sweetmeadow for more years than he wanted to count.

But with over eleven thousand export licenses issued each month in the United States, for more than one thousand types of strategic commodity, Brewer hoped he would slip through with the crowd.

Later that day, the last parcel of Rooley Attashah's parts arrived at JFK's Cargo City from a public warehouse near Bush Terminal in Brooklyn. Brewer then filed his papers and waited.

He spent the evening drinking beer and reading.

CUSTOMS IN NEW YORK noted that all the items on Brewer's documents were on the Rated Commodities Watch List and so sent a copy to the Export Import Control Systems offices in Washington by overnight Guard Mail.

Export Import the next morning sent a copy of Brewer's document to McCall's office by messenger, along with eight other documents. Joanie Walsh put the envelope on Borden's desk. And there it sat, waiting for Borden to open it.

THAT MORNING, the weather was perfect for flying when Poke strolled around to Cargo City terminal and presented his papers for Brewer's cargo. Then he waited.

About nine-thirty, a customs man walked into the cargo area with his clipboard and a briefcase bulging with papers and envelopes, tags and tickets, stamp pad and various official rubber stamps. He stepped up to the cargo and ran his eyes over the cartons, taped, strapped, and labeled. Then he looked at his clipboard for the carrier's name—Poke. And he frowned.

He called Poke. "Where are you going with this material?" he demanded. "Every item on here is on the Rated Commodities Watch List. Every last thing."

Poke shrugged. "I just fly it to the address." He pointed at the destination. "England. I've already filed my flight plan."

"Well, you're not flying anywhere. I'm putting this on hold until I hear from Export Import Control."

"How long will that take?"

The customs man shrugged. "You know Washington."

"I'll lose my shirt if I sit here for long. How about making a phone call to them?"

"I've six other loads to check. After that we'll see."

Poke took a shuttle over to the passenger terminal and hunted up Brewer. Brewer went to a pay phone and made a credit card call to London. He identified himself as Mr. Cricket. The Minister came to the phone promptly.

"They're shitting all over your End User's Certificate," said Brewer. The Minister telephoned the British consulate in New York.

Brewer and Poke sat down to wait. Something had to give. If someone came around the corner and clapped a pair of handcuffs on his wrists, Brewer would know who had won the Great War of the Washington/London Bureaucrats. Not his side.

POKE ARRIVED BACK in Cargo City in time to see the limousine from the British consulate arrive. He heard a U.S. Customs man say to the British consulate man: "You guys are making a joke out of the End User's Certificate. We're blowing the whistle this time. That cargo is going to sit there until hell freezes over."

"You people," the British consulate man replied, "are trying to compel Britain to enforce American law in Europe. I'm here on orders of my government to make an official protest."

Poke went back to Brewer.

"That's tough old beans," said Brewer. "I know at least thirty ex-spooks from the U.S. who are importing American stuff into London and Vienna and everywhere else. There are other guys in Hong Kong and Montreal and Buenos Aires and Christ knows where else. The minute they get the stuff they tear up the End User's Certificates."

"Then what do the Feds do it for?"

"It makes it very tough on the Russians." He shook his head. "But what the hell. Why did they have to pick on my cargo to make their point?"

AT NOON, IN WASHINGTON, Borden came in from a long meeting to check his phone messages before going to lunch. He saw the envelope from Export Import and opened it. Nine new cases to check out. He shuffled through the documents, and at the bottom he found the JFK sheet. "Holy shit."

He called New York Customs. Everyone was at lunch. He tried McCall, who was attending a conference in Manhattan, and had him pulled out of the meeting room.

"I want to read something to you," Borden said. And he commenced reading the parts list.

"Where?" demanded McCall.

"JFK. They're all out to lunch."

"You keep calling them, Borden," McCall said. "Make them hold up on that shipment until I get there."

McCall ran down the marble steps two at a time. When he got to the street, he couldn't find a cab. He had half-run all the way to Seventh Avenue before he got one.

The cab started across town to the Queens Midtown Tunnel. The cab driver shrugged at McCall as he encountered one traffic snarl after another. "Crosstown," he said. "It's always the toughest way to go."

"How about the Brooklyn Battery Tunnel?" McCall asked.

"It's a lot longer," said the cabbie. "This way I can go out Queens Boulevard to Van Wyck Expressway right in to JFK. The other way you got to go all around Brooklyn on the Belt Parkway."

"I spend one half of my life in cabs chasing airplanes," McCall said. "And the other half on airplanes, chasing cabs." He looked out at the traffic.

It took more than twenty minutes to get to the Midtown Tunnel. Once they got through it, the Expressway was fairly clear. But they were stopped by road-surfacing work on the Van Wyck and crept for nearly fifteen minutes. It was well after one when they reached the airport.

McCall hunted up the customs officer. "Where is it?" he demanded.

"Ha!" exclaimed the customs officer. "You should have been here before lunch. It was Bunker Hill all over again."

"But where's the cargo?"

"It's about a quarter of the way to England . . . if that old kite hasn't crashed somewhere. You never saw anything loaded so fast in all your life."

About half a mile away, Brewer was stepping aboard his jet flight.

McCALL WAS YELLING into the phone at Borden. "Of course I'm sure! Brewer got every jot and tittle on Attashah's list and flew it the hell out of here. We have to catch him on the other side. You get your butt on the next Washington flight to London and I'll meet you there. And—hey, Borden, bring Dice. Don't fail to bring Dice. You hear me?"

MADELINE HALE received a cable from Malta that morning: RE YOUR REQUEST FOR CRIMINAL RECORD OF ANTON RUMBH UNABLE TO COMPLY. NOTHING IN OUR FILES ON ANTON RUMBH OR SEVEN VARIANT SPELLINGS.

Another cable arrived from New Delhi: REFERENCE YOUR WIRE (XC2790) NO SUCH PERSON AS ANTON RUMBH SEVEN VARIANT SPELLINGS IN OUR CRIMINAL RECORDS LAST TEN YEARS.

The cable at three made it conclusive. Athens reported no criminal record for any person named Rumbh, seven variant spellings.

Anton Rumbh had obtained an American passport and an Interpol criminal record—both fraudulently. Why would anyone want a false Interpol criminal record?

In the mail, she received a confirming carbon of Interpol's profile on Russell Pines a.k.a. Peno Rus. The last sentence in that report noted that Peno Rus was an avid collector of American Colt .45's. And that suddenly told Madeline Hale a great deal. It was time to find out who had put the red flags on Brewer's personnel file and on Rumbh's INS passport file.

Hale called a friend in the FBI.

"I need a favor," she said. "I need some sub rosa information."

Illegally legal, Brewer had called it. Then legally illegal. The salami tactics of relativism. Brewer had started with phone taps; she with illegal information. A slice at a time; a step at a time.

MCCALL MET Borden's flight at the passport control gate in Heathrow Airport outside London that evening.

"Where's Dice?" McCall asked.

"Behind me in the line somewhere. Has Poke arrived yet?"

"Late," McCall said. "He left Gander for Shannon but he's bucking stiff head winds. He's overdue at Shannon."

Borden chuckled. "Can you imagine anyone flying one of those old bats anymore? I can walk faster than that."

"Listen," McCall said. "When Poke lands we have to move fast on this. We're not going to get any cooperation from our British friends on this. After that flap in New York, they're sticking to their story. Okay?"

"How are we going to destroy that stuff?" Borden asked.

"Modern technology," McCall said. "Gasoline and a match."

"Remember," Borden said. "You're dealing with a real fox."

"How can I forget it?"

He and Borden went into an airport pub to await the arrival of Poke's old Connie.

AT 1:00 A.M. they received word that Poke had landed in Shannon, complaining of engine trouble. Estimated repair time five hours. McCall and Borden and Dice all went to bed in the airport motel.

AT 6:00 A.M. Borden woke McCall in his motel room. "Poke took off from Shannon shortly after two."

"Two!" McCall sat up in his bed. "When did he arrive here?"

"He didn't."

"What! What are you telling me, Borden?"

"He left Shannon more than four hours ago and he hasn't arrived here."

"Quick. Query the other airports."

"I have. No word yet."

By seven they had their information. Poke had landed at Orly, Paris. "The cargo," Borden said, "was unloaded and cleared French Customs an hour ago. Brewer made a clean getaway."

By eight McCall and Borden and Dice were booked on a flight to Paris.

On the plane McCall said to Dice. "This is your baby, Dice. You find Brewer and that cargo."

Dice looked solemnly at McCall. "I think you're out of your mind. You're not smart enough to catch Brewer."

A GREAT AUTUMN FOG rolled over much of Normandy and muffled the entire city of Paris right after the three of them arrived. In a drizzling mist McCall and Borden started spreading some money around Orly. The old airport had been overshadowed by the Charles de Gaulle Airport, and with less freight volume flowing through it than formerly, they were hoping someone had noticed the truck that carried the cargo away. French Customs was distinctly icy.

McCall followed a different tack. Leaving Borden and Dice to search for Brewer and the Iranian cargo, McCall set out to find Poke. The Connie couldn't have gone far. He contacted flight control and learned where Poke had gotten to: Weary from its flight against Atlantic head winds, the old Connie had gone to Brussels for maintenance.

McCall hit a snag. Due to flying conditions, commuter flights from Paris to Brussels were either booked solid or canceled. So McCall cabbed into Paris and took the train to Brussels. "I'll be back tomorrow," he told Borden.

The autumn fog had rolled over much of the Netherlands, Belgium, and France. Car drivers and plane passengers alike had taken to the rails, and they all seemed to be on the train to Brussels. McCall managed to get a boarding pass but no reserved seat. He stood during the entire ride.

McCall watched the red lights go flashing by in the muffling fog and thought about Brewer. It was incredible for even one as gifted as Brewer to have rounded up all that contraband and gotten it this far. It was a brilliant job. Now there was only one last barrier between Brewer and Iran: Bobby McCall. If Brewer got by him, he had a clear run to his goal.

It was strange being Brewer's adversary. They'd fished together, sailed the Chesapeake together, gotten kited on beer and laughter together, and, especially, handled a number of dangerous assignments together. Brewer was the best of companions, charming, endlessly cheerful, full of wit and humor. McCall had probably come closest to glimpsing the inner Brewer.

Of all the spooks in Washington, Brewer was the only one who lived for the game itself. He loved those sharp contests with the arms dealers. When most agents were playing it safe or demanding other assignments, Brewer was out working a scam, setting a trap, dodging a deadfall. He came closest to making it all seem like a suspense film. But one thing astonished McCall. He would never have believed Brewer could turn traitor.

Furthermore, McCall had always secretly believed that he himself was the better all-round agent. And it would have been fascinating to go up against Brewer just to find out, except for one thing: the package he'd sold Wainwright.

McCall had to either call off the whole operation or add one more name to the list of assassinations of Rus and Rock and Slane. Charlie Brewer.

WHEN HE got to the Brussels Airport, the fog was lifting and the terminal was packed with passengers queuing up for their long-delayed flights. There were lines everywhere.

He found the Constellation in a nose hangar. Two men were working on one of the engines.

"How long is it going to take to fix that?" he asked them.

One of them shrugged eloquently. "Who knows? It is difficult to find mechanics who know how to fix these old engines. And getting parts is impossible. This belongs in a museum."

Well, at least Poke wasn't going to be hard to find. He was never far from his plane. He often slept on it. McCall went back to the passenger terminal. He searched out the places that sold cold soda.

In ten minutes he found Poke and his large girl friend— at Le Cheeseburger.

Poke wouldn't look at him. "We got nothing to talk about, McCall."

"One shouldn't make enemies in your business, Poke," McCall answered.

Poke smiled bleakly at him. "Would you want Charlie Brewer for an enemy?"

"But he's off and gone! You don't need to protect him anymore."

"Maybe."

"I'll make it worth your while," McCall said. In his hands he held a $100 bill.

Poke looked at it, then at his girl friend. "Very nice, McCall. I love portraits of great men."

"How about two?" McCall asked. With his thumbs he revealed a second $100 under the first.

"I do love two, McCall. I truly do."

"Then talk to me. Where did Brewer go? Do you know?"

"It's a possibility," Poke said.

"Three," McCall said. His hands now fanned a trio of bills. "Talk to me."

"I got the license number and the make of the truck," Poke said.

"Four," McCall said. "Tell me."

Poke grinned at his girl friend. "Want another beer?"

"Five," McCall said. "A perfect poker hand."

"Write it down, McCall." Poke nodded at his girl friend. "Tell him."

McCall wrote it on a paper napkin with a felt pen as the woman spoke. "O-I-K, one-nine-one," she said.

McCall pocketed the napkin. "Good show, Poke." He handed him the five bills. He held up five others. "I was ready to go for a grand."

Poke clucked his tongue. "Never was good at poker."

SURVEYING THE ROWS of used cars, the Fat Man, Georges, drew a deep draught on his cigarette and sighed a cloud of smoke stoically: he had the toothache. After fourteen years of neglect he knew he had to see a dentist. The dying molar twinged deep in the root and drove sharp pain through his right eye. Each time it made him hunch his shoulders. Today, he said to the pain, he would go to the dentist. Today.

He watched his men furtively working—as usual. It was just past dawn, and a November sun pushed weak light into the Montmartre district of Paris and through the clouded windows of the old factory building.

The American was supervising the opening of the cartons. Inside each were many small packets wrapped in pink plastic sheeting and bound with plastic tape. His men were fitting them into the huge pans that were to be welded to the bottom of the cars. Twenty pans in rows waiting to be filled.

Aimable: that was the word for the American. Patient. He explained without irritability, answering the same questions over and over. He could make a joke. The men smiled. Still in all, Georges looked at the set of the man's head on the shoulders, the slope of the arms and the way the man moved: No, he would not like to have to explain to that American why the plan failed. He would not like to see that man angry.

Georges got up and walked over to Brewer. "Why do you have to stop the cars at night?" he asked. "I can put two drivers in each car and they can drive day and night straight through."

Brewer stood up. "I want a roll call each night. If any cars break down we can double back to find them before we've left them too far behind."

Georges nodded. "*Eh, bien.* The caravan will leave tomorrow morning first thing." Georges walked back to his desk. Twenty cars; twenty drivers.

ARRANGED IN ROWS behind him inside the old factory, twenty cars waited in the faint light of predawn. They seemed innocuous enough: There were old Volkswagens and Renaults and Peugeots and Fiats and Saabs and Volvos and English Fords, all worn beyond their prime, all put into satisfactory running condition for the long trip, all destined to finish their days in the harsh, baking climate of Syria.

With one eye squinted against the smoke of his cigarette, Georges studied his maps. From Paris to 'Stamboul and from 'Stamboul to Damascus, the auto traffic would be at its peak: Long lines of overland buses would be carrying their hordes of travelers and pilgrims; endless caravans of truck traffic would be hauling oil pipe and cement and machine tools and air-conditioning equipment and tons of other items into the Arab world, all at the beck and call of money from those bottomless oil wells.

With such traffic, border checks should be nominal, especially for used cars with temporary transit papers, consigned to a car dealer in Damascus.

MCCALL FOUND BORDEN and Dice back at the hotel in Paris, still flogging their way through lists of cab drivers and truckers who might have seen the unloading of Poke's old Connie. No luck. And now Dice was on the telephone, wearily calling more trucking companies.

McCall held out the bar napkin from the Brussels Airport. "Okay," he said to them, "we've got it."

Borden took the napkin. "What is it?"

"It's the license number of the truck that offloaded Brewer's goodies."

Dice settled down in a chair, staring at the napkin and chuckling. "Christ, am I glad to see you," he said to the napkin. "No more fractured French conversations with truck drivers."

"Let me call that in," Borden said. He dialed the phone and read the number off. Then he hung up. "It could take a few hours, Bobby, to get the name and address of the truck owner."

"We also need more men," McCall replied. "At least four, I'd say."

Borden made another phone call. Then another. He talked for nearly fifteen minutes. When he hung up he said, "People aren't as friendly as they used to be. You know that? Disgraceful. You'd think we worked for the competition."

"So?" McCall demanded.

"Four grunts coming from Brussels," Borden said.

"That's the best they can do? They might not get here until tomorrow."

"They said they're rounding them up now," Borden answered. "They should have them on the way in a couple of hours."

GEORGES'S MECHANICS had labored all through the day and into the evening, packing the bundles in the pans. Twenty pans, each filled with pink-wrapped little packages. Brewer had fussed at them all the day, shifting parts from one pan to another like a crapshooter trying to cover all his bets, improve his odds. He was asking himself one question over and over: What if any of these pans failed to get through—what would that mean to the total parts list? He tried to make the loss of any one do minimal damage.

It upset Georges. Brewer was playing dice against the Fates, trying to thwart their will. He was defying God. Only fools and madmen did that. All was written.

Throughout the evening, the little stars of the welding torches created cascades of sparks in the semidarkness of the garage as silhouettes moved in and out of the light. Smoke drifted in the air. Perhaps it was his ailing tooth, but to Georges the garage in the darkness gave an impression of Purgatory.

Nine P.M. had just passed when the last pan was welded to the underbody of the last used car. The caravan was ready—twenty cars, four files, five ranks, sitting there like lumps in the dark garage. The air was heavy with the odor of welding torches and gasoline.

Now, with the smuggling work finished, it was time to examine the drivers. Under the small light of a green lampshade, the Fat Man waited for them. He was seated behind a large tin box that rested on an old kitchen table, and he waited with his habitual cigarette hanging from his mouth, one eye squinting against the rising smoke.

He glanced at the twenty shadowy hulks behind him. Normally, if more than ten of the twenty got through, Georges's reputation would be well served. But if half of these cars failed to get through the border checks, Monsieur Brewer would be disappointed. Georges preferred to deal with Arabs who could take disappointment philosophically. How would this man react? Badly. A growing premonition of failure possessed George's thoughts.

He drew a deep draught on his cigarette and sighed a cloud of smoke against the sharp pain. In the morning, after the cars had left, he would go to the dentist.

In a few minutes the first driver arrived. He approached the table, a young dark-skinned man, sniffing at the very strong odor of gasoline and frowning at the cigarette.

"Driver's license and passport," said Georges. He spoke French with a heavy Syrian accent. The driver handed him the documents and Georges checked the name against his list, then studied the passport. He now spoke exclusively in Syrian Arabic. From the open square tin box he searched through the twenty paper pouches and lifted one out. He opened the pouch and spread the documents on the newspaper.

"These are all the papers you need. These are the transit visas. This is the insurance certificate. It's the one paper they check at every border. If you lose it they get very difficult. This is the temporary registration of the vehicle's ownership. It is consigned to this automobile dealer in Damascus. These are your strip maps. They show the route you must take. You will go by way of A-six, Autoroute du Soleil, straight down the Rhone Valley, across the Riviera and the Italian Riviera, around Genoa, across Italy into Yugoslavia, and so forth. Here the way is marked—you see? All through Turkey and into Syria.''

The driver pointed at a road on the map. ''Why did you pick that route?''

''Because that is where our way stations are set up. Here are your gasoline vouchers. On these maps the gasoline stations are marked with blue crosses. And here is where you will sleep, and here, and here—where the red circles are. The addresses of the approved houses are on this sheet of paper. At each one, you will be given dinner when you arrive, breakfast in the morning, and a box lunch to eat on the road. If you have any trouble, any trouble at all, you will call this number, or this, or this—depending on where you are. If you fall behind schedule for any reason, call. If you lose any of these papers, the authorities may impound the vehicle. If they want to get nasty they may impound you. This envelope contains money for your tolls in the right national currencies. Do you have any questions? No?''

The driver shook his head.

''Good,'' said Georges. ''Let me see your bag.''

The driver put it on the table. It was an old suitcase, the leather so dried out it was cracked and flaking at the creases and edges and would tear easily. It was closed by two new leather straps.

The Fat Man lit a new cigarette with the end of the old one and hung it from his lips and resumed his pained, one-eyed squint. His hand groped through the contents of the suitcase, the striped shirts, the still-damp cloth bag containing toilet articles, the towels and a second suit, carpet slippers, and a photograph in a glass frame of a seated woman with a child in her lap.

"You have any drugs? Guns? Property without papers?" He watched the man shake his head with each question. "Plants? Seeds? Cameras? Radios? Money? Currency of any kind? French francs? How much? Show me. That's all? Any diamonds or jewelry? You will be questioned at the borders and you can be searched, so you must be absolutely clean. No free-lance smuggling? No? If you do, you will receive a visit from us in Syria at your home. Your whole family is accountable for you. You understand?"

The driver nodded. The strip map directed him to the Porte de Clichy and from there to the Boulevard Périphérique to A6—Autoroute du Soleil—which runs south to the Riviera.

"Departure time is six A.M.," Georges said. "I will wake you." The driver was assigned to one of the twenty-odd cots behind the parked cars.

The next driver sat down and Georges looked briefly at him, unable to shake the premonition that hounded his thoughts. *Eh, bien.* By morning he would be rid of the cars, the monsieur with the strange eyes, and the toothache. God is good.

BORDEN SAT IN THE HOTEL with McCall and Dice. His elbow rested on the table by the telephone. Next to it was the bar napkin with the truck license-plate number McCall had gotten from Poke.

They all waited for the phone to ring.

Borden looked at Dice, who drummed fingertips on a chair arm. "If this number pays out, Dice," Borden said, "I'll let you sleep with my mother. Free."

Dice didn't laugh.

The phone rang. Borden picked it up. "Yes." He nodded and wrote on a small white pad a little parade of black numbers and letters. He smiled at McCall.

"The Fat Man," he said.

"Georges?" McCall asked. "Back from Syria?"

"And back in business. Up in Montmartre." Borden got out a street map of Paris and the three of them studied it.

"Here," McCall said. He pointed to a street behind the Sacré Coeur. "Let's hit it right now."

Borden looked at his watch. "We're short-handed, Bobby. We don't know what we're going to run into. If we make a hash of this, it's going to cause a real fracas between Washington and Paris."

"We can't wait much longer," McCall said.

"Give it another hour or so, Bobby," Borden said. "Those four grunts should be here any minute."

"They should have been here hours ago," McCall replied. "Minutes count."

"They'll be here," Borden said. "It's a long ride from Brussels."

AT 5:00 A.M. there was a light tapping on the hotel door. McCall and Borden had fallen asleep fully dressed on the two double beds. Dice slept fitfully in a small chair.

Dice answered the door. "Who's there?"

"Brussels."

Dice admitted four men.

McCall splashed cold water on his face and put on his shoes. Then, without a word, he led them across the city in two cars to Montmartre. By 5:40 they had located the building. There, in the street like a paid informer pointing the way, was the truck itself.

"Seven come eleven," McCall said. "Get someone to check the back."

Borden took one of the agents with him and slipped down a dark alley. They returned in a few minutes.

"I don't think there's anyone in there," Borden said.

"That's not Brewer's style," McCall said. "What's back there?"

"An old wooden door. No braces, no bars. One kick should do it."

"Kick," McCall said. He looked at his watch by the pale streetlight. "In five minutes. And we'll go through this side door. Looks like it leads into an office of some sort."

"You want to wait for daylight?" Borden asked.

"No," McCall said. "We'll draw a crowd. Five minutes."

Borden was gone with three agents. McCall and Dice and the fourth agent waited at the front. At exactly 5:45, McCall drew back his foot and kicked. The old latch hardly made a sound. It just swung open.

They scrambled into a small office. By flashlight, McCall found an open doorway that led into the main garage. From the back he saw flashlights coming at him: Borden and his men. The garage was completely empty.

Everyone stood looking at Dice as though he knew where Brewer had gone.

"Well," one of the agents said. "It's a long way to Brussels." He walked toward the front door.

McCall watched him. Was it a long way to Iran?

GEORGES FOUND OUT about the raid later in the day when he returned and found his doors broken. His premonition had been right.

So had Brewer's. Brewer had awakened at 4:30 and roused everyone. "Six o'clock is dangerous," was all he said. The last car left at 5:31, less than ten minutes before McCall arrived.

Immediately after the last car had driven out of the garage and down the hill, the Fat Man himself left the building, intent on the tooth pain that was forcing him now to shut his right eye. The whole side of his face throbbed.

He struggled into his own car and drove, with his right hand gently against his jaw, in quest of a dentist with merciful woman's hands. He decided to go to a hospital for a painkiller until the dentists of Paris should open their offices. He even forgot to smoke.

Georges was less than four blocks away when the raid on his garage occurred. He later said the toothache was a gift of God.

IN THREE DAYS the seminar would commence, and Peno Rus felt as though he were making his debut at Convent Garden. British executives, born and bred to Western business techniques, might take such things in stride; Major Mudd, in fact, regarded the preparations as beneath him, something for clerks to handle.

But for Peno Rus, even with his recent years of arms dealing, a seminar was a vast unknown continent fraught with mysteries and traps. Each day he discovered new uses and new implications in this seminar. Should the slide presentation on Small Arms Management and Control precede or follow Comparative Firepower and Uniform Calibers? What was the idea he wanted to get over in the symposium titled Third World Armaments: Where to Get Military Financing?

Most important, was the seminar doing its main job of making everyone forget that African famine? He was still astonished at the number of hard-bitten men in the trade who continued to criticize him for it. Really, what difference did it make? Just a bunch of mindless gooks and their brats. Rus still considered it one of his masterstrokes. He just didn't like being called a monster for it.

But, by trying to erase the memory of the famine with his little dog-and-pony show, he feared making a fool of himself. He was greedy for praise and success. In the end he'd hired a London agency specializing in business meetings and trade shows. And now he fussed and fumed at every detail—agenda books, sharpened pencils, arms catalogues, cut flowers in each room, all persistent worries. The London agency was earning every penny of its fee.

Three days to go.

Rus stood in the marble lobby of his penthouse, ready for his daily cup of wormwood: the ride in the elevator. In his hand he held a list of things to do for his seminar—the product of a sleepless night. The elevator arrived with the ding of the bell chime. The door slid open and the car waited for him. Silent and menacing. An empty, upright, upholstered coffin. Peno Rus adjusted his tie, cleared his throat, stepped resolutely into the car, and pushed the ground-floor button. He fought back his never-gone terror as the doors shut.

SLANE WAS PLEASED. His hundred mercs had shaped up very quickly. Taking over the island was going to be a piece of cake even if there was organized resistance—which was extremely unlikely.

He smiled at the endless discussions and disputes that engrossed the movie makers. In three days he would come wading ashore into the lens of the camera, the most unlikely stand-in for the Benevolent Presidente that ever was. Three days and his fortune was made.

ROCK called Rumbh in Paris.

"I can handle your deal," he said.

"Good. I was sure you would," Rumbh said. "What kind of protection do you need?"

"Not much. Just keep the girl's family out of the way for a couple of days."

"Done. No problem at all."

"Okay. I'll be in Cairo on the twenty-sixth with all the equipment."

JAMIL LOVED the Leeward Island Free State. The trade winds flowed constantly over the land, cooling it and creating a constant springtime. The country was dirt-poor; the economy was badly handled and struggling. But the people were warm and the terrain was beautiful. Jamil, with his soul still damp from the autumn rains of Paris, reveled in the sunshine on his back.

The beach where Slane would come ashore was easy to find. The Benevolent Presidente had marked it with a huge monument that bore a statue of himself at the top. Jamil strolled along the beach watching the rolling surf languidly heave up, curl, and spill its water in a booming white spume. All the Europeans in their gray, wet, cold, drafty cities—and here, this magnificent beach and surf. The Benevolent Presidente had to be the world's worst salesman if he couldn't fill those beaches.

Jamil turned away from the beach and walked up into a line of palm trees. He would need an elevated platform of some sort from which he could get Slane in his sights. He needed to be able to get rid of the weapon. He needed a getaway vehicle and then an immediate flight from the airport to, probably, Miami.

As he stood studying the terrain, idly he scooped up some sunwarm sand and let it sift from his fingers. He watched the grains fall away in the breeze. The wind could be a factor in his sniping. He had to do the job with one shot.

Jamil watched the blowing sand drift from his fingers. It reminded him of an hourglass. Three more days.

AT HIS HOME, in his library filled with books with leather bindings and uncut pages, Major Mudd calmed himself with a cup of tea, his ears blistered by Rus's furious complaints about the choice of cut flowers.

Before him on his desk lay the maintenance manual put out by the manufacturer of Rus's elevator. Major Mudd had spent hours closely examining each schematic. The electronic relay panel got his greatest attention. He felt that his best line of attack was through the starter and controller units, although for some time he'd felt the motor generator set was the solution. He leafed through the schematics: The counterweight and its buffer, the traveling cables, the secondary sheaves, the governor, the roller guides, the terminal stopping switch cam. Which one?

His eyes asked the drawing for the best way to drop the 50,000-pound car down its shaft. That would end that silly seminar. And make him a free man.

Peno Rus would not be able to criticize the choice of cut flowers the major planned to send to his funeral.

15

South of Lyons a chilly autumn rain began, a light but steady soaking drizzle. Brewer looked through a pair of swaying windshield wipers at the dotted white line that twisted and turned, rose and fell through six countries, five border checks, and innumerable stops to Damascus.

He felt like a shepherd herding his flock. As he drove he examined Georges's car with a critical eye, looking for telltale signs of trouble.

He told himself over and over that he was a fool to have agreed to make delivery in Damascus. He should have drawn the line at New York or Boston and let Attashah get the stuff home from there. That way his work would already be finished. He would have done the job Attashah couldn't do, and Attashah would have done the job he didn't want to do. Instead, Attashah got him to do two jobs for the price of one.

Worse—if he failed in the smuggling operation, it would cancel out the job he had done assembling the parts. And that disaster could happen at any border inspection. Certainly Attashah would accept no excuses. For failure there'd be no payoff—except perhaps a shot in the back of the head.

BECAUSE OF THE RAIN and the poor road conditions, the cars made no attempt to stay together. It was well after dark before the last of them arrived at their first rest stop. Over a soggy, half-warmed meal, the drivers chatted eagerly of home. They were one day closer.

After they were asleep, Brewer walked around the cars in a downpour, kicking tires and checking for loose exhausts and other signs of trouble. Then he tried to sleep, wondering how far behind him his pursuers were. Surely Dice had cut his deal with McCall by now.

THE CARAVAN hit a crisis the next morning at its first checkpoint, the French-Italian border.

Brewer was the first to go through. Then he waited for the twenty-car caravan. Ten of the caravan got through without incident, the guards merely checked passports, green insurance cards, and auto registration. Then one of the cars, an old red Renault, was stopped.

Two Italian Customs men opened the Renault's back doors and lifted the seat. They reached under the dashboard, groped under the front seat. They required the driver to open the trunk. They felt under the spare tire and lifted the trunk mat. Then they stood looking critically at the rear tires. They pressed down on the car trunk to depress the springs.

"Why is this car so heavy?" one asked the driver. "Your springs are almost flat." The driver shrugged. The two customs men conferred briefly in low voices, then signaled the driver. They wanted him to drive the vehicle onto a weighing scale. One of them wet his finger and turned the pages of a directory that listed all the makes and models of cars and their standard weights.

The driver was complying when, abruptly, thick black smoke wrapped around the customs station. Horns blew and voices shouted. Soon everyone was coughing, and many were covering their faces with handkerchiefs. A truck's cargo was burning, fanned by high driving speeds, and now that it had stopped, the smoke billowed out of the truck body and crept along the ground. Vehicles in the smoke's path blew their horns, and the customs men hastily began waving all vehicles through in order to get the truck downwind of the station.

Brewer, waiting by the side of the road, counted all twenty of his cars as they drove by. Then came the truck. The driver stopped it, jumped out, and ran as the cargo burst into leaping flames. A towering pall of black acrid smoke ascended. Brewer drove off after his flock.

He caught up with the caravan and drove behind the red Renault to examine it. It had an undulating, laboring quality. The shock absorbers were shot. They would have to be replaced and the tires would have to be overinflated before they reached the next checkpoint at the Yugoslavian border. But that was on the other side of Italy. They had a lot of road to traverse first.

With twenty elderly cars, veterans of Parisian traffic wars, Brewer knew he had to expect breakdowns soon.

THE STRAIN was beginning to tell on Madeline Hale. She went everywhere in cabs. She always walked the last two or three blocks to her furnished apartment in Georgetown, sometimes walking in a complete circle to mislead anyone who was following her.

The slightest noise would awaken her. And there were many noises in the old brownstone building, creaks and snaps in the woodwork, doors closing, footsteps in the hallway.

One morning the mail girl walked into her office with a quizzical expression on her face, holding a letter. It was a piece of ordinary white paper that had been sent in an ordinary white #10 envelope. On it was written one word: BOOM.

On another day, she was told she had a phone call from a referee in a court case. But when she picked up the phone it wasn't the referee.

"Hello," she said for the third time.

And the voice on the other end said, very softly: "Boom."

She tried not to let it shake her. But it terrified her. And Brewer's attack on her came back vividly. With a shudder she felt anew his fingernail being drawn down the length of her torso, across her throat. She thought of being dropped seven stories off her balcony. And she remembered with nightmare clarity the explosion of her automobile.

One sleepless night she recalled her childhood prayer: "If I should die before I wake, I pray the Lord my soul to take."

The phone call when it came was unexpected. Her mind was on other things. Her friend in the FBI said: "Meet me in the Lizard Lounge."

He wasn't hard to find. He was sitting with a soft drink and a bunch of papers, a busy FBI attorney with too heavy a caseload and too short a workday. All the world was his office. When she walked up to the booth, he was busy editing a brief.

"Hurrah for the Red and the Blue," she said.

"Yay, Pennsylvania," he replied. When she sat down he pushed a piece of paper to her. "This is the guy who put the red flag on Brewer's personnel file."

She read the name. Robert McCall. "Oh," she said. "That's his boss."

"No surprise there," he said. "That's the kind of thing bosses do, I would say. And here's the name of the guy who put the red flag on the Anton Rumbh file over at Immigration and Naturalization."

It was a name she'd never heard before: Roger Hardy.

"Who's he?" she asked.

"A ranker. Career man. GS-sixteen or so. My contact tells me that when Hardy put the flag on, he said to her: 'A little favor for a neighbor.' "

HER UNLISTED PHONE rang at two in the morning. She had been sleeping fitfully and she straggled through her dark apartment to the phone, sure it must be trouble from home.

"Hello," she said.

There was no reply.

"Hello," she said again.

And a voice said, "Boom."

SHE DRESSED and called a cab and rode to her office. It was now two-thirty. She heard the night bell ring in the office lobby somewhere, and soon an old man in a guard's uniform came strolling to the entrance. He studied her through the glass doors, then slowly unlocked them.

She signed in, then took the elevator to her office. When she entered she turned on all the lights and put her coat on her desk. Then she went to the library and searched for the U.S. government *Who's Who*. She found Roger Hardy's name and title. Middle initial T. She dialed the emergency number listed.

"This is State," she said. "London desk. Urgent message for Roger Hardy. Home phone number, please."

The operator read it off. Hale then went to the master phone number directory and ran her finger down the columns of numbers. She found Hardy's address. She got the cross-check directory down, a house-by-house listing of all the phones in the area. She found Hardy's house address, then studied the names of the families on either side, across the street, and around the corner. A favor for a neighbor. Directly behind Hardy's house was the neighbor. Madeline Hale recognized the name immediately. She had found Anton Rumbh's true identity.

Now she had to find Brewer. If there was one person who knew where Charlie Brewer was, Hale knew who it must be. She dialed the home of Joanie Walsh, Bobby McCall's secretary.

While the phone was ringing, she looked down at a white piece of paper that had been tucked under her telephone. It contained one word.

BOOM.

FIVE HOURS after they'd crashed Georges's garage, McCall's team was still stonewalled.

They had quickly gone through Georges's neighborhood, interviewed the family, tried to interrogate shopkeepers and pedestrians. Many people pretended not to understand French.

McCall met Borden and Dice at a café at eleven to compare notes. McCall drummed his fingers frantically on the tabletop. Each minute that cargo got farther and farther away.

"How?" he demanded of Borden and Dice. "Plane? Truck? Boat? Camelback?"

Borden shrugged. "The Fat Man uses them all, Bobby. One time he shipped small handguns into Algeria inside vacuum cleaners. I don't know where to look next. But I'll say one thing. If we ask enough people, someone is going to say something, some little thing that we can use to pry open the other people. Sooner or later we'll come up with something."

McCall sat under the dripping awning, watching the drizzle pimple the puddles. He snorted at Borden. "Sooner or later Brewer will make delivery to Attashah. We're out of time, Borden."

"And out of ideas," Borden said.

"Not quite," McCall said. He raised his umbrella and walked off in the rain.

EARLY IN HIS CAREER McCall had been taught the proper attributes of a policeman: to be systematic, plodding, patient, and thorough. And to trust to luck. Above all, one must put oneself in a position to receive the breaks. In desperate times, he learned, one must not panic; stop chasing and become the chased; let the world come to you. Return to the scene of the crime.

The door to Georges's garage was still ajar when McCall arrived before noon. He stepped in and shut the door firmly behind him. He began systematically to search the building.

Rain muttered in a downspout. Mice scurried in a dark corner. Under a tarpaulin he found an ancient Citroën in the process of restoration. There were many tools on benches and in old metal toolboxes. Grease and oil stains everywhere.

Brewer was proving too smart for him, too cunning. He seemed to know what moves McCall was going to make before he made them. And the passage of each succeeding hour increased Brewer's chances of success. Maybe the game was over already.

With the odors of oil, gas, and acetylene in his nose, McCall poked morosely among abandoned papers in a nearly empty office file.

MCCALL STOOD BEMUSED in the middle of the garage, studying a large pan that leaned against a wall and wondering what it was for. He examined the welding torches. And he asked himself why there were so many cots stacked against a wall. Why so many blankets? What kind of business was operated here? He searched the drawers of the old desk in the office. He asked himself, if he were Brewer, how would he smuggle those parts to Iran?

Through the wet garage windows he watched the people of Montmartre hurry along the twisted streets, with umbrellas and sheets of paper over their heads, women hurrying home with noontime loaves of bread. Children in hoods, bearing school knapsacks, went by.

Footsteps approached and paused at the door. McCall stepped quickly up to it and waited. The doorknob was tried. Then the footsteps hurried away. Through a grimy window McCall saw the retreating back of a young woman under a large red umbrella.

It was maddening. Brewer's contraband had come to this place in the truck that was still parked on the apron in front of the building. The parts had evidently been brought into the garage, been placed where he now stood, been processed somehow, repacked, and now were gone again.

He sat and propped his elbows on the old kitchen table in the corner. With his chin on his hands he glanced at the headlines of the loose newspaper pages that covered the tabletop. They were from a French scandal sheet—tales of infidelities, improbabilities, and impossibilities. Man, eighty, marries childhood sweetheart after fifty years in jail. Man discovers that his wife had been keeping a lover in their attic for seven years. Woman gives birth to a monkey. Male girl makes self pregnant.

Bobby McCall admitted to himself he was beaten. He stood up to leave, brushing the loose newspaper pages. And found himself looking at several sheets of paper peeking out from under the newspaper. He sat down to read them.

One sheet contained a list of names with passport numbers—twenty of them. Another contained a list of automobile serial numbers and license-plate numbers—twenty of them. Twenty names, twenty cars, twenty-odd cots—and one pan.

McCall stood up and hurried to the door.

To BORDEN the problem was simple. "Why don't we just turn the license numbers over to the border checks?" he asked.

"No, no," McCall said. "This is not our turf. If this story gets out, half those countries might provide Brewer a god-dammed armed escort all the way to Iran, just to embarrass the U.S. The papers over here would have a bloody party. It would raise hell in Washington. No, that's not the way to do it."

"Then what is?" Borden demanded. "Christ, Brewer has a full day's head start on us already. Even if we started right now we could never catch up with them."

"Not by car," McCall said.

"Then what?"

"Airplanes," McCall said.

"What about airplanes?"

"Small private ones," McCall said. "We can fly low over the main roads from here to Syria until we spot the cars with the right license numbers."

"Smart," Borden said. "Very smart."

McCall said, "When you want to catch a Brewer, think like a Brewer."

THE AUTO ROUTE across Italy led them south of Milan toward Verona. Not far from Verona the red Renault commenced blowing heavy smoke from its exhaust. It lost power and drifted over to the shoulder. And there it died. Brewer wondered if the Renault was going to become his Nemesis.

Brewer and two other cars in the caravan stopped. They raised the hood and fiddled with the carburetor. The automatic choke had jammed. The driver adjusted it, started the engine, and watched it shudder and die, emitting more black smoke.

One of the drivers quickly pulled out the oil dipstick, stroked his finger along the oily rod, then wiped the oil drops onto the hinged flap of the automatic choke. It worked; the car started without smoking.

"Are you a mechanic?" Brewer asked him in French.

He shrugged and smiled. "In Syria most cars are old, so everybody is a mechanic."

DURING THE DAY, when they stopped for gas, Brewer watched each driver check his own oil, cooling system, battery, belts, and tires. Georges had chosen his drivers well.

But the caravan was spreading out. It was scattered along a sixty-mile length of Italian roadway. Some cars were more than an hour ahead of others. Brewer looked down the long white ribbon of roadway. The next major test was the Yugoslavian border.

Then he looked back. That's where the real trouble would come from. He was nursing twenty old wrecks, fixing breakdowns, stopping for meals, for sleep, for road checks, for fuel, for regrouping, for customs barriers. McCall could travel light, day and night.

Now he knew how the old cattle barons had felt on their long cattle drives through hostile Indian territory. It would be a miracle if he got this wandering herd of exhausted cars through the shooting gallery of customs checkpoints and into Damascus before McCall caught up with him.

He was sure that trouble was hatching under every hood, lurking at every customs post, and pursuing him from the rear on greyhound's legs. Trouble was coming from every direction—like Nemesis in Act Five.

INTERPOL-AID helped McCall get two small police planes from the Italians, with pilots and air clearance through Yugoslavia, Greece, and Turkey to Syria.

He and Borden made a rendezvous with the Italian pilots in the airport near Venice. The morning was wet and windy, and they stood inside the briefing room, over the air maps and the coffee cups, looking at two slowly shaking Italian heads.

"Too risky," one of the pilots said. "Low-level flying is too risky. Wind shear at low levels. Later today."

McCall stood at the window and looked out at the red windsocks that veered in the quixotic wind. Somewhere out in the weather, Brewer's cars were bounding over the roadway, slipping away from him mile after mile while the two pilots sat and played cards.

He and Borden drank coffee, flipped through magazines, and watched the two pilots play cards until noon. Then they all went to lunch in an airport restaurant crowded with people. All that light banter and relaxed meal-making seemed to mock him. The frustration was like a lump in McCall's throat, and he was unable to eat anything. He believed he was an inch away from madness.

A ray of sunshine lit up his lap. Abruptly he, Borden, and the two pilots got up and ran to the briefing room. The winds had shifted and dropped, and the wet weather lifted. They were cleared to fly. Both McCall and Borden had binoculars, maps, and a list of the car license plates. Within twenty minutes they were airborne toward Yugoslavia.

THEY HAD a bumpy time of it. And staring through binoculars at the license plates was dizzying, especially with the large number of vehicles; the main road through Yugoslavia was jammed with traffic in both directions.

At last McCall saw a long string of cars that seemed to be riding in a convoy. As they approached, he saw that many of them exhibited the French auto symbol. It took the driver two passes to get low enough to read the plates. The pilot called them off as McCall checked his list. He shook his head at the pilot.

"No. None of them match," he said. They flew on to the next section of roadway, to more license plates and more rough flying.

The onset of darkness forced them to quit for the day.

"We'll start again at first light," McCall told Borden.

Borden nodded unhappily. "Every goddammed vehicle in Europe must be driving through Yugoslavia. We're never going to be able to check them all."

McCall said, "I think Brewer must be in a hell of a sweat, too."

LATE IN THE MORNING, Brewer's caravan approached the Yugoslavian border. There were extended lines of crawling traffic waiting for clearance, with long delays. The Yugoslavian Customs was searching every car and truck.

They were weighing many more vehicles than normal, checking manifests, examining cargoes. They were going through personal belongings, opening suitcases.

The caravan finally reached the checkpoint, and the guards began a thorough check of all twenty cars.

"Are you carrying any books?" they asked in six languages.

They removed the car seats, searched under the dashboard, opened the hood of the engine, opened trunk lids. All bags were opened.

"What do you seek?" Brewer asked in Italian.

"Books," said the guard. "Italian books. A very bad book about President Tito. A scandalous biography. It's full of lies about the Trieste settlement."

Not one of the Syrian drivers was carrying a book of any sort. By noon all twenty cars had cleared the border check and were racing to the Bulgarian border, more than six hundred miles away. It was nearly dark.

THE TWO PLANES reached the Yugoslavian-Greek border that afternoon. Crawling traffic at the checkpoint required a number of overflights. Even so, it was almost impossible to read the license plates of the bumper-to-bumper traffic.

They landed at dusk, tired and discouraged. McCall said, "We must have overflown them. They couldn't have gotten this far unless they were driving day and night and they would need forty drivers for that, not twenty. I figure they're still in Yugoslavia somewhere."

"You mean we're going to have to double back?" Borden asked.

"Yes. All the way back to Trieste almost. And start all over again. But tomorrow we're bound to find them. I'll bet you a big lollipop those twenty cars are in Yugoslavia right now, getting ready to stop for the night.

AT BREAKFAST McCall and Borden announced the day's program to the two Italian pilots.

"Today should do it," McCall said. "By doubling back along the Yugoslav highway, we should spot them quickly."

The two pilots exchanged glances. "We hope so," said one of them. "This low-level flying with those winds coming off the mountains is very dangerous. We'll be glad when it's over."

"We should spot the cars in the next two or three hours," McCall said.

Half an hour later the two planes were back in the air, headed toward Trieste. The auto traffic below was as heavy as ever.

By nine McCall began to feel frustrated once more. By ten he was frowning. They couldn't have overflown the caravan again. Those cars had to be down there.

"Hot damn!" he said suddenly.

"What?" demanded the pilot.

"The bastard's driving at night!" McCall shouted.

THEY REFUELED before eleven. McCall asked the two pilots: "How long to the Turkish-Syrian border?"

The two pilots consulted their air maps. "Five or six hours."

"Okay. Borden, you stick to the air patrol. Ezio, you can take me to the Turkish-Syrian border."

"What are you doing that for?" Borden asked.

"If my calculations are right, before dawn tomorrow Brewer and his little black sheep are going to drive through the Syrian customs there. And I'm going to be there watching."

BY SEVEN THAT NIGHT, McCall was posted in a car overlooking the Syrian Customs check at the Turkish border, a well-lit oasis in the darkness. It was also heavily guarded.

The Ottoman Turk had been driven out of the Mideast in the aftermath of World War I. But he had occupied the Arab lands, including Syria, for more than four hundred years. The Arab has a long memory, deep pride, and an unforgiving nature. Unfriendliness, therefore, between the Turks and Syrians fairly crackled at the border points. All traffic coming through Turkey was regarded with suspicion by the Syrian guards.

There was an incredible collection of competitive nations stuffed into the confining area of the mideast. Turkey and Syria. Syria and Lebanon. Lebanon and Israel. Israel and Syria. Iraq and Iran. Iran and Saudi Arabia. Russia and Iran. Sticks of dynamite, packed tightly, rubbing together—an explosive friction.

And every hour brought Charlie Brewer closer, with a lighted match.

Borden's parting words had been: "He's a goddam fox, that Brewer. Watch your step."

By six the next morning, McCall was sure, he would see Charlie Brewer and his little flock drive right by him. McCall stepped out of the car, rubbing his eyes, and stretched, then paced up and down in the cold air to fight off drowsiness. Falling asleep could be a catastrophe. When the binoculars grew so cold it hurt to hold them, he got back into the automobile.

The car traffic tapered off after eight that evening but the truck traffic kept coming all night. And the Syrian guards checked over each one with care. They went strictly by the book, checking the trucks and their cargo and their documents, then the drivers and their bags and their documents. Often there was shouting between the guards and the truck drivers.

The weight of each truck was verified on the scales. And the underside of each car was examined by angled mirrors on a pole with wheels.

Brewer was going to have one tough time. If the guards used their mirrors, they would quickly discover the welded pans.

THERE WAS SOMETHING hypnotic about the passing night traffic. Whenever McCall felt drowsy he stepped out of the car. The steady cold breeze would soon chill him, and he shivered and paced. He did knee bends. And he touched his toes. And hummed to himself. Then, stiff with cold, he would get back into the car.

The hours passed slowly. On the back of an envelope, with pencil marks, he began collecting vehicles from different countries. Most European plates looked alike. One had to look at the letter in the oval ring on the trunk above the license plate to identify the country. F for France. CH for Switzerland, and so forth. The commonest European vehicle plates in his count were German. France was second, Italy third. But the Italians had a decided run at eleven o'clock and nearly broke into first place. At midnight the German plates were well in the lead again. Then some French trucks and two Renaults put France back in contention.

At one, he gave a violent lurch. He had dozed. Momentarily, but nonetheless he'd dozed. He stepped out of the car and strolled up and down. It had gotten colder.

McCall versus Brewer. It would be gratifying to best the legendary Brewer. McCall would serve his country and add to his own legend. He would be rated better than Brewer.

He ran in place. "Don't you fall asleep, you son of a bitch," he said aloud. Then he drew back his hand and slapped his own face as hard as he could. The inner wall of his cheek was cut on a tooth and he tasted his own blood.

"Brewer, I'm going to get you."

BUT BREWER stubbornly refused to arrive. By two, McCall had to reassure himself. He reestimated Brewer's average speed and calibrated an arrival time of 4:00 A.M. Two hours to go.

At three he discovered an error in his calculations and revised the time of arrival to 5:00 A.M. Still two hours to go.

He went into long reveries now, recalling his father. The broken hockey stick. He envied Borden, who was sound asleep in his hotel room. Then he heard the long falling scream of the Flying Tumbler. He was wide-awake. It was five o'clock. And no Brewer.

The tarot deck and the falling Tumbler were a long way back down the road.

He got out of the car and strolled up and down, up and down, for the hundredth time that night. A group of trucks arrived. Italian and Spanish plates.

He had been beaten. There was no night caravan. He'd guessed wrong. The fox had fooled him once again. Somewhere in Turkey, Brewer must have switched everything to trucks—or planes or balloons.

McCall realized with a start that it was the morning of November 26. He had been so intent on Brewer he'd forgotten about the three other assassinations. Today was the day.

McCall got into his car and started the engine. He fought off a wave of despair. As if to mock him, two more trucks and a car arrived. Almost as a reflex action, he put the binoculars on the car—an old red Renault with a French license plate.

Bingo.

GETTING THE BINARY explosive into Cairo was the easy part. Rock shipped it in two packages, inside new copies of the Koran published in Damascus. They were air-freighted to his Cairo hotel, where he'd reserved an expensive suite.

Planting the bomb in the Royal Nile Hotel was going to be very dicey. Rumbh had really done his homework, and Rock had brought with him all the floor diagrams, photographs of room settings, and, most important, keys to the conference room. But the security was so tight in the Royal

Nile, he was going to have a tough time getting close to the conference room.

There was really only one possibility—through the air-duct system.

He made the bomb in his hotel room. Discreetly then, he got rid of the cut-out Korans and other debris in trash piles in various parts of the city. By noon of the twenty-sixth he was all set. The bomb fit neatly into an expensive attaché kit he'd bought just for it in Paris. And the attaché case fit neatly inside a larger executive case, very expensively made of natural leather with white-gold fittings.

Just before he left his room he laid out the photographs and floorplans of the hotel and conference room. He'd memorized the route he would take and the precise location of the closet for the air-conditioning system.

He dressed carefully and expensively, then left his room carrying the large executive case. When he reached the Royal Nile, the doorman held the cab door open for him and he stepped into the coolness of the glassed-in lobby. The kiss-and-tell conference was set to commence at 3:00 P.M. and already the lobby was awash with government security men, Cairo police, and representatives of both sides who would make their own final checks.

All eyes were on Rock's attaché case as he crossed to the elevator. A security man stepped on the elevator with Rock and pretended to read his newspaper. The man watched Rock get off on the sixth floor. He held the elevator door open with his foot as he watched Rock walk down the corridor. Rock stopped at 612, put a key in the lock, and entered the room. He waited there for fifteen minutes.

At twelve-thirty Rock walked down the stairway to the conference floor. He strolled down the carpeted hallway, past the two entrances to the conference room, and turned at the corner. There was a security man at each door, and inside, through a partly open door, he saw several men setting up chairs around a large conference table.

The air-conditioning system was closeted behind two latticed doors. He could feel the hum of the massive unit when he put the key in one of the doors. It turned; the door opened; he stepped inside and pulled the door shut behind him. Halfway home. He took out a pencil flashlight and aimed it up at the wall behind the unit. By stretching his head up, he could see through the wall opening under the main duct. He saw little slits of light coming through the wall from the conference room around an air outlet.

Voices came down the corridor toward him. They drew closer: two men, one with a two-way radio unit. They paused before the doors of the air-conditioning system. Rock had not locked it behind him. If they opened that door, Rock was a dead man—possession of that bomb would put him right in front of an Egyptian firing squad. One of the men gripped the door handle and turned it. The door opened. Light from the hallway fell in a vertical stripe on Rock's form. The two voices discussed this. Then the door was shut; a key was inserted in the lock and turned. The two men walked away.

Rock told himself to hurry. With both hands he reached the attaché case up and through the opening in the wall under the air duct. It just fit. With his right arm extended, he reached the case up against the conference room wall and left it resting upright against the side of the air duct. Surely any idiot would find that. It stuck out like a bull fiddle in a phone booth. The bomb was set to go off at precisely five o'clock.

With his key Rock unlocked the door of the closet and stepped into the hallway. This time he walked away from the conference room to another stairway and walked back up to the sixth floor. There he summoned the elevator and took it down to the lobby, carrying the empty executive case.

He crossed the lobby and got into a taxi. Then he relaxed. It had been a piece of cake after all.

BEFORE ROCK had left the building, the closet door was unlocked. An arm reached in and retrieved the attaché case. Two brown hands opened it and, with great care, lifted out the bomb from the case. The hands then deftly fitted the bomb into a child's schoolbook knapsack. On the blue canvas fabric of the knapsack were printed in white the initials UCLA.

NOW CAME THE ONE PART of the operation Slane didn't like. The ship was less than twenty miles off the coast of the Leeward Island Free State. In an hour and a half, he would wade through the surf with his troops, dash up on the beach, and commandeer a taxicab which would carry him to the presidential palace.

In the original event the Presidente had been picked up by his cousin, who owned the cab, and carried to the palace concealed in the trunk of the vehicle. That was the part Slane didn't like. He had a premonition he would die in there, gasping for air. Everyone has assured him there was plenty of ventilation in the trunk but he was still apprehensive.

And in recent nights he had dreamed of his first murder. Carson was his name. It was the only killing that had ever bothered him, probably because it was the one that had carried him over that forbidden line from which there was no turning back. It was the irrevocable act. And Carson had died badly, shouting at him, terrified of death, a man with fears of damnation.

His words had come back to Slane many times. "There is a hell, Slane, and that's where you're going."

Just before dawn the ship turned toward shore as the mercenaries began working the fittings of the landing craft. Slane told himself that after the ride in the taxicab trunk, everything would be all right.

PENO RUS slept fitfully. The seminar was going splendidly. There had been nothing but praise from the attendees. Word had gotten out as Rus had intended, and already other arms buyers from all over were calling to sign up for the next seminar. Rus had said to Major Mudd in jest: "We may have to start our own war college, Mudd, as a rival to Sandhurst." But there was a real possibility that they would have to form a permanent program of some sort.

Yet, each day brought new surprises. Rus had kept careful notes and in the next seminar there were many things he would do differently. What kept his sleep so fitful was his apprehension that before the seminar ended he would make a major gaffe. So he woke and reviewed the scheduled events in his mind, made notes, and went back to sleep, only to wake again and make more notes.

At 2:00 A.M. he woke and wrote, "Make a large chart of the Morston military maneuver for Schmidt's talk."

Then he listened to the slow-paced breathing of the young man beside him and drifted off into sleep again.

16

The streets of Damascus were full of soldiers. Truckloads of armed infantrymen drove up and down the rainy avenues. It was the second limited alert within a week, and the civilians seemed as bored with it as the military did. They barely glanced at the olive-drab vehicles that struggled through the narrow, winding ways.

Earlier in the day the sun had appeared briefly through the clouds to strike the minarets of the holy Umayyad Mosque on the northeastern outskirts of the city. Then the clouds had closed in once more, and a steady autumn rain commenced.

The Fat Man, Georges, sat in the coffeehouse across from the car dealer's garage, smoking and watching the rain. He waited to read his fate in the number of his cars that would arrive. Like giant tin tea leaves.

He drained the last of the coffee from his cup and scooped the quarter inch of residual sugar into his mouth with his forefinger. He would count himself fortunate to lose only eight cars. Six would surely have been detected. He signaled for another cup of coffee.

Idly, his tongue probed again the three new empty spaces among his teeth, deftly touching the sunken hole in each space in the still-tender gums. He remembered the loud crack each tooth had made, torn from the gums by the dentist's rocking extraction tool. And all the while the dentist's suppressed sighs of horror.

"Oh, monsieur. Your mouth. A catastrophe. [Crack!] Three extractions. Five root canals. And seventeen fillings. [Crack!] Oh, monsieur, what an unnecessary waste. Fourteen years of neglect is a tragedy. [Crack!] You must never, never, never [drill, drill, drill] neglect your teeth like this again. Never." Georges licked his sticky forefinger and mourned his three lost teeth.

Abruptly, while his mind was wandering, a red Renault turned into the lot. He recognized the French license plate immediately and sighed with pleasure: Red was his lucky color. He calculated that if just ten cars appeared, he would not receive a bullet through the head from his irate client. The tenth arrival would save his life.

Across from him, toothless and white-bearded, sat an old Bedouin with skin the color of chocolate from a life in the desert, murmuring of the dying old ways. He was a haji and therefore revered and ignored. In the traditional singsong of the Arab storyteller, he crooned to himself an epic of desert strife and of a brother's betrayal of brother, the old story. It was filled with the familiar characters who are called forth in every age and every generation to reenact the immemorial tragedies without end. So it is written.

Next to the haji three men talked of the old quarrels among the Shi'a and the Imamis of Iran, the Alawites, the dominant orthodox Sunni, and the ferocious Ismailis of Syria. One poked a finger at the vein in his arm. "Ismaili," he said. The other two laughed and pointed at their arms.

Georges uttered a comfortable sigh: Two more cars entered the parking lot. It was one-thirty. Only seven more were needed to save his unworthy neck. His mind roved over the different checkpoints on that long route from Paris to Damascus. He knew every mile of it, how many cars had he himself driven over the years? He recalled the few that were impounded. The Turks always gave him the most difficulty. But his driving days were over.

Two more arrived—a total of five cars by 1:45. Four more appeared at two o'clock. That made nine. One more was all he asked. Time passed. Georges squirmed in his chair. Was that all that got through? Nine? Eleven had been taken?

A CATASTROPHE. He sat with his chin on his fist, squinting his left eye against his cigarette smoke, disconsolate. It was not two-thirty. Monsieur Brewer had offended the Fates with his endless rearrangements of the cargo in the pans. At quarter to three, Georges was convinced. Only nine had gotten through. At three, he prepared to leave. It had been an hour since the last arrival.

A red Volkswagen drove up the street and turned into the lot. It was number ten. Georges snubbed out his cigarette, stood up, then sat again. He rubbed his hands on his trousers and lit another cigarette. Saved by a Volkswagen. Red, his lucky color again. God is good.

Then two more cars arrived almost together. Before Georges could draw an overjoyed breath, three more arrived. An incredible total of fifteen cars. Extraordinary. He celebrated with another coffee with cardamom. Any more cars were extremely unlikely. But the sixteenth arrived minutes later, and while he was standing in wonder, paying the waiter, numbers seventeen, eighteen, and nineteen arrived. He tipped the waiter heavily.

After twenty-six years in the business he never permitted a feeling of elation. Resignation, yes. He was always prepared for that when, as expected, things went poorly. There was safety in a little misfortune. But when things went too well he grew suspicious: Too much luck is dangerous. And when things went this well, surely the Great Bestower of Fortune was raising him for a disaster.

As he stood in the doorway, pulling his raincoat over his swelling bulk, the twentieth car turned into the lot. Incredible. The Fat Man's heart was filled with dread. It had to be the herald of a major catastrophe.

He strolled across the lot in the pelting rain, his eyes counting the cars once more. There they were: twenty cars. He looked at the smirking faces of four drivers.

"How did it go?" he asked.

"Very well indeed, monsieur. Only a few breakdowns, easily repaired."

"No trouble at the borders?"

No. There had been none. Georges stood looking at the twenty automobiles for a moment and listening to the sounds of Damascus—the chorus of car and truck engines, occasional horns, and the sounds of construction, hammers and riveting—and wondering what went wrong. He threw his cigarette down. Filled with dread, he needed to sit. He went back to the coffeehouse for another cup. Twenty cars. Georges did sums in his head: He had earned a fortune.

He thought of his assignations at the Hotel Taft—Margot and her red umbrella. Would he lose his Wednesday appointment? He yearned for her. A certain stirring in his loins. He hungered for Paris. Having grown old there, he had become a Parisian to his gizzard. Margot. And couscous. And Paris. He would go back there and hide from the baleful eye of Fate.

As he raised the cup to his lips, his client Brewer drove into the garage lot. He remembered how Brewer had agonized over the apportionment of the parts in the various underpans. How the man had tormented Fate. And now, was Fate taunting him with twenty cars?

Brewer walked across the road in the downpour, bearing an attaché case, and entered the coffeehouse. He held a thumb up to Georges as he sat down.

"So," Georges said. "It went well."

"Yes," Brewer said. "Very well. Total success."

"And now?"

"And now I will load my inventory on a truck and deliver it to my client. The mechanics have already removed a number of the pans."

When the thin man in the polka-dot tie arrived, shaking his umbrella, Georges knew where the parts were going. Attashah stepped up beside the seated Brewer and leaned forward to whisper a question.

"All," Brewer answered.

"All? Everything?"

"Everything," Brewer said.

Attashah clasped his hands together and shuddered in violent joy. Georges thought of the old Arab proverb: "How doth the serpent smile?"

BOBBY MCCALL stood bare-naked before the bathroom mirror of his hotel room in Damascus. Ever since he had watched the red Renault roll through the Turkish-Syrian border check, just when he had almost quit in despair, his luck had changed. He felt invincible now.

With care, he applied the dark-brown makeup to his face, his ears, his neck. He fitted brown contact lenses in his pale-blue eyes. Over his curly brown hair he adjusted a straight-haired black wig. Then he applied the dark-brown makeup to his hands and wrists and midway to his elbows. Next he coated his feet and ankles with the same hue.

From a brown paper bag he took a white pullover shirt with no collar and struggled into it. Then a pair of trousers made of a coarse material and gathered at the ankles. He stepped into them and cinched a woven belt around his waist. Next he took out a burnous, a heavy woolen hooded cloak broadly striped in brown and orange. He pulled it over his head. Lastly he stepped into a pair of leather sandals. As the finishing touch, he wound around his head a flat porter's turban made of a length of twisted cloth. He tucked in the end just above his right ear.

He examined himself critically in the full-length mirror. A sun-brown Damascus street porter with brown eyes and straight black hair looked back at him. He took a can of makeup remover, plus a large box of cotton pads, and put them in readiness on the sink. On the bed he had laid out his suit, shirt, socks, shoes, necktie, and personal items including his airline tickets. His suitcase and garment bag waited by the door. He was nearly ready.

From a bureau drawer he took a .38 pistol and broke it and checked it, then snapped the cylinder back into place. He attached a silencer to the barrel, tucked the weapon into his trouser belt, and adjusted the burnous over it.

McCall took a last look at himself in the mirror.

"Don't miss," he said to the porter in the glass.

ROCK SAT in the Cairo café, pretending to read the newspaper. But he kept watching the same corner a block away. She would come swinging around there and then cross the street and walk by the café as she did every day.

A thousand times he told himself she wasn't coming. She was late. She'd gone another way. He writhed in his chair. And then at last she appeared, walking around that corner, crossing the street, and as he watched she drew closer. Closer. He studied her figure. Her face. Had she changed? It was only a few weeks. No more than two months. She came in brilliant sunlight with her schoolbag slung across her back. Tawny skin. Golden skin. Long tresses. Rock felt poetic. His heart sang. *The coast is clear.*

She drew closer. Rock laid aside the paper, threw some money on the table, and in his new white linen suit and new white sun hat, stepped out on the sidewalk.

She stopped and gasped and hung her head. He spoke to her. She nodded at her name. He invited her to walk with him. They strolled together.

"Are you pleased to see me?"

She nodded her head but kept her eyes averted.

"I have a present for you," he said. "A very nice present all the way from Paris. Would you like to see it?"

She nodded again with lowered head.

"Let me carry your schoolbag," Rock said. He walked happily with her to his hotel, the bag slung over one shoulder. It was a blue canvas knapsack with the legend UCLA on it.

MAJOR MUDD SAT in the foyer of Peno Rus's penthouse, facing the door of the elevator. In five or ten minutes Rus would come up to take his regular afternoon nap with his latest bedmate, a seventeen-year-old boy, a truant from one of England's best public schools.

Major Mudd sat with the cable-box between his feet. Several electrical lines trailed along the marble floor and up the wall into an open junction box.

He checked the connections for the last time, then looked at his watch. Three minutes before two.

THE CARIBBEAN SUN never merely rises. It ascends. Majestic and dazzling, it mounts the dawn sky, bestowing its rays like largesse. On this day, November 27, it found the early-morning beach filled with people. The great sea stirred, the surf hissed, and the sound of many people on foot and in vehicles filled the air as they scraped and shuffled and murmured and laughed and slammed and tapped and hammered.

All eyes watched the ocean for the arrival of the landing craft. The grandstand was filled. El Presidente was given the foremost seat; it was a director's canvas chair with one word across the back: EXCELENCIA. Others—members of his cabinet, his family and close personal friends, including his official biographer, his official photographer, his official recording secretary, his mother, his four children as well as the children of his cabinet members—all were present and murmuring excitedly as they watched for the landing boats.

Servants went among them, passing out picnic foods on paper plates printed for the occasion. With the rising of the sun, El Presidente could now see the crowds extending along the brow of the beach in both directions. They stood obediently behind wooden sawhorses that fenced the beach off from traffic. On the beach, at strategic locations, three cameras and their crews waited.

The crowd cried out and cheered when they spotted the ship approaching. It headed directly toward the beach.

Jamil stood on the roof of a van that was parked on the brow of the sand dune. His slender boy's body was dressed in a yellow ensemble. On his head was a wide-brimmed straw hat. His binoculars searched the sea.

On the ground beside the van stood a tripod with a camera. Inside the van under a blanket lay an Ingram rifle with a silencer attached.

Next to the van was parked the taxicab that the President had commandeered for the ride to the presidential palace. His cousin who had driven the original cab was waiting today to reenact the drive. The two ladies who had ridden in the original cab were waiting with the cousin to make the same ride again. Slane would emerge from the surf, cross the beach, tumble into the trunk of the cab, and be whisked off to the palace.

Slane's cab ride to the palace would take fifteen minutes. Jamil's van ride to the airport and the waiting private jet would take ten minutes.

Jamil glanced at His Excellency and laughed to himself. The man sat there in his official director's chair with his official Hollywood sunglasses, casting a critical eye on the performance of one hundred troops who were about to take over his island, topple his government, arrest him, and then execute him in the basement of the presidential palace. He had a front-row seat to his own downfall. Within an hour he should be dead.

Jamil was witnessing an ironic reenactment of the story of the Trojan Horse.

ROCK QUICKLY STRIPPED and got on the bed. He held out to her the package tied with ribbon. "Go ahead," he said. "Open it."

The girl carefully untied the ribbon and saved it. Then deftly she slipped off the wrapping paper and saved that. Her hands were trembling as she opened the lid of the small box.

"It's from Paris," Rock said.

Inside was a gold necklace, and she stared at it with open mouth. It was the first gold she'd ever touched. Rock helped her put it on, fumbling with the clasp like a bridegroom. She stood before the mirror, nude save for the necklace, and gaped at her image. Then she flung herself on the bed and into the waiting arms of Rock.

It was precisely five o'clock, and Rock's bomb behaved flawlessly. The explosion blew out the wall of the hotel and left a gaping hole where the room had been.

MAJOR MUDD heard the elevator start in its shaft. He looked at the floor indicator above the door, then at the flashing light on the cable box between his feet. He reached down and unclasped the safety cover from the red button. Then he waited.

The little square of light on the floor indicator danced along the numbers: 2 3 4 5 6. Mudd looked at his little black box; 9 10 11 12 13 14 P. The light stopped at P. Mudd heard the two voices murmuring in the elevator and watched as the door slid open. Peno Rus stood framed in the doorway with his right arm draped over the shoulders of a handsome young man. The youth's eyes widened when he saw Major Mudd.

"Father!" he called. "I can explain."

Major Mudd reached his right forefinger down to the red button and pushed. The cable brakes short-circuited. The lighted elevator car disappeared in the wink of an eye. One instant it was there, and the next there was nothing but rattling cables against a brick shaft wall. The elevator car fell. If Rus and the boy screamed all the way down the elevator shaft, Mudd never heard them. The only sound was a great whistling rush of air.

A moment later, the major heard the loudest boom of his life. He would hear it ever after.

SLANE, IN THE FIRST BOAT, brandished a pistol at the beach, then jumped down into the surf. The grandstand broke into prolonged applause and shouts of encouragement. Swaying from side to side, Slane struggled through the surf to the shore.

He took three steps out of the surf, drew back his left arm, and waved the troops forward. The throng was applauding loudly and shouting instructions to Slane and the troops. Everyone was standing. Slane drew back his right arm and waved the troops forward. The crowd cheered as though at a soccer match.

Slane trotted up the beach toward the waiting cab. Jamil stepped forward and waved Slane onward to the open car trunk. Slane came at a fast run. Jamil picked up the rifle and held it out for Slane. Slane came closer at a dead run. Jamil waved Slane on. "Hurry!" he shouted. Slane sprinted.

Jamil nodded at the driver, who jumped into the car with the two ladies. Slane arrived and tumbled into the trunk, holding out his hands to receive the rifle.

"So long, you son of a bitch," Jamil said.

Slane began to sit up with shocked recognition on his face. Jamil reached the rifle out to put it into the trunk. With scarcely a pause in his motion, he pulled the trigger at point-blank range. Pfft! Pfft! Pfft! Pfft! Four shots into Slane's head. Jamil pushed the rifle into the trunk and slammed it. He waved the driver off.

17

In the steady downpour Bobby McCall stepped out of the rear entrance of the hotel and walked up the street to the coffeehouse, his ragged costume blending with those of other pedestrians who hurried and skulked on their rainy errands. On his head he bore a nondescript cardboard carton with the legend CHAMPION MOTOR PARTS. The rain made tapping noises on it.

McCall turned into the covered market street, Suq al Hamidiyah, and walked in the semidarkness. Over his head, the steady rain pelted the metal sheeting of the roof. Shafts of gray light lit the bazaar here and there. The street led through the Old City directly to the Umayyad Mosque. The bazaar was impossibly crowded and McCall slowly picked his way through.

Vendors' voices sang out their wares.

"Almonds."

"Cuuuuucumbers."

"Figs. Pomegranates."

"Walnuts."

"T-shirts. Japanese radios."

At the stand of the oil merchant, McCall turned and walked down an alley. He came out into the rain again and walked a wet street to the garage where the twenty cars were being worked on. At the side of the building stood a truck with its back doors open. McCall walked across the parking area to the truck and without hesitation slid the carton from his head into the truck beside a number of other small boxes. His thumb and forefinger gripped a piece of short flat wire that protruded from a hole in the side of the box. He gave a quick tug, then turned on his heel and walked back across the parking area.

He crossed the road to the coffeehouse, glanced inside, and saw Brewer sitting with Georges. He stood against a wall and waited.

IT WAS a very good bomb. It exploded within three minutes. The entire back of the truck went up, carrying with it all of Brewer's parts. A great black ball of smoke tumbled skyward and soon a shower of smoldering debris fell on the parking area and the street.

McCall stepped away from the wall and looked into the coffeehouse. Brewer and Georges were standing, staring at the burning truck. McCall pulled out the weapon from his gown, held it in both hands, drew a bead on Brewer, and pulled the trigger twice. With the silencer, it barely made a sound. Brewer flung his arms up and tumbled backward over his chair. No one noticed; they were all staring at the bombed truck.

McCall turned and quickly walked back the way he had come into the jammed bazaar. In the crush he pitched the pistol under the oil dealer's stand and blended into the crowd, picking his way back to his hotel and the makeup remover.

An hour later he was airborne on a flight to Paris.

AS IF IN CELEBRATION, the weather in Paris had finally turned magnificent. The street cleaners were sweeping up the last of the chestnuts from the Champs Élysées, and the streets were crowded with people enjoying the last good weather before the wet winter set in.

McCall was making his final arrangements, preparing to return to Washington a hero. He was the founder and sole proprietor of one of the great intelligence coups of the decade. The arms world talked of nothing but the assassinations, the Iranians had been thwarted, and McCall had a fortune in Wainwright's money. The only payout had been in black casino chips to Jamil, and McCall waited for the man's return to Paris to make the final payment. It was the single piece of unfinished business.

There was one other slight expense: the few dollars for the blue UCLA knapsack he had given the girl's family in Cairo to carry the bomb from the Royal Nile Hotel to Rock's hotel. McCall regretted the death of the girl, who had unwittingly carried the bomb to Rock. But that was her family's idea. Arab justice.

THIS TIME McCall took no chances. Rather than meet Jamil in another public brasserie, he picked him up at the airport.

"Well," he said to Jamil. "It was one of your masterpieces?"

"My two great masterpieces," Jamil said. "Major Mudd was a masterpiece in its own right but I feel my job on Slane is unsurpassable. I was almost to Miami before they realized that Slane was dead. I laughed all the way back here." He took a newspaper out of his hand case. "You did see the London papers?"

McCall glanced at the headline. "Poor Mudd. A very unhappy man, Jamil."

Jamil pulled his trench coat around his thin body. "I think I shall spend the winter somewhere warm." He glanced at McCall. "With a friend." He chuckled. "A warm friend."

They drove back to Paris in the car McCall had rented. In the long slow sunset, Jamil chatted, telling McCall in detail how the operation went.

They entered the city from the west. "Where are we going?" Jamil asked.

"Payday," McCall said. "I have your fee for the Mudd job. And I have reconsidered your fee for Slane and decided that you were right. Slane was worth a quarter of a million."

"Seriously?"

"Seriously. I have another job coming up and I want you absolutely comfortable with me. Are you available?"

"But of course."

McCall drove to the bus terminal near Les Invalides and parked. "Perhaps we may dine together somewhere—a little victory celebration."

"Delighted," Jamil said.

"It's all cash, small bills in an attaché case, as you requested," McCall said. "No more black poker chips."

They both chuckled.

"Don't forget to count it," McCall said. He handed Jamil the key to a baggage locker.

Jamil shook the little key in his fist. "I'll be right back."

Jamil entered the bus terminal, found the bank of lockers, and searched out the number on the key. He opened the locker, found the attaché case, laid it flat, popped the latches, and lifted the lid. The case exploded in his face, killing him instantly.

"It's called deniability," McCall said to himself as he drove away. Inside the bus terminal a woman was screaming over and over.

THE LAST LEG. Homeward bound. McCall packed his bags and checked his papers—passport and airline tickets. There would be no broken hockey stick for him.

The phone rang. McCall turned and looked at it. His phone was not supposed to ring. He was expecting no information, no visitors, no contact from anyone. And without warning McCall felt dread in his stomach. It was the announcement of Nemesis's arrival in the final Greek scene—in the form of a shepherd with a piece of information, a messenger with an item of devastating evidence, the final tampering with man's fate by the gods. He told himself not to answer the phone.

It rang again. An insistent, unpleasant, shrill ring. Commanding: Answer me immediately.

McCall looked at the door. He could leave the room with his bags and go to the airport with the phone ringing behind him, never to know who was calling.

It rang a third time. McCall picked it up.

"Bobby? It's me. Borden."

"I'm just leaving for the airport."

"I'll meet you at Dulles."

"What's up?" McCall demanded.

"You're not going to like it."

"Skip the buildup, Borden. What is it?"

"Those Iranian parts got through," Borden said. "The whole order."

"What are you telling me?"

"We just got a report from our British cousins in Tehran. They're dancing in the aisles there. And Attashah is a big size-fourteen hero. They're fitting out those surveillance planes with new navigational equipment and new black boxes. The fat's really in the fire now."

"This can't be true."

"I'm looking at the report, Bobby, right in my hand."

"I'll see you in a little while." McCall hung up.

He sat down on the edge of the bed. Brewer. Brewer had slipped him a mickey: a decoy truck. While everyone was watching the explosion, another truck was carrying the parts to a rendezvous with Attashah somewhere—probably in the Syrian desert.

McCall stood up, trying to salvage his operation. There had been four brilliant hits. And Major Mudd's assassination was the added fillip. The arms world was abuzz with the whole matter. The prestige of the United States had risen enormously. No one would pluck the lion's beard with such casual aplomb anymore. All this was just as McCall had planned it.

On top of that, the Arms Control Committee had complete deniability. Rock and the girl were dead; Mudd and Rus were dead; Slane and Jamil were dead, and he himself had taken care of Brewer. There was no one left to point a finger at Washington except himself.

But how to explain away the Iranian parts disaster?

The phone rang again. McCall let it ring. "No more," he said. He gathered his baggage.

It rang again. "No," he said. The image that had crossed his mind so often lately was too appropriate. Messengers were arriving with disastrous news from all over his kingdom. The final payment for hubris. "No," he repeated.

He picked up his baggage and walked to the door. He opened it. As he turned around in the hallway to close it, the phone rang again. He started down the hallway. It rang again through the door. He put down his bags and dashed back. In three strides he'd crossed the room and snatched up the phone.

"Hello."

Was the line dead?

"Hello. Who is this?"

The voice was low, almost a whisper. "Bang bang, you're dead. Fifty bullets in the head."

"Who is this?" demanded McCall. But the caller hung up. McCall hurried back to his baggage and took the elevator to the lobby. He paid his bill, stuffed the receipt into his inside jacket pocket, and hurried through the lobby doors.

Bang bang, you're dead. Fifty bullets in the head.

At the curb he beckoned a taxi from the cab stand. He stooped with his two bags to enter the cab and paused, drew back almost violently.

"Hello, Bobby." A hand reached out to grip his lapel and pull him in. "Let me help you."

McCall tumbled into the cab. And looked at the last messenger of the gods. Brewer.

"Mr. Rumbh, I presume," Brewer said. He signaled the driver to move on.

McCall sat rigidly, staring at him.

Brewer smiled. "Look at that face. Mouth wide open. Amazed expression. Bobby, you are a classic screw-up. It took Madeline Hale forever to figure out what you did. And do you know why? Because it was so damned dumb."

McCall retreated to a corner of the cab. He sat with his fist pressed against his mouth, looking with fury at the passing street scene.

"When you blew up Madeline Hale's nice powder-blue Mercedes, Bobby, you should have done it with her in it. You'd still be on top of the world if you had. You know that?"

McCall didn't answer.

"Cat got your tongue, Bobby?"

McCall finally spoke. "You're a traitor, Brewer. They're going to send you up forever."

"Cellmates, you and I, ha?" Brewer laughed at him.

"Shit." McCall sat up angrily. "How did I miss you? I drew a bead at less than fifty feet. And I fired twice right at the head. Right between the goddammed eyes. I couldn't have missed."

"It was all the Fat Man's doing. He's got relatives all over Damascus, and you were spotted the minute you got off the plane. You're just not a born agent, Bobby. You're not paranoid enough. You can't arrive in a town like Damascus with an assassin's pistol in your suitcase without having people figure out what you're up to."

"I checked that piece before I fired it."

"Nah, the bullets were fakes, Bobby. Very clever fakes. Blanks. Georges made them and then he had one of his cousins slip them into your piece right in your hotel room while you were sound asleep. Wrong bullets and wrong truck. Christ, we waited forever for you to blow that damned decoy up."

"Where are we going?"

"One place you're not going is home, Bobby. Madeline Hale has you made for at least six federal raps. Jesus, Bobby. You put your own name on the red flag. You can't get any dumber than that."

"It was only on the State Department file."

"But who do you use to put the red flag on the Rumbh file in Immigration and Naturalization?"

"I don't want to talk about that. Will you tell me where we're going?"

"A neighbor," Brewer said. "For Christ's sake! A straight-arrow neighbor. When Hale got his address, all she had to do was look at a street map of Alexandria. And she had you right in the cross hairs."

"Where the hell are we going?"

"Why didn't you ask me to help you, Bobby? I could have done a job on Rus for you. All you had to do was ask."

"What do I need your help for?"

"Madeline Hale and I finally figured out just what you were up to. You were trying to clean Peno Rus's clock for causing that famine in Africa."

"That goddammed animal."

"Striking a blow for mankind and all those dead women and children who starved. How noble. To get a monster like Rus, you turned yourself into a monster. All in the name of love for mankind."

They rode in silence. The driver was taking them by way of the Périphérique.

Brewer finally looked at McCall. "Christ, what you did to me."

"Up yours, too," McCall said.

"You should have known better than to try to get Rus on a gun charge."

"Spare me the lectures, Brewer."

"Everyone knows he collected forty-fives. But that didn't mean he was dumb enough to fly to New York and walk into your dumb-ass trap. And what was worse was breaking into that military arsenal to swipe those pieces. And trying to cover it up by taking a bunch of rockets and terrorist crap. If you'd been caught, you would have drawn ten-to-twenty."

McCall made no answer.

"But worst of all, Bobby," Brewer said, "worst of all: when Rus blew the whistle and ratted to the cops, what do you do? Quit? Ha! Did you cut your losses and go on to the next round? No. Not you, Bobby. Never say die. You stick my hand in the fire. Mine and Marvel's. You're figuring that maybe we'll nail him, and if not, then we can take the fall with no harm to you. Rus never came near New York and you screwed your two best men."

"Stop the violin music, Brewer. You're breaking my heart. I got you the hottest young lawyer in the business. I raised a fortune in legal fees. You could have beat that rap standing on your head. You could have pleaded to a lesser charge, gotten a suspended, and walked. You're the screw-up, not me. If you hadn't made that harebrained not-guilty plea, it would have all worked out. You and Marvel would have both walked."

"Walked. Sure. Walked away with our reputations ruined forever. A couple of dishwashers or door-to-door encyclopedia salesmen. If that was such a good idea why didn't you take the fall yourself?"

McCall had half-turned his back to Brewer.

Brewer reached into McCall's coat pocket and drew out his airline ticket.

"What are you doing?" McCall demanded.

"I'm going to the airport. You don't need this ticket to Washington—unless you want to go straight to the slammer."

McCall rolled his head in anger.

A short time later they reached Charles de Gaulle Airport.

"Well, have lots of fun, Bobby," Brewer said. He tapped a finger on McCall's attaché case. "With all that dough. A lifetime of fun and sun on the run. You know, you could always get a nose job. In fact, with a little eye work, they could even make you look Chinese. Just remember to always wear gloves so you don't leave fingerprints."

McCall pointed a finger at him. "You go back to Washington and they'll hang you from the White House Christmas tree. We're both permanent exiles."

Brewer smiled at him again. "Four Iranian surveillance planes crashed today, Bobby," he said. "Count them—one, two, three, four. All those new parts were either defective or wrong or sabotaged."

"What are you telling me?" McCall demanded. "You deliberately sandbagged the Iranians?"

Brewer said, "It looks like I got the girl and the gold cup and the happy ending. And now you're the one who's on the lam, Bobby Mack."

Brewer stepped out of the cab. Then he leaned in the window. "Maybe they'll give me your old job, Bobby. Chief of the whole operation. That would be fun. And maybe they'll give me the assignment of catching you. That would be even more fun. *Arrivederci*, love. Pay the cab, will you?"

He stepped back. "You ended up with the broken hockey stick after all." He turned and walked through the terminal doorway and disappeared in a melee of human bodies and baggage.

"Where to, monsieur?" the cab driver asked.

"Oh, God," McCall sighed. "Make me clean again."